JESSICA ANN DISCIACCA

AWAKENING THE
DARK
FLAME

DARK FLAME
PUBLISHING

JESSICA ANN DISCIACCA

AWAKENING THE DARK FLAME

DARK FLAME
PUBLISHING

To those who had to walk through the fire in order to be reborn stronger than before.

NOTE TO READER

CHAPTER ONE

T he Kingdom of Doonak was only an hour's flight from the Kingdom of Urial. I was exhausted and frightened, but I didn't dare fall asleep. The world below was so much more magnificent from this height on the back of Erendrial's ragamor Eeri. Everything looked new as if I was truly seeing our world for the first time.

Erendrial and I didn't speak on the way to the kingdom of horrors. I tried to hold myself together as best as I could, scooting away from him whenever I got the chance. He wasn't King Lysanthier, but that didn't mean he wasn't just as bad, if not worse.

I tried to focus on Lily, my beautiful, kind little sister, for whom I had risked everything to rescue from our current destination. She would be waiting for me when I arrived, but in what condition would I find her? Would she be beaten? Missing limbs? Underfed? If she was hurt, I would have Otar tear through their court just like I had him do to the light court.

We began our descent around a tall mountain that stretched across the land. The rocks that made up the tall peaks were black and grey. The colors of the dark court ... how fitting. I couldn't see a castle anywhere in sight. There were no settlements or cities around the mountain.

"Where are we landing?" I asked Erendrial.

"The Kingdom of Doonak, of course. Your father made me promise no pit stops," he replied in a husky voice.

"But where is the kingdom? The cities and settlements? I don't see anything but a mountain."

"I guess you'll just have to learn to look a little closer, princess." He stretched across my back, easing Eeri down towards a rocky ledge carved into the side of the mountain. The ragamor slammed into the floor, causing me to reach for Eren's arms to support myself. I let go as soon as we were safely on the ground. Erendrial slid off the back of his scaled, dragon-like creature, reaching up to assist me.

"I'm good, but thanks," I said, not wanting to feel his hands around my waist.

He furrowed his brow as his silver, swirling eyes questioned my standoffish behavior. His dark, shining black hair blew freely in the wind as the last of the evening sun kissed his smooth tan skin.

The rest of the dark alfar warriors that accompanied us landed on the rocky platform, one after the other. I followed Erendrial into the mouth of the cave cautiously. There was no light while we descended further into the cavern. Fear flickered inside of me.

We finally stopped at two large glistening stone doors. Erendrial stepping up to the entrance, placing a hand on each of the panels. An illuminating, purple light blazed from his hands as the magic shuddered through the door, traveling in a vein-like pattern throughout the stone. I heard the latch unlock from within.

"Princess ... welcome to your kingdom," Erendrial said, smiling while he pushed open the doors.

Light streamed through the seam. I shielded my eyes, trying to take in the grandeur of the hidden kingdom I was now expected to call my home. I stepped through the doors waiting for my eyes to adjust. Multiple hallways connected to the massive foyer we entered. The sounds of music and laughter filled the halls. The floors were made of unblemished white marble. Long golden rugs ran down each hall. The walls were black, just like the stone the mountain was made of. Massive golden chandeliers were hung from the forty-foot ceilings.

Groups of dark alfar huddled around human musicians, listening to them play. Paintings were displayed along each wall, changing, and shifting as dark magic reconfigured each frame, causing a new scene to take the place of the one before. Large metal floor lamps stood every ten feet, lighting the way with purple fire spewing from their tops.

"This way, princess," Erendrial said, leaning down to my ear.

I followed him through the halls as the dark alfar stopped and looked at what the ragamor had dragged in. Erendrial smiled and nodded to each one as we passed. The music stopped as they peered at me, their new princess. The title, princess, was still so foreign and new. I could only imagine what they thought of this whole shift in power. A disgusting half-breed would sit on their throne someday.

As we got further into the castle, humans and dark alfar alike ran through the halls, chasing each other in a playful manner. One of the alfar males caught a girl he was pursuing, slamming her into one of the doors just before he began undressing her.

She laughed and moaned while she reached for the doorknob to a room. They both tumbled inside, shutting the door behind them. She didn't seem afraid or hurt. She seemed to enjoy the contact, which caught me off guard. In the light court, the humans were terrified of their alfar masters, with good reason. I had been the mistress of the next light king Gaelin Atros, and even that hadn't protected me.

We stopped at another set of double doors. Carvings of dragons and fire were scattered across the beautiful grey stone. The fire was painted in gold, creating the most captivating contrast with the dark colors that surrounded it.

"You all are dismissed," said Erendrial to the twelve warriors behind me.

They nodded respectfully to Erendrial and then each locked their eyes on me, bowing in unison.

"Oh, you don't have to do that," I said without thinking.

They hesitated, looking from me to Erendrial for instruction.

He laughed, stepping to my side. "You are their princess. Time to get used to the formalities. Also, the perks," he whispered, winking at me.

I turned back to the group of dark alfar that had been ready to fight for me an hour ago. "Thank you all for your help. Your kindness will not be forgotten." They smiled at me, laughing under their breaths. I looked at Erendrial, unsure of what I said that was so funny.

"We're going to have to work on that kind streak of yours too. The list just keeps getting longer, doesn't it," he said, turning around. "As promised..." He pushed open the doors to a room which was set up like a living space.

There were decadent couches, chairs, and a massive lit fireplace to the right. There was a table with a feast set out at the back of the room. Thick fur rugs covered the floor. I stepped inside, taking in the riches of the space. Erendrial stepped behind me, shutting the doors.

A small figure popped up from one of the chairs. As she stood, her long gold dress fell to the floor. Her golden-brown hair was curled, pinned away from her face, catching the light of the fire. Her cheeks lit up as a smile stretched from ear to ear.

I could feel my legs beginning to tremble. My body went limp with relief. Tears trickled down my cheeks as I tried to formulate words. Unsuccessful, I covered my mouth with my hands and collapsed to the floor with relief, shock, and joy. She rushed towards me, wrapping her arms around me while she laughed and cried.

I slowly allowed myself to embrace her, needing to make sure she was real. That this moment was real.

"Lily," I whispered, shaking.

She began laughing, pulling away from me. She took my face in her hands, wiping away the tears from my cheeks. "Yes, yes, you stupid girl, it's me," she said. She kissed me on either cheek before wrapping her arms around me again.

Everything I had gone through, everything I had endured was for this moment. I tried to focus, but the feeling of her cheek on mine sent my skin crawling. The way her hands ran down my back. How hard she embraced me. It all made me want to throw up.

I pulled away from her violently and got to my feet, not wanting to feel physical contact for another moment. I wrapped my arms around myself, trying to soothe my stinging flesh. She looked at me, seeming confused and hurt. She didn't know what I had went through in Urial. She couldn't. It wasn't her fault. *Damnit*, King Lysanthier had even managed to ruin this moment for me. He was dead, yet he was still making my life a living hell.

"What is it? What's wrong?" she asked, taking another step towards me.

I backed away, trying to get a hold of myself.

"Gen darling," she said.

"Don't call me that! Don't ever call me that!" I snapped, remembering the sound of my name on the king's lips the night before.

She froze, looking at Erendrial and then back to me.

I backed up into the wall, trying to force away the image of his cold, thin body on top of mine. His smell, his disgusting smile. The way he felt inside of me. How he beat and tortured me for weeks just because he could. I slid to the floor, holding my head, willing the memories to catch fire and burn away.

"Please, go away. Both of you," I whispered. I was about to have one of my panic attacks. I didn't know what had set it off, but I could feel it building.

Erendrial looked at me without emotion. "I'm sorry, princess, but I've been ordered to stay with you until your father arrives," he replied.

Lily approached me cautiously, kneeling to the floor. She gently reached out, touching my shoulder. "It's over, Genevieve. You're safe now. You're here, with me," she whispered reassuringly.

I looked up at her, taking comfort in those familiar brown eyes.

"What happened to you? You can talk to me, Gen. You can tell me anything."

I looked back at Erendrial, uncomfortable with his presence. He didn't return my gaze.

"Not now," I whispered. I took a few deep breaths, gathering what control I could. "Are you okay? Has anyone hurt you?"

"Not for a while now," she said. "At first, they weren't so pleasant, but now it's bearable," she said with a sweet smile.

"Has ... has anyone ... forced you?" I asked, remembering what Erendrial told me about her alfar lover. He had to have been lying.

He was just trying to get a rise out of me that day in the hallway, taunting me with information regarding Lily.

She smirked, leaning back on her heels. "Why don't we just focus on getting you cleaned up and fed for now. Then I will fill you in on the past six months. Oh, and remind me to kill you for risking your life for mine, *Your Highness*," she said, mockingly.

I snickered, pulling myself from the floor. She led me over to a washbowl and vanity.

"Please turn around, Ambassador Lyklor," she said sarcastically.

He nodded, doing as she insisted.

"He listens to you?" I asked her.

She laughed with amusement. "No. He is only doing as I ask out of respect for you. Now take that hideous rag off and let's get you cleaned up."

I did as she instructed, keeping an eye on Erendrial the entire time. She washed my body, stopping at the Lysanthier sigil that adorned my chest. Her eyes traced the twirling lines of the tree design that wrapped around the circular edge.

"Don't worry," I said softly. "The new queen of the light has a similar brand, except hers is of the dark court sigil, thanks to Erendrial and his friends."

"I see," she said, still seeming uncomfortable. Lily continued to wash me, slowing as she approached the black sigil on my left wrist. She didn't say a word. I shivered the entire time, trying to reassure myself it was only Lily who was touching me. It wasn't the king.

She dressed me in a beautiful floor-length formfitting black silk dress. It dropped low in the front with delicate gold beads along the neckline. The back was revealing, exposing some of the scars that resided on my lower back. Lily led me to the vanity and began work on my hair. I closed my eyes, imagining we were back under the church. She pinned my curls up off my neck, exposing my ears for the first time in my life.

"You can turn around now, Ambassador Lyklor," she said.

He gracefully turned towards us, stopping abruptly as I stood from the vanity chair. His swirling eyes caught the light of the fire. His gaze began at the silk slippers that now adorned my feet before trailing up the length of my body. His eyes linger on me for an uncomfortable number of seconds before he resumed his blank stare at the back wall.

Lily reached for my star pendant that was now on display around my neck. "That is pretty. Where did you get it?" she asked.

I grabbed it defensively, shielding it from her and Erendrial. I dropped my eyes to the floor. "It was a gift," I replied shortly.

She pulled away, as something like hurt flashed in her eyes.

I reached for her, realizing how cold and unfeeling I was being. "I'm sorry, Lily. I am just going to need some time to get used to everything and to—" I stopped, not wanting to reveal any more than I had to.

"It's okay," she whispered. "I understand. Come, let's get you something to eat. You look skinnier than when I last saw you at the summer solstice. I didn't even know that was possible."

I stood, feeling the weight of the dress trail behind me. It was the most luxurious thing I had ever worn. I felt out of place and a little silly. I dropped my head, fiddling with my hands in front of me as I followed Lily to the table of food. Erendrial tracked me with his eyes until I took a seat.

"Erendrial, have you eaten?" I asked.

"Not yet, princess," he responded.

"Please join us. I can't eat all this anyways and it will be better than having you stand there like a statue," I said.

He smiled, nodding his head in compliance, and walked elegantly towards us. Lily sat next to me, while he took the place farthest from us. Lily gathered an assortment of foods, placing them in front of me like I was a child. I took the fork and slowly began eating. I wasn't hungry, but I knew it would soothe Lily's worries. Her smile beamed brightly as she waited for me to say anything to her.

Lily's eyes suddenly widened with terror. Cautiously, she pushed her seat away from the table as her eyes fixated on something behind me. She began to shake while she tried to forced words from her mouth but failed.

I turned around quickly to see Otar standing behind me, smiling at Lily as if she was a snack. I exhaled in relief, laughing under my breath.

Erendrial snorted in amusement, as he took a sip of wine. "Calm yourself, sweet Lilian. It is only your sister's pet," Erendrial said.

"What ... what is that? It sure as heck isn't a dog," she exclaimed, taking another step back.

"She looks lovely. May I eat her?" Otar asked, drool dripping from his lips.

I looked back at his leathery black face and those haunting yellow eyes. His white flesh-eating teeth bared towards her. "No, absolutely not!" I snapped.

His shoulders fell in disappointment.

"Lily, this is Otar. Otar, this is my *sister* Lilian. Lily, it's okay, you can take a seat, he won't hurt you." I got another plate and filled it with the different meats on the table. I placed the plate to my right. "Sit and eat, Otar."

"But it is so much better when it's fresh," he hissed, walking closer to Lily.

"Otar, she is off-limits. Period!" I said again.

"Ooooh, no fun, wicked one. But I will do as you ask," he said, walking over to the plate and taking a seat in the chair.

Lily watched his every move as he dug savagely into the stack of meat. "What is he?" she asked.

"Still not really sure how to answer that," I said, watching him with curiosity.

"This is what killed the light king," added Erendrial. "At your sister's request."

Lily looked back at me for answers.

I took a deep breath and exhaled. "Otar was dead. Then I resurrected him and now he obeys my commands," I explained.

"Yes, and how exactly did you resurrect the creature?" asked Erendrial, leaning into the table.

I gave him a look that said, *'you wish'*.

"Wait, you are the reason the light king is dead?" asked Lily. "Why would you want to kill him?"

I diverted my eyes, not wanting either of them to see the truth. "I had my reasons. Now, tell me what you do here. Tell me everything that I've missed," I said.

"Well, I sing for the dark alfar mostly. I help around the castle, and I've begun to learn how to sew. The dress you're wearing right now, I made it," she said with pride.

I looked down, admiring her work with a smile.

"I made it for the size you used to be. Now, it just hangs on you like a bag. Sorry."

I reached out, taking her hand in mine. "It's beautiful. I love it," I said, smiling at her.

A knock came at the door. I sat up straight in defense.

"Come in," Erendrial said, popping a grape into his mouth.

A massive male made of nothing but muscle entered the room. He was over six and a half feet tall, with mahogany brown hair tied back into a bun against his neck. His face was strong and broad, with indigo eyes, thin lips, and a shapely nose. He wore black fighting leathers that was distinguishable by the unique texture imprinted on his vest resembling ragamor scales.

I stood up as he approached the table, not knowing what he wanted or who he was. Lily smiled, popping up next to me. He looked at her softly and then back to me, in an assessing manner. Lily gently took my arm in her hand.

"Gen, I'd like you to meet Zerrial. He's one of Erendrial's men," she said with a beaming smile.

I looked back at Erendrial. He had a smirk on his face as his hands were laced across his stomach. He gave me a small shrug.

"See, I didn't lie," Erendrial said casually.

"No, no, absolutely not!" I yelled.

Lily looked at me with confusion. I grabbed her arm, taking her to the other side of the room. Otar stood from the chair, looking at Zerrial as if he could be dessert. His venomous smile stretched across his black, leathery skin before he disappeared out of sight.

Lily inhaled sharply, looking around the room, panicked. "Where," she muttered, "where did it go?"

Before I could answer, Otar appeared behind Zerrial, slashing his claws down his back. Zerrial groaned, arching his body in response while massive, bear-like claws of his own appeared from his right hand. He turned just as Otar disappeared again. Otar solidified again slamming his body into Zerrial's legs, sending him to the cold floor. My creature pounced on the dark alfar's chest, widening his mouth, revealing his sharpened set of murderous teeth.

"Otar, don't kill him," I ordered.

Otar turned to me, his face enraged by the command.

"Not yet, at least," I finished. "Go back to the table and sit down until I'm finished ... please."

The creature did as commanded. He sat slowly back in his chair, grumbling, and throwing the meat off his plate in a tantrum.

Lily helped Zerrial from the floor, checking him over to make sure no real damaged had been done. She then rushed over to me, taking me by the arm, leading me to the far corner of the room.

"What is the matter?" asked Lily.

"Him. Zerrial. He is the matter." I was so flustered I couldn't even organize my thoughts. "Erendrial said Zerrial had taken you as his mistress. Is that true? Because if so, just say the word and I will have Otar rip him from limb to limb," I growled, feeling the heat from my rage ripple through every nerve ending in my body.

She grabbed both of my arms, shaking her head. "No, no, it isn't like that at all. And I am not his mistress. We don't use words like that here," she said, dropping her head.

"Then what? What is it like, Lily?" I asked, trying to calm myself.

"I ... I chose to be with him," she whispered.

I shook my head in disbelief. My little sister. My God-fearing, nun-loving sister chose to give her maidenhood to a dark alfar.

"I don't understand. Why would you ever give yourself to one of them?" I asked in disappointment.

Her face blushed with embarrassment. "He's … different. It's true, some of the alfar here are brutal and cruel, but not all. They do things that sicken me and repulse me, but he isn't like that. He takes care of me. He has never hurt me. He's … gentle."

I laughed, standing with my hands on my hips, trying to wrap my head around the two of them together. "What happened to the church? I don't think you'll qualify to be a nun now, Lilian. They'd probably burn you at the stake for what you've done."

She stepped back away from me with pain written all over her face. I couldn't believe she would be this stupid. How could she? Why would a sane person ever give themselves to one of these things? It made me sick. Knowing he had touched her and taken a part of her.

"Gen, I love—" she started to say, but I held out my hand to stop her from continuing.

"Don't even say it. You have no clue what love is. These things don't know how to love, Lily!" I shouted. "They only know how to use and take and fuck. They take and take and take until there is nothing left of you that they want!"

Erendrial and Zerrial watched as I screamed at Lilian with anger.

"You are foolish and stupid!" I continued. "Everything I did, everything I've been through was to find you. To save you from this. And yet here you are, freely sharing a bed with one of them."

Tears fell from her face as her bottom lip quivered.

I took a deep breath in, unable to look at her for a moment

longer. "Just leave," I demanded.

She looked up at me, trying to formulate a sentence, but I walked away from her, not able to deal with her childish views of love.

I sat on the couch, looking into the fire, willing myself to disappear. She and Zerrial left the room without another word. Erendrial walked over and handed me a goblet of wine before taking a seat.

"You are just full of surprises," he said, looking into the fire.

"You have no clue," I replied.

He waited for a moment before responding. "Do you think you might have been a little harsh on her?"

I looked at him in shock. "What do you care? She's just a human to you and him. She made her choice, now she has to live with it." I took a sip of wine, trying to calm myself.

Erendrial didn't approach the subject further. "Your father will be here soon. What do you want to do about your pet?" Erendrial asked.

Otar appeared next to Erendrial's ear, snapping his sharp teeth only inches from his face. Erendrial didn't even flinch. "I am not her pet! I am no one's pet! If you call me that again, I will cut off your pathetic excuse for balls and make you choke on them, you piece of shit," Otar wheezed in his ear.

Erendrial turned to him and just smiled.

"Otar, I'm liking you better by the minute," I said with a smile. "Otar will stay in whatever room is next to mine. He will have free reign of the castle and grounds. Otar, you may go wherever you wish, but you cannot kill anyone. If someone is trying to kill you, you must try to escape first, before defending yourself. Do not steal. You are my guest. If you want or need something, just ask."

Otar nodded at me and snickered before disappearing from the room.

"You really think that thing sleeps in a bed?" asked Erendrial.

"We will soon figure that mystery out," I said, finishing the last of my wine.

We sat in silence as I waited for my long-lost father to pay me a visit. I focused on the fire. The red and orange swirls of the flames. How they licked and danced over the dried wood. I closed my eyes, trying to process the past few days. I wondered what kinds of hell I would have to endure here. I wondered how much of myself I would lose to this court.

CHAPTER TWO

T he two large doors to the room opened without warning. Erendrial stood to his feet as the King of Doonak entered ... my father. I turned on the couch to look at the male who sired me. The male who I had so desperately wanted to know about for so many years. The male I had hoped would come and save me from a life of starvation and loneliness.

The king stopped as we made eye contact. I stood slowly, my heart racing, and my nerves on edge. He looked no older than thirty, with white skin and a flawless complexion. His face was strong and sculpted: high cheekbones, a straight and dominant nose, and familiar lips. His eyes were a vibrant green, just like my own. Long, straight, black hair trailed down his back. His frame was lean and muscular.

A gold crown sat on top of his head. He wore a black suit and vest with satin detail work covering the canvas of his attire. A black cape lined with gold trim and fur fluttered behind him. Veins popped from his forehead and neck, and his jaw tightened as he took in the sight of me.

I looked back at Erendrial for instruction on what to do or how to act, but all he did was smile at me before bowing his head. I began to play with my hands, uncomfortable by the awkward silence. I had imagined this moment for so long and now that it was here. I didn't know what to do.

"Ambassador Lyklor, how did the trade go over with the Queen of the Light?" asked King Drezmore.

Erendrial stepped forward, taking a deep breath in. "Not as planned, your majesty," he said, holding up my left wrist to show the king the sigil that controlled Otar. I pulled away, uncomfortable. King Drezmore's eyes widened.

"You rose Otar? You're the reason King Lysanthier is dead?" he asked.

I nodded, still unable to find my voice.

He turned away from me, back to Erendrial. "I expect there was conflict?"

"Just a little, but everything was handled without an ounce of bloodshed, your majesty. The queen was also branded as requested with your house sigil," smirked Erendrial.

"And where is the creature now?" asked King Drezmore.

Erendrial laughed lightly, shaking his head. "He has been offered a room, next to the princess's, per her request. The situation with Otar is more than we could have expected. Though, she won't reveal many details about the resurrection or the bond with the creature," he said, shooting me a side glance, "the creature follows her commands and seems complacent to do so."

The king tilted his head towards me with interest. "Is that so? A very interesting development indeed. One we can use to our advantage in the future, I hope. Thank you Erendrial. As always, you serve our kingdom and your king with honor. Please, wait outside until I call for you," instructed the king.

Erendrial nodded, taking his leave from the room.

Once the doors were closed behind him, the king slowly approached me. I didn't realize how tall he was until he stood towering above. He examined my face, my figure, and then my hair. I couldn't read his expression. I couldn't tell if he was pleased with me or not, but I still was hesitant to say a word. He reached out his hand slowly to a loose curl that dangled near my ear. He rubbed the curl in between his fingers gently before dropping his hand back to his side.

"You look so much like her. You even smell like her," he said in a deep voice.

I brought my eyes up to his, seeing the same shades of green flicker through them as my own. "You ... you remember her?" I asked shyly. I still didn't know what type of relationship my parents had.

He smiled, for the first time as he dropped his eyes to the floor. "Yes, I remember her. Every detail," he said, gesturing to the couch for me to sit.

I did as he requested, never taking my eyes off him.

He took off his cape and sat down next to me, leaving a cushion between us. "After I found out about you, I sent my people to your town to look for her. They said she passed eleven years ago." He paused for a moment. "How did she die?"

"I don't really know. I went out to the market and when I returned home, I found her dead in our bed. The healers said she was perfectly healthy. They couldn't find any evidence of illness or disease."

He sat silent for a few moments. "I didn't know she was with child. If I would have, I—" He stopped, putting his hand over his mouth.

"What ... what was she ... to you?" I asked. I had a long list of questions, but I needed to know what type of alfar I was dealing with first.

He turned to me, straightening his back, sitting tall and elegantly. "You mean to ask if I raped her?"

I dropped my eyes, not wanting to think of my mother enduring that kind of pain.

"I didn't," he said shortly. "She wanted me as much as I wanted her. There was consent."

"And how do I know you're not lying to me? Humans are nothing more than cattle to your kind, am I right? Why allow yourself to sink so low for a messy human?"

He studied me for a moment. His face gave away nothing of his thoughts or feelings ... if he were capable of experiencing them, that was. "I can see trust with you will need to be earned," he said, matter-of-fact.

I took a deep breath, gathering my thoughts. "Did she live here with you?"

That question seemed to take him off guard. "She told you nothing of me?" he asked.

"No. I tried to ask when I was young, but she would always change the subject. At night, after she would put me to bed, I would hear her crying softly at the kitchen table. I thought you may have died by the way she acted, but no, she never said a word."

His eyes flickered to the fire. "She never lived on this side of the border. I met her in town one evening. I was hurt and she showed me kindness. I was captivated by her. After that night I couldn't forget about her, no matter how hard I tried. I went back just to watch her at first and then eventually I made contact. She accepted me for who and what I was."

"Then, why did you abandon her?" I asked.

"I had no choice. If certain members of this court had discovered her and what she meant to me, they would have done awful things to her. Just because I am king does not mean I am untouchable. I had to end our relations, which meant leaving her."

"I understand," I whispered. A dark alfar doing something selfless. Hell must have frozen over, I thought.

"Did she ... did she ever marry another?"

"No. She focused on raising me and helping the people in our town. That was her life."

"After she died, how did you survive?"

"I learned to steal. Begged for scraps from people I knew who were sympathetic to what I was. Eventually, I was taken in by a nun. She clothed me and provided a place that kept me safe."

He rubbed his hands together, dropping his eyes uncomfortably. "I'm sorry you had to go through that. I'm sorry you had to endure everything you've experienced, but I can promise you, your suffering is over." He reached out to touch my arm, but I recoiled from him, afraid of another king's touch. Even if he was my father.

He stopped, taken aback by the reaction.

"I'm sorry," I whispered. "I've just ... been through a lot in the past few months."

"Understandable. I must warn you: I don't know how to be a father. My own father was a cruel and violent man when it came to children. I try to be better, but the fact that you are sitting here next to me is still hard to wrap my head around."

"I don't expect anything from you. I had a mother, that was enough," I replied.

He stiffened. Did my honesty make him uncomfortable?

"Is what Erendrial told me the truth? You have announced me as your heir?" I asked.

"Yes."

"Why? Why a half-breed? Your court must think you're mad."

"Some do, others are loyal to me and my judgment. You are as much a part of me as any other child I would ever sire."

"And … if you do sire a child with the queen … what happens to me then?"

"Nothing. You will still be the rightful heir to the throne. I have publicly announced and claimed you. Your position is safe." He stood. "We have much to discuss, but for now, I am sure you would like to rest."

He held out his hand to help me from the couch. I took it reluctantly. His grip was soft and gentle. I stood in front of him for a few moments as he took me in one more time. He slowly cupped my left cheek with his hand, rubbing my face endearingly. I was taken back by the kindness of this dark alfar. His eyes were locked on mine. I wondered if he was thinking of my mother.

"Erendrial," he yelled, without removing his eyes from me. The doors opened as Erendrial re-entered the room.

"Yes, my king?" Erendrial said with a small bow.

"I will escort my daughter to her rooms this evening. In the morning, you will assist her with a proper tour of her new home and anything she needs or desires. You will make sure the court treats her with the utmost respect and no harm comes to her. Am I clear?" he said firmly.

"It would be my pleasure, your majesty," Erendrial said, standing off to the side of the doorway.

The king … my father held out his arm to escort me out of the room. I gave him a small smile before sliding my arm through his. He placed his hand on top of mine and grinned. I could tell smiling was a foreign thing to him, but he was trying.

We walked towards the door, passing Erendrial on our way out. He kept his head down, not making eye contact with either of us. As we ascended the hall the groups of dark alfar and humans stood and bowed towards us. Some of the court members had black hair, others dark shades of brown. A few dyed their hair vibrant colors like purple and blue. They wore revealing fashions, makeup dramatically contouring the features of their faces.

My father held his head high, ushering me along beside him. We passed two large red doors as we entered the residential wing.

"These are my chambers," explained my father. "If you need anything, feel free to come to me. The white doors are Queen Nora's chambers. The four blue chambers belong to my brother and his children. These are yours," he said, stopping at a set of purple doors. "Ambassador Lyklor mentioned you like lavender. I thought the color fitting."

"Thank you," I said, forcing a small smile.

He nodded, pushing the doors open. The room was broken up into three different compartments. The chamber we entered was a seating area. The walls were smooth and flat compared to the rest of the castle. White wallpaper adorned the surfaces, bringing a lighter feel into the room.

Two couches and four chairs were placed around a low table. A massive fireplace greeted us as we walked in. Rugs covered the marble floor, providing some warmth.

The second room off to the left was a study. There was another fireplace behind a large rich brown desk. Floor-to-ceiling bookshelves covered the walls. A few extra seats were scattered around the area along with a meeting table.

The room to the right was my bedchamber. A deep purple comforter and gold pillows were scattered over a massive bed placed on the far wall. A wardrobe sat in the corner, along with a vanity and another seating area. A third fireplace was next to the bed. Another entrance that I presumed was the bathroom was off to the back of the room. The chambers were beautiful and lavish, but there wasn't a window in sight. I guess that shouldn't come as a surprise since we were in the middle of a mountain.

Candles were mounted to the walls. Gold accents were placed throughout the room. Artwork brought color and movement into the space. It was truly beautiful, and it was all mine. I wouldn't have to share the room with anyone. For the first time, I had a bed to myself.

"Are you pleased?" asked my father.

"It's wonderful. Thank you," I said, still taking in the space.

"I'm pleased you are happy. Atalee," yelled my father.

A young female came into the room behind us. She was wearing a charcoal grey dress. Her hair was long and draped around her shoulders. She was a simple beauty, with brown hair and eyes. Her cheeks were pale, and her lips were covered with a light shade of pink.

"Yes, Your Grace," she said in a soft voice.

"Atalee, this is my daughter, Genevieve. Genevieve, this is Atalee, your lady. She has the gift of telekinesis. Anything you need on a personal matter she will assist you," he said.

I smiled at the young girl. "Nice to meet you," I said.

She curtsied. "It is an honor to be in your service, Your Grace," she replied.

All this still felt so odd. My father turned back to me.

"If there isn't anything else you need this evening, I have matters to attend to before I retire," he said.

"I think I am good. Thank you," I replied.

He walked towards me until he had to bend his head to look down at me. "I am glad you are here, Genevieve. I will do my best to do right by you. That is my promise."

I smiled at him and nodded. He left, closing the doors behind him. I looked at Atalee uncomfortably. "So, what's next?" I asked her.

"Anything you wish, Your Grace," she responded.

I laughed at her. "Please, just call me Gen."

"As you wish, Gen."

I walked over to the young girl. She was taller than I was, but somehow seemed like a child.

"If we are going to be spending a lot of time together, I would just like you to look at me as another alfar or human, whatever I am. No formalities, please. It will make this whole situation a lot more comfortable for both of us."

She smirked, nodding her head. "Are you hungry? Or would you like to bathe?"

"Actually, I think I am good for tonight. Can you just show me where all the clothes are?"

"Your dresses are in the armoire. Pants, shirts, and your night-wear are kept in the tall dresser. Are you sure you don't want me to turn your bed back or run you a hot bath?"

"I am sure. It was nice to meet you, Atalee. Have a good night," I said, ushering her to the door.

When she was finally gone, I exhaled, relieved to finally be alone. I went to the dresser, pulling a silk nightgown from the drawer. I made my way to the massive bathroom. The tub could fit five people easily. I ran the water and undressed slowly.

Even though my body was healed from my last encounter with King Lysanthier, I could still feel the residual pain of his affection. I slid into the tub, pondering on how crazy this all was. Even though I now had seen Lily with my own eyes, a part of me still felt incomplete. I missed Levos, Madison ... even Gaelin. I wondered what he was thinking at this moment. Was he mad, enraged, or hurt?

I had to try and put the light court behind me. I had to focus on the dark court now and figure out how to survive this place. If Lily could do it, then so could I. I just didn't know what was expected of me. And how was I ever going to be queen? The thought was so foreign and yet it was now my future. Me ... the heir to the dark alfar kingdom. I snickered at the thought. Gods, how things had changed.

I got out of the tub, dressed, and headed to the bed. I stopped before removing the pillows. The bed was so big and intimidating. I was in a foreign place, surrounded by alfar who the humans had told horror stories about. Even though everything had gone smoothly thus far, I still felt unsafe. I looked back at the armoire behind me.

I removed the dresses from the hooks and then grabbed a pillow and blanket from the bed. I shut myself in, imagining I was back in the linen closet at the light court. My secret safe place. I closed my eyes, trying to force from my mind the memories of what used to happen to me at night. King Lysanthier was dead. Gaelin was miles away. My body was safe. My body was my own for the first time in what seemed like forever. I cried myself to sleep.

Chapter Three

The doors to the cabinet cracked open slowly allowing the light from the fire to stream within. My head felt heavy and my body protested as I pushed myself up from the floor of the armoire. Erendrial stood above me with his arms crossed over his chest. He was in black leather pants and a thin black shirt with the sleeves rolled up: more casual than I had ever seen him. He wore a thick gold necklace with a pendant at the end bearing the Drezmore sigil.

"Is there something wrong with the bed, princess? If you don't like it I can have someone bring you another," he said sarcastically.

I pulled the covers over my body, stepping out from the armoire. "That won't be necessary, but thanks," I replied.

Atalee was in the corner of the room. Once I moved out of the way she took the dresses from the bed and put them neatly back into the chest.

"Are you going to make me ask why you were in the armoire?" Erendrial said.

I rolled my eyes. "Now that I am a royal, are you still allowed to talk to me like that?

"I respect your position, but I am still entitled to have my own personality, princess. It's one of my most attractive traits."

"Ha, says who?" I snapped back.

"It will grow on you in time. Now, regarding the agenda for the day," he started.

"Erendrial, I don't mean to be rude, but isn't there someone else that could show me around? I am sure you are far too busy for this, and I don't know if I can deal with your snarky personality all day. I might beg to return to the light court by the end of this little informative session."

"Back to King Atros, you mean?"

I stopped halfway to the bathroom.

"Is that why you were in the armoire?" asked Erendrial. "You couldn't bear to sleep in the bed without him? I am sure we could arrange a monthly visit for the two of you if—"

"No!" I snapped in rage. I walked over to him, clutching the blanket close to my chest. His expression fell. "Don't you dare begin to assume what I want. If I were you, I would focus on doing what you are told." My tone, firm and threatening, surprised even me. I hadn't seen this side of myself in a long while and boy, did she feel good to wear again.

He smiled, nodding his head. "As you wish, my princess," he said.

I turned around, walking away from him. "No possessive pronouns either, Lyklor. I am not your anything." I slammed the door to the bathroom.

I took another bath and then exited to find a beautiful black lace dress awaiting me. Erendrial turned around as I dressed behind the dressing screen with Atalee's assistance. The gown dropped down my chest to my mid stomach, the full length slit up to my midthigh. The back was completely exposed. Long sleeves fell off my shoulders and trailed down my arms to my hands.

I could feel the cool air kissing the exposed skin. My hands trembled while I tried to cover myself.

Atalee froze, unsure of what I was doing. "Is ... is everything alright with the dress, Your Highness?"

"I ... is there something less revealing I could wear?"

"It is the fashion of your court, Your Grace."

"My court?" I said, still reeling from the turn of events. Atalee nodded. "Are all the clothes this revealing?"

"This one is actually very modest in comparison to most," she whispered.

A chuckle fought to escape from my lips. I covered my mouth with my hand. "This is what you all consider modest?"

She nodded again, now looking very confused.

I turned to the mirror, taking in the sight of myself ... my body. The body that had been used, beaten, and scarred. The body I had learned to detach myself from in order to survive. *It's just flesh, Gen*, I heard myself repeat the phrase I had clung to so many times during my nightmares.

I exhaled, turning back to the young alfar female. I forced a smile to appear on my face. "I suppose it will do."

Atalee pinned my hair up away from my neck. She dusted my face lightly with powder and then dragged black eyeliner across my eyelids, elongating the appearance of the shape.

While the alfar worked her magic, I pondered my reaction to Lily and Zerrial. For the life of me, I would never understand why anyone would choose to be with one of these things out of free will, but had I reacted too harshly? Was I taking my own pain out on my sister? Shouldn't I be glad that she had found some kind of happiness here? I needed to talk to her.

Atalee ended with a bright red lip. I didn't look like myself. I looked like one of them, and for some reason I loved it. I could start new here. I could be stronger ... better. If Lily could find happiness here, so could I.

Atalee bowed behind me before leaving. I sat at the vanity, still taking in my appearance. Erendrial appeared in the reflection of my mirror, holding a wooden box. He opened it slowly as I watched closely. It was a beautiful gold crown. It came down to a point in the middle with a black stone fastened in the center. The edges of the crown were shaped into small leaves and branches.

"Your father had it designed specifically for you when he discovered you were indeed his daughter. May I?" Erendrial asked, taking the crown from the box.

I nodded.

He placed it on top of my hair gently. The black stone lay in the center of my forehead as the gold of the crown glistened. It was breathtaking. "Now, you look like a queen," he said, leaning down next to my face.

I smiled. "It's a bit much, don't you think?"

"Nonsense. You are royal now, Genevieve. You will have to get used to the extravagant lifestyle and people being under you."

"I don't know if I will ever get used to all of this." I stood up, with my back still towards him. His eyes shifted to the scars I wore from my time in The Frey. He turned away quickly. "It's okay. No need to act like they're not there. I got them when I was fourteen. I stole from an advisor's wife. I got caught and received seven lashes. The guard that was administering my punishment knew what I was and wanted to make me suffer, so he tied pieces of ulyrium to the end of the whip."

"Did you kill him?" he asked.

I laughed under my breath. "No. It just motivated me to get better at stealing from them. That was the last time I ever got caught."

"Is the guard still alive?" His face was stern. I was still learning to read him, but I knew where his questioning was headed.

"I don't know. And no, you cannot kill him. Understood?" I asked.

He exhaled and gave a single nod. "Come, we should be on our way. Breakfast will be served in the throne room."

"I'd like to go see Lily first."

"She's busy at the moment, but I can arrange for her to come to your rooms later this evening."

"Busy doing what, exactly?"

His head turned slightly in my direction. With one eyebrow arched, a devilish smirk appeared at the corner of his lips. "Don't worry, princess. Your sister is completely safe and well cared for. Zerrial would have it no other way."

"Erendrial!" I snapped.

He laughed with amusement. "Calm yourself. She is working on new dresses as we speak. Something she has come to love."

I exhaled with relief, trying to refocus. "Will my father be at breakfast?"

"No, he is in meetings this morning, but your uncle and cousins will be," he said with a smirk.

"Oh yeah, I have an actual family," I said, still amused by the fact.

We headed out of the room into the halls of Doonak. "Can you tell me about them?" I asked.

"Where to begin? Your father and your uncle, Rythlayn, are very close. His gift is a paralysis shock like your fathers, but his gift only mutes other powers that are directed at him. Which means, no one can magically harm him. He can't affect the body like your father can."

"So, who is more powerful?" I asked.

"Your father, of course."

"And are they close?"

"Inseparable."

I allowed myself to smile. The two of them were close. Like siblings should be. I was comforted by the normalcy.

"Rythlayn has two daughters and a son. Icici is the oldest, then his son Toreon and his youngest daughter is Vena. Icici can control nightmares. Toreon can control metals and Vena is a healer."

"They all sound extraordinary," I said in awe.

Erendrial huffed. "I wouldn't go that far. Icici is their ringleader. She is very striking and has a strong head on her shoulders. Toreon follows her lead and Vena is too kind to be related to the lot of them."

"Do you think they will like me?" I asked.

"You shouldn't be worrying about whether they will like you or not. You need to make them fear you, princess. Strength and power are what they respect. That goes for the entire court."

I nodded, trying to set my feelings aside. Family or not, I was their princess ... their future queen. The pressure was almost unbearable, but I had to make do. I had to find my place amongst this court.

We entered the doorway of the grand throne room, and I stopped dead. This place was absolutely magical. The ceiling swirled with red, purple, and black fog that danced and created new designs with each motion. Hundreds of candles floated out in the open, suspended by nothing. The ceiling sparkled like it was covered in glitter or stars.

The ground was made of pure gold with a single, black runner going down the center aisle. At the front of the room, steps led up to a platform covered in black fabric. Three thrones sat in the front, made of black stone. The largest throne had skulls covered in gold at the base of the chair. A red velvet curtain hung behind the thrones. Food was laid out on handcrafted tables of black wood, their legs and sides swirling with different designs and pictures.

The alfar sat at the tables enjoying their breakfast. One by one they stopped and stared at me as I inched into the room. I felt like I was on display, which I suppose, I should have been used to by now. I took a deep breath, holding my head high in the air. I needed to earn their respect. I couldn't be weak.

"That's it," said Erendrial in my ear. "Come, this way. For the record, you do not bow to anyone except your father. You are now second, which means no one other than the king is higher than you." He led me to the table in the front where a beautiful female with dark brown hair and radiant blue eyes sat waiting for us. "Queen Nora, may I present Princess Genevieve."

The woman stood without a smile on her face. If looks could kill, I would have been dead. She curtsied slowly. "Princess Genevieve, how wonderful to finally make your acquaintance," she said in a deep and haunting voice.

"Thank you, Queen Nora. It is nice to meet you as well," I

replied.

"Princess, these are your cousins, Icici, Toreon, and Vena." Erendrial gestured to the other end of the table.

Icici, the dream weaver according to Eren, was stunning. She had black slick hair that was braided away from her face with one white stripe running through its length. She had deep black eyes and smooth tan skin. Her nose was small and fit her high cheekbones perfectly. She had a desirable figure with a full chest.

Toreon, the manipulator of metal, smiled softly at me and nodded. He was tall and well built. His hair was dyed blue and cut short against his scalp. His eyes were also black.

Vena, the healer, was the smallest out of the three. Her face was soft and kind ... almost human-like. She had a cropped haircut with the edges of her hair dyed red. She had yellow eyes and small features.

They all bowed, without a single smile or word. I could only imagine what they thought of me. The half-breed that took the crown away from their father.

"And this is your uncle, Prince Rythlayn," continued Erendrial.

A tall man came from around the table towards me. He had shorter hair than my father but looked almost identical to him. His eyes were the same shade as Vena's. He was dressed in a black suit with a thick gold chain around his neck. He took my hand and kissed it gently as he bowed.

"Niece, it is so good to finally meet you. We have waited for this moment for a long while," he said in a deep, caring voice. He smiled at me as he rose to a standing position.

"Thank you, Prince Rythlayn—" I started to say.

"Please, uncle, if you would do me the honor. I am at your service. I can't tell you how happy I am for my brother. That you both have found each other," said Rythlayn.

"Thank you, uncle. I am also glad." I smiled at him, looking around the room for my sister. I leaned into Erendrial. "Where is Lily?"

"Working on dresses, remember? Would you like me to find her?"

"No thank you," I said, taking a seat next to my uncle. Erendrial sat on the other side as the human servants brought us plates of food and drink. Now that I had some time to ponder my conversation with Lily, I realized I may have overreacted a bit. I should have at least heard her out before lashing out like I did. I would make things right.

"How do you find our court, Princess Genevieve?" asked Queen Nora.

"From what I have seen, it is very ... entrancing," I replied.

"Better than the light court?" asked Toreon.

"They're both beautiful in their own way," I said, trying to sound unfazed by the mention of that hellhole.

"Is it true that you were King Atros's whore?" Icici asked.

Here we go, I thought to myself.

"Icici, do not speak to your cousin in that manner," snapped Rythlayn.

"If we are ever to have a relationship, honesty is a must. So, how was he? I find him most delicious. Last time he was here I tried to lure him to my bed, but he refused. I wonder if that was because of you." She smirked at me from the other side of the table.

I looked at Erendrial, not sure of how to respond. He focused on his food, apparently not willing to get into the ring with the two of us. I took a drink, trying to think.

"I was his mistress, yes," I replied shortly.

"Lucky girl you are. I can only imagine fisting all that white hair as he rode me till—"

"Icici, that is enough!" demanded her father.

She shut her mouth, her eyes still taunting me.

I focused on the fruit on my plate.

"I'm sorry about my daughter, niece," said Rythlayn. "She forgets her place far too often."

I smiled at him and nodded.

"Lily is your friend, right?" asked Vena.

"Yes," I replied.

"Her voice is lovely. She is my favorite singer. She is quite gifted for a human. I could only imagine what she would be like if she was an alfar," said Vena.

"She's perfect just the way she is," I replied firmly.

Vena nodded with a smile and then finished what was on her

plate.

"So, when is she going to begin training, Lyklor? If she really is a Drezmore, she will be a quick study," said Toreon.

"Tomorrow, once she is more familiar with our customs and the castle. Are you volunteering to get your ass kicked by the princess, Toreon?" asked Erendrial.

"I can be of assistance if you wish. Though, by the looks of her, I don't think I will be the one getting my ass kicked," said Toreon, sizing me up.

"Don't underestimate her. I have, and we lost our inside man in the light court. King Lysanthier did as well, and now he is dead," added Erendrial. I smiled at the memory of the king's mutilated body on top of his dinner table.

Two guards barged into the throne room carrying another alfar towards us, who was beaten and bleeding profusely. The alfar in the room smiled and began to gossip as they all stared at the blood being dragged across the floor. The guards dropped the male in front of us before exhaling with exhaustion.

"What has happened?" asked Rythlayn with authority.

"Excuse our interruption, Your Graces, but our men were attacked by a demon-like creature out in the woods this morning. It was hideous, with black skin and razor-sharp teeth," said one of the guards.

"Shit," I mumbled under my breath.

Erendrial began laughing at me as he looked down at the

wounded guard.

"What is so funny, Lyklor?" asked Icici.

He caught my eyes and crossed his arms, gesturing his hand for me to take the floor. I sat straight up in my chair, not sure how this was going to play out.

"Otar!" I tried to yell, but my voice sounded weak and pathetic. I waited a few moments before calling for him again.

"Yes, wicked one," I heard him whisper behind me.

The crowd of alfar gasped as they stood to their feet, readying their weapons and their powers to kill him. The dynamic of the two courts were complete opposites. Where the light court would have hid in fear, the dark court jumped into action, readying to attack in a moment's notice. Levos wasn't joking when he said they were all trained warriors.

"That's it! That's the ugly thing that attacked us this morning," yelled the guard.

"Now, now, now," rasped Otar. "I am not the ugly one, you all are. With that ugly color of skin and those dull and useless mouths of teeth you all have. And for the record, I was not the first to attack; he was." Otar nodded at the bloodied guard on the floor.

"Otar, what did I tell you about hurting anyone?" I whispered to him.

"I did as you asked, yes, I did. I didn't attack, I only defended. He was trying to kill me with his sharp pointy stick," Otar said, smiling down at the alfar.

I exhaled, trying to figure out what to say to him. I looked out on the court and cleared my throat. "This is Otar," I started to say. "He is under my control. He will not steal, harm, or kill anyone here as long as you do not attack him." Blank looks covered the alfar's faces. I didn't know if I was the thing that shocked them or if it was Otar. "Understood?" I asked, with as much authority as I could muster.

They all nodded, taking their seats.

"He is your ... pet?" asked Icici.

Otar appeared behind her in the blink of an eye, snapping his teeth at her throat.

She flinched away, her face frightened.

"I am no one's pet!" yelled Otar. "Please, punch me, so I can tear that pretty little head from your shoulders. Or maybe I will play with you first. You aren't as ugly as the others," he whispered, running a talon down her arm.

She pulled away from his touch with disgust.

"Otar, stop," I demanded.

He growled, appearing back at my side.

"I've had a room made up for you by mine," I relayed to him. "If you would like to stay here, you are welcome. Just don't hurt anyone else, understand?"

"Only if they hurt me first, right?" he said, twirling his finger through a loose curl on the back of my neck.

"Only if they physically mean to harm you, yes," I clarified.

"But I am hungry," he whined. Everyone at the table was still looking at me and Otar.

"Well, what do you eat?" I asked.

"Flesh is usually good, but blood is what keeps me alive and strong. I have had none since the light court," he whined.

"Are there no animals out there you can hunt?"

"They don't taste as good, and they don't restore my health. Not like humanoid beings do."

I exhaled, trying to come up with a plan that would keep everyone safe. I stood up from the chair gesturing for Otar to follow me. Erendrial stood.

I stopped him. "Can you give me ten minutes on my own, please? Then I will be ready to do whatever is on your agenda for the day," I said.

He looked at me and then Otar and nodded.

"I'll be in my chambers," I said before leading Otar out of the throne room. The court examined both of us with wonder, terror, or disgust: I didn't know which.

I got to my chambers and shut the door behind us. I took the apophyllite dagger that I still hid on my thigh and cut along my forearm. Otar watched with excitement as the blood spilled from my arm. I held the dagger firmly, ready to kill him if I had to.

"You can feed off me. You will not use your teeth. You will be gentle and only take what you need. When I tell you to stop, you will obey. You will not take any flesh, only blood," I said.

He nodded, taking a step towards me. He took my arm in his leathery hands and lifted my wound to his mouth and began to drink. He was indeed gentle, but the feeling still made me want to vomit.

In some way, I felt indebted to this creature. I didn't view him as a weapon or a slave, but as my salvation. He had freed me from the nightmare that had destroyed me. If he needed to feed, it was the least I could do. The sight of the light king's mutilated body would forever be my favorite memory.

After a few moments of feeding, he pulled away, licking his lips with satisfaction.

"You taste better than I could have imagined, wicked one," he said, looking at the blood that was smeared across my arm.

The door opened behind us. Erendrial stopped, looking at my bloodied arm and then at Otar. I grabbed a nearby piece of cloth, wrapping my arm to stop the bleeding so it could heal.

"Otar, go," I said. Otar disappeared in an instant.

"What did I just walk in on?" asked Erendrial.

"Nothing. Are you ready to begin?" I asked, moving past him into the hall.

He followed. "Princess, if he poses any threat to you, he will have to be eliminated," Erendrial said.

"He doesn't."

"Then why are you bleeding?"

"I gave him my blood willingly. He needs the blood of a humanoid to survive. I didn't want him snacking on anyone else, so I gave him what he needed."

He pulled at my arm gently, stopping me from moving ahead. "You willingly allowed that *thing* to feed on you? Teeth and all?" he asked.

"I told him he couldn't use his teeth, but yes. Would you rather he tears out your artery?" I asked smugly.

He smiled, exhaling with frustration. "For the record, I don't like this. We will have some of the servants donate blood from now on."

"No! I will not force an innocent to sacrifice such a thing." I said instantly. "Otar is my responsibility, and I will deal with him the way I see fit. Now, onto the tour please." I pushed past him, back into the halls of my new prison.

CHAPTER FOUR

E rendrial led me through the massive Kingdom of Doonak for the rest of the day. The city was built into the center of the mountain below the actual castle. After descending staircase after staircase, we approached a large archway where sounds and light seemed coax me closer. As I reached the threshold, the confining space opened into a massive, cavernous room. Shops, restaurants, metalsmiths, jewelers, and other professions lined the carved pathways on either side of every street. Balls of light floated aimlessly, illuminating the entire city.

At the top of the ceiling, dark purple and blue fog hovered above the buildings—the same type of fog that was in the throne room of the castle. Erendrial told me that it was the raw dark magic that ran through our blood. Its power was used to create the kingdom and remnants were scattered throughout the mountain.

The buildings and shops were well kept. Spotless glass in each window reflected the sparkling flame of the candles lit within. Each handcrafted door depicted the logo of their family sigil or business. Some sigils contained flames, others stars, and some displayed symbols I had never seen before.

The cobblestone streets wove and twirled throughout the city, connecting the different levels of the structure. Fountains of water were scattered throughout the different meeting areas. The water ran blue and purple and had a sparkle to it, as if the stars were caught inside. Beautiful sculptures were spread throughout the streets, made of a marble and black stone I had never seen before. The eyes of the sculptures turned and followed us as we walked past. The dark magic in the city enchanted them, giving them animated tendencies.

Humans were scattered throughout the city busying themselves with work. Some swept the streets; others ran errands for their ladies and lords. I came upon male and female alfar along with some humans, stripping and exploring each other's bodies in plain sight for all to see. Down the alleyways in between the buildings, sounds of sex and ecstasy filled the air as they screwed each other against anything that was in reach.

I turned away, trying to block out the sights and sounds of them. It made my skin crawl to even be nearby. Erendrial seemed to notice my discomfort and pulled me back into a busier part of the city. I took a few breaths, calming myself as I felt his eyes lingering on me.

"You will need to get used to that kind of behavior if this is to be your kingdom someday, princess," said Erendrial.

"I didn't ask for this, and I don't think I will ever get used to seeing people screwing each other in public," I responded, feeling my anger rise.

"Besides the public displays of affection, what do you think of the main city?" he asked.

"It's actually quite remarkable, minus the creepy statues."

He laughed at me as we descended further into the mountain. "I'm glad to hear you think so."

Everything I had seen thus far didn't match the rumors and terrors I had heard of the dark court. I had to be missing something.

"Where are all the human dissections and torturing conducted?"

He arched his eyebrow at me. "We're not as bad as some like to think. We like our humans, and we like sex, but we don't torture them like the light alfar would have you believe. In the beginning, after we created the Kingdom of Doonak, there were experiments and testing conducted on every species. The dark alfar are knowledge- and power-hungry. Sometimes, in order to accomplish your goals, morals have to be broken.

"We crossbred species. Dissected them. Pushed their bodies, abilities, and minds to their limits, to understand what we were up against. After the war with the demons, our world was forever changed. There was a very small number of us and a lot more of every other species out there, so we had to be prepared. But those kinds of methods stopped about two thousand years ago. We learned all we needed to, and we became more powerful than any other thing in our world as our powers and numbers grew.

"We decided to foster relationships with each species and race of creature. We sent out ambassadors to broker peace with the other races and eventually created a working network with the different groups of fae. As far as humans go, we still need them to assist in the operation of our kingdom. Though there are still cases of rape and abuse that we must combat, most of the humans here are taken by request, not against their will."

"Is that what you tell yourselves?" I said sarcastically. "That the humans back in The Frey wanted to be kidnapped?"

A small smirk rose at the corner of his lips. "No, princess. We don't ask the humans for their permission when we take them as workers, but when it comes to the sexual side of their involvement with our kind, we give them the curtesy of declining."

Anger flared inside of me. "So, what about the sacrifices to Azeer?" I asked.

"Two sacrifices happen a year. During the Winter Solstice, three humans are burned through the longest night of the year. We try to choose humans who are sick, in pain, or willing to be sacrificed. We take away their feelings of pain and fear as the fires are lit so they are sent to him peacefully. The second sacrifice happens during the Summer Solstice. A virgin alfar no older than fifteen sacrifices themselves on a blood altar as payment for our powers."

"What is the purpose?"

"It is the deal Maleki made with Azeer in order to obtain the Dark Flame. The virgin represents the innocence our kind sacrificed in order to win the war against our enemies. The three human sacrifices in the winter symbolize our metamorphosis from the common race we were before the Norse gods transformed us into alfar: first to kind and nurturing beings the light court still possesses, and now, to the powerful darkness that saved our world from extinction."

"Disgusting," I said, a chill of fear and rage fluttering under my skin.

"It is what it is. We do not have a choice. This is what was demanded of us. Even though our generation did not make the bargain, we must uphold our end of it."

"What happens if you stop the sacrifices altogether?"

"I don't know, and I never will know. Regardless, if we like it or not, this is what we must do." He stopped at one of the bistros in the middle of the city street and flagged another alfar over who owned the place.

He approached us with a blank expression, looking at me and then Erendrial. "Ambassador Lyklor, it is a pleasure to serve you. What can I do for you today?" asked the male.

"First, you can show respect to Princess Genevieve Drezmore with a bow," Erendrial said with authority and annoyance.

The alfar's eyes got wide, looking towards me in shock. He dropped his head and bowed low. "Please forgive me, Your Highness, I did not know who you were," he said.

"It is okay, thank you," I said.

He lifted his head and nodded to me in thanks.

"Two of your hot chocolates, please," Erendrial said to the man. "And make sure to add a dash of fire."

The alfar nodded, heading back into the bistro. We took a seat at a small table in front of the window of the shop. I smiled, amused by Erendrial's order.

He looked at me and smirked. "Find something humorous?"

"The ambassador of the dark court drinking hot chocolate," I laughed as the words came out of my mouth. It was the first time I had really laughed that I could remember. It felt good and freeing.

He smirked at me and nodded. "Well, I am glad I could be of amusement to you, princess, but don't judge me too harshly until you taste this specific brew. It is a favorite of mine. There is no other like it."

"What is a dash of fire?" I asked.

"A shot of whiskey is added to the mix. The owner, Hertus Yesper, grows his own beans and creates his own whiskey for the recipe. Every ingredient he touches, he has harvested," Erendrial said, leaning across the table.

"Whiskey," I said, chuckling to myself.

"What? You don't like whiskey?"

"Quite the opposite. It's just ... whiskey is what your gift smelled like when you used it on me the last time I saw you. Whiskey and oranges," I said, feeling a bit warm at the admission.

He sat up, looking out into the crowds of people. "Huh, is that so? And you liked the smell?" He didn't turn his eyes to me.

"It was ... comforting in an odd way," I admitted.

"My gift affects people in different ways. Each time I use it on a new being, they experience different feelings, tastes, and smells. Never had whiskey and oranges before though."

Hertus came out from the shop with two steaming cups of hot chocolate. He placed them down on the table in front of us and then gave another small bow.

"On the house, Princess Genevieve. It is a pleasure to have you here," he said before returning to work.

Erendrial picked up his cup and held it out to me for a toast. "To a wonderful beginning and a powerful reign," he said.

I knocked my glass against his before bringing the liquid to my lips. The aroma filled my nostrils, making my mouth water, and my stomach yearn. I allowed a small amount to pass through my lips before an involuntary moan of satisfaction escaped.

Erendrial smiled, dabbing his lips with a napkin. "Told you."

"This is better than anything I have ever tasted," I said, taking another mouth full.

"Well, I am glad you are pleased. It is my job to make you happy," he said, winking at me.

I dropped my face, uncomfortable by the action. "When does the Jestu celebration take place?" I asked, trying to put us back on track. It was the all-night sex party I remember Levos telling me about that their court hosted each month.

"Twice a month. We just had one two days ago, so we won't be having the next for another two weeks. Why? Interested in joining?"

"No," I said quickly, turning in my chair.

"It is custom that the heir to the throne be present during the festivities. You don't have to partake, but you will be expected to be there."

I held the warm cup close to my chest, feeling the panic rise inside of me. "How long do I have to stay?"

"An hour or so. It is usually an all-night event."

I pinched my eyes together, not even wanting to think about sex. "Is there any way out of it?"

"Unfortunately, no." Erendrial leaned forward, trying to catch my eyes with his.

I turned away, trying to hide my fear from him. "So, what will my days look like from now on?" I asked.

"The only meal you are expected to attend in the throne room is dinner with your father amongst the court. During the day you will be educated in our ways, on the races of our world, and in combat. You will learn how to defend yourself and work as a unit against the beasts coming from the rift."

"Will I be able to kill those things out there?" I asked, anxiously. The thought of being able to not only protect myself, but to hunt and kill, excited me. More than I thought it would.

"Is that something you want?"

"Yes," I said, all too quickly.

He laughed softly. "Then yes. You will be able to fight and be a part of the diplomatic negotiations with the other races until you are with child."

I stopped, straightening my back at the word child. My stomach turned. "What?"

"Until you are with child. When you are pregnant you will need to remain here, protected and out of harm's way."

"And who am I supposed to be creating this child with?" Surely, there would be an arranged marriage as I had seen happen in the light court. I wouldn't get to choose. I would be forced to lay with yet another alfar I did not want.

"There are three candidates that have been chosen to compete for your hand. Soddram Yositru, who is an air caster and is currently helping settle a political matter in the Draugr court. He comes from a very old and high family. Therosi Servi is a blood sifter. His father sits at the king's table. He is very respected and holds a lot of sway among the dark alfar. Then there is Avalon Flarion, who is a shapeshifter like Queen Nora. He is her nephew."

"How long until a decision is made about a ... husband?" I asked, choking on the word.

"It won't happen until after the winter solstice, so you will have some time to get your bearings. The king will conduct a tournament where each male is tested on three things: intelligence, strength, and will. The winner will become the next King of Doonak."

"Fantastic," I said sarcastically. I sipped the rest of the hot chocolate, signaling for Hertus. "Hi, yes, can I please have three shots of whiskey, thank you," I said, matter-of-factly.

Erendrial nodded to Hertus, never taking his eyes off me. "Not so thrilled about your impending prenuptials I take it?" Erendrial asked.

Hertus dropped the three small crystal glasses off in front of me on the table. I slammed them back one after another, allowing the warm smooth whiskey to run down my throat and take hold of my nerves.

"I'm being forced to be with yet another male I do not want. How would you feel? Being forced to take a wife and have a child with them?" I paused to let him speak, but he said nothing. "Exactly." I stood from the table, feeling the smooth arms of the whiskey wrap around me.

Erendrial stood slowly. "Come on, we need to get you fitted for your wardrobe," he said, reaching his arm out to me. I took it, only to steady myself.

The dress shop was extravagant. Hundreds of bolts of fabric littered every wall. Mirrors and platforms were stationed at different points in the room where alfar females gushed over their revealing fashions that left little to the imagination.

My eyes scanned the room, taking in the textures and shades of the beautiful fabrics and detail of each design. I had never seen anything like this place. A small smile began to creep along the edges of my lips but was instantly muted as my eyes landed on Icici, my new bitchy cousin. I groaned, a little louder than I had intended.

Erendrial smiled, looking down at me. "You'll need to learn how to handle her sooner rather than later, along with your alcohol."

"Yeah, thanks for that little tidbit," I whispered, already slurring my words.

She saw us approach and smiled gracefully. She looked like a royal. Her hair was perfect, not a strand out of place. Her figure was smooth and sinful. Her eyes drew one in and held them captive. Gold hoops pierced her long-pointed ears, which only added to her appeal. I exhaled, taking in my beautiful, flawless cousin.

"And may I ask what new revelation you just made?" asked Erendrial. "We're going to need to work on those facial expressions of yours,"

"I am just now realizing I got hit with the ugly branch on the way down from the family tree," I said, bringing my hand up to my small, pointed ears, a constant reminder that I would never fully be one of them.

Erendrial gently took my hand from my ear and brought it back down to my side. "Never reveal your weakness to anyone, including me. I know this is a lot to absorb, but you need to appear strong, no matter what you really feel. If you waver, they will eat you alive, understand?" he whispered softly.

I nodded, turning back to Icici as she headed in our direction.

"Ambassador Lyklor ... cousin," she said, giving me a small curtsy. "Are you here to get fitted for your winter wardrobe?"

"Yes, and you?" I asked.

"Of course. The wind is beginning to chill, and I need to make sure my skin is protected. I know a few males in particular who would hate the thought of my flawless skin being scarred," she said, looking at Erendrial seductively. Her eyes drifted back to me and then stopped abruptly on the Lysanthier sigil burned into my chest.

I shifted from embarrassment of the marking but felt Erendrial's arm stiffen in warning.

"Yes, that would be a shame," I said, giving her a small, unfeeling smile.

"Well, don't let me keep you. I have things I must attend to before dinner," she said, moving beside Erendrial. She placed a hand on his chest. "I presume I will see you a bit later, once your courtly duties are fulfilled?" She looked up at him with desire and hunger.

He gave her a small smile before she continued out of the shop. I took my arm from his, covering my open-hanging mouth with my hand.

"You're sleeping with my cousin?" I asked in disbelief.

He shrugged, walking past me. "From time to time," he said, taking a seat in one of the red velvet couches in front of the wall of mirrors.

Two human girls came out from the back, ushering me to a small platform in front of the mirrors. They began taking my measurements as I stared Erendrial down in the mirror.

He exhaled in frustration. "If you have something to say, princess, just say it."

"Oh no. I have nothing to say at all about where you choose to put your dick," I replied.

The two human girls snickered with amusement as they worked around me.

"A bit judgey now, aren't we?" he replied.

"I'm sure you were disappointed when you learned Icici was no longer going to be queen. What influence you would have had."

"Please, Icici would have been a terrible queen. She's too selfish," he said without emotion.

"So, should I expect your wedding to be before or after mine? Just so our themes and colors don't clash," I said, arching my brow at him.

He laughed, leaning his upper body over his knees. "It is not like that. Here, sex is just that, sex. You can have it with anyone and then go about your business without any promises or consequences. Plus, I've already told you. I will never take a wife. Your cousin is just a means for a good time. That is all."

"So, you've never had feelings for anyone? You can just fuck and move on without a single feeling?"

"Yup, pretty much. As I told you, alfar do not love. It is an inconvenience and a weakness."

I dropped my eyes from his, realizing how cold my life would be here. At least I would have Lily, even if only for another fifty years. But then, what would I do? What would I look to for a glimmer of hope and happiness?

"Seems like a cold and lonely life," I replied, turning my attention to the fabrics and designs the two girls had set out for me.

Erendrial stared at me, not saying another word.

I chose dark blues, purples, and black for most of my dresses. I threw a couple of red ones in there just to mix it up. Fur, lace, silk, and velvet were in for the season, so I conformed to the norm. Erendrial escorted me back to my rooms, as he discussed how the politics worked within the kingdom. I discovered I would have a seat on the board next to my father.

I would have to learn how to be a politician along with a warrior, diplomat, queen, wife, mother, and ruler. So many hats, so many responsibilities. I could do this. I had to. As if my wish had been granted, I would now have the power to protect myself and those I loved, but at what cost? Would I lose myself to the dark court? Becoming as cold and unfeeling as they appeared? Maybe that was okay. Maybe that was better than feeling the claws of the monster that tortured me day and night. Feeling nothing, was better than feeling this pain.

CHAPTER FIVE

The two guards stationed outside of my room bowed to me before opening the purple doors. Erendrial followed me in, making his way to my study. On the table across from my desk were stacks of books that hadn't been there this morning. I went over to them, peering down at the writing on the leather covers.

"Homework?" I asked.

"We will have to first teach you to read, but yes," said Erendrial, sorting through the stacks of books.

"I can read," I whispered.

He stopped, looking back at me with surprise. "Well, I am glad to see Gaelin was good for something other than—"

"—It wasn't Gaelin," I interrupted him, knowing where the comment was headed, "it was Levos Atros. He is … was a friend to me, when I was there." The mention of Levos tugged at the empty part in my heart. Surely, he hated me and never wanted to see me again after learning the full truth. I dropped my head, trying not to show my weakness, as Erendrial had instructed.

"Levos Atros is an intelligent and well-rounded young alfar. They don't put him to use effectively in my opinion, but I am glad he was a friend to you. Well, that makes my job easier. Never liked teaching much. Go sit at the desk and we can begin."

I did as I was told, pulling the large velvet chair from the wooden desk. I had a feeling I was going to be spending more time in this chair than my bed.

Erendrial placed three books on the desk. He opened the first book to a page that had my family's sigil marked at the top. "This is your family history. A detailed account of each member's magical abilities and talents along with who they married. The rest of these books consist of every high and low house of alfar in our court. The first thing you need to learn is who possesses what abilities. This is a way to protect yourself and it will allow you to understand exactly who you are dealing with. Start with the high houses."

I pulled the book closer towards me and began to read. For the next two hours, Erendrial answered any questions I had and filled in the blanks for me.

The magical powers of the mother and father didn't necessarily fall to their offspring. Some alfar would have only one gift, while others had two. There was no way of knowing exactly what a child's gift would be, which made keeping track of who could do what that much harder.

A knock came at the door and Atalee entered my room with a rack of clothing. I exhaled, thankful for her interruption. Erendrial perched on the edge of the desk looking down at me.

He smiled, seeming amused by my exhaustion. "When dinner is

over, I want you to go over this again. Remember, the faster you learn, the faster you will be able to protect yourself. Also, try to sleep in the bed tonight. You begin training tomorrow morning and you will need a good night's rest," he said before heading to the door. "See you at dinner, princess." He turned and gave me a small, exaggerated bow with that devilish smile spread across his face.

"Erendrial," I said, before he could take his leave. "I know you're just doing what my father asked but, thank you ... for today. You were a lot of help. I appreciate it." I forced a smile.

He nodded with a soft grin and took his leave.

I made my way over to Atalee, who was waving her hands across my armoire.

"What are you doing?" I asked.

She smiled and reached for the doorknobs. "Watch," she said, pulling them open. Inside the armoire, a room as large as my study had appeared. It was filled with dresses, shoes, coats, covers, crowns, and jewelry, so much jewelry. I stepped inside in awe and shock.

"This was not here last night," I said, remembering the small armoire that provided me with a sense of safety and comfort.

She laughed at me, rolling the rack of clothing inside. "Only you and I can access this. It's enchanted to hide the more expensive pieces of your collection. Impressive, wouldn't you agree?"

"Oh, I do," I said, running my hands across the different types of fabrics of my gowns.

"This one is what you will wear tonight," she said, pulling a bloodred dress out from the cart.

"Is there a holiday I wasn't informed about?"

"Tonight, your father will officially introduce you to the high houses. They all know of you, but for him to recognize you in public among the court solidifies your place. It's a formality of sorts."

I nodded, not looking forward to being put on display. I was tired of being gawked at by these beings: judged for things I had no control over. I didn't ask for this, nor did I want it, yet here I was being paraded out in the open like some show horse. I was well aware of the target on my back. No title would be able to save me.

I sat at the vanity in my room as Atalee worked my hair into a slick and perfect masterpiece. She redid my makeup, with a more dramatic black liner and a vibrant red lip. My lashes stood out from my lids, long and heavy. She glued gold jewels around my eyes and down my cheekbones.

The red dress was stunning, which I was learning would be the norm for my new wardrobe. It was a floor-length dress with a train in the back. The bodice was tight, accentuating my waist. The neckline plunged down the middle, wrapping the stiff fabric around my breasts stopping just before my navel. The top of the neckline reached up on either side of my shoulders and curved into sharp tips that were capped with gold pieces.

The dress fell long and formed to my body the rest of the way down. Black feathers scattered the bottom of the hem and followed the slit up the left side of my thigh. I wore gold diamond high heels that matched the jewelry Atalee placed on me. My neck was left bare, until she brought out a jar of gold dust. She started under my jaw and then dusted my neck, chest, and down the center of my rib cage with the gold flecks. My crown sat on top of my head, completing the look.

I turned around to look at myself in the mirror. The Genevieve I once knew back in The Frey was gone. The scared, desperate young woman who was willing to sacrifice every part of herself to save her sister no longer stared back at me with tears in her eyes. I was a royal, and I damn well looked the part.

My green eyes blazed under the dark makeup. My lips seemed fuller than I remembered and my body— the body that I hated for so many months, was now draped in gold and riches. Atalee smiled behind me with pride.

"You are an artist," I said to her.

She smiled, dropping her head. "You're easy to get ready. Quite fun actually," she responded.

A knock came at the door. She rushed over and bowed as she opened the door for my father. He stepped in, draped in a long black silk robe with red trim. It hugged his strong form as did the stiff pants he wore underneath. His gold crown, in the shape of flames, sat on top of his head. He rounded the corner, stopping dead in his tracks as he looked upon me. He didn't smile, he didn't blink, he just stared.

"Thank you, Atalee, that will be all," he said.

I brought my hands in front of my stomach, fidgeting uncomfortably. He took slow strides towards me until he hovered above, lifting my chin with a single finger until our eyes met. He gave me a small smile and nodded. "You look stunning, my daughter." He kissed me softly on the cheek before extending his arm towards me.

"Thank you ... father," I said with a forced smile.

Everything inside of me wanted to trust him, but how could I? He was the ruler of the dark court. He allowed the terror that occurred here. How would I ever grow to fully trust him?

I felt his eyes searching my face. "Is something wrong, daughter?" he asked.

"No ... it's just ... I still have so many questions."

He smiled softly. "We have time, I assure you. I know this all must be a lot to take in, but you are safe now. You are home."

Home. A faint memory of safety, warmth, and laughter. Something I hadn't felt since in the basement of the church back in The Frey. Would I ever feel that sense of safety—of peace—of happiness again?

We walked towards my door to exit into the hall. I held my head high with my shoulders back. My father was the king, and I was to be queen. I had to act like it.

We got to the doors of the throne room. The halls were mostly empty, besides a few servants. Everyone was waiting for us inside. Waiting for me. He looked at me one more time and nodded. I smiled, tightening my arm around his, and nodded back. We faced forward as the guards opened the doors slowly. The announcer at the threshold spoke loud and boldly.

"Everyone rise for the king and princess of Doonak. King Avalmon Drezmore, and his daughter and heir, Princess Genevieve Drezmore," the male said.

Hundreds of people packed the throne room. They rose and bowed as we descended the aisle towards the thrones. The moment passed slowly while I took in each of their faces. Each of the court members smiled at me. I didn't know who to trust: who would be my ally, and who would try to kill me. Each of them, rehearsed in the art of deception. A game I would need to learn how to play if I were to survive.

The purple and blue magic that swarmed overhead began to spark with lightning as we approached the platform. I kept my eyes forward, acting as if I was unfazed. We got to the steps and ascended to stand in front of the thrones. The queen bowed towards us with respect. I looked at my father as he took my hand in his and held it up. He looked out into the crowd, allowing a moment more to pass.

"High houses of Doonak, it is my pleasure to present my daughter and heir, Genevieve Drezmore of Doonak," said the king. He turned to face me and lowered on one knee, smiling up at me with pride for the first time. His face in this moment would be a memory I would never forget.

The court followed his lead and bowed again. I took a deep breath in, uncomfortable at the gesture. I tried to steady myself, but anyone who knew me could see through my mask. I looked to the right where Erendrial bowed. He drew his eyes to mine and smiled softly with a slight nod.

The court finally rose as my father, the queen, and I took our seats on our thrones. The rest of the members sat at their tables while the servants began to serve them the first course. Each house of the court appeared in front of us one by one, introducing themselves before kneeling in front of my father and I to pledge their loyalty to us, as custom called for when the reigning monarch announced their heir.

I tried to memorize their faces, noting unique things about each alfar. House Sollerum's heirs were twins. Both of the male's names started with H's but I failed to remember them. House Tiflon's patriarch seemed to be a kind, older alfar male. Even though I didn't know him, something inside of me told me he was trustworthy.

He unleashed his magic, creating beautiful snowflakes to fall around me. Each white flake caught in my dark hair. I felt myself smile, entertained by his gift. The male grinned with glee, before bowing and taking his leave.

I was overwhelmed. I kept my expression cold and unfeeling,

as I had seen my father do, yet, on the inside my paranoia was getting the better of me. Each court member that came before me I assessed, praying to the gods I would be granted a vision in order to see who would attempt to rob me of my poor, pathetic life. A few nights ago, I was prepared to die; yet now, something inside of me begged to live.

We eventually made our way to the dining table where we were greeted by my uncle and three cousins. We ate with pleasant conversation. Icici was on her best behavior with my father present. Vena spoke the most, trying to get to know me with personal questions about my likes and dislikes. If I didn't know better, I would have thought she was genuine, but she was Icici's sister.

An alfar woman with dark brown hair shot through with white stripes made her way over to me. She had white eyes to match her hair and a long face. Everything seemed long about her: her nose, lips, neck, ears, all of it. She was skinnier than most alfar females I had seen. She bowed in the presence of my father and then nodded to my uncle. I noted the smile that appeared on his face. Almost as if they were romantically involved. If they were she did not reveal any sign of satisfaction from his gesture. Her eyes turned back to me.

"What a joyous occasion, princess. My name is Lady Winnow Fellwood. I am the court's seer... well, *other* seer," she said softly.

"A seer," I said with excitement. "It is a pleasure to meet you."

"The pleasure is all mine," she replied. "I hope to host you in my chambers soon. I am curious to discover if there is any links between our gifts."

"I would very much like that," I replied.

She bowed without another word before taking her leave.

After dinner, we took our seats back on our thrones. The members of the high continued to line up, paying their respects to their king and new heir. Erendrial came up behind me and began to whisper who each member was and what their powers were. Some of them I recognized from my studies, but most of the information was new to me.

Once the formalities were through, the tables were cleared and music began to play. Lilian's voice flooded the air as she sang in Latin. I turned to see her standing in front of the musicians on a small stage. I stood from my throne, walking towards her with a smile, remembering what joy and comfort her voice brought me. The alfar and humans began to dance on the open floor. They were elegant and fluid as they danced in a style I had never seen before. Red goblets of wine were passed around to the humans and alfar. As they drank, they became looser and more relaxed.

A male appeared in front of me that I recalled from the introduction ceremony. His eyes had been full of something like hunger, as they were even now. He was about six feet tall, with skin the color of caramel and brilliant green eyes, only a shade duller than my own. His black hair was combed away from his forehead, cleanly shaped and highlighted with red streaks. He had thin lips and a strong chin.

His black imprint started under his neck and traveled down his chest disappearing into his black shirt. Silver piercings lined each of his pointed ears. He smiled at me, revealing a beautiful white set of teeth that could light up a room. His broad, muscular shoulders pulled the fabric of his shirt taut. He might have been the most handsome male alfar I had ever seen.

He extended his hand to me.

"Princess Genevieve," he started as he bent down, kissing the top of my hand softly. "I am sure you don't remember but. I am—"

"—Therosi Servi," I interrupted with a sly smile. "You're one of my suitors?".

He laughed, rising to a standing position. "Most likely your future husband, but let's not get too ahead of ourselves on our first date," he said, winking at me.

"Date?" I asked, pulling my hand away from his.

He examined me from head to toe. His eyes wandered over my figure slowly as he lingered at my hips and then chest. "I may have spoken too quickly. How about I ask for a dance first and then we will go from there," he said, extending his hand back out to me.

I took it with reluctance, cringing at the physical contact. I looked back at Lily, knowing I would eventually have to smooth things over with her. He pulled me into him, placing his hand on my lower back while the music slowed. My body lit up and not in a good way.

I forced my eyes down to the floor, trying not to feel his warm breath breathing down onto my face. He led us across the floor, twirling and gliding me along with him. My feet fumbled trying to match each of his steps. I had no clue what I was doing. I looked up into his mesmerizing eyes. He was smiling down at me, his eyes hesitant and curious.

"You are more than I had expected. Being what you are." he said.

"A half-breed, you mean?" I replied with an attitude.

He laughed, spinning me around once. I almost lost my balance as he pulled me back into his chest. "Direct. I like that about you. There are a lot of things I find that I like about you in a short period of time."

"Oh, besides my crown," I said, trying to pull away from him.

He tightened his grip on me, pulling me back in. "You do not have to fear me, Genevieve. If I am lucky enough to become your husband, I will treat you with respect and honor. Your happiness I will strive for, I promise you this," he said softly.

I looked back into his eyes, trying to read him, like I had seen Erendrial do to so many others back at the light court. "Why would my happiness mean anything to you? Marriage here is just a contract. A power play, nothing more."

He nodded, with a smile. "Usually, yes, but I would like something different. I've had my fair share of affairs and Jestu's, and frankly I am bored."

"So, I would be just a means of entertainment? How romantic."

"A bit of romance wouldn't be so bad, now, would it?" he said softly, dragging the side of his thumb down my cheek.

I trembled at the action. He pulled back. Someone passed a red goblet to Therosi. He took it, still looking at me, before taking a drink. He smiled, licking his lips, and then passing the cup to me.

"What is it?" I asked.

"Ambrosia, from the Greek gods. It gives you quite the high if the right amount is consumed."

I took the glass, looking down at the clear sparkling liquid inside.

"If this is the first time you've had it, take a small amount and wait to see how it affects you."

I brought the cup to my mouth and hesitated before the liquid could touch my lips. Therosi gently tipped the bottom of the glass up, encouraging me to take it. Before the ambrosia could slip past the rim, a hand snatched the cup from mine. I looked up to see Erendrial passing the red goblet to a human servant as he stood facing Therosi.

Erendrial casually slid his hands into his pockets, squaring off his shoulders while he cooly sized Therosi up. "Is this your plan to win her heart, Servi? Getting her high so she will forget who you are?"

Therosi laughed, shaking his head in annoyance. "Lyklor, why is it that you show up at the most inconvenient times?" asked Therosi.

"Inconvenient for you maybe, but not me. I find my timing quite spectacular." said Erendrial, taking a step closer towards Therosi.

"No harm done. If Genevieve didn't want the ambrosia, I wasn't going to force her. I wouldn't do that to my future wife. I do want her to like me, after all," Therosi said, winking at me.

"She is Princess Genevieve to you, and she is not your wife yet, Servi," Erendrial said. "The king would like a word with you, Lord Servi," he said, placing his body in between Therosi and I.

Therosi looked as if he wanted to shred Erendrial to pieces. He took another step forward, now chest to chest with the ambassador. He moved around Erendrial and bowed in front of me.

"It was a pleasure to get to spend a few brief moments with you, Princess Genevieve. I hope we get more chances like this. And please, remember what I said to you about our future. I hope you consider my proposal," said Therosi, kissing my hand before taking his leave.

Erendrial turned, taking me in his arms as he began to dance with me to the sound of Lily's voice. "What was his proposal?" Erendrial asked after a few seconds of dancing.

"Therosi said that if he were to become my husband, he would want a real marriage, where my happiness would mean something to him," I said, feeling stupid for even letting the words pass my lips.

Erendrial huffed, tightening his hand around mine. "Therosi

wants to be king, that is all. Don't believe any promises he makes you."

"Just like I shouldn't trust anything you tell me?" I asked him smugly.

He stopped, looking down at me with amusement. He leaned down to my ear, hovering there for a moment before speaking. "If you want a monogamous relationship, I suggest you take a human lover. You will never get it from an alfar. Especially not one from this court." He pulled away, looking into my eyes, the silver mercury inside swirling around his dark pupils.

"I know," I responded unfeelingly. I dropped my gaze from his as we drifted across the floor. He held me close enough that I could smell the faint scent of oranges and whiskey coming off him. I looked out in the crowd and watched as alfar and humans began to let their guards down as the ambrosia took effect.

A female came up from behind Erendrial, placing her hand on his bicep. He stopped dancing and turned towards her. She was a beautiful dark alfar with chestnut brown hair and black eyes. Her figure was tall and curvaceous with a full chest and a nice set of legs. Her eyes were large and almond-shaped. Her mouth was plump, and her nose was small and shapely. She looked at Erendrial and then back to me.

"Your Highness, my name is Rismera Calavi. It is an honor to meet you," she said with a curtsy.

"Nice to meet you, Lady Calavi," I replied.

Erendrial's grip tightened on me before he pulled away, an odd reaction for him.

She rose and smiled at me and then looked to Erendrial. "Ambassador Lyklor, may I steal you away from the princess for a bit. I have a few matters to discuss with you," she said.

"Of course, Lady Calavi," replied Erendrial. He turned to me and nodded with a half-hearted smile. "Princess, I will see you in the morning. Please, remember what I said about your sleeping arrangements. I can assure you the bed is much more comfortable than your former sleeping place." He winked at me before following Lady Calavi out of the throne room.

I made my way back to my father to tell him I was retiring for the evening. Two guards escorted me back to my room where Atalee was waiting. She helped remove all the makeup and the jewelry. Once she stripped me of my dress, I finally felt like myself again. She pulled my bed back and tidied the room before getting ready to leave.

"Atalee, before you retire for the evening, can you please send Lilian Thomas to my room?" I asked.

She nodded, taking her leave.

About twenty minutes later, a knock came at my door. A guard stepped inside the seating area of my chambers and announced Lily. I slid on my robe and made my way to the other room.

Lily was in a beautiful gold dress that complimented her hair and skin color. She held her hands together in front of her with her head down, trying not to look at me. Once we were alone, I gestured for us to sit on the couch. I could tell she was uncomfortable and didn't know what to say to me after our last conversation. I took her hand in mine, trying to give her some sense of comfort.

"Lily ... I am so sorry for the way that I spoke to you the last time we were together. I had no right," I said.

"You're the Princess of Doonak. You have every right to speak to me the way you see fit," she replied.

I turned her to face mine. "I am your sister first and foremost. Always," I said, taking her face in my hands.

Her bottom lip began to curl over as her chin shivered. "Do you really think that of me? That I should burn because—" she started to say.

"No, no of course not. I was just taken back by your choice. I am still trying to understand this place. It's nothing like the rumors warned us, and when I saw Zerrial and the way you acted towards him, I just went into overprotective mode I guess."

"I didn't expect this to happen, Gen. I promise," she said, with tears rolling down her face.

"Are you happy? Does he make you happy?" I asked.

She waited a few moments and then began to nod. "Very happy," she whispered.

I exhaled with a forced smile. "Tell me about him. How you met, what he does. I want to know everything."

She smiled at me, wiping her tears from her face. "I didn't start singing until week three of being here. That was the first time I really got a good look at the dark court. He was captivated with me from the start. He made his intentions to bed me very clear." She laughed at the memory. "I was naturally taken aback by his pursuit and didn't return his attention. He never gave up. He started sending me gifts. Jewelry, instruments, poetry, flowers, the works. The poetry was my favorite. At first, I thought it was from a book he had found, but he told me he wrote it just for me.

"Then we started talking on a daily basis. He would sneak away to have lunch with me out in the forest. He would make me laugh and he didn't look down on me for being human. For being a big brute, he is really sweet and thoughtful. After two months of getting to know him, I finally gave into my feelings and admitted that I cared for him.

"Our first time together he was so gentle with me. He made sure I was okay with everything that was happening. That night was the best night of my life and since then I've spent every night with him. He's claimed me as his and the other alfar fear him enough to not try anything."

"Are you two exclusive?" I asked.

"We don't really talk about that part of our relationship, and I don't push it. I don't know if I want to know, but we fall asleep together every night. And when I wake up, he is still there, so I like to think so," she said.

"And ... he has told you he loves you?"

"No, but he shows me every day. I know the alfar have different opinions and outlooks on relationships than us humans, but I've never been happier than I am with him. As long as I am with him, that is all I care about."

I gave her a small smile, trying to look happy. How could she not want to know if she was the only one he was sleeping with? How could she tolerate not hearing that she was loved and that she was enough? She wasn't me, and I didn't ask. I had to be happy for her, regardless if I agreed with the male she chose to be with.

"You said he works for Erendrial?" I asked.

"Yes, his right hand. Zerrial is a soldier and one of the deadliest alfar from what I have gathered. He doesn't talk a lot about his work because Eren doesn't allow it, but I know enough to know that Erendrial Lyklor is very dangerous and you should not underestimate him, Gen."

"Yes, that seems to be the reigning consensus. What else do you know about Erendrial?" I asked.

"The court calls him the ambassador of lies and manipulation. He started from nothing and worked his way to your father's table by outsmarting and outmaneuvering anyone who got in his way. The rumor is that he slept his way to power by bedding some of the high ladies. In return for his services, they offered to pay for his school and other materials and resources he used to get where he is.

"He has a group of dark alfar that are loyal to him to a fault.

Zerrial, who can take the form of a beast. Leenia is a pusher and can levitate. Twin boys, Oz, and Voz who can hold any living thing in place. Doria who controls lightning and Evinee who can shoot bone spears from her hands. She can also turn her skin into armor. There is also his secretary, Firel. He is very young, but he can see and walk through objects."

"So, he has his own private army?" I asked.

"They're more like his family, but yes. Zerrial is loyal to him to a fault. He only ever speaks highly of Eren. Besides those seven alfar, everyone else despises him. I've seen him in action, and I can see why."

"So have I," I added, trying to commit his army to memory.

Lily let a few moments pass in silence before she reached out and took my hand. "Whatever happened to you ... at the light court, I am here if you want to talk."

I smiled at her, knowing I would never tell her of the horrors I endured. She would blame herself and frankly, I didn't know if she could handle it.

"Do you miss him?" she asked.

"Who?"

"King Atros. Zerrial said you were his mistress?"

Did I miss him? A part of me cared for him, but no, I didn't love him, that was clear to me now.

"I was his mistress," I admitted.

She paused uncomfortably. "Did you ... are you still a—"

"A maiden? No. He didn't rape me, I agreed to it, but what he and I had wasn't what you and Zerrial have. If I had a choice, a real choice, I wouldn't have given myself to him. Especially under those circumstances."

"I am sorry to hear that, Gen. Did he hurt you?"

"No, he never did. He was always gentle and caring, but he wanted me more than I wanted him. I could never love him the way he did me. Knowing I would only ever be his mistress. How could I love someone who kept me as a slave?"

"I understand," she said while shifting uncomfortably. "Did he protect you from the others?"

I turned my head away from her, trying to stop the images of King Lysanthier from replaying through my mind. I began to shake, my skin on edge as if he was there, taunting me, touching me, forcing me. Everything in the room faded besides the crackling of the fire. My eyes grew heavy as tears fell from them.

Lily wrapped her arms around me and held me. She rubbed my hair as I cried into her chest. I sat in her arms for what seemed like hours before I could finally get myself together enough to pull away from her. Her face was wet with tears as she tried to give me a reassuring smile.

"Will you stay with me tonight? I don't want to be alone," I said.

"Of course I will. It will be just like back home in the church basement," she said.

I laughed, taking her hand. "Yes, except, our bellies are full, and we have a bed adorned with fabric and material that is worth more than the whole church."

We laughed together, making our way to bed.

CHAPTER SIX

The next morning, I awoke to an empty bed. Lily must have already been working on her latest fashions at the seamstress shop. She had told me this was how she earned her keep within the castle walls, designing dresses for the upper class. I got up and put on a pair of leather pants and a formfitting sleeveless shirt and jacket. I pulled my hair back into a ponytail just in time for the knock that came at my door.

"Your Majesty," said one of the guards. "Your cousin, Lord Toreon Drezmore, is here to see you."

I turned slowly, trying to think of what he could possibly want. "Send him in, but please stay stationed at the door," I instructed.

Toreon stepped in casually, taking note of my rooms. Blue-dyed hair that was longer on the top of his head shined radiantly in the light. He was dressed in the same fashion as I: leather pants, a tight black sleeveless shirt that showed off his muscular build, and a leather jacket to top off the look.

"Good morning, cousin," he said, bowing towards me.

"Morning. Can I help you with something?" I asked.

"I've come to escort you to your first day of training. I will be helping with your lessons from now on. We Drezmore are quite skilled in the art of battle, so I expect you to catch on quickly."

"I see. So do you just plan on killing me and making it look like an accident during training, or are you going to pretend to care so I begin to trust you, and then you'll stab me in the back later?" I said.

He laughed, taking a step towards me. "I'm not out for your head little Genevieve. I am not my sister. The crown was never going to be mine anyway. Honestly, I am glad you appeared out of nowhere. You should have seen the temper tantrum Icici threw when our uncle announced you as his heir. It was priceless."

"So, you're not loyal to your sister?" I asked, trying to read his face.

"I am loyal to whomever I want to be. And for the record, no. She would have been an awful queen."

I tried to search out any signs that he was lying. I didn't believe him, but I could still try and use this to my advantage … somehow. "We will see. Shall we be on our way?" I said, moving past him to the door.

"I like you, cousin," he said, catching up with me as we made our way into the hall. "You have the family's brassy personality. It will get you far. Believe me. Now, shall we go over what you will be doing today?"

"Do I have a choice?" I replied, following him down under the castle to another area Erendrial had briefly mentioned yesterday during our tour. This was where every member of the dark court trained. It didn't matter if you were upper-class or lower-class, everyone learned to fight. This was what gave their court the advantage over the light court.

"We will start with hand-to-hand combat. Alfar are usually quick learners so we will work on this for a few days and then move onto swords, arrows, and axes. It is going to be hard, and you will be very sore, but you will recover each day before your next lesson. Erendrial will come and get you after lunch for your other lessons, so that gives us about five hours."

We entered through two large, frosted glass doors. A large fighting gym appeared where multiple sets of alfar were practicing and training. Some with swords, some with powers, others with weapons I had never seen before: long slender pieces of black metal that lit up with blue lightning. They cut clean through pieces of wood without even trying. They were curved into a hook at the end and had black writing down the shaft of the sword.

"What is that weapon?" I asked Toreon.

"That is one of our newest toys. It is a weapon that can harness the dark magic inside of us. The handle has a small needle on it that pierces our skin, pulling from the dark magic within us to activate the enchanted sword that can cut clean through anything we've tested it against. We call them black weapons," said Toreon.

"Did you create it?"

"I wish. No, it was created by the mad genius twins Voz and Oz

Telgarie. They have come up with all our weapons and toys that we use to defeat the creatures we're up against."

No wonder why Erendrial befriended the twins, I thought to myself. He had two little masterminds in his pocket able to create whatever he needed.

"Come, we're over here," said Toreon, leading us to a private room, separate from the other members of the court. "I thought you might want some privacy while you get your bearings."

"That's very thoughtful," I said, feeling inadequate. "Thank you."

We made our way to a clearing in the cave where another male stood waiting for us. He bowed towards me and forced a smile. He was a tall lean man with no hair. His imprint covered his head and part of his forehead as the design swirled around like a river. His ears were pierced all the way to the tips, and he had a ring in his lower lip. He wore no shirt, revealing his well-toned body. His eyes were white and haunting.

"Princess Genevieve, meet your other teacher, Varches Llrune. He is our military trainer. His gift is multiplication. He can create mirror images of himself that make it quite impossible to defeat him," said Toreon.

"Please now, Lord Drezmore, you speak too highly of me," said Varches in a deep voice.

"I only give praise where it is due," said Toreon, bowing in his direction. "Now, he will take the lesson from here and I will evaluate. Good luck, cousin. You're going to need it."

The next five hours consisted of Varches beating the shit out of me. I bled so much, I was surprised I was still conscious. Thank the gods for my healing abilities. Just as I thought I had a move figured out, Varches would switch it up and prove me wrong. I learned proper form, the soft places on a humanoid body, and the places I should aim for to take down my opponent.

Toreon laughed at me mostly, taking notes on a piece of paper as he sat back and watched me fail repeatedly. Varches barely broke a sweat. I, on the other hand, was a mess. My hair was tangled, my face flushed, and my skin wet from exertion. We broke for lunch and moved to a back room where a table of food was already waiting. I drank four glasses of water before even picking up a piece of fruit. Toreon watched me closely, noting my every move.

"Can I help you with something, or are you just going to stare?" I asked, shoving a piece of meat into my mouth.

"There's a lot of alfar in you, but the human parts are still a surprise," he responded. "Your cheeks are flushed. That doesn't happen to us often. I guess because we run a bit colder. It's a good look on you though."

"Thanks, I think," I said, taking another swig of water.

Erendrial appeared in the doorway in a clean black shirt and a leather pair of pants.

"How did the hunt go?" asked Varches.

Erendrial nodded with a smile. "We caught the little beast, so I would say good. It was a nasty one though. Swords for hands that could shoot spikes from the tips. It moved faster than anything I have ever seen, but it isn't moving anymore," Erendrial said.

"Excellent. Will you be at the dissection?" asked Varches.

"Have I missed one yet?" replied Erendrial.

"When is it?" I interrupted. They all stopped and looked at me as if I spoke out of turn. "I would like to attend."

"You want to see the insides of that thing?" asked Toreon.

"Yes. I am curious about the creatures that are coming from the rift. I've seen a few, and resurrected one, so yes."

Erendrial smiled. I could have sworn I saw pride on his face. "Tonight, after dinner. I suggest eating a light meal. Come now, princess. Time to get you to your next lesson. Maybe we can throw a shower in there before we go," he said, taking in my current state.

I stood, looking back at Varches and Toreon. "Thank you both. I will see you tomorrow," I said politely.

They both stood and bowed.

"Of course, Your Highness," said Varches.

"It's been fun, cousin. I can't wait to get to know you better," added Toreon.

I followed Erendrial to my room where he told me about the hunt and how they took down the beast that now sat in the examination room of the castle. I quickly showered, eager to know what I would learn next. I came out of the bathroom in a robe and made my way over to the wardrobe. Erendrial sat in one of the chairs off in the corner.

"What lesson am I going to next? What should I wear?" I asked.

"Something light and comfortable. You're going to meet our other seer. Hopefully, she can help you with that very special gift of yours," he said.

I nodded, rolling my hands over the armoire as I remembered Atalee doing. I opened the doors to the room full of clothing. I shut them behind me, putting a magical barrier between Erendrial and I.

I slipped on a dark plum purple dress that had long sleeves and came to a point in the center in between my breasts. The fabric was sheer but hid everything well. It was formfitting, as was everything I now owned. It rested at the ends of my shoulders. I left my hair down as it curled along the length of my back. I placed a crown on my head and made my way back out to Erendrial.

He took a hard look at me as I exited the wardrobe. I turned nervously to face him.

"I don't know how to do the whole makeup thing and I was never good with hair," I said as he kept his gaze on me.

He stood, walking over slowly towards me. "You're the princess. You get to look however you want. Come, let's not keep the seer waiting," he said, walking towards the door.

We went to the residential wing of the castle where the other high lords and ladies took residence.

"Are your rooms over here?" I asked.

He smirked at me with a side look. I already regretted the question. "Why do you ask? Are you planning on ruining another night of fun for me, like you did back in the light court?"

"Would you rather I had let you go for round two, only to end up dead the next morning? Not very smart for such an intelligent alfar," I said innocently.

He laughed. A real laugh. I stopped dead in my tracks. It was the same sound that I had heard for the past three years in my dreams. The same sound that brought so much joy to me in my times of need and despair. He turned back to me. I dropped my eyes from his, trying to push the thought of my visions from my mind.

"Are you alright?" he asked.

"Yes. I'm sorry, I just ... your laugh," I said honestly.

"Yes, I occasionally do that from time to time when I find something humorous. You should try it. It does wonders for your health, so I hear."

"I don't think I have much to laugh about anymore, but thanks for the advice. Can we continue?" I said, gesturing down the hall. We passed a pair of black doors that had an engraving of a dragon on it. Erendrial pointed to the doors.

"These are my quarters, just in case you get lonely," he said, winking at me.

"Oh please."

"Was that not why you were asking after my rooms? I just figured—"

"You figured wrong, Lyklor."

"Your loss," he said with a smile. I couldn't help but smile a bit back at him. He did that on purpose to get a rise out of me. He was always doing that. "See, a smile. Laughter won't be too far behind, I promise."

I rolled my eyes.

"Can you teach me how to read people like you do?"

"I suppose I could share a few secrets with you, but it is honestly a gift. It takes years to learn the tells, and each being is different. All your senses have to be aware and alert."

"Well, I guess I am at a disadvantage there," I said, feeling inadequate once more.

"How so?"

"My nose doesn't work like a full-blooded alfar's. I can only detect things as humans do. Same with my hearing."

"Then we'll just have to refine those senses and make them work a little harder. I've known many humans over the years that are just as skilled at reading others as I am. If they can do it, I don't see why you couldn't."

"Thank you," I replied as we stopped in front of two black doors. A carving of an eye covered both doors. How poetic. Erendrial knocked twice and then stood back. A human girl came to open the door and bowed at the sight of us. Erendrial passed her without a look and entered the room.

Winnow Fellwood stood from her chair as we entered and made

her way over to us. She bowed towards me and then nodded at Erendrial "Your Highness, Ambassador Lyklor, what an honor it is to receive you in my private quarters," she said in a formal voice. She walked over to me, taking my hands in hers. "You are brighter than I had seen," she said, tracing her eyes around my face. "Your light is exquisite."

I looked at Erendrial with confusion. He mouthed the word 'later' to me.

"Thank you, Lady Fellwood," I said.

"Please, come sit. Tasha darling, bring us some tea and refreshments please," she said to the human girl. We sat on the couch and Erendrial took a chair next to us. "Now, I hear you and I share a very special gift. I would like to know all about what you have experienced thus far. Start from the beginning, please."

I hesitated, knowing where I was going to have to begin. "Well, I started having dreams three years ago. Just one dream really. It would play over and over in my head when I would sleep. Same details, same images, same sounds. I thought I was just going crazy until I saw what I was dreaming in person," I said, trying to keep the details of that special dream brief.

"And what was it," she said eagerly.

"I'd rather not say, but when I got to the light court, I started having more dreams. I saw the day Erendrial and the others arrived for the battle with Otar. I could feel the hatred between the courts. My ... my hand was smashed," I said, looking down at my palm, remembering the pain I had endured. "I saw and felt it before it happened."

"Interesting, so you actually felt your own pain?" she clarified.

"Yes. Then ..." I looked at Erendrial and laughed a little. "Then this one over here pissed me off, so I wanted revenge on him. I thought of how to get back at him, but I couldn't come up with a clever enough way to hurt him. That night, I had a vision about the light alfar high lord he was working with. I saw them conspiring against King Atros. The next morning, I confirmed it was the male I saw and then spoiled their plans." I turned back to Erendrial. "Sorry about that."

"All is forgiven," he said, winking at me.

"So, you wanted something, and your gift gave it to you? How interesting," she said.

"Does your gift not work like that?" I asked.

"Oh, no. The details of my gift are sparse and sometimes hard to understand. It has never given me a vision for personal gain. I only see the future, or visions that will help others. Most of the time I can't control when they come or what I see. It seems that your gift is far more advanced than my own. Have you used your gift for personal gain since that night?" she asked.

"Yes. When I ... when I wanted King Lysanthier dead. I dreamed of Otar and how to revive him. I saw myself controlling him and speaking with him," I confessed.

"And your visions only come in dreams?"

"No. I had one when I was awake. I was looking at a map before the battle with Otar. When I saw the northern border of Urial it triggered a vision, but it was painful and sent me to the floor. I had to recover from that one."

Winnow stood from the couch and began to pace back and forth. "Interesting. Maybe because your body is in a relaxed state when you are asleep, the power doesn't affect you as greatly because you have time to heal and recover. But when you are awake and they come, they affect you due to your human side. Humans were not meant to have power. Their bodies cannot contain the gift, so it taxes them on a physical level."

"Will the pain I feel eventually ease as I get used to my powers and learn how to control them better?" I asked.

"I'm afraid not. The pain will be something you have to live with, but if you can control and manipulate your vision to see the things you desire, I would say the pain is well worth the gain," she said.

I nodded with a small smile. *Nothing can ever be easy*, I thought to myself.

"So how do I control it?" I asked.

"Premonition isn't a gift you can necessarily control. Sometimes visions will come to you of things you didn't even know to look for. Other times, you can focus on a topic or a detail and will yourself to see into the past, present, or future. For example, when you raised Otar. We knew the creature had died in battle and yet somehow, he rose weeks later and killed the light king. I focused on Otar and his life. It took some time, but that was when I saw the sigil on your wrist. Very clever by the way, princess. I am already a fan," she said, patting my hand.

"So, I need to focus on specific things I want to see?" I asked.

"Yes. Once a vision is triggered you need to focus on the smallest details. Sounds, noises, colors, symbols. Anything that will help you make the connection out here. Unfortunately, that is all the help I can provide. Premonition isn't something that can really be learned. You just have to get good at understanding what you see. But if you ever have questions or need help, I am here for you," she said, sipping at her tea.

Erendrial rose from his seat, offering me his hand. "Thank you so much for your time, Lady Fellwood. Though we would love to stay, we have a very busy schedule to keep," said Erendrial.

"Of course, Ambassador. Princess Genevieve, it was such a pleasure to meet you."

"It was a pleasure to meet you as well, Lady Fellwood. I am sure we will be seeing a lot of each other," I said, taking her hands in mine.

"Oh, I do hope so," she said, smiling at me.

"And thank you for finding me. You don't know how truly thankful I am."

Her smile softened as she took my face in her hand. She kissed my cheek and then placed her lips to my ear. "He got exactly what he deserved," she whispered, pulling away from me slowly.

My heart sunk in my chest. My eyes widened as I looked at her. "You ... you saw?" I asked her in disbelief.

She nodded. "Every moment. I am truly sorry for what you had to endure to get here, but it is in the past. It doesn't define you. You will rise from the ashes of this fire into who you were truly meant to be," she said.

I dropped my head in shame. Her grip tightened on my hand.

"That's what I try to tell myself," I said, pulling away from her. I took a deep breath and headed to the door. Erendrial and I left her rooms. My heart still felt heavy. I felt embarrassed even, knowing someone else saw the abuse I endured. Why hadn't she told anyone? Surely, she could have found a way to use it against me.

"What did she see?" asked Erendrial. His voice broke me out of my own head.

"Nothing important," I answered, as we made our way back to my rooms.

"Zerrial tells me you and sweet Lily made up last night. I am glad to hear it," he said, changing the subject.

"Yes. I was wrong to lash out at her like that, but ..."

"But ...?"

"Does Zerrial still take others, even though he is with her?" I asked.

Erendrial scoffed. "I don't keep track of who my friends fuck, princess." He paused for a moment. "But I know he is eager to get back to her every chance he gets. He's turned down late-night drinks, strip parties, and no longer attends Jestu. So, if I were to guess, I would say no."

I smiled, feeling truly happy for Lily. "Does he love her?"

"You know how I feel about love and alfar."

"Yes, but that is your opinion. It doesn't mean it couldn't happen," I smiled brightly at him, still reeling with joy for Lily. "For whatever it's worth, she loves him, no matter what he is or what he does."

"The love of a human ... how—"

"Worthless?"

"I didn't say that."

"No, but you were thinking it. The sheer fact that he is friends with you would have been a deal breaker for me, but Lily has a bigger heart then all of us, I guess," I said playfully.

"Or she is just very, very stupid," he said.

I looked at him, searching his face to see if he was playing.

His smile stretched across his cheeks, revealing those deep dimples. "I'm teasing. I am glad my friend has found happiness. I am just sorry it will be so short."

"What do you mean?"

"Her human lifespan. She will have another thirty good years if she is lucky before things begin to change."

"Oh, right." Yet another reminder I would have to live most

of my life without my best friend. Would this world ever become normal to me? Would I carry her loss with me for the next 900 years? What a life to live: watching as everyone around me died.

Chapter Seven

The dissection that night of the creature was fascinating. It had five hearts, breathed out of a hole in its neck and the swords of its hands were almost indestructible. Its blood was orange as it spilled out of its body. I watched and listened while the scientist rattled off theories of how it reproduced, what it ate, and where it was from. Erendrial watched me closely the whole time, seeming intrigued by my interest.

The next two weeks were repetitive, but educational. I became obsessed with fighting and killing. It was a form of release for me. A way to expel the pain that still resided in me from being raped. Sword fighting was my favorite. Bow and arrows came naturally. With a sword, I had to learn how to estimate my opponent's attack.

Toreon was a skilled fighter and taught me everything he knew when it came to weapons. He was strong and fast. I grew to like him, more than I should have. I still was unsure if I could trust him, but only time would tell. Vena, his little sister, started coming to practice with us. She was small but fast. She was deadly with small daggers and could rip a giant in two if given the chance.

"Come on, cousin," taunted Vena, crouching into an attack stance. "You're going to have to move faster than that if you expect to take down those beasts outside the walls."

Without warning, she charged, daggers positioned to strike. Her left hand flung out low towards my abdomen while her right came down above her head, aimed for my shoulder. I spun, narrowing my body (her target) just before I caught her right wrist, preventing her from sinking the blade into my flesh.

I took a breath, and in that moment, my error was revealed. She sliced the blade she had in her right hand across my side, causing me to release her and stumble back in pain. I held the bleeding wound, taking shallow breaths.

"Oops ... sorry," she said, placing the daggers in her belt.

"It's fine," I replied, feeling the wound already healing. "Lesson learned; don't let my guard down around you even for a second."

She laughed, approaching my side. "Thankfully, I can heal you as well." She placed her hand on top of my wound. A comforting warming sensation spread through my body almost like warm honey. When she removed her hand, the wound was gone. No scar left behind.

"Thank you," I said, amazed by her gift.

She grinned and shrugged, as if her power was nothing to be proud of.

I quickly learned that Vena was chatty with an explosive personality. She seemed to be trying to earn my approval, as if it mattered to her. I was kind, but I kept my guard up.

After combat training, I would meet Erendrial in the massive library, which was my favorite place in the entire kingdom. Books filled every wall from floor to ceiling. The dark court obtained records about anything anyone could ever want to know about. A three-hundred-year-old treatise on Nymph lineages. Poetry written in languages I neither understood nor had ever heard of. Books about races that had long been extinct. Ladders scattered throughout the shelves reached to the highest ledges. It made the light court's library look like a joke.

I committed the members of the high and low classes of alfar to memory, along with their powers. I now understood everyone's station and where they fell in the lineup of importance. Erendrial taught me about politics and how to work the room. He shared the councilmember's weaknesses with me and where to strike and when. He also began to teach me how to read a being's facial and body cues. It was like trying to understand a different language, but I was determined to learn.

Despite trying, I had no visions. I focused on the light court, Queen Daealla, Gaelin, but nothing. The court I once saw as the better of the two had now become my enemy. There were still those in Urial whom I wished to punish for what they had done to me and my friends. So much for my visions giving me what I wanted.

Creatures continued to come through the rift on our side. The dark soldiers were heavily skilled and talented, always coming home with one or two of the creatures to study. I began taking notes on their anatomy and powers.

I asked Otar about them every third day when he came for his feeding session. He looked at the drawings of the creatures but couldn't remember a thing about them. Tonight was no different. Zerrial had just killed a large lion-like creature with the tail of a scorpion and the wings of an eagle. Otar finished feeding on my wrist as I pulled out the picture from the pile of my notes.

"Do you recognize this one?" I asked him.

He wiped his mouth while I cleaned my arm. He stared, tilting his head curiously as if he was on the edge of something. "I ... I can't remember," he answered.

"What do you remember? You must remember something from your time working for whoever controlled you."

He paced in front of me, aggravated. "I have tried, believe me, but I can't remember, I just can't. There is a block in my mind," he spat, knocking on his head with a fist, "that I can't remove, wicked one. Sometimes I see flashes of things, humanoid figures, but they are unclear, and I can't remember who they are or where I was. I don't know what happened to me, but I will find out who controlled me, and I will kill them, yes, I will," he said, smiling with his sharp teeth.

"And when you're free of me, will you kill me then too, since I control you?" I asked.

"Would you like me to kill you?"

I stopped, looking at him in shock. "Why would you ask that?"

"I hear you sometimes, calling out for me to come and end you. To take away the pain and the memories. It's the worst when you sleep, which ruins my favorite time of day."

"You can hear my thoughts?" I asked.

"Not your thoughts, only your desires and feelings. That is how I knew how you wanted me to end the light king and his bitch."

I was stunned. I had no clue the connection between Otar and I was this intrusive. My inner thoughts ... feelings ... desires, were no longer my own.

"Why don't you just end me then?" I asked, feeling violated in some way. "If you have to do what I want, and you can hear me asking for it."

"Self-preservation, I suppose," he said.

Right, I forgot his life was tied to mine.

"Your keeper isn't very sneaky, wicked one. He's been hiding behind the wall listening to our conversation." Otar turned to the entrance of my room, where Erendrial stepped into the doorway.

I stood up, praying he didn't hear the part about me wanting to off myself. "How much did you hear?" I asked.

"Enough that I am questioning whether leaving you alone is an option," Erendrial said, walking slowly towards us. "Are you done with your meal?" he asked Otar. "If so, I think you should leave."

Otar turned to me. I nodded for him to go. I finished wiping the spilled blood from my arm and placed my crown on my head acting as if the conversation with Otar had never happened.

"Are we going to talk about your desire for death?" Erendrial asked.

"There's nothing to talk about," I replied, praying he would just let what he heard go.

"Princess, I must inform your father of this."

I swung quickly on him while my panic set fire within. "No, Eren, please," I begged. "I'm still dealing with ... with things from the light court, but I assure you, each day I feel better ... stronger. It will pass."

He studied me for a brief moment. "What are you running from, Genevieve?" His voice was soft.

I turned away from him, closing my eyes while my nightmares flashed behind them. "Nothing you need to be bothered with." I forced my gaze to meet his. "Please don't say anything."

His jaw tightened before he dropped his eyes from mine and nodded, silently agreeing to what I was asking.

"Thank you," I whispered.

It was my favorite time of day. I got to talk with my father and uncle. My uncle and father were ornery and playful with one another, like I had always imagined siblings being.

"You bore her, brother," said my uncle, pulling new books from the shelves.

"Are you saying our ancestry is of little importance?" asked my father.

"Oh, we've had some colorful characters in our family tree, that's for sure," replied Uncle Rythlayn, "But they hold nothing on this one." He slammed a book down in front of me. The binding was old and worn. The brown leather was faded and torn around the edges. On the front of the cover, there was no title or author listed; only the image of a flame burned into the surface.

"Maleki," I whispered.

My uncle looked at me in shock. "You know of the first?"

"A little," I answered. "Levos Atros told me the story of how the dark court came to be."

My father and uncle looked at each other before bursting into laughter. I was confused by the action.

"What?" I asked.

"Leave it to a prissy light court know-it-all to think he can properly retell our history," laughed Rythlayn.

My father placed his hand on top of mine. "The light court knows very little about what truly happened and how we conduct our court, as you've already come to see."

My uncle slammed into the chair beside me and flipped open the cover. "Here is the truth about our heritage and why this planet survived, no thanks to those pathetic excuses for alfar over in the light court."

"Now brother," piped in my father, "everyone had a part to play."

"Ha," laughed my uncle. "If I were Maleki, I would have allowed the demons to finish off those cowards before sending their asses back to the Hell plane."

"What did the Atros boy tell you, daughter?" asked father.

"Basically, after the demons had destroyed a large portion of our lands, we were helpless. Maleki and his armies were the only ones that stood a chance. They met Azeer and when the deal was proposed, Maleki brought it before the council, but they denied his request. He took the deal anyways and when he and his forces knelt before Azeer, their lives were the final sacrifice to complete the bargain.

"Maleki and the others were resurrected with new gifts, Maleki's being the Dark Flame. The most powerful of them all, able to destroy any celestial being. Once they had rid this world of the demons, the light court would no longer accept them. They then broke off and made their own kingdom here, within this mountain."

"So many details left out," mumbled Rythlayn.

"What is the true story then?" I asked.

My father turned the page to the first chapter. "The beginning of this story was correctly retold." He flipped the page again. "The alfar once lived among each other and the other species of this planet in peace. Even those courts who are now depicted as barbaric, like the fairies, were once our equals and friends.

"We tended to this planet and in return, this planet was our sanctuary. No race was higher than another ... even the humans. There were no laws when it came to who you could love or mate with. Each was able to choose freely. This world was once filled with half breeds ..." my father paused, taking in my face, "...like you.

"When the demons descended, we were completely unprepared. None of the courts had ever had to fight. We had been raised in a utopian society. We only killed out of necessity. The fallen angels were ravenous: stripped of any humanity they once contained. They saw our planet as a playground, where they were free to kill, rape, and eat whatever they desired.

"The Norse gods did not want to disrupt their treaty with the Christian God. The demons, once his own angels and warriors, were still beloved to him. When we turned to our friends ... our creators for help, they turned their backs on us, shutting the Bifröst bridge that had been opened to us since the beginning.

"We were completely on our own, abandoned by the gods that we loved and served. Little by little, each court weaponized their gifts and natural abilities, learning how to defend themselves against the demons. But nothing we possessed killed them completely or prevented them from coming back once they had been slain.

"Maleki was our most revered general in the war. He was betrothed to the king of the light's daughter at the time... Shevira." My father turned the page to an illustration of a beautiful female with golden red hair and bright golden eyes. "Everything Maleki did was to protect his beloved and the future they had planned for.

"Azeer came to the king of the light and the council directly. He offered them unimaginable power and abilities. He would not interfere with their way of life after the war had concluded, but if they took the deal, they needed to understand that the gifts bestowed upon them required a sacrifice.

"Azeer is a selfish god. He knew the love our people had for the Norse gods. To ensure our allegiance to him and him alone, we would have to prove ourselves. Three people from the weakest race would be sacrificed each year. This represented our three transitions as a race. It also proved that we were placed above all others in power and station. Where we once protected those who were weaker than us, we would now have to look them in the eyes every year and murder them in cold blood.

"The next sacrifice would be that of a virgin of our own race. An offering to Azeer to show our thanks for the gifts he would bless us with." My father paused, looking down at the next page with something like sorrow in his eyes.

"Is this where Maleki goes against the council?" I asked.

"No, dear niece," said my uncle. "This is where we were betrayed." My uncle turned to the next page where a picture of a red, horned god stood above an alfar male.

"The council," continued Rythlayn, "including Maleki, banished Azeer from these lands. Even though the Norse gods abandoned them, they would not subject themselves to such an evil celestial being. The alfar, at this time, valued all life as equal. They would never murder in the name of such a diabolical god.

"As the war continued, our numbers dwindled. The demons began to attack the inner council members and their families. Our people didn't stand a chance. The light king met with Maleki privately after Shevira had been attacked attempting to protect young ones.

"The king informed Maleki that the council had reconvened and decided to take Azeer up on his offer. The small sacrifices he required would be worth it if it meant their people and their world survived. Maleki was taken aback by the decision of the council, but with Shevira laying in the medical wing fighting for her life, he was desperate.

"Maleki and his unit went deep into this mountain and summoned the fire god with the spell the king had given them. When Azeer appeared, the god was offended that the king did not come himself to accept his generous offer. Instead, he sent his future son-in-law, someone of no royal birth, along with a handful of lowborn foot soldiers.

"Azeer restated the terms and then informed the alfar of the final payment ... the sacrifice of their own lives. Maleki would do anything to ensure Shevira lived. The others had families back in the castle and felt the same. It was unanuimous. Each alfar who stood under this mountain that night agreed to sacrifice themselves so this world could survive.

"Azeer, being the vengeful god he is, kept his word and bestowed the group of alfar with powers that could kill celestial beings. But instead of spreading the power through our entire race, he tied it to those who were brave enough to come before him in our greatest time of need.

"Maleki and his forces ascended from this mountain, fueled by powers that were unmatched by any other," my father explained. "They tore through the demon legions, sending them back to the pits of Hell from hence they came. The war ended within a week's time and our planet was saved.

"When Maleki and his unit returned to the light king victorious, the council placed each of them under arrest in the dungeons below. The king denied giving Maleki the orders to make the deal with Azeer and accused him of being a power-hungry usurper who only desired his throne.

"In reality," interrupted my uncle, "the light king was pissed. He thought when Maleki made the deal with Azeer that he too would possess the power of a god. He didn't account for how shifty gods could be with their loopholes."

"The king and council," continued my father, "decided that Maleki and his army would be put to death. Their powers and the deal they made with the fire god was unhinged and that of a devil. Maleki was willing to take the sentencing of the council, since he hadn't planned to make it out alive in the first place.

"But Shevira wouldn't accept her beloved's fate. She refused to believe that Maleki would ever go against the word of her father. She conceived a plan to free Maleki and the others. They would leave her father's kingdom and create one of their own. Maleki tried to talk her out of it, but there was no use. She refused to live without him, even if it meant dying alongside him.

"The night Shevira set her plan into motion, Maleki discovered a traitor in his ranks. One of his closest friends had informed the king about her attempt to free Maleki and the others. As they used their new powers to try and escape, the king ordered his own daughter to be killed by Maleki's friend who then accused Maleki of administering the final blow.

"Maleki, devastated by the murder of his love, lost control of his power, burning everyone in his path to the ground including his treacherous friend. He set the entire light kingdom on fire, destroying the original castle.

"Maleki's men managed to get him out before the king and his men were able to kill him. Even with the powers they possessed, they were heavily outnumbered by the light alfar and the other races who now believed them to be murderous devils.

"They returned to this mountain and built the Kingdom of Doonak. Maleki vowed to destroy the king of the light no matter the cost. The light king had seen the power the dark alfar possessed. To rally the other races to his defense, he ordered the killing of all half breeds, pinning the massacre on Doonak."

"His narrative was believable," muttered my uncle. "I'll give the bastard that."

"What was it?" I asked.

My father inhaled. "He told the others that the dark court revered themselves as gods, and refused to be rivaled by any other being of mixed race or power who could potentially become a threat to our station. The light court banned the creation of half-breeds from that point on, saying it was to protect the races from our evil court. In reality, the lines between the weak and the strong had been drawn.

"The light king knew he was no longer of the strongest race, and he had made an enemy out of a male who could easily destroy him. This way, the courts would only ever reproduce with those of the same race, not risking the creation of another being that could become an unknown threat, adding to the light king's paranoia."

"My gods," I whispered, in complete shock of the details I had learned. Father shut the book, allowing a moment of silence for the pain and sacrifice our ancestors had experienced.

"The other races," added Rythlayn, "like the fairies, had lived in a world where they had to fight savagely to survive for so long, they no longer knew another way of life. The light court banished them and others like them that they no longer found civilized.

"The Draugr had been born out of the war and were also banished from their lands, even though they had fought at our sides in the end. Our kingdom took them all under our banner, helping each court establish new homes and systems to support the way of life they chose. Thus, their loyalty to our plight."

"How does no one in the light court know this?" I asked.

"Reality is perception, I suppose," answered Father.

My uncle put the book back on the shelf. "Plus, those little pissants removed any account of the truth long ago from their records. The light king killed anyone who refused to live under his lie. A lot of those alfar had a family member who followed Maleki. He was thorough, I'll give him that."

"I thought it impossible to hate the light kingdom more than I already had, but now—"

My father reached across the table and took my hand. "We no longer fight the battle of Maleki, dear daughter. The light kingdom is a means to an end. If they chose to allow their court to remain blindly in the dark, then so be it. Now, we must band together until this unknown threat is illuminated. But it is important you know this history ... the truth of how we came to be."

"Well," my uncle said, pouring himself a glass of wine. "After that little history lesson, I am famished. How about you two?"

Father and I both chuckled, shaking our heads.

CHAPTER EIGHT

While I was readying for dinner, Erendrial appeared in my rooms to escort me. I felt his eyes on me in the reflection of the mirror. I looked back at him, not sure of what to say.

"Shall we go?" I asked. He didn't answer. I exhaled. "You have nothing to worry about."

"I am loyal to your father," he replied. "If something were to happen ... and I knew about this ...."

"You must have only heard part of my conversation with Otar. That's what you get for eavesdropping." I said playfully, trying to divert anymore interrogation.

He grabbed my arm gently, pulling me back in front of him. "Why would you want to kill yourself? Have we not been good to you here? Have you not found the family you always wondered about? You have your sister, an education, a purpose."

I looked at him, trying to figure a way out of having this conversation. "It has nothing to do with any of you or the dark court. There are things in my past that I can't seem to escape, no matter how happy I want to be. When I close my eyes, I relive those moments over and over again. The nightmares devour me, but I am working on it. I am not going to kill myself," I said, giving him a small smile.

He nodded, still seeming unsure of my response.

We made our way down the hall and stopped to talk to some high alfar. The court was buzzing. Tomorrow night was their beloved Jestu celebration which I was not looking forward to. They spoke of who would be in attendance and what they planned to do. I tried to block the details out, but it was almost impossible. Icici came around the corner with a male alfar I recognized as Soddram Yositru, one of my suitors. Great, every male I knew was screwing my cousin.

"Princess Genevieve, Ambassador Lyklor," he said coldly, before entering the throne room.

Icici smiled from ear to ear as she approached us. "Good evening, cousin ... Eren. Hasn't today been lovely?" she asked, watching Soddram from behind.

"Dessert before dinner, cousin?" I asked coldly.

"I do like to break the rules now and then. I will let you in on a little secret. If he ends up being your husband, you will not be disappointed, I can vouch for that," she said with a giggle.

"If I ever have a question in regard to any male at court, I know who to ask," I said.

Erendrial choked on a laugh, clearing his throat to cover the sound.

Icici's eyes deadlocked on me as if she was about to attack.

"What can I say? I may not be as warm as the lowly humans, but that doesn't mean I'm not gifted in every other fashion when it comes to sex. Isn't that right, Erendrial?"

"I don't believe this is the time or place to be talking about your sexual explorations, Lady Icici," replied Erendrial.

"Oh, come on now. The sounds you were making when I did that thing with my tongue on you the other night. I thought the fun was going to be over before we even got started," she said, smiling at me.

"And why do you think revealing your sexual relationship with Erendrial would have an effect on me?" I asked.

She shrugged with a beautiful smile. "Call it a hunch. Anyways, are you excited for your first Jestu tomorrow night? My people tell me you haven't taken anyone into your bed since you arrived. I am sure you're going to be happy to alleviate some of the pent-up tension. It isn't a good look on you, princess," she said.

"It is going to be an experience, I am sure," I replied shortly.

"I don't blame you for not taking a lover. I mean, who would compare after you've had both King Atros and King Lysanthier on top of you. What could a dark alfar offer that they couldn't?"

My stomach flipped and bile rose in my esophagus. I was going to be sick. I tried controlling my face, but I was taken off guard and I didn't know how to react.

"Tell me," she continued with a smile, "was Gaelin or King Lysanthier better in bed? My spies tell me the former king could be quite rough. I guess it could be enjoyable if you like that sort of thing."

My vision went black as the anger and rage inside of me let loose. I slammed into Icici with the full force of my body, pinning her neck with my forearm to the wall while I restrained one of her hands. She fought to breathe as a smile still crept across her face.

"You shut your fucking mouth; do you hear me?" I growled in a low and threatening tone. "You know nothing of what you speak, and if I find that you have told *anyone* else about this, I will personally have Otar tear you to shreds. Then you can go fuck the king yourself in the afterlife. Am I clear? You jealous, narcissistic whore?" I yelled.

The crowds of alfar were silent as they looked at me with astonishment. Otar appeared out of nowhere next to us with a wicked smile on his face.

"I can kill this one now? Oh, please, wicked one, please!" Otar said, jumping with excitement.

"As you wish," Icici said, still fighting to breathe, her eyes locked onto Otar with fear.

"Thank you Otar, but I have this one handled," I said, releasing her as she slouched over, grasping her neck.

Otar growled and disappeared.

I turned away and walked through the crowds of people as if nothing had happened. Erendrial followed without a word. I stopped before we entered the throne room and turned towards him, still fuming with anger.

"I know you have an agenda up your sleeve and somehow winning me over is part of your twisted plan for power and control, but I swear, if you ever use what you just heard against me, I will make it my life's mission to destroy you and everyone you have ever cared for. And I will not stop until you are below whatever station you rose from. Am I clear?" I said.

He looked at me in shock as if he was trying to figure out why he was now on the receiving end of my wrath. "Princess, I would never—"

"Don't princess me, Lyklor. Am I clear?" I demand.

He swallowed hard, straightening his figure. "Perfectly."

I turned from him, walking into the throne room with my head held high and ready to kill something. I made my way over to Toreon, no longer hungry.

"Care for a sparring session?" I said to him just before he brought a turkey leg to his mouth.

"Now?" he asked.

"Yes, now. Finish your leg and I will meet you in the gym in five minutes," I said, nodding to my father and uncle before heading back out of the room.

Erendrial tried to follow but I stopped him, unable to look him in the eye now that he knew about Lysanthier. "You've got the night off. Go fuck someone or something. I don't care," I said, before returning to my rooms to change.

Toreon and I fought for the next three hours without a word. I was still beaten and sore from the morning session, but I didn't care. I imagined he was his sister and beat the shit out of him every chance he gave me. I fell into bed exhausted and spent.

That night I dreamt of the first time King Lysanthier took me violently. All the blood ... *my* blood that stained his sheets. The way the red looked on his white skin. How he licked at my wounds. I woke up, sweating and crying as I held myself, trying to get my head under control.

The next morning, I went to my combat session, sore, tired, and hungry. By the end of the match everything hurt so badly I was surprised I was able to make it back to my room on my own. To my surprise, Erendrial was waiting for me in my study.

"What are you doing here? I thought we were supposed to meet in the library?" I asked.

"I figured the confinements of your room would be the safer, more private option, just in case you decided to have another outburst for the whole court to see," he said, dragging his finger along the edge of the desk.

I slammed the door, walking over to him with fire flickering behind my eyes. "You forget who you are talking to, Lyklor. Watch your tone," I snapped, face to face with him.

He dropped his eyes. "You're right, Princess Genevieve. Please forgive my rudeness."

I turned, making my way to the bathroom. I showered and

dressed, barely able to bring my arms through the holes of my sleeves. I walked over to the desk and took my seat in front of a new pile of books.

"Next time you go on a hunt, I want to come with you," I said bluntly.

"Do you think that is wise, Your Highness? You've only just begun to train."

"I'm not pregnant, so there is nothing preventing me from going on the hunt. I will attend," I demand.

"As you wish," he said, opening the book to the new section of history I was to learn today.

After the first thirty minutes of listening to him talk, it became a challenge to stay seated in the chair. My back was in so much pain I could barely stand it. It was still bruised and sore from the fifteen hours of combat in the past twenty-four hours. I fidgeted in my chair, reaching for my back, trying to rub the discomfort away.

"What is wrong?" asked Erendrial.

I looked at him and exhaled. "I'm just a bit sore is all. Nothing that won't pass in a few hours."

"Yes, but it appears to be a distraction during our lesson. Let me take a look," he said, moving behind me. He gently peeled back the thin edges of my dress, making sure not to touch me. He came back around and rotated his wrist with a snap. A jar of cream appeared in his hand out of thin air.

"I want to learn how to do that?" I said quickly.

He chuckled, bringing it down to his side. "Yes, I guess we will have to teach you how to mist soon, won't we? I am going to put this on your back. It will help with the discomfort until you heal."

"There's no need. I can do it myself," I said, reaching for the jar.

He pulled it out of reach. "Unless you've developed a gift that allows your arms to grow in length, I doubt you can reach most of yourself." He moved behind me causing my entire body to stiffen. The back of my simple dress already exposed much of the bruised flesh, but I felt him unbutton the few buttons at the bottom, revealing the area entirely.

I closed my eyes tightly, trying to anticipate the feeling of another's touch. I am fine, I told myself. He is not King Lysanthier. He isn't going to hurt me. I can endure another alfar's touch without screaming or throwing up.

The cream was warm as he gently applied it in between my shoulder blades. I stiffened, holding my breath while he to slid his hand down my lower back. I felt myself beginning to shake as he reached the middle of my area. He removed his hand to get more cream and then resumed the same gentle motion. I sprung from the chair, moving out of his reach.

He stopped, frozen in place. I dropped my head, trying to calm myself. I rubbed my arms, shaking the images out of my head.

"I'm sorry. I didn't mean to startle you. I know you are just trying to help, but I can't—" I stopped, taking a few deep breaths to calm my racing heart.

He put the jar on the desk and held his hands up in a surrendering gesture. "It's okay. You don't have to apologize or tell me anything. I'm sorry I made you feel uncomfortable. That was not my intention. Why don't we just focus on your studies. We can call it a day after this chapter, agreed?"

I nodded, returning to my chair. I rubbed my face, trying to focus on the words in front of me.

Once the chapter was over, Erendrial began to gather his personal belongings. I watched him closely, building the courage to ask the question I wanted answered.

"Eren," I whispered, trying to hide my hesitation. "Do you have time for one more lesson?"

He smiled softly, latching his bag before reclaiming his seat. "Maybe a small one," he replied. "What would you like to know, princess?"

I swallowed, closing my eyes to steady myself. "Jestu ... what purpose does it hold?"

He nodded, seeming to understand why I had been so hesitant to ask. "Well, from my understanding, it started a few decades after our court was formed. It began as a way to bring our people and other races together. A way to build trust between each other. A place we could explore and celebrate each being's unique physical attributes, our gifts, and sate any growing desire between races.

"As time went on and the relationships between the courts calmed, the celebration had become an event everyone looked forward to so much that our court decided to continue it, in remembrance of how far we had come and the bonds we now continued to strengthen."

"Does ... does my father or family attend?"

"Your father, no. It is informal for the reigning ruler to attend the celebration, but your uncle occasionally attends. Your cousins almost always do as well."

A disgusting feeling slithered down inside of my stomach. "Leave it to this court to weaponize sex for their diplomatic agendas."

Eren laughed. "Well, when you stop and think about it, when is one most exposed?"

"Ha, ha," I said, the nerves of having to attend the event festering inside of me. "I don't want to go," I admitted.

Eren stood moved from his seat to a kneeling position in front of me. He took my hand in his and looked up into my eyes with something like compassion. "It is custom for the next heir to celebrate this event. Whether it be for physical enjoyment or a political one, you are telling those who see you that you are open to the unity the celebration represents. It won't be forever, princess."

I nodded, trying to settle the fear that blazed under my skin. Eren stood and went to the door without another word. I sunk myself into the corner of the room and cried.

CHAPTER NINE

A fter dinner, the throne room cleared quickly as everyone eagerly made their way to the Jestu celebration. Atalee gave me a mask to wear, as it was tradition to cover your face during the celebration. I made my way to the bottom level of the castle into a room I had never been in before, on purpose.

It was a large room, poorly lit with couches, chairs, tables, and platforms surrounding the outer edges. A beautiful crystal-clear pool was center stage in the room, fed by an indoor waterfall that fell from the ceiling. Glasses of ambrosia lined the trays of the human servants as I walked into a room full of eager and horny beings. A servant girl gestured for me to follow her to a throne that sat on the highest platform. Great, a front-row seat.

Alfar and humans alike were scattered around the floor. Their faces were covered in masks which I was thankful for. At least I couldn't easily make them out from one another. Music played heavily in the air while everyone began to drink and flirt. Ten minutes in, the clothes began coming off as they kissed, licked, and sucked on each other in the most intimate yet vulgar ways. I tried to focus on the music and not look, but as time went on the sounds got louder.

Even though I didn't have an alfar's nose, I could smell the scent of sex as it filled the room. The sounds and moans saturated the air, taking precedence over the music. I tensed my fists, trying to focus on anything but what was happening around me. I felt a hand slowly slide up my arm. I snapped open my eyes to see a male alfar I didn't recognize.

"May I serve you, Your Highness?" he asked in a deep voice, running his hand up my leg.

"No," I snapped, pushing his touch away.

He bowed, backing into the crowd and out of sight.

I looked around me to see flesh glistening with sweat and alfar and human bodies intertwined with one another. The flashes and memories began to flicker behind my eyelids once more. This time it wasn't just of the king. It was of Gaelin too. How he felt. How he sounded. How he smelled. The memories made me sick. I was going to be sick.

I pushed myself from the throne and darted through the crowded room to the door, eager for fresh air. I ran up the stairs and through the halls until I finally reached my bedroom. I barely made it to the toilet as the contents of my stomach came pouring back up. I wiped my face, trying to calm myself, but I was shaking and crying, unable to see through the spots that clouded my vision.

I hated sex. I hated everything about it. The sounds, the smell, the sight ... everything. How was I going to endure this twice a month for the rest of my life? How was I going to endure a husband in the next few months?

I made my way to the bed and crawled into a seated position against the headboard. I curled my knees to my chest and wrapped my arms around them as I rocked, trying to soothe myself like Levos used to do to me.

I closed my eyes, trying to shake the images from my mind, but I couldn't. I pulled at my hair, trying to make my mind stop, but it was no use. I was in the middle of a full-blown attack, and I would just have to ride it out.

A soft hand touched my forearm.

I opened my eyes quickly, pushing myself against the back of the headboard in fear. Erendrial sat in front of me on my bed. His mask lay next to him. His hair was tousled, and his shirt was opened lower than normal. I recoiled away from him, trying to put as much space between us as I could.

"Please leave. I don't want you to see me like this," I said, still shaking.

He placed his hands on either of my arms, turning me towards him. "Gen, look at me," he said. I kept my eyes shut, trying to squirm away from his touch. "Genevieve, open your eyes and look at me." he demanded.

I did as he said, trying to focus on the motion of his silver swirling eyes. "Please leave," I cried.

"I'm not going anywhere. Not when you're like this. Now, focus on me and breathe. Deep breaths. In and out. Just focus on your breathing. Nothing else. In and out," he said softly.

I did as he said, feeling my tired heart finally begin to slow as the shaking eventually stopped altogether. He slowly released his hands from me as I relaxed against the headboard. I couldn't bear to look at him. I was so embarrassed and humiliated.

"Thank you," I whispered.

He nodded silently. He went to the bathroom and returned with a cold cloth. He handed it to me. I wiped my cheeks, removing the warm sweat and tears that stained my face. He swirled his wrist around in the air. A clear ball the size of a grapefruit appeared in his hand, with tiny clouds swirling in the center.

"What is it?" I asked, too exhausted to take a closer look.

"This is a projection sphere. It will show you anything you desire on a larger scale. A memory, a sound, a visual ... anything. All you do is hold it in your hand and think of what you would like it to project. I want you to think of something that brings you comfort," he said, placing the smooth, cold ball in my hands. "Oh, and princess I swear, if Gaelin Atros appears naked on the ceiling, this will be the last favor I ever do for you."

A laugh unexpectedly erupted from inside of me. The action felt odd and foreign. Erendrial smiled and nodded towards the ball.

I held it close, closing my eyes and imagining the one thing that always brought me comfort ... the stars. I opened my eyes to see beautiful balls of bright light scattered around me. There were constellations and clusters of suns and planets that filled the room. I smiled, feeling like I was finally home.

"Stars, huh. I wouldn't have guessed. Is that why you wear the pendant?" he asked, gesturing to my necklace.

"One of them," I replied, touching the green stone in the center.

Erendrial got up from the bed and left the room. When he returned, he had a quill and paper in his hand. He sat on the bed and looked at me intensely. "Gen, I am not going to try to understand what you've been through, but I know for a fact that the only way you are going to truly be able to move past it is if you face the thing that haunts you out in the open. You need to admit to yourself that it happened and realize that you survived. You have two options. You can either let it continue to destroy you, as you are allowing it to do now, or you can own it and allow it to make you stronger."

"I don't know how," I admitted.

"You need to tell someone. Everything. Every detail, every feeling, every memory."

"No, absolutely not. I can't."

"You can and you will. He is dead. You got your revenge. Don't let him continue to torment you from the grave. You have a chance at a new life, a new beginning. Take it, and leave the prick behind. Do you remember what I told you before I left the light court the first time?" he asked.

I shook my head, unable to think clearly.

"The greatest power comes from surviving the darkest of nights. This is your darkest night." Erendrial handed me the piece of paper. It read:

I, Erendrial Valor Lyklor, swear never to repeat, use, write, or depict the accounts of Princess Genevieve Drezmore shared with me on this night, the second of November. If I fail to uphold this contract, I will take my own life as penance.

"You want me to tell you? Why?" I asked.

"Tonight, I am not Ambassador Lyklor, I am not Erendrial the liar or schemer, I am just a pair of ears for you to talk to. You need to do this for yourself. Once it is out there, you can begin to truly heal and move on. I promise," he said, taking a dagger from his waist and slicing the center of his palm. He dipped the quill and signed the contract in blood. He then took my hand and sliced a shallow line in my hand. I took the quill and signed my name to the contract. He then placed his wound over mine. I inhaled in astonishment feeling my open wound acting as a suction to his blood.

"What is happening?" I asked.

"It's the bonding taking form. My blood is now in you, tying me to the contract, and yours is now inside of me, accepting my offer."

"Amazing," I said. I pulled my hand back and watched while the wound began to heal.

"Now, turn around and place your back against mine," he said, taking his shoes off.

"Why?"

"I find it is easier when you don't have to look at the person you are telling your experiences to. Being back-to-back will provide you with the comfort of knowing someone is there, but you won't have to look me in the eyes."

I nodded, doing as he told me. I felt his broad back push up against mine before he exhaled, settling in.

"Now, remember every detail. Leave nothing out. You will speak of it once and then never again."

For the next hour, I told him everything. I started with Gaelin and then worked my way to King Lysanthier. The things he did to my body. The things he used on my body. What he made me do to him. The way I felt. How sick I was after every session. How I considered giving myself to the fairies to end my suffering. I told him how I didn't feel worthy of another's love or desire. I saw myself as a disgusting used rag, not worth the soap it would take to clean it.

At the end of the tell-all session, I took one final inhale and let the pain of my past go. I could feel the weight leaving me. I no longer felt trapped or suffocated. It worked. It actually worked.

I pulled away from Erendrial, still hesitant to look at him after he now knew the darkest and most shameful parts of me. He slid his legs over the edge of the bed and slid his boots back onto his feet. I stood, not sure of what to say or do.

"I'm sorry you got stuck being my babysitter. I can talk to my father if it's too much," I said, now feeling guilty that I just wasted an hour of his night.

He stood, turning towards me. "That won't be necessary. You are a lot of work, but not because of this. And for the record, you have every right to feel the way you do. That wasn't just rape, princess. That was torture and mutilation. Many alfar wouldn't have lasted through all of that."

I dropped my head.

"I also feel that I am to blame for the torment you had to endure."

I snapped my eyes to his. "What do you mean?"

"If I would have known the light king would have reacted in such a way to the poison we administered, I would have never allowed—"

"It's not your fault, Eren," I quickly interrupted, trying to abolish any guilt he may have felt. "I don't blame you for any of it. The poison didn't cause the king to become a rapist. That was already inside of him, hidden somewhere deep and dark."

Eren nodded, seeming to understand my need to end the conversation. "What are you thinking?" he asked. "Whomever I end up with ... how am I ever supposed to tell them this and expect him to want me after? I know emotions aren't your thing and all, but whoever he is, I want him to be proud to be my person. I want him to accept and want me and only me completely. Who would want this?" I said, gesturing to my body.

"Whoever you end up with will be very lucky to have a strong wife or lover. They won't care because you aren't that situation. You've risen above it, and you are now free of whatever bondage it had over you. You have conquered the darkest parts of this nightmare. Your body is healed, your heart still desires love, and in time, your mind will heal as well."

I smiled, feeling comfort in his words. I walked back over to the bed, crawling in between the sheets, ready to finally, truly sleep. "Eren, can I ask you one last favor before you leave?"

"See, needy," he said, smiling at me. He came and sat on the edge of the bed.

"Can you ... can you use your gift on me to make sure I have a good night's rest?"

"You haven't been sleeping well?"

"No, not since I got here, really. I have recurring nightmares of Lysanthier, or others being raped and harmed. Some of the images I've haven't witnessed first hand."

Erendrial stopped and looked at the wall next to my bed as he thought.

"What is it?" I asked.

"Nothing you need to worry about. I will take care of it, but yes, I can give you a good night's rest. Don't make this a habit though. I can be very addictive," he said with a devilish smile.

I laughed, laying my head back on the pillow. "So says every woman at court."

"They do, huh? I think that's the nicest thing anyone has ever said to me."

I hit him on the arm, laughing at his ego. "If that's so, you need new friends."

He smiled, leaning in towards me. "Lie back and relax. Clear your mind."

I closed my eyes as his hand reach out to my face. His skin was smooth and soft like velvet caressing the side of my cheek. I leaned into his touch, welcoming the comfort. Whiskey and oranges filled the air. I breathed in deep and smiled at the delicious combination.

"You will rest completely tonight," he said. "You will not dream, you will not think, or worry. You will close your eyes and your body will relax, offering you the most refreshing night's rest you have ever experienced." His thumb traced my chin gently before I felt the heaviness of sleep settle upon me. He went to pull away, but I managed to grab his hand, preventing his fingers from leaving my face. I opened my eyes heavily.

"I know I say this a lot, but thank you, Erendrial Lyklor. For everything," I whispered allowing a single tear to escape my eye.

He smiled at me softly and removed the tear with his thumb. "Sleep well, my princess. I will see you in the morning."

I fell asleep before I could remember his hand ever leaving my face.

I woke up with a smile on my face. My body was no longer sore. My stomach no longer hurt, and my heart no longer burdened. I stretched, feeling like a new person. I *was* a whole new person. I was better than I had ever been. Erendrial was right. I had been given another chance at life and I wasn't going to waste it. I may be the princess of the dark court, but I was a princess. I had power and money. So much money. I laughed as I made my way to the bathroom to bathe.

I got dressed and tied back my hair before making my way down to combat practice. I thought of Erendrial. His words, his demeanor. How gentle he had been with me last night. He could have easily exploited my trauma, but he didn't. He helped free me from myself. He spoke about the events of my experience as if he understood. As if he had gone through something similar. He knew what to do to set me free. Had he experienced a similar situation?

I pushed the question from my mind before I made my way into the ring with Varches and Toreon. That day I fought with a clear mind. I was able to anticipate attacks and counter strikes. I was no longer just reacting. I was fighting. I was reacting like an alfar. Calm, cool, and collected.

I rushed to my room, after to shower and change. As I left my chambers, Erendrial was waiting for me on the other side of the door. He smiled with a small nod. I returned the gesture. He extended his arm to me. I took it without fear.

"How did you sleep?" he asked, eyes forward.

"Incredibly. I can understand why females think you are so addictive."

He laughed a real laugh while he shook his head. "I don't think that is what they are referring to, but I will let your innocent mind believe whatever it wants."

"Where are we going? The library is the other way."

"Since you're so eager to go into battle, you will need something to ride—since you can't mist yet."

I stopped, moving in front of him. A smile stretched across my face from ear to ear. He chuckled at the sight of me.

"Ragamors? I get to learn to ride a ragamor?" I exclaimed.

"No, a horse. Yes, of course, a ragamor. What do you think we are, light alfar?"

I clapped with excitement. He took my arm and continued down the hall.

"Finally, something fun."

"What? My lessons aren't fun for you?"

"They are ... educational." I snickered to myself as he looked at me with an eyebrow raised.

"As I said, I don't like teaching."

"You're a good teacher."

"Well, aren't you just full of compliments today? I like this version of Gen. And thank you." We walked towards the exit as a lingering question ate at me.

"Eren, can I ask you a personal question? You don't have to answer it if you don't want to."

"I think you're entitled to a few personal details of my life, princess. Ask away."

"Last night, you knew exactly what to do and say to help me through my situation. Almost as if you had personal experience with it yourself. Almost as if—" I stopped, unable to finish the sentence.

He looked around us to see if anyone was watching. He exhaled before pulling me into an empty hall. He looked at me seriously for the first time. "This stays between us," he said, removing his hands from my arms.

"Of course."

He dropped his eyes to the floor. He began to pick at his thumb uncomfortably. "After my parents died, I was left with nothing, less than nothing, actually. I was in a very similar situation that you were in back in The Frey. I had to steal and beg for anything I got. I knew that wasn't the life I wanted, so I promised myself I was going to find a way out. That I would do anything to accomplish my goals and I would let nothing, and no one, stand in my way.

"When I was fourteen, I began sneaking into the castle. A high lady caught me stealing jewelry from her room. Instead of turning me in, she made me an offer. She would pay for my education, provide me with whatever I needed to succeed in life, and introduce me to the other high houses when I was ready. She would do this, if I would in return sign a contract binding myself to her physically for the rest of her life. Any time she wished to be ... serviced, I would have to willingly accept and fulfill my duty. I agreed. I signed my first blood contract and in return, I made myself into who I am today."

I chewed on the bottom of my lip nervously. "Is she still alive?" I asked. *Please be dead, please be dead.*

He laughed nervously, still not making eye contact. "She is alive and well and regularly serviced," he said, looking at the nearby wall. "And please don't ask who. I can't tell you, even if I wanted to. Part of the contract."

We stood in the hall for a few moments in silence. I reached out my hand to his arm. I knew he wouldn't like pity, but I couldn't prevent myself from trying to provide him with some comfort. I pulled him into me, wrapping my arms around his neck. He was hesitant at first, unsure of what was happening. Eventually, he wrapped his arms around my waist lightly, hugging me in return.

"Here's to hoping the bitch dies soon." I said, pulling away from him.

He laughed, still not bringing his eyes up from the ground. "I've been praying to Azeer for centuries. He must enjoy her cruelty. Come on, let's get you on a ragamor. I can't wait to see how you fair on one."

"Thee of little faith," I said playfully.

"I'm not Christian, so I have no faith, but I do have a sense of humor, and I can't wait to see this." We walked out of the hall, arm in arm as we headed outside into the Kingdom of Doonak.

CHAPTER TEN

E rendrial called Eeri to the front gates. We rode her to a place where Eren told me ragamors usually nested in the nearby forest. Eren was cautious of our contact, but it didn't bother me as much anymore. It would still take time before I would be comfortable with a male's touch, but last night had been a huge breakthrough. And against my better judgement ... I was beginning to trust him.

We landed at the bottom of a waterfall where swarms of ragamors nested. They came in all colors and sizes. Some were small, some were big. They were yellow, blue, red, and green. Their wingspans differed in size and shape, each perfectly designed to their structural design of their bodies.

Their hides shimmered as their scales reflected the rays of sunlight that broke through the clouds above. Their bodies were long and sleek, perfectly designed to navigate through the air. Massive retractable claws hid beneath their long toes, sharp enough to tear any creature to pieces.

Each of their faces was unique, decorated with different markings and colors. Their eyes, so vibrant and aware, seemed to be gateways into their souls, as if they could experience emotions of their own. But inside each of their mouths hid rows of sharp, flesh tearing teeth.

"First thing you need to know is that each ragamor has its own personality. Some are sweet, like Eeri here. Others are feisty, and some are straight-up deadly. If a ragamor bows when you approach, that is a good indicator that they will allow you to ride them. If they ignore you or make any threatening action towards you, back away slowly, head down. Never turn your back to them, or they won't hesitate to attack."

"So how do I mount one?"

Erendrial started laughing. "We are really going to have to work on your wording of phrases."

"Oh, shut up. If you didn't have such a dirty mind this wouldn't be a problem."

"You're the heir to the dark court. It's going to be a problem. Anyways, when you *mount* the ragamor, slit your palms and slide your hands into the slits gently. A flash connection will happen instantly. You will be able to see the ragamor through its own eyes. You will feel its power and be able to harness it. Then, once you are in your right mind again, you will be able to control the ragamor with your thoughts. Before you take flight, let me mount the ragamor with you so I can talk you through the navigation. When the first flight is complete, the ragamor will lean his neck back into the sky revealing a very sensitive patch of scales if he accepts you as his rider. You will take one and we will form it into the calling beacon you will use to call him or her."

"Got it. Find a ragamor, mount ragamor, pluck ragamor."

He laughed again, which sent an odd sense of joy spiraling through me. "You've got it."

I took the dagger from him and headed into the heart of their swarm. Some ragamor seemed interested in me, while others didn't even look in my direction. After studying their faces, bodies, and wings, I came across a ragamor that was unlike any other. Its scales were black as night. Its face was long with a strong jaw and vibrant white teeth. Its eyes were red, and it had green markings going down the center of its faces.

The other ragamor seemed to steer clear of the massive creature. I didn't know if ragamors had alphas, but if they did, this one was clearly superior. It spread its wings as I approached, revealing its inner green lining. It was magnificent.

I moved forward slowly, looking for any sign that it would accept me. It looked at me for a moment and then huffed, turning its back to me. I walked around to face the creature again, but got no response. I was becoming agitated with the stubborn beast, but I didn't give up. I circled around to face the creature one last time. It saw me out of the corner of its eyes and extended its head forward releasing a loud roar, as a warning to stay away.

My eyes narrowed and my determination flared. I had overcome so much. I had been gifted this new life ... a life where I got to start over and choose who I wanted to be. I needed this ragamor. It symbolized the strength and power I wished to possess.

Oh, no you don't. I climbed on top of a high boulder nearby that lay parallel with the beast. I slit two gashes in my hands and dropped the dagger to the floor, then took a leap of faith.

I slammed into the silky scales of the creature's back. It began to lash and growl as it fought to get me off. My thighs tightened around its strong back while I searched for the slits. As the ragamor inhaled, two pink pockets appeared by its shoulder blades. I could hear Erendrial yelling for me to stop, but I didn't listen. I slid my palms into the slits, wrapping my hands around two bones that acted as handles.

Images of the ragamor soaring in the air flashed behind my eyes. Battles and fights for dominance. Memories of the beast killing creatures of all sizes and shapes. Defending his territory. My vision returned to normal while the ragamor stomped his feet in protest of my action. I felt his power, strength, and ferocity streaming through me like a wave of delicious energy.

I couldn't wait a moment longer. I had to get into the air. I held on, leaning low against his body. The ragamor flared his wings, shooting into the sky so fast tears began to pour from my eyes. As he broke through the clouds the air thinned. He twirled and flipped forcing me to hold on for dear life. His wings were strong and glorious, catching the beams of sunlight.

He steadied out, gliding at a calm and easy pace. Eeri and Eren broke through the clouds, evening out next to us. I looked over at him with a smile on my face.

"You're insane! You know that?" he yelled, shaking his head.

I shrugged, still enjoying the thrill. "You only live once! Well, unless you're Otar, that is."

"Yes, easy for you to say. If you die, then my life is over as well. Do you know what your father would do to me if you were killed on my watch?"

"Skin you. Isn't that what you told me last time?" I laughed at his overprotective behavior.

"That's if I'm lucky."

"Get the stick out of your ass, Lyklor." I said before leaning into the ragamor, sending him hurtling down to the ground. The rush was unbelievable. It was like breathing for the first time. I didn't think I would ever get enough. The beast flew across a massive body of water, skimming the surface with his clawed feet before we shot back into the air, tumbling through the clouds and atmosphere. I smiled, allowing the feeling to consume me.

We made our way back to the hive of ragamors. I landed the beast and pulled my hands out of his slits. My wounds healed automatically. Eren landed a few paces away, sliding off Eeri and rushing towards me. I slid off the ancient creature, hoping he would offer me a scale so he would be mine, forever.

"So, you're an adrenaline junky—good to know," Eren said.

I laughed, walking towards the front of the beast. He looked down at me with his radiant eyes and stomped his feet again. He snapped at Eren to back away before returning his fierce gaze to me. Eren did as he was instructed. The ragamor stood with his head bent, assessing me for a long time, before finally raised his neck to the sky.

I smiled, walking slowly towards him. I pulled a black scale from the soft part of his neck, trying to be as gentle as possible. He lowered his head, allowing me to touch his beautifully sculpted face.

"You are incredible," I said. "Tarsyrth, is that your name?" I said, pulling the name from his memories while I ran my hand over his scales.

"That's an interesting name," added Eren, coming up behind me slowly. Tarsyrth snapped his head to him and growled. "I can see the resemblance between the two of you."

"You mean the black scales and green markings?" I asked.

"I mean the stubborn, impulsive behavior, along with a side of snarky attitude."

I laughed, turning to face him. "Better watch it. My collection of creatures keeps growing. Odd how none of them seem to like you. It must be a sign."

"It's a sign that you have terrible taste in pets. Come on, we should be heading back to get ready for dinner."

"Why don't we skip dinner and go for a ride instead? Maybe we can fly over the light court and take out some of their buildings."

"Though I like where your head's at, we are not allowed over there right now. We have to wait until they make contact with us before we can fly in their skies again. They're still pissed about someone killing their king." he said.

"What can I say, he was a dick."

"You will hear no argument from me. Here, cut your palm again and cover the scale with your blood." I did as he instructed. "Now, hold it in your hands. I am going to encase your hands with mine and then you are going to blow between them. This will create the calling beacon." I covered the scale with my hands. Eren wrapped his long fingers around mine as a bright light beamed from them. He nodded signaling for me to blow in between my palms. When he removed his hands, I looked down at a small, whistle-shaped instrument.

"Amazing," I exclaimed.

"Try it out."

I brought the whistle to my lips and blew. A deep, booming echo sounded, like a war call. Tarsyrth nudged my back, letting me know he was there. I smiled, taking his face against my shoulder.

"Okay, one more ride, and then we have to get back," said Eren.

"Deal," I said, mounting Tarsyrth. I used Eren's dagger to cut my palms before throwing it back down to him. I slid my hands into his slits and shot back into the air. My new favorite escape.

We got back to the castle thirty minutes before dinner. Eren showed me how to open the doors to the kingdom before I took off down the hall to my room. Atalee was waiting for me on my bed. She got to work on my windblown hair and chapped face. I slid on the black dress that was lined with fur before Eren reappeared in my sitting room.

I took his arm as we headed down to the throne room for dinner. I was still buzzing with happiness from having my very own ragamor when I felt a familiar lightning zap up the back of my spine. I stopped, turning to Eren before it reached my brain.

"My head—" I muttered, before my whole body gave out as a vision took hold of my mind in a savage, painful embrace. I saw St. Paul's Church up in flames. My human family stood outside, crying while they watched their home burn to the ground.

Another image appeared of a light alfar exiting from behind the burning church with a smile on his face. He wore a necklace with the Lysanthier sigil. Then I saw Sister Ester's body, burned, and charred. My family stood over her, praying and crying as they mourned.

My eyelids opened slowly. I blinked a few times, trying to will the pain behind my eyes away only to realize I was in Eren's arms, off to the side of the hall. Groups of humans and alfar stared at us in curiosity. I sat up pulling away from him, reaching to rub the back of my neck. My head was killing me, and I felt weak, but it wasn't as bad as the last vision I had.

"How long was I out?" I asked Eren.

"About five minutes. I was about to call for help."

"I need to get to The Frey, now," I said, forcing myself up. I was still weak, and my legs protested wobblingly unsteadily. Eren helped me lean against the wall. My father came around the corner and beelined straight for us.

"Are you okay? One of my guards saw you collapse," he said, taking my face in his hands as he checked me over to be sure. My uncle came up next to him, looking worried for my sake.

"I am fine. It was just a vision," I replied.

"What did you see?" asked my uncle.

"My church, burning. The sister that took us all in didn't make it out. She's going to die. I saw a light alfar with the Lysanthier sigil leaving from the burning church. I think Daealla is going to burn my home down as revenge for killing her father. I have to warn them. Please, father. I know they are only human, but they are important to me. I owe them," I pleaded.

My uncle placed a hand on my father's shoulder and whispered something into his ear.

"I will give you five hours. Be back by midnight, or I will send a rescue team out to find you," said my father. "Erendrial—"

"Of course, your majesty," answered Eren before bowing.

"Thank you, father," I said, reaching up to kiss his cheek.

He froze, looking down at me in shock. That was the first time I had ever kissed him with affection. I guess breaking King Lysanthier's hold over me had taken down other barriers I hadn't even known I had built. My father smiled and nodded before returning to the throne room.

"I am going to change. Get Zerrial and Lily. Lily will want to come," I said to Eren.

He nodded before I took off to my room.

I changed into a more practical dress with a long black fur coat that trailed to the floor. I removed my crown and let my hair fall around my shoulders. I rushed to the entrance and called for Tarsyrth. He appeared in a few moments with a loud roar. Eren, Zerrial, and Lily appeared at my side. Eren and Zerrial called their ragamors. Within minutes their beasts soared down out of the air, landing by Tarsyrth. My creature snapped and hissed at the others.

"See what I mean? You two are one in the same," joked Eren.

"And you expect me to believe you are soft and fuzzy like Eeri?" I asked.

"You've never been in my bed," he laughed, mounting her.

Lily looked at the ragamor with sheer fear.

"You haven't ridden one before?" I asked her.

"Uh, no. Why would I?" she answered.

"It's okay, angel, I won't let you fall," assured Zerrial, reaching for her. She smiled up at him and took his hand. He positioned her carefully underneath him. Eren looked at me and made a puking face.

"Oh, very mature," I said. We both laughed, taking to the sky.

The flight to The Frey was a bit rough. I was still getting use to flying on the back of a dragon and how to navigate and control the creature. Tarsyrth was accommodating, banking every time I nearly slid off his back, to prevent me from plummeting to my death. Flying felt natural, but it would still take time to get good at it.

We followed Eren to the border, where we dismounted. Eren handed me a small, blue stone.

"What is this?" I asked, rolling the smooth, flawless crystal in between my fingers.

"It's so you can cross through the border whenever you want. Your father wanted me to give it to you. Since you're only half alfar, this will allow you to walk through on your own."

I nodded, sliding the stone into my pocket. We crossed into The Frey, where the air was thicker, and the land was barren. Zerrial found us two horses at a nearby stable, one for he and Lily, the other for Eren and I before we rode through the streets towards home.

An hour later, we arrived at the church, which was fully up in flames. I dismounted quickly, rushing towards the building in disbelief. A crowd of humans surrounded the burning pile of stone and timber, completely silent while they watched the structure fall into the thrashing flames.

I froze, feeling the sorrow envelop me. "We're too late," I whispered, as the others joined me. "Why did my gift show me this, if we were going to be too late?"

"Sister Ester," Lily whispered, tears streaming down her face.

Zerrial held her while she wept for the kind woman. From the back of the church, I saw a blonde-haired figure move into the crowd. Without thinking I took off towards them. I pushed my way through the onlookers until I had a clear path to the culprit. I flung myself towards him, tumbling us both to the ground. He began to fight me as I pulverized his face with my fist.

He rolled on top of me, wrapping his hands around my throat, trying to suffocate me. His body suddenly stiffened. His eyes bulged and the veins in his neck protruded. He fell off me shaking and convulsing in pain. Eren appeared above me, offering a hand to before pulling me from the ground. I dusted myself off.

"What are you doing to him?" I asked.

"Bursting the veins in his brain over and over again as he heals."

"Remind me not to piss you off."

"Don't piss me off," he said with a sarcastic smirk.

Zerrial appeared, wrapping ulyrium cuffs around the light alfar's wrists. Once the restraints were secure, Eren released his hold on the male. I turned back to the church that was now falling in on itself.

"Do you think I can still save her?" I asked.

"If everything in your vision has already come to pass, I doubt it," answered Eren.

Lily appeared by my side, taking my hand in hers while we watched our haven burn.

"We can at least find the others," suggested Lily. "Just to make sure they're okay." I nodded, turning back to Eren.

"We will secure the prisoner and join you shortly," Eren said to us.

We made our way through the crowd in search of our family. A group of young, dirty boys and girls stood off to the side, watching as their home burned to the ground. I approached Jordan, touching my hand to his shoulder lightly. He turned, taking in the sight of both of us.

"Gen, Lily, is it really you?" he asked in disbelief.

"Yes," I said with tears in my eyes.

The others turned around at the same time, tear-filled faces turned into smiling ones. Jordan exhaled in disbelief, picking me up and swinging me around until I thought I was going to be sick. Kara and Nil bulldozed into me, as they clung to my waist. Evan picked up Lily, kissing her on the cheek. Zerrial appeared behind her with his eyes deadlocked onto Evan.

Jordan and Evan pulled us behind them as Eren stepped out of Zerrial's shadow. Zerrial stood face to face against Evan before reaching around him, taking Lily by the arm, and pulling her to him. Evan reacted, pulling her back, but Eren stopped him before he could succeed.

"I wouldn't do that young man. My friend here is very territorial. You wouldn't want to lose an arm now, would you?" Eren said to Evan.

"She is no one's property, you filthy dark elves," spat Evan.

Eren cleared his throat, walking closer to Evan and Jordan. He noted Jordan's hand on my waist before clearing his throat. "Princess ... are you going to cut in here or am I going to have to kill your friends?" Eren said, smiling as he restrained his hands behind his back.

"I was enjoying watching all of the steam coming from your ears," I replied.

He chuckled, nodding his head. "Clever as always," he mumbled.

"Princess," said Jordan. "Gen, what is he talking about?"

"Why don't we go somewhere quiet, and we will explain," I suggested, looking at each of them.

Nil and Kara were in each other's arms, shaking at the sight of Eren and Zerrial.

"The stables are cleared out for the night. No one will be there," Evan said.

"Fantastic, the smell of horse shit and filth. Let's go," Eren said sarcastically, turning to lead the way.

I laughed as my eyes caught Jordan's. He looked at me with confusion. I cleared my voice to chase away the laughter.

Once we reached the stables, the questions began pouring in.

"Okay, what in the hell is happening here? How did you both manage to survive?" asked Stefan.

"Luck, mostly luck," I replied.

"Don't forget the magic, scheming, oh, and murder. Your friend here killed the light king. She's very impressive," added Eren.

"You did what? How? Tell me everything," demanded Stefan.

"Yes, I did, but that isn't the point. We are both alive and well. Happy even," I said, looking at Lily. "Where is Conner?"

"Gone," answered Stefan. "He left the day after you went with the light alfar. He said he had to start over. We haven't heard from him since."

"How are you happy with these things?" Evan blurted out, still sizing up Zerrial. "Are the legends not true?"

"Most of them are wrong or exaggerated," answered Lily. "In the dark court, they don't rape any more than humans rape here. They don't experiment on humans or torture us. We have jobs, and are treated well, for the most part."

"If you are taken by an alfar that is," said Evan, still staring Zerrial down.

"He didn't take me, and no. You are treated well regardless of who you are sleeping with," added Lily.

Evan made a disgusted face and walked to the back of the barn.

Lily chased after him.

"Where is your covering?" asked Jordan. "If they know who you are, why aren't you dead?"

"Turns out my father is the King of Doonak. I am the heir to the dark court," I said slowly.

The girls' faces went blank. They stared at Erendrial, still shaking with fear.

"He isn't going to hurt you girls, I promise," I said, kneeling in front of them. I rubbed both of their dirty faces, kissing each on the head.

"What about the law against half-breeds?" asked Stefan.

"My father got rid of the law in his kingdom before he claimed me as his heir," I answered.

"How did you know about the church?" asked Kara.

"My gift ... I have visions. I saw the church burning and I saw Sister Ester ... dead."

The girls began to sob, falling to the floor in each other's arms.

"I'm sorry," I said softly. "I tried to get here before it happened, but I was too late."

"Princess, we need to be getting back," said Eren from behind me.

I looked back at my family, feeling the pain of having to leave them again.

Jordan looked distressed as he walked over to me. He took my hand with his and my face in his other. "You don't have to go. Stay.

Stay here with us. We need you now more than ever. I will protect you. We can protect them," he said, leaning in close to me.

"Jordan, I wish I could, but I—" I started to say. "I didn't realize ..." Jordan started, but then stopped and hesitated for a moment. "I didn't realize what was right in front of me until you were gone. Please Gen ... stay," he pleaded, leaning his head into mine.

A slow clap of hands disrupted our moment. Eren strolled over to us with an amused smile. "How sweet. The poor boy from the church basement is in love with the Doonak princess," he said, moving a curl away from my face.

Jordan looked at him and then back at me. "Is he your ... are you two?" asked Jordan.

I looked at Eren, connecting what he was trying to ask. "Oh, gods, no. He is our ambassador," I replied.

"Oh, thank the Lord," exhaled Jordan.

"Doesn't mean it couldn't happen though. Right, princess?" Eren said, winking at Jordan.

Jordan's face tightened with rage as he peered at Eren, who was calm and collected.

"Jordan, I can't stay. I just found my father, and there is so much I have yet to learn and experience," I admitted.

"So, we're not enough. That is what you're saying?" asked Jordan.

"Exactly," Eren said happily.

I pushed him behind me, trying to calm Jordan. "Not at all. I am saying that I will never fit here. I didn't belong in the first place. There, I am learning how to use my gifts and magic. I am learning who I am."

"You fit with us," he said, dragging his hand down my hair.

I looked at him tenderly. "I'm sorry, but I can't stay." I took a large pouch of gold coins from my jacket and placed it in his hands. "This should buy each of you a chance at a good life."

Jordan dropped his head in disappointment.

"You may have to go, but Lily can stay, right?" asked Nil. Lily and Evan made their way back over to us.

I looked at Lily with a heavy heart. "If she chooses to stay, then yes," I said. I heard Zerrial take a step forward behind me before Eren stuck his arm out to stop him from continuing. Lily looked at our family and exhaled. Tears filled her eyes as she took the girls in her arms.

"I love you all so much, but I too have found where I belong. I am sorry, but I won't be staying," she said.

I was surprised how quickly she turned down the offer to return home. I stole a glance at Zerrial, noticing the relief that consumed his face.

"Will you both at least visit?" asked Kara.

"Of course. As soon as it's safe and we can, we will visit," I said.

"Princess, we really should be going," said Eren.

We hugged each of them one last time before we took our leave. We retrieved the light alfar prisoner and made our way back to the horses. The light alfar dragged behind us as we rode to the border.

"Did you really have to be so rude?" I asked Eren.

He leaned in from behind me and whispered in my ear. "Would you have me any other way?"

I shoved my elbow back into his stomach.

He grumbled and laughed.

"They were grieving and in shock," I replied. "You could have at least just stood there and brooded like Zerrial."

"Now, where is the fun in that? Plus, little Jordan was too easy to torment. I couldn't help myself. If he didn't realize what he had when it was right in front of him, then he never deserved it in the first place."

"You don't know him. He's a good man. Any woman would be lucky to have him as her husband."

"Yes, but you are not a woman, and he will never be a king."

"And to think, at the beginning of this day I actually liked you."

"See, I told you I would grow on you."

"You're like a fungus. You just keep spreading," I said.

"Oh, so you like to be consumed. Duly noted."

I laughed, feeling my cheeks blush. I felt Eren stiffen behind me. I turned to see a look of surprise on his face. "Wha's wrong?" I asked.

He inhaled deeply. "Do you smell that?" he asked.

I took a deep breath and shook my head. "No. What is it?"

"Sandalwood and ..." he took another breath, "... lavender."

I laughed, shaking my head. "Probably some perfume your last victim was wearing."

"Jealousy is a good look on you, princess."

Taken aback by his arrogance and assumption, I allowed my aggravation to get the best of me. "Do you have a comeback for everything?"

"Yes, but so do you. That is why I enjoy our little tiffs. You can keep up. Most people give in by now, or end up trying to kill me. You just keep firing back. Then, once I am done, I can just shut you up."

"Oh, and how do you plan to do that?" I asked.

He smiled as the horse galloped down the road, bouncing both of us in the saddle. I felt Eren's fingers gently caress the back of my hand that held the horn of the saddle. Whiskey and oranges drifted into my nostrils. I inhaled, welcoming the comforting and familiar scent. I relaxed back into him as my whole body loosened. He wrapped his arm around my waist, preventing me from falling. He chuckled in my ear, resting his head against mine. "I win," was the last thing I heard before I drifted into a deep sleep.

CHAPTER ELEVEN

We got back to the castle ten minutes before midnight. I had to ride Eeri with Eren, unable to sit upright long enough to fly Tarsyrth home as my body still fought for sleep. His damn magic was like a drug and had lasting effects. He laughed at me the entire way home, teasing and making fun of me. Gods, how I wished I had an offensive power. I would torment him with it every chance I got.

I awoke the next morning and began to prepare myself for combat training, when Atalee appeared.

"Your father has requested you attend breakfast with him in his private chambers," she informed me.

This was an unusual request. Usually, my father took his political meetings with other houses in the morning—never for personal benefit. Something had to be amiss.

I nodded. "Tell him I will be right there."

She bowed before leaving to relay the message. I quickly pulled a plain, black dress from the wardrobe and trailed a brush through my curly hair before heading to his rooms.

When I entered, the smell of fresh pastries and fried meat greeted me. My mouth instantly began to water. I rounded the corner of his study and was surprised by the display of food set out for just the two of us. It was truly a table fit for a king.

My father came out from his bedchamber dressed in a casual shirt and pants. His hair was pulled away from his face; his green eyes, identical to my own, placed on display.

He embraced me, kissing my head softly. "Good morning, Genevieve. How did you sleep?"

"Okay, thank you," I said with a suspicious smile. "Is something wrong?"

He looked at me with curiosity. "Not at all. Why would you think that?" He shooed the help away, leaving only the two of us in the room.

"You've never called me to breakfast before." I followed him to the table, sitting in the chair he pulled out for me. He began filling a plate without a word. "Usually," I continued, needing to fill the silence, "you conduct courtly matters during breakfast. So, I just figured it had to do with something political."

He set the plate in front of me and took a seat across the table. He folded his hands in front of his chest, smiling down the rectangular surface at me. "You're very observant for one so young. An excellent trait to possess."

"What is it, Father?" I asked, trying to get to the point.

He exhaled, leaning towards the table. "I wish to discuss the upcoming tournament. The one that will decide your future husband. Our future king."

My stomach dropped. I took a deep drink of the juice in front of me, trying to keep my calm demeaner. "What about it?"

"The tournament will soon be upon us. It is important you take the time to get to know each candidate. Has Ambassador Lyklor shared with you those who wish to claim your hand?"

The word 'claim' made me sick—as if I were another's property. "He has."

"Good. The tournament will consist of three trials. Each will test their abilities, whether they be physical, mental, or political. The winner will have the honor of claiming your hand."

"Why have the three candidates been chosen? Can no one else join the tournament? Do I have no say in who I am tied to for the rest of my life?" I felt my confidence grow as each word passed through my lips.

"Each candidate was chosen based on the alliance and strength they would bring to the throne and to our bloodline. These are families we trust, loyal to us for generations.

"During the tournament, it is a formality that we open the floor to any last-minute contenders that wish to toss their coin into the race. But it is just that: a formality. No one has ever dared to go against the chosen three. It is a death sentence socially and physically. These candidates are the strongest of their generation and are best equipped to face the challenges the tournament will deliver.

"And as far as choice goes ..." my father paused, looking down at the table. Something like guilt fluttered across his face. "I am sorry that you haven't been able to choose how your life has unfolded. It pains me to take this choice away from you, but you must understand ... as a royal, in this matter, we will never have a choice.

"Though, as I am sure you are now aware, marriage is mostly a formality here. After the ceremony is complete and an heir conceived, you are free to take who your heart desires. No one will ever question you."

"Marriage means something to me," I spat, the anger of the situation getting the best of me. "I wasn't raised like the rest of you. I don't want a political match. I want a husband. A real husband, who loves and desires me just as much as I desire him. A male who I've chosen to give myself to. Who I can trust ... who makes me happy."

Father took another deep breath while he shook his head. "I wish I could give you that, but this is not the way our world works."

"You are the king. You have the power to change that, just like you changed the law about half-breeds."

He slammed his hand into the table, rattling the glasses on the surface. I sat back, surprised by the outburst. I had never seen my father enraged before.

He took a moment and steadied himself before finally looking up at me. "I desire nothing more than to make you happy. After everything I've missed out on ... after everything you've had to endure, truly, I want to see you happy, but our station requires sacrifice. Yes, we are royal. Yes, we have power, but we serve our people. Our court comes first ... always.

"Daughter, if there was a way that I could guarantee you a male who loved you the way you described, who cherished you and could make you happy, I would stop at nothing to ensure that life for you—to find you a partner who would put you above anyone and anything else.

"Yet, that is not the life we were born to. So ... I must ask you to make another sacrifice, to ensure our kingdom remains strong, powerful, and united."

I pondered his words, taking in all he said. "Yes, Father. Whatever is needed, I will do."

"Genevieve," he whispered. I drew my eyes up to him. "You will find your happiness. I know you will."

I forced a smile and nodded. "I am sure I will." I dug into my breakfast, changing the subject to stories about his childhood, trying to seem interested in his retellings while a part of my heart withered and died.

After breakfast, I rushed back to my room, needing a moment to myself while I processed my future. I tore the dress from my body, reaching for my fighting leathers. I would process my fate while I pulverized someone's face in the ring.

Eren barged in without even being announced. I threw on my clothes as fast as I could to cover myself.

"Uh, excuse me. Heard of knocking? I could have been naked," I said, pulling my shirt down over my midsection.

"Princess, what makes you think I haven't already seen you naked? You've seen what my powers are capable of," he said, throwing a black bag onto my bed.

I stopped, trying to recall how many times I remembered the smell of whiskey and oranges. Only three times, right? Or maybe he took my memory of the smell away altogether.

He started laughing. "Calm yourself, I am just kidding. I haven't laid eyes on you, I promise."

"You're the Ambassador of Lies. I can't trust your promises," I replied, pulling on my boots.

"And manipulation. Ambassador of Lies and Manipulation. Glad to hear my reputation is still going strong."

"What's in the bag?" I asked.

"Armor and weapons. You, little Genevieve, are going on your first hunt this morning."

I smiled, rushing over to the bed in excitement. "Finally! This couldn't have come at a better time. What are we hunting? Does it have hair, scales? Does it run in a pack?"

"Calm down already. It is only one creature that we know of. It spews some type of acid from its mouth and its blood is toxic as well, so you will have to be extra careful when you attack. None of it can touch you. We don't know how potent it is."

"Fantastic," I exclaimed.

He pulled out a black leather vest, plated in silver armor. It was light and breathable. There were matching leg coverings and gloves to complete the set. I put the armor on, still trying to contain my excitement. Eren pulled out a black magic sword that I had only practiced with a handful of times. It was brand new. It had a black hilt wrapped in leather, with the Drezmore sigil stamped into the metal base at the end of the sword. It curved into a hook at the tip like the other swords I had seen. Black markings were inscribed into the neck of the blade.

"Your very own black sword, created just for your small stature," he said, handing it to me.

"Oh, this day just keeps getting better," I said, turning the blade from side to side.

Eren strapped a belt around my waist that contained daggers and a sheath for the sword. He then bent to strap another belt around my leg. As the leather slid across the thin fabric of my pants I giggled.

He stopped, looking up at me with an arched eyebrow. "Princess?"

"Sorry, it ... tickled."

He shook his head and continued to fasten the belt to my leg. "We'll have to make the hunt fast. I have another surprise for you when we get back," he said, standing to his feet.

"You're giving me gifts now? Are we that close of friends?" I said.

"No. If I had it my way, this 'gift' wouldn't be coming, but I have no say in the matter."

I stopped, realizing he was talking about a person. "Who, Eren? Who is coming?" I asked more seriously.

"The new ambassador of Urial. Ambassador Levos Atros. He should be here for dinner. He is coming to negotiate the release of Queen Daealla's cousin."

"Wait. The light alfar we caught is her cousin?"

"Apparently."

"And Levos is now their ambassador? When did this happen?"

"About a week after we rescued you. Apparently, the queen was not thrilled with the previous ambassador's skill set. Gaelin suggested Levos, which was a smart move, but now it means I have to up my game. He's a smart little prick, but don't tell him I said that," he said, strapping his own belts onto his body.

My face fell, wondering how he would be towards me. I never got to tell him goodbye. I never had the chance to explain myself. Out of everyone at the light court, I loved him the most.

"You okay, princess?"

"Yeah, just thinking," I answered, trying to focus.

"Don't think too hard. When you do, people end up dead, or creatures we've already killed come back to life. Speaking of, why don't you call your little pet to assist on the hunt?"

"He's going to rip your throat out for calling him that."

"Only if you give him permission, and I know you won't."

"What makes you so sure?"

"Whiskey and oranges," he winked at me with his wicked smile.

"Gods, I hate you," I mumbled, walking past him to the door.

"Glad to hear I've made an impression. Let's head to the rag-amor. The rest of the team should be there."

"Who is coming with us?"

"Zerrial, Leenia, the twins, and Evinee."

"Beast, pusher, the mad geniuses who immobilize things, and bone spears with a side of armor, check," I said as we walked through the halls.

"Very good."

"Lily filled me in on your group of friends. Quite the collection you have."

"She did, did she? It's almost complete. Now all I need is a wicked queen to complete the set." He turned to me, looking for a reaction.

I rolled my eyes. "Is that why you are still assisting me? So I will be under your control once I take the throne? You would basically be king."

"I am ambitious, aren't I?"

I laughed as we exited the castle. I called for Tarsyrth. He appeared in a moment, slamming into the rock platform with a loud roar announcing his presence.

"She got the black one?" asked Evinee in awe. "How? I tried to get him to accept me for weeks before he finally struck at me."

"She basically raped him," replied Eren.

The twins snickered while they mounted their ragamors.

"Oh, so he likes it rough, does he?" said Evinee. "Dammit, why didn't I try that?"

I laughed at her, kissing Tarsyrth on the nose. We took off into the sky, soaring low enough to search the treetops for the creature. After an hour of scouring our surroundings, we finally caught a glimpse of the hideous thing, climbing up a nearby mountain.

We landed behind the creature, blocking any chance for their escape once the fighting began. I withdrew my sword, allowing the needle to puncture my palm shallowly. The blade illuminated with green lightning. Usually, the stream of light was blue, but not this time. Oz and Voz came up on either side of me, taking in the new color.

"How did you?" asked Oz.

"I don't know. Every other time it's been blue like the rest of the black weapons," I replied.

"But this sword was specifically made for you. We used your DNA to comprise it. Maybe that has something to do with the color change," added Voz.

"Why does the color not change for every alfar that uses them, then?" I asked.

"Very curious. I do not have an answer for that, but I will research it once we get back," said Oz, returning his attention to the beast.

"I guess green is just your color," commented Eren, coming from behind. "Don't do anything reckless. If you feel tired or get in over your head back away and let us handle it."

I nodded before we approached.

The creature's hairless skin was a pale, sickly flesh color. It sagged all over its body, like its hide had been melted off or stretched. It had three long fingers on each hand and three long toes that allowed it to climb. It had no eyes and no nose, only two large holes on either side of its long, oval head and a mouth full of black teeth. It was tall and gangly like Otar.

As we approached, it snapped its head towards our position, noting our arrival. We stopped, waiting for it to make the first move. Zerrial transformed into a large hairy beast the size of a massive bear. His snout was long, and his teeth made for ripping flesh. His ears stuck out from his head. The muscles of his body bulged and tensed with power as he came crashing on all fours to the ground.

"Wow," I whispered.

Without warning the creature jumped from the rock it was perched on, landing in the center of our group. Its long legs and arms swung like whips as its body contorted into unnatural positions. It bent backward flipping and slithering on the ground like nothing I had ever seen before. Yellow bile began to spew from its mouth, burning anything it touched.

We all attacked, taking turns trying to land hits on the creature.

It dodged as if it could see us coming before we even engaged. I ducked and dove out of the way as its long claws sliced at my face. Leenia used her power to throw the creature against a nearby tree, which only worked for a few moments before the thing pulled itself away from her magic, now unaffected by her gift.

"How did it—?" asked Leenia in shock.

"It must be adapting to our magic somehow. I will try to stun it with pain so someone can land a blow. Don't use your gifts until I say," ordered Eren.

He held his hand out, focusing on the creature. The thing grabbed at its head before it erupted with a scream more haunting than anything I had ever heard. It lashed back and forth, trying to escape Eren's power. Leenia came from behind, slicing at its back. Blood sprayed forcefully from the wound, coating her arm. The acid began to eat into her armor, heading straight for her skin. She quickly removed her cuff and barely got the thing off before it began eating her flesh.

"Its veins are like a fountain. Everyone be on guard," yelled Leenia.

The creature broke through Eren's power, heading straight for him. Zerrial came out of nowhere, slamming the beast into the ground. He jumped back, unable to land a final blow because of the toxic blood. He changed back into his alfar form and picked up his sword, readying himself for a fight. Evinee launched bone spears into the creature's abdomen, causing blood to spew out everywhere. We all dove and ran for cover as the creature pulled the spears from his hide.

It reared its ugly head back and launched the liquid bile towards Evinee. She jumped out of the way, turning her skin into another layer of armor before tumbling into Eren on the way down. The creature healed in moments while it continued to shoot its dangerous bile from its mouth. I looked over at Oz and Voz, who were on opposite sides of the clearing. With the creature distracted by Eren and Evinee, this was our chance.

"Oz, Voz, hold the thing still for as long as you can," I yelled.

They nodded, throwing both hands out towards it. Their dark power locked onto the creature, creating a magical cage. It yelled and thrashed, trying to get away already, pulling free from their magic. I took off as fast as I could towards it with my black sword ready to attack. The green power zapped and flickered through the air as I brought my sword across the creature's neck, severing its head from its body. I rolled to the ground, rushing away from the fountain of blood that was now spouting from its neck.

The creature collapsed to the floor, defeated. I got to my feet, looking back at the hideous thing. I noticed smoke coming from my chest. I looked down to find a pool of its blood, making its way through my armor. I dropped the sword, working as quickly as I could at the buckles on the sides of the vest.

Eren appeared next to me in an instant, unfastening the other side as we raced to free my body from the burning mound of armor. I pulled my head through the hole, throwing it to the ground as I checked my shirt and skin for any acid. I exhaled in relief while I watched the acid eat through the vest until there was nothing left.

"You could have been killed," Eren said in a hasty tone.

"So could have you," I pointed out. "Was there a plan I was unaware of? I thought we were just making the moves up as we went."

"I told you not to take any risks. It could have broken free of the twins and melted the skin off your skull."

"Well, it didn't. And now it's dead," I said with a smile.

He shook his head in aggravation.

"Way to go, princess," said Evinee. "I like her, I think we should keep her," she said, nudging me in the arm.

"Irresponsible, but effective nonetheless," said Leenia, walking towards us.

"May we take your sword when we get back to Doonak? I would like to run some tests on it," asked Voz.

"Sure," I responded. I looked back at the creature's body as blood pooled from its neck.

"Now, how are we going to get that back to the palace?" asked Oz.

As if my gift was listening, my spine began to tingle and zap. I felt a quick and powerful bolt of lightning travel to the base of my skull. I collapsed to the ground.

I saw the alfar pouring salt onto the blood of the creature. I watched as the blood sizzled and burned until it eventually clotted, rendering the liquid harmless. I opened my eyes, taking a deep breath as I looked around at the group staring down at me.

Eren had my head in his hands. I sat up, rubbing the base of my neck and then dusted myself off while they all continued to stare. I felt weak and my head was pounding from the vision. Everything around me blurred and it was a struggle to stand without tumbling back to the ground. I noted that with each new vision, the pain worsened.

"Salt," I said. "That is how you deactivate its venom. Pour it on the blood and it will clot, rendering it harmless."

"Interesting," said Voz and Oz at the same time.

"I can get used to having that gift around," said Evinee. "Yeah, we should definitely keep her."

"Hey, guys, come look at this," called Zerrial, poking the creature with a stick. We made our way over to its headless body. On the back of its shoulder, there was a rune burned into its flesh.

"It's the runic symbol for D, which stands for dagaz," Leenia pointed out. I looked at the butterfly-shaped symbol, recalling the same symbols on Otar's chest before I brought him back to life. Once he was reborn, the symbol vanished from his flesh.

"I've seen this symbol before. It was on Otar's body when he was dead, before I resurrected him," I said.

"Maybe we should ask him if he remembers it," suggested Eren. I nodded and stood to my feet.

"Otar, please come," I yelled. A few moments passed before I called again. "Otar!" Suddenly, the sigil on my wrist began to burn. I looked down to see the black-inked triangle begin to turn like a compass as the lines glowed red. I grimaced, trying to refrain from screaming. The dotted side of the triangle finally stopped, steadying out as it pointed north.

"What in Azeer's name?" said Evinee.

Eren grabbed my wrist, turning it, watching as the compass continued to point north.

"Has it done this before?" he asked.

"No. I think something is wrong with Otar. I need to find him," I said, the sigil steaming and burning in my flesh.

"Evinee, Oz, return to the castle and get as much salt as we need to get this thing back. The rest of you stay here and keep watch. I will take Princess Genevieve to find Otar. We will meet back at the castle," instructed Eren, calling for Eeri. I went to call for Tarsyrth, but Eren stopped me before I had the chance.

"I don't think so, princess," he said. "That last vision took a lot out of you, and don't lie and say it didn't. You can barely stand up straight, let alone fly. I will not be the one to explain to your father why you fell off your ragamor to your death."

I rolled my eyes just as Eeri landed. "Overprotective nursemaid," I grumbled.

"What was that?"

"Nothing. Nothing at all."

We climbed onto her and took flight, following the guidance of my sigil that also doubled as a compass. Twenty minutes passed before the sigil began to spin out of control on my wrist. The thing burned hotter than before.

"Land," I demanded. "He's close." I followed the compass while we traveled through the thick woods. We finally stumbled across Otar hanging from a tree. His stomach was split open, allowing his guts to fall out onto the ground. His flesh was carved away in certain areas. His ears were missing, along with his eyes.

I did all I could to keep my breakfast down, but the sight and the smell was putrid. Eren walked towards the creature, taking in the gruesome display.

"Artwork look familiar?" he asked, testing me.

"Fairies," I replied.

He nodded.

"What now?"

"Let's get him down. I think I can bring him back to life again."

We cut him out of the tree. I took off my jacket and wrapped him, trying to keep the remaining organs inside of his body. We loaded him onto Eeri and then took flight.

It was almost winter. The air was cold and unforgiving on the skin. Without my jacket I shivered. Eren, without saying a word, wrapped the loose edges of his jacket around me as he pressed his body into my back for warmth. I held the fabric close to my skin, not saying a word. It was an uncomfortable situation, but I was desperate.

We got back and made our way to my room with Otar's body. I opened the pocket doors that led to my bedroom and beheld a beautiful tunnel that led out to a balcony on the outer wall where my bed used to be. My bed was now against the left wall. I stopped, taking in the natural sunlight that streamed into the space. The balcony was separated from my room with a beautiful pair of glass doors that had black ironwork swirling around each panel.

"What is this?" I asked Eren as he placed Otar on the floor.

"I may have mentioned to your father that you like the stars. Now you can have the real thing at night. The entrance is enchanted, so from the outside of the mountain no one knows it is there, but it is an exit for you, nonetheless. It is runed, so no one or thing can come through without your permission."

I pulled the doors open allowing the fresh air to fill my quarters. I looked back at Eren and smiled.

"Thank you," I said softly.

"Thank the king, princess. Your happiness means a great deal to him, it seems."

I nodded, closing the doors to keep the cold air out. "I'll make sure to do that. Thank you for your help. Now, leave," I said, making my way over to Otar.

"What? Oh, no, no, no. I get to watch," he said, making himself comfortable on my bed.

"I'm sorry, but no. I made him a promise that I wouldn't share his secrets with anyone. Especially a power-hungry politician."

Eren exhaled, standing to his feet in frustration. "Fine, but when that little shit wakes up, will you ask him to tell me? His species baffles me, and I want to know his secrets."

"I will ask, but he will say no. He doesn't like you much. Maybe it has something to do with you calling him my pet."

"Is that not what he is? An animal on a leash?"

"Go, Eren. Tell the guards I will not receive anyone for an hour."

"Fine. Then I will see you in an hour." He nodded towards me and left my room.

I slit my palm and fed my blood into Otar's mouth. I lit him on fire, watching as his form was encased in a black charred cocoon. I left him be while I bathed and cleaned the dirt from my skin. I was able to dress and brush my hair before he finally began to move.

He shook the ashes from his skin before he took a deep breath. I slit my wrist, offering him more blood. He looked at me with hesitation and then took my arm and gently fed. When he was done, he pulled away from me, still locked onto my eyes.

"Who do you want me to kill this time," he said, tilting his head towards me.

"No one just yet," I laughed.

"You saved me, again, wicked one," he said, still sounding surprised.

"Eh, you've grown on me." I got to my feet and walked back into my room. "Are you going to tell me how you died this time?"

He stood, strolling towards me with his long gangly legs. "Fucking fairies. I hate that race. I want to destroy all of them and feast on their children," he said with rage.

"How many did it take to kill you?"

"Twenty of the little flying fuckers. I killed a group of five before they sent for reinforcements. Cowards."

I laughed at him as a knock came at the door.

Eren strolled through, cleaned, and dressed. "Ah, good to see you up and alive, Otar. Since I helped with your little rescue, I feel I am entitled to know the secret of how you keep coming back to life," Eren said.

Otar laughed, baring his teeth at Eren. He appeared directly in front of Eren, taking a deep breath in as if he could taste him. "Wicked one, may I kill him yet?" asked Otar.

I turned around, looking at the two of them squaring off in front of each other. "He did drug me last night with his powers," I said.

Otar turned his head slowly towards me, revealing his profile. "Yes, but you liked it. I felt your satisfaction," Otar revealed.

My mouth dropped as I felt my cheeks blush with embarrassment.

Eren chuckled, looking towards me. "Is that right, princess? Told you I was addicting," said Eren.

"Otar, please keep whatever you feel or see in my head between us, thank you," I said, turning away from the both of them.

"If she didn't like you so much, I would tear you to shreds right here and now," said Otar, growling into Eren's face.

"Otar, what did I say," I snapped, feeling the heat rise inside of me.

"As I said, I grow on people," Eren laughed.

"Don't worry. I will poison her against you. Then, I will devour you, slowly. I will feed on your flesh, then allow you enough time to heal, and feed on you again," sneered Otar.

"Okay, that's enough of that," I intervened, walking towards the both of them. "Otar, do you remember anything about this rune?" I held out a piece of paper that had the butterfly-shaped rune drawn on it.

He looked at the symbol for a moment, shaking his head as if to dislodge the memory. He grimaced and whined as he tried to remember. "It ... I, I had it on me. Burned into me by a ... by the son of a bitch that captured me before you," he said, smiling at the memory. "Narella, yes Narella. Her name. She has ... is power." Otar jumped up and down in excitement, happy he was able to recall his memories.

"Is she the one that is controlling the rift?" I asked.

He stopped, trying to think. He shook his head violently. "No, no, not her. She is dangerous but there is another. I ... I can't remember his name. I can't see him, but he is the one I hate. He is the one I want to destroy," Otar growled.

"Thank you, Otar. If there is anything else you recall, please tell me as soon as you remember. You are free to go. Just don't get killed tonight," I said.

He nodded, taking one of my loose curls into his fingers.

Eren smacked his hand away from my face.

Otar growled in anger before he charged Eren. "She is mine. Mine, mine, all mine! I do not like you and I do not trust you. You do not touch her. No touching. No touching at all, you disgusting filth," Otar snapped at Eren.

I was taken back by Otar's possessive behavior, but kind of touched. Oh, gods. What was happening to me? I was flattered by a demon creature's affections? I really was broken.

"Awe, so the pet has a crush on its master? How touching," said Eren.

Otar screamed and stomped, enraged that he couldn't touch him.

"Otar, please. I need to get ready for my lessons. I will call for you later," I said, reaching out to his shoulder.

He rolled his head with satisfaction as he purred at my touch.

I pulled away, taken aback by his reaction.

"As you wish, wicked one." He snapped his head back to Eren. "No touching!" he yelled before disappearing.

Eren started laughing as I held my head in my hands with embarrassment. "I think you have another suitor. Interesting turn of events," Eren said, taking a seat by the wall.

"He's never done that. I don't know where all of that came from."

"Well, you are looking for love. I guess you found it."

I threw my brush at his chest. He laughed, catching it without flinching.

"Your Highness," said one of the guards at my door. "A letter has come for you from your uncle." I rose to take the letter, nodding in thanks.

"What does Prince Rythlayn want now?" asked Eren.

"It's an invitation to a private lunch with him. I guess I am getting out of all my studies today," I said smugly.

Eren rose, taking the letter from my hands and reading it for himself. He looked down at me with a stern look. "What is rule number one?" he asked.

I rolled my eyes.

"Princess?"

"Don't trust anyone," I responded.

"Good."

"But he's family. He's been nothing but kind and helpful. The only one I can see driving a dagger through my back is your bed warmer," I said, referring to Icici.

"I have the ability to separate pleasure from business. Something you should probably learn to do."

"Yuck. Please do not share any more details of how my cousin pleasures you. I might never be able to look at you again. I'm surprised she hasn't murdered you in your sleep by now."

"Oh, she does plenty of things to me while I sleep. None that I won't recover from thankfully."

"Erendrial, please. I don't want to know," I snapped, feeling my skin crawl.

He laughed, bowing his head towards me. "As you wish, princess. Enjoy your lunch. I will see you tonight in the throne room to welcome the new ambassador of the light," he said, before leaving my chambers, still chuckling.

Chapter Twelve

I finished getting ready and made my way to my uncle's private chambers. I knocked on the blue door and waited for the servant to let me in. She bowed towards me as I passed through the doors. A table of fresh fruits and meats was set with only two places. My uncle came from his study, arms stretched out towards me with a smile on his face.

"Genevieve, my darling niece. I am so glad you accepted my invitation," he said, taking me into his arms for an embrace.

"Thank you for the invitation. I was excited to receive it."

"Come, come, sit, and eat. Tell me all about your first hunt. My servants tell me you were the one that dealt the final blow today."

I took a seat while the servant began to fill my plate. "It was exciting. I've been wanting to go on a hunt for a while now, so I jumped at the opportunity. The creature was very interesting, to say the least. I can't wait to see what they discover once they cut him open."

Rythlayn laughed as he dug into his meal. "And the killing part? How did you find that?"

"Easy and satisfying," I answered truthfully.

He smiled, raising his glass to me. "You are a true Drezmore, my dear niece. I am glad to hear it." I raised my glass to him and took a sip. "And how is combat training going? My son tells me you are quite the little fighter."

"Favorite part of the day, hands down."

"Good, good. I am glad you and your cousins are getting to know each other better. Family means everything to your father and me. He has been devastated for so long without an heir. When he discovered you, his spirits were instantly lifted. Now, to watch him with you. It brings nothing but joy to me. Our family grows stronger by the day. Azeer has truly blessed us."

"Yes, the more I learn about Azeer, the more questions I seem to have."

Rythlayn chuckled and took another sip. "I am sure our beloved ambassador has been more than willing to answer all of your burning questions. Seems like you and my daughter have more in common than you think."

Instant discomfort took hold of me while I assessed my uncle. "I'm not sure what you mean."

"Not that it's my business," he said, filling his glass, "but I am sure you've heard the rumors of Lyklor's ... other talents, outside of political matters, that is."

I took my own glass of wine and took a large gulp. "I'm not sure what Icici has told you, but I can assure you Ambassador Lyklor and I are not sleeping together."

Rythlayn evaluated me for a silent moment, seeming to assess if I was telling the truth or not. "Well, regardless, I'd keep my guard up. Always up to something, that one is. Being a royal myself, I know how hard it can be when you're trying to tell friend from foe and believe me, dear niece ... the foes come in all shapes and sizes. Some more desirable than others."

"Thank you for the advice, uncle."

He took another moment, focusing his attention on the wine that he swirled around the sides of the glass. "I would also watch out for the queen. She has been oddly silent since your arrival. I've known her for centuries. She doesn't wear jealousy well. Experienced that one first had two decades ago when your mother entered the picture."

"Did you know about my mother?" I asked.

"Yes. Your father told me about her once he began to develop ... *feelings*. I encouraged the relationship. She made him happy, and he had been so low for so long. It was nice to have the older brother I once admired back. She was the light of his life for those few short months they had together."

"Did you ever meet her?"

"Unfortunately, I did not have that honor. If I am being honest, I thought my brother foolish to develop such feelings for someone who was so weak in comparison to us. But now, after meeting you, I see I was wrong. I think I would have liked her very much." My uncle fiddled with his fork for a few moments.

"I owe you an apology, niece," he said hesitantly.

"For what?"

He took a deep breath, looking up at me behind his dark eyelashes and grinned softly. "I have a confession to make, and I am unsure how you will respond."

I set my fork down, giving him my full attention. "I'm listening."

Rythlayn took another moment before he spoke. "When my brother came to me with the idea of removing the ban on half-breeds, I was against it. I uphold our customs and traditions, even more so, I would say, than your father. It was how things had always been done, and I do not take kindly to change.

"I opposed him during the vote. One of the very few times I had ever done so. I didn't see his reasoning and could not understand this need to change a law the rest of the lands would continue to uphold. But when he finally told me about you, my heart softened.

"I knew how desperately he wanted children of his own and now that there was a chance he could have that ... I love my brother. I have always worked to help strengthen his throne. I honor the sacrifices he has made and respect him for them. The thought of him finally obtaining something he so desperately desired brought me nothing but joy.

"With that being said, I know you had no say in your genetics. Getting to know you and seeing the joy you bring to everyone around you, I can confidently say I was foolish and petty in my former decision, and I ask for your forgiveness in the matter."

I assessed my uncle for a moment. No signs of ill will or lies were present. He was a smart male, more educated than anyone I knew, but he had never done anything to make me question his intent. "I forgive you," I whispered with a small, forced smile.

He grinned from ear to ear, raising his glass to me. I followed suit. "Here's to new beginnings and a fruitful reign," he said in a happy, hopeful tone.

"Agreed," I said before taking a drink. I continued to assess him, trying to figure out why the alfar continued to look their noses down at the humans. There had to be more to it. "May I ask, have you spent much time in The Frey? Have you studied the people there and how they live? I only ask in hopes of understanding the alfar's outlook on the human race."

"No. The Frey doesn't provide much interest to me. My place is here, with my children. Speaking of, how are they treating you?"

Changing the subject. Clever male.

"Toreon and Vena are wonderful. Very smart and skilled. Icici, I am still working on," I said, sugar-coating the truth.

"She can be a handful. Has been since she was born. She is still sore about not being queen someday I fear." He leaned in across the table. "Honestly, she would have made a terrible queen. Too temperamental and selfish to run a kingdom."

We laughed as I remember Eren telling me the same thing. I had this weird sense of having lived these moments before. I stiffened my posture while my mind fluttered to the worst possible scenario.

Eren was sleeping with Icici on a consistent basis. His words about her becoming queen and my uncle's matched, too perfectly. Maybe this was his plan. Eren was getting me to trust him so he could be an easy person to take me out and put Icici on the throne. Then, she would take him as her husband, and he would be king. He would have the position and the power he's always wanted. All they had to do was kill me and then the path would be wide open. I swallowed hard, choking on the thought.

"Is everything okay, niece?"

"Yes, I just swallowed too much food," I said, taking a drink of wine. Gods, I was such an idiot. I rose from the table, wiping my mouth. "Uncle, I am so sorry to cut our lunch short, but I just remembered I have a meeting with Ambassador Lyklor before Ambassador Atros arrives. I was close to the new ambassador, so he will want to know all I can tell him."

"Of course, of course, I understand. Well, I am glad we got to have this time, even if it was cut short. We should do this again soon. I enjoy watching you grow, Genevieve. You are truly special," he said, before embracing me.

"Yes, we should make these lunches a weekly event. Gets me out of my studies," I said with a small laugh.

"Let's," he replied, escorting me to the door.

I made my way across the hall to my father's study where I knew he had a collection of ulyrium daggers and slid one under my sleeve. I marched through the residential quarters to Erendrial's room. I pushed open the door without even knocking, slamming it shut behind me with force. He was at his desk, hunched over a pile of papers. His head popped up and he frowned in confusion.

"Lunch didn't go so well?" he asked. I marched over to him, taking the dagger out of my sleeve and placing it at his neck, pinning him against the chair. I pressed hard enough that a sliver of blood trickled down his skin.

"Oh, it went quite well," I snapped.

He moved a hand slowly, trying to make skin contact.

"Don't even think about touching me or I will cut off your hand, do you hear me?"

"What did he tell you? I can assure you whatever it is, it is a lie," he said slowly.

"Of course, you would say that. The master of lies that you are. Tell me. How were you going to plan on doing it, hm? Were you going to make me suffer or were you going to make it quick?" I said pushing the blade deeper into his neck.

He swallowed hard. "I promise, I do not know what you are talking about."

"Don't play stupid with me, Lyklor. I figured it out. The whole fucking plan. Tell me, how were you going to kill me?" I yelled.

"Princess, I have never had any intention of killing you. I swear to it."

"Stop denying it and just admit it!" I yelled.

"I will sign a blood contract as proof if you still do not believe me. I have never planned to kill you. I swear on my own life."

I looked into his eyes, searching for signs that he was lying, but there were none. He was calm and did not make a move to hurt me. Even though I had a dagger to his neck, I was certain he could have me hunched over in pain in a few seconds, rendering me helpless.

I took a deep breath, slowly removing the dagger from his neck. I backed away, feeling a bit foolish, but I had to be certain. He took a handkerchief and wiped the blood from his neck as the gash continued to trickle from the shallow cut.

I sat on a chair next to the table, thinking over the conspiracy I was sure that had taken root. He came over silently, with two glasses and a bottle of whiskey. He poured mine first, handing it to me. I looked up at him in shame and took it. He poured one for himself, throwing it back before pouring a second. He sat across from me, twirling the glass on the table.

"So, are you going to tell me what you thought I was planning to do?" he said in a heavy voice.

I drank the whiskey and reached for the bottle. "I thought you were working with my uncle and cousin. You were being nice to me, so you would have an easy shot at killing me. I wouldn't see you coming. Once I was dead, Icici would take the throne and marry you, and then you would become king, having the position and power you so desperately desire," I said, taking another shot of whiskey.

He laughed underneath his breath, shaking his head. "And what led you to this?"

"You and my uncle made the exact same remark about how horrible of a queen Icici would be. The wording and phrasing were exact."

"Paranoid ... are we?" he said, sipping on his drink.

"I wonder whose fault that is," I replied, glaring at him.

"You're right, that is my fault. I just want you to be on guard is all. Though, I can see now that your imagination is very active."

"Can you blame me? You share a bed with her regularly. She throws it in my face for whatever reason every chance she gets. She wants the crown; you want power. The only thing that is standing in the way is me."

"And what makes you think Icici would ever marry me?"

"She seems to like you well enough," I said.

He laughed, finishing off his whiskey. "Icici doesn't like anyone, even her own father. We use each other in one way and one way only. That's it, I promise you."

I looked into his fireplace, unsure if I should believe anything that was coming out of his mouth.

Gods, it was exhausting not being able to trust anyone. I held my head, swirling the amber liquid. Eren appeared in front of me, slowly kneeling. He took the glass from my hands and placed it on the table and then lifted my chin, so my eyes met his. His face was calm and serious.

"Genevieve. I am a clever male, and yes, I have ambitions, but none of which require you to be dead. I am loyal to your father and to his bloodline, which includes you. You never have to fear me in that way. I promise," he said with a nod.

I pulled my eyes away from his, feeling foolish. I stood from the seat as he rose from the floor. "I should go get ready for dinner. Sorry about your neck," I said, looking at the unhealed wound.

"If it scars, I am not going to be happy. I am flawless and would like to keep it that way," he said in a lighter tone. I couldn't help but smile, though I tried to hide it. He smiled back, feeling the air between us lighten. "I'll see you at dinner, princess."

I turned and left his rooms.

Atalee prepared me for dinner. Extra makeup and extra glamor, since members of the light court would be attending this evening. My dress was made completely out of leather. It was tight and hugged ever curve. I felt naked, even though everything was covered for a change. She glued diamonds to my shoulders and down my arms. Silver glitter dust was added until I shimmered brighter than a star. I wore a silver crown tonight, with a green stone attached in the middle of the setting.

My father came to escort me. We had to appear as a unified front, which to my knowledge, we were. I rushed towards him and embraced him tightly. I pulled away, looking into his fierce glowing eyes.

"Thank you so much for the balcony. You don't know how happy it makes me," I said.

"I am glad it had the intended effect, daughter. As I promised you in the beginning. Anything you want, you will get." He leaned down and gently kissed me on the forehead.

I felt the warmth of love spread through me. I enjoyed having a father, more than I ever could have imagined. I dropped my head, nervous to speak from my heart, but I wanted him to know the truth.

"Father, I know the alfar don't like to discuss emotions, but I want you to know … I want you to know that I am so grateful that I found you. I've come to love you in a way I always hoped to love a father. I thank whatever god that sent me to you."

His eyes softened as he took my face into his hands. A smile, small, yet tender stretched across his perfect face. "I am the one who is thankful. I not only got a daughter but a piece of the woman I came to care so much for. Your light glows just as brightly as hers. Protect that light, my child. There are those who will always look to destroy it, but never let them. It is what makes you special."

I nodded, still confused about this light that everyone spoke about. I would have to ask about that another time. "Now, shall we go intimidate the hell out of the light court?" I asked with a smile.

He laughed under his breath. "Nothing would bring me more joy," he said, extending his arm towards me.

We made our grand entrance into the throne room. Levos and seven other light court members stood in the front next to our dining table. I held my head tall as my father escorted me past them. I felt Levos's eyes lock onto me, never once straying. We took our seats in the middle of the table and sat, signaling for the rest of the court to begin dinner. Levos and the others appeared in front of us, giving a small bow.

"King Drezmore, Princess Genevieve," Levos tensely said between his teeth. "Thank you for receiving us in your court. I am glad that you agreed to meet with me in regard to the release of Lord Areon Lysanthier."

"Ambassador Atros," said my father, "congratulations on your newly appointed position. I have heard high praise in your regard. I hope that our two kingdoms can come to an agreement that will begin to restore the rift between us. Though, I doubt your king and queen will ever be able to make up for the disrespect they and their court showed my daughter in her time under your protection." My father's voice dropped an octave as fire blazed behind his eyes.

"With all due respect, King Drezmore, our court was unaware of your daughter's true identity," replied Levos.

"Really? I've been told the resemblance is uncanny. Don't you agree?" My father said, looking at me with a smile. "Also, isn't it true that you and your king were well aware of my daughter's alfar blood long before I announced her as my heir?"

Levos swallowed hard. "Yes, we were aware of her alfar blood. Though you have removed the decree to kill half-breeds, our kingdom's law in regard to them still remains. Your daughter's life would have been in danger if we revealed who she was, so we kept her secret."

"Are you expecting a thank you, Ambassador Atros? Because you won't receive one from me, I can assure you that," growled my father.

"Of course not, King Drezmore."

"Please, sit and eat so we can begin negotiations," said my father.

Erendrial appeared on the other side of my father, taking the seat where the queen usually sat. She was pushed down a place setting.

"Now, please enlighten me as to why your queen ordered her cousin to burn down a human church on the other side of the border in the dead of night."

"My queen had nothing to do with the actions of her cousin. He is to be reprimanded by our court once we return for acting without her consent," said Levos.

My father tapped his fingers on the table, letting a moment of silence pass. "Ambassador Atros, I hear you are an intelligent male. I also know that you were kind to my daughter. She shared a lot of her personal life with you during her time in your court. Please, do not insult my intelligence with blatant lies. Your queen knew what the church meant to my daughter and what the nun meant to her. If this is your queen's attempt to throw a temper tantrum because my daughter killed her father, then stop dancing around the truth, so we can get to the business concerning the rift," said my father.

"Whatever action my queen may or may not have taken would be justified in retaliation to the brutal murder of her father and our king. In regard to the rift, yes, we would like to continue to work together until the threat is eliminated from our lands."

"I will release the Lysanthier bastard if your king and queen agree to come to Doonak in four days' time for an in-person meeting. They will be welcomed and treated with the respect they deserve. If we are to work together, I need to know there is no bad blood between them and my heir," insisted my father.

The thought of seeing Daealla and Gaelin again set every nerve ending in my body on alert. My time here had begun to heal the parts their court had broken and damaged. I didn't know how I would react seeing them again.

But I *was* healing. I had come so far. I was no longer the slave and concubine they knew. I was a Drezmore. I was the heir to the dark throne. A dark alfar.

Levos thought for a moment before responding. "I will present the invitation to their majesties, and we will respond by tomorrow evening," said Levos.

"Very well. Until then, the prisoner stays. As insurance," said my father.

Levos nodded, taking a sip of wine.

"Now, please," my father continued, "enjoy our hospitality. If you will excuse me, I have other business to attend to."

We all rose as my father stood. He kissed me on the head, his first public display of affection. I smiled up at him proudly. "Ambassador Levos," the king said, "please take my seat. I am sure my daughter and you have much to discuss."

Levos nodded, coming around the table. Eren dismissed himself, working the room as he usually did after dinner. I sat back in my chair, unsure of how to act around my old friend. I missed him terribly. I wanted to ask him and tell him so much, but I would wait until he made the first move. My cousins watched us curiously from the other end of the table as we finished our meal in silence.

The dancing began among the court members. Lilian's beautiful voice flooded through the air as the music sped up. The dancing was flawless and fluent, yet seductive, like the dark court members themselves.

"So that is the human who started all of this?" Levos said, gesturing towards my sister.

"Lily, yes," I replied.

"I can see why they've kept her alive. Her voice is truly majestic. You look well also. Better than the last time we saw each other."

"I've learned how to cope and move past what happened. I get a little better each day. Thank you for noticing," I said formally.

He exhaled deeply, reaching from his chair to grab my hand. He pulled me towards him, leaning into my face. "Enough with the formalities, sweet Genevieve. I've missed you terribly and I would like to talk freely with you, since I will soon be on my way back to the light court." His eyes traced my face, taking in every detail.

The other members of court stared, but I didn't care. I smiled, leaning to embrace him. "Thank the gods. I thought you hated me. I've missed you so much. You have no idea how much," I said.

He laughed, pulling his head away from mine. "I don't hate you. I may not have agreed with your methods, but that monster deserved to die. I understand why you did it, and I can't tell you how glad I am to see you glowing again. What is your secret?"

I dropped my eyes, glancing at Eren as he talked among the high houses. "I learned how to let go and not look back. I faced it and conquered it. I decided I wasn't going to let him control me from the grave. I was given a second chance at life, and I wasn't going to waste it."

Levos stroked his hand across my face, looking at me endearingly. "I am so glad to hear that. You are strong. I always knew that, but this just proves how much stronger you really are. And your father seems to adore you as well. How are things with him?"

"Wonderful. Better than I thought it would be. He ... cherishes me," I said, feeling a flutter deep inside.

"What's not to cherish? And your uncle and cousins?"

"My uncle is wonderful. Very accepting and attentive. My two younger cousins and I get along well, but Icici on the other hand ...she's a raging bitch."

Levos started laughing, covering his mouth so the others couldn't see. "Mad about your succession, I presume?"

"More like royally pissed. She does these stupid taunting little things to try and get a rise out of me. Most of the time I can remain calm, but I've snapped a few times and it hasn't been pretty. I don't trust her one bit."

"So, what have you learned since you've been here?"

"How to fight, kill, be a politician, a princess. I've learned all about the alfar's history. I know everyone at court and their powers, along with my own family's heritage. And I've begun to learn how to read people, to tell if they are lying or being manipulative, which comes in handy around here."

"I can only imagine how useful a tool that is. Especially when you have to deal with Lyklor daily."

I paused, biting the side of my lip, trying to refrain from laughing.

"What is it?" Levos asked.

"Eren is actually the one that has taught me everything I've learned. My father assigned him to me when I arrived." I started laughing as his face fell in shock. How good it felt to laugh with him.

"Oh, no, sweet Gen. What have I told you about him?" he said, leaning towards me.

"I know, I know. He is a liar, a cheat, a manipulator. On and on and on. But he is also smart, useful, and funny at times."

Levos tilted his head, his expression suspicious. "Please tell me you and he aren't—"

"Oh, heavens no. He is sleeping with my cousin. I am not into that whole sharing thing, as you well know."

"Oh, thank Thor."

I giggled again at his reaction. "But he really isn't so bad. He's been very helpful and kind in his own way."

"Just be careful. I don't know what I'd do if anything happened to you. I can't bear losing another person I care for." His eyes filled with sadness.

"Levos, what is it?"

He paused, taking a moment. "Madison. I sent her back to The Frey a week after you left. She protested, but it had to be done."

"What? Why? What happened?"

"The queen appointed me as the new ambassador, which meant I couldn't be a Lord as Gaelin promised, which means I couldn't protect her. I would have had to spent the rest of Madison's life watching her be abused, powerless to stop it. So, I took her and made the trip to The Frey. I sent her back to her brothers and father where she'd be safe."

I reached for his hand, tightening mine around his. "That is the most selfless thing I have ever heard. You're a good male, Levos."

He scoffed. "I'm not. I've been screwing everything that walks past me since she left. I'm trying to fill the void inside, but nothing works. So, I bury myself in work and pray to the gods that I will forget her."

"Well, the dark court is a good place to come and forget things. You finally got your wish to peek behind the dark curtain. Too bad it's not Jestu. You'd love it."

He laughed lightly as his eyes met mine. I kissed the back of his hand as Eren approached the table.

"Ambassador Atros," said Eren. "Good to see you elevated to this position. I will have to be on my game from now on, since they've finally appointed someone with a brain."

"I plan to destroy you little by little, Ambassador Lyklor. It's at the top of my to-do list," replied Levos smugly.

Eren laughed, turning his eyes to me. "Princess Genevieve, may I have the honor of this dance?" He extended his hand towards me.

We walked to the middle of the dance floor as the music strummed.

"You were quiet during negotiations," I said.

"Your father is a smart man. He handled the situation perfectly. You and Levos seemed to have made up rather quickly."

"Yes, and I couldn't be happier," I said while he twirled me around him.

He smiled at me as we faced each other.

"I have a question," I said.

"Don't you always," he mumbled, laughing before I hit him in the shoulder.

"Why do people keep saying there is a light about me? Winnow has said it, Gaelin, my uncle, you. What is it?"

He tightened his grip on my back as we drifted across the marble floor. "Humans have what we refer to as a light about them. It's their humanity. It's their kindness, gentleness, love. Each human has a different radiant of light about them. The stronger the light, the stronger the pull we feel towards it. The light alfar bask in the light, but our darkness tends to want to possess it.

"I've seen many humans come through this court with their light, only to lose it after they get involved with one of us. Their spirits are broken, or sometimes their hearts. A part of us craves the light that we will never be able to possess ourselves, so we learned to treat the humans with kindness and respect in order to preserve it. Selfish I know, but the arrangement has worked for centuries."

"Interesting. So, you all want the thing you say you're repulsed by. Emotions?" I asked.

"I wouldn't say that. Humans possess a part of us that was consumed by the dark magic so long ago. I guess we are trying to fill the void in our souls," he answered.

"What is my light like?" I whispered nervously.

He stopped moving, looking down at me with a softly, vulnerable smile. "Blinding," he said, pushing me out into a twirl.

I smiled as he coiled me back into him. "I'll try to keep it in check for you. I know how much you hate those pesky emotions." We both laughed in unison.

"How generous. By the way, I have my people looking into the name, Narella, that Otar gave us. Hopefully, they can find something. It's the first I've heard of her, but if she is as powerful as Otar remembers, the mending of the two courts couldn't have come at a better time."

"You'll keep me updated?"

"Don't I always?"

"No. You probably have more secrets than I have dresses."

"Now that is a hard comparison. I have no clue why someone needs so many. It seems like a waste of fabric."

"Ha, you're telling me. Still trying to get used to the excess of this lifestyle."

"Well, you're doing an excellent job."

I stopped, looking at him in surprise. "Did Erendrial Lyklor just pay me a compliment? Hell must be freezing over," I said.

"I'm polite ... sometimes." He smiled down at me genuinely. His eyes lingered on mine for longer than normal. He was happy. Truly happy.

A hand appeared on Eren's shoulder. We both turned to see who it belonged to. Lady Calavi stood in a scarlet red dress in front of us.

"Your Highness," she said bowing to me. "Ambassador Lyklor, I would like to discuss a trade matter with you, if your responsibilities have concluded for the night."

I watched Eren's face closely. His breathing was calm, but his jaw lightly tensed in the back. His fingers curled against my back ever so slightly.

"Of course, Lady Calavi," he said, pulling away from me.

I tightened my grip, preventing him from leaving. "Actually, his services are still needed. He's an excellent dance partner, and I am not yet ready to part with him," I said, putting his arms back around me.

She glared at me in a cold, challenging manner. "I am sure one of your three suitors would gladly take his place. Or maybe the light alfar ambassador you were just cozying up to, *Your Grace*," she said.

"I don't want them. I want the ambassador," I said firmly. "Now, if you will excuse us, I would like to return to my entertainment. You are dismissed, Lady Calavi." I turned away from her and pulled Eren back into the middle of the dance floor. She was the woman who had been forcing him to please her for the past two millennia. She was his contract.

"You shouldn't have done that," he whispered. All feeling and joy was now drained from his voice.

"I am the princess; I can do whatever the hell I want."

"Gen, please don't take this on your shoulders. This is my battle, not yours."

"So, she is the one?" I said quietly.

"You know I can't answer that."

"Just kill her and be done with it," I said adamantly.

He smirked. "Is that your solution to every problem?"

"It's effective, isn't it?"

He laughed, pulling me closer into him. "The contract states I can't harm, kill, plot against, or hire someone to kill the being I am bound to. If I know of someone who is plotting to hurt the being, I must inform them of it. So please, don't be you, and don't do anything stupid."

"I would never," I said playfully.

"Gen, I am serious. You have enough to worry about. I was young when I made the deal, but I knew what it entailed. Now I must see it through." The music stopped as he slowly pulled out of my arms.

His face fell and his demeanor sunk. I tightened my grip on him. "Don't go. Just stay. Stay here with me."

"It doesn't work that way. I will eventually have to go, regardless of what you demand." He dropped his hands, straightening his perfectly pressed black jacket as he held his head high. "Go have a nice night with Levos. I'll see you in the morning," he said, turning and exiting the throne room.

I stood watching as he marched to his own living hell, just like I had done so many times before. My heart felt heavy for my friend. I wanted so desperately to save him, but I didn't know how. There was no way of breaking a blood contract. The only way out was if one of the parties died. Killing wasn't beneath me, and surely the world would be a better place without the molester Lady Calavi. I would find a way to help my friend. I would get him out of this, whether he wanted my help or not.

CHAPTER THIRTEEN

L evos stayed in my room that night. We caught up and told each other everything that had transpired the weeks we had been apart. I tried to stay away from the topic of Gaelin and so did he. We fell asleep laughing together, even though a part of me was dying a little for Eren.

The next morning, we sent Levos and the rest of his members back to their court. If everything went well, I would see him in three days. My father had set up three separate lunch dates with each of my suitors; I was desperate to be rid of them.

Therosi was lively as ever, attempting to seduce me with his promises of a real marriage. He had obviously studied the ways humans valued marriage and hoped to lie his way into my bed and my heart to give him an advantage. He was attractive, yes, but I knew better than to trust him.

Soddram was polite and civil. He asked me about my life back in The Frey and what I now enjoyed most about court, but I could tell he was disengaged. I had heard the rumor of his and Icici's physical escapades. Was it too much to ask for a male who hadn't shared a bed with my cousin?

Avalon was the most uncomfortable date of all. He barely spoke, didn't eat or drink the entire time, and then excused himself, claiming he needed to deal with some political matters involving the Incubi.

Finally, I returned to my room, skipping combat practice while I planned a way to set Eren free. I called on Otar for his expertise in killing. He was eager to assist. He laughed and jumped for joy as we discussed the possibilities of how to kill the high lady.

"Heart removal," suggested Otar.

"Too brutal," I replied.

"Head removal?"

"Too evil."

"Fairy bait?"

"It will take too long?"

"Tearing her into little pieces and spreading her throughout the kingdom," he said, clapping his hands together.

I nodded, furrowing my brow. "That could work."

"Really?"

"No, Otar. We need to find a way that kills her that won't start an investigation. She is a careful female who tends to stay under the radar. If she just up and disappears, the court will wonder what happened to her and begin to look into it. Whatever we plan needs to be flawless, leaving no clues to connect us to her."

He thought on the matter, then went over to my wall and pulled a book from one of the upper shelves. He slammed it down in front of me. It read, '*Poisons*'.

I shook my head. "No, her nose would detect anything we tried. Plus, it would have to be mixed with ulyrium dust if it were to truly kill her."

He smiled at me with his teeth sharp and deadly. "I'm not talking about poisoning her, wicked one."

It was a moment before his plan took root in my head. I smiled. "You are brilliant, Otar. Truly brilliant," I exclaimed.

He smiled and giggled in an unsettling way. "We will pick a poison that is hard to come by, so there is no question it came from her when we plant the evidence. You rally her up for the next few days in public, so the court sees how she detests you. Then, you call her into a private meeting in your chambers, where you insist she brings a drink to serve to you. You fight with her loud enough for the guard to hear outside your doors.

"I will plant the evidence in her room. Once she leaves your chambers, you take the poison. Atalee will be along to help you settle in for the night, where she will find you unconscious. They will call for your cousin, who will attempt to heal you. I will appear, rattled, and ballistic, spouting accusations about Lady Calavi. The others will believe me because of your interactions with her the past few days. They will find the poison in her room, along with the book that contains the antidote.

"They will give it to you, and you will recover by morning. She will be arrested and sentenced to death, where you will have a chance to drive a blade through her heart. The bitch of an ambassador will be free of whatever she has on him, and you will be happy. Sound like a plan?"

I shook my head in awe of the masterful little creature. I was beginning to understand why whoever controlled him before me had given him reigns over a military unit. I reached over, grabbing his face and kissed his black leathery cheek. "You are truly a mastermind. It's perfect."

He swayed a little, smiling in an unsettling way. "Now, to find the right weapon." He flipped through the book, stopping at a poisonous plant that was rare and found hundreds of miles from the castle. It was called guneria root. "I will search for the root while you piss off the bitch."

I nodded at him before he disappeared out of sight. I closed the book and put it back on my shelf before leaving my room.

My uncle came down the hall with a smile on his face. "Ah, there you are, niece. Your father has asked you and I to attend a meeting in his study," he said, extending his arm to me. I took it with a smile as we headed to the king's chambers.

My father and Eren were already inside. They were looking over documents of the creatures we had killed. I joined them at the table as my uncle closed the pocket doors behind us. My father and Eren looked up and smiled at me.

"Daughter, brother," said my father, nodding to us.

Eren bowed.

"What's going on?" I asked.

"The light court will agree to our little meeting in three days' time," explained my father. "They are desperate for our help, according to our sources in their castle. We need to plan a way to unravel them, so we can get them to agree to a new treaty which favors our kingdom."

"What does the new treaty suggest?" I asked.

"It's not so much about what it suggests as much as what it protects, which would be our interests," said Eren. "We've begun to be able to use the research that we've gathered from the creatures we've killed to create weapons. That is how black weapons were discovered. The twins got the idea from a dark magic creature we killed last year. It was able to harness its own magic into objects by feeding them its blood. Now, they have begun to experiment with acid explosives, lightning traps, and impenetrable armor.

"The new treaty will remove the sharing clause of our findings, so the light alfar do not stumble upon the same discoveries we do. It will also give us access to their lands to continue to track beasts that originated from our side, without their involvement. We are more powerful than them. Regardless of what we've told them, we've never truly needed their help to take down the monsters.

"The royals must also agree that they will not harm you and you will be welcomed and respected while at their court, if you choose to visit. This will put your involvement with King Lysanthier's death behind us, so we won't have to worry about your safety while we continue our scientific advances," finished Eren.

"I see. So why do you need me here?" I asked.

"You need to start seeing how we conduct business, daughter," my father stated. "I want your opinion and outlook on all matters from this point on."

I nodded.

"So, how are we going to unravel the light queen and king?" asked my uncle. "From what I've heard, King Atros seems to be the levelheaded one, while Daealla is quick to act and has a temper."

"Not an exaggeration," said Eren. He paused, looking at me for a long moment. "I think I have it. Princess Genevieve will do the work for us."

"What do you propose?" asked my father.

"I noticed Daealla was extremely jealous of the affection Gaelin showed Princess Genevieve while I was at her court. If we placed the princess in Gaelin's way, long enough to drag his attention away from political matters, it will ignite Daealla's jealousy, allowing us to catch them both when they are distracted," explained Eren.

"And what do you purpose I do, Lyklor?" I butted in. "Walk into the throne room naked?" How dare he even purpose this? He knew how I felt about Gaelin.

My uncle choked on his wine at my comment. "Of course not. We play on Gaelin's *feelings*."

"You're assuming he still has *feelings* for me," I pointed out.

"He does, believe me," said Eren. "He has yet to take another mistress since you left. The night they arrive, the king will already be seated on his throne. You will enter, alone, as the music begins to play in the background. We will have each of your three suitors dance with you intimately in front of him. Gaelin was very territorial if I remember correctly, so any other male that touches you will set him off, in return setting Daealla off."

I scoffed under my breath. "If your goal is to make him enraged, then all you would have to do is touch me," I said.

Eren smirked. "That can be arranged," he said.

"Explain," said my father.

I exhaled, annoyed at the plan. "Gaelin hates Erendrial more than any male alive. He was furious and jealous every time he made contact with me during his visit at court. The day Erendrial retrieved me, Gaelin was more concerned about the way Erendrial was touching me than the fact that I had just murdered his king," I finished.

The room went silent for a moment as everyone thought.

"Then it is settled," said my father. "Genevieve will dance briefly with all three suitors, to not raise suspension. Then, towards the end, Ambassador Lyklor will step in, making sure to put on a believable show for the light king. You will sit next to my daughter at dinner and continue the charade until we have successfully completed the treaty."

"As you wish, Your Grace," said Eren.

I nodded, still annoyed with the stupid plan. I didn't want to upset Gaelin, but I would, once again, be forced to use him to get what I wanted.

"I can't wait to see what transpires," added my uncle mischievously.

I elbowed him with a smile as he wrapped his arm around me, pulling me in for a side hug.

"Thank you all for your assistance. You may go," said my father, taking a seat behind his desk.

We exited, heading towards the library. I looked at Eren in annoyance.

"What are you pissy about now?" he asked.

"I don't want to play on Gaelin's feelings. I wish you wouldn't have suggested that. He's been through enough," I said.

"How else would you have suggested completing the task at hand?"

"You piss everyone off. Couldn't you have just run that smartass mouth of yours for a while? I bet the queen would be more inclined to fall on a sword than to listen to you."

He laughed, revealing his bright white smile and his cheek dimples. "I like that you recognize my talents."

"Don't get me started. And I wouldn't call it a talent exactly. Maybe a defect," I said, spotting Lady Calavi in one of the seating areas up ahead with a group of ladies. I quickly wrapped my arms around Eren's waist as we continued towards her.

He looked taken aback by the gesture but placed his arm around my shoulder.

"I am just glad you don't want to kill me," I said, looking up at him playfully.

He smiled cautiously, likely wondering why I was clinging to him. Her gaze locked onto us as we passed. "And I am glad you believe me," he said, looking down at me. His smile reached his eyes. "For a moment there, I thought you were going to kill me. I understand why Otar calls you 'wicked one' now. There is something dark behind those entrancing eyes of yours."

"How can someone so bright be so dark?" I asked with a playful tone.

"You're an anomaly in every other way. I don't know. You tell me."

I pulled away, wrapping my arm around his. I looked back at Lady Calavi with an evil glare and smiled tauntingly. Her eyes darkened with jealousy at the sight of us.

I continued this overdone display of affection every time we were in her presence for the next two days. Otar finally returned with the root we needed. He made the potion and then a remedy, just in case something went wrong with the original plan. I trusted him, since my life kept him alive. The only thing that was left was for her to make a spectacle of herself in front of a crowd.

At dinner that night, I asked Eren to dance. He accepted as we made our way to the floor. "So, are you ready to make a king go crazy over you?" he asked. The light court would arrive the next day.

"Easy as breathing," I said as I spun around him.

He chuckled. "I see your arrogance is coming out to play. It's a good look."

"I'm just stating the truth."

"Well, you're right ... in regard to Gaelin, that is."

"Thanks for the morale boost, Lyklor. Great friend you are," I said, offended.

"I'm just saying, he goes weak when you're around. It will be easy for you. It's a good plan. That is why I suggested it."

"Whatever," I said, focusing on the crowd around us. "You can't think I am that ugly, since you bed my cousin every chance you get," I whispered under my breath.

"You're comparing yourself to Icici now?" He reeled back to look at me.

I turned my head away. "No. I mean, I know we don't look that much alike. She's full alfar, and I'm only half, contaminated with the hideous human genes."

He scoffed. "Is that jealousy I hear in your voice? And here I thought you were above that petty feeling. I learn something new every day."

"I'm not. She can have you. You're too much work."

"Now I am the offended one," he said, smiling down at me.

I returned the gesture, unable to stay cross with him.

Lady Calavi made her way towards us as we pulled off the dance floor.

"Your Highness, Ambassador Lyklor," she said with a bow. "You both seem to be enjoying yourself out on the floor tonight."

"Why wouldn't I be enjoying myself? I have the most handsome dance partner in the room," I said running a hand down his arm.

Eren shot me a sideways glance.

She smirked, looking at Eren and then back to me.

"Yes, I am curious. Why don't you show your suitors as much attention as you do the ambassador? Surely you should be spending this time getting to know your future husband, instead of galivanting around with a male who will never give you what you want." She smiled at me as if hoping she had struck a chord.

Eren stood silent while he watched the drama unfold.

"Who's to say he doesn't give me what I want? He's exactly who I need him to be, and he does exactly what I want, where I want it, and when I want it."

I paused to read her face. Her jealousy was rearing its ugly head as she tried to calm herself. I took a step closer to her, holding my head tall and proud.

"It's nice to have a male who desires you, isn't it," I whispered. "Who will please you in any and every way you could imagine. To have a male who truly enjoys your body and the way he makes it respond to his touch. For him to want you so badly ... so often, that he takes you wherever you are, without a care of who is watching." I pulled away, looking at her with pity. "Oh, wait. You wouldn't understand, since you have to force the males you want into a contract, just to feel the slightest hint of pleasure."

"How dare you speak of our arrangement to me!" she snapped, getting into my face. "You know nothing about our relationship or what I mean to him! How could a half-breed like you ever please a male alfar? You are disgusting and a disgrace to our kind. You should have been put down the moment you left your whore of a mother's womb. You will never be one of us. No matter how many males you screw, or what you wear on top of that flawed head of hair!" she yelled.

The crowd turned towards us, watching in silence as she threatened and insulted their heir. Two guards approached either side of me as I peered down at her with a wicked smile. She fell right into my trap. I took a deep breath, collecting myself.

"Lady Calavi," I said loud enough for everyone to hear. "I think we've gotten off on the wrong foot. I have offended you and for that, I am sorry. I know you didn't mean to threaten me with death, when you said I should have been killed the day I was born.

I for one know my father doesn't have the same opinion."

Her eyes grew wide as the reality of her words came back to haunt her. "No, Your Grace, please forgive my lack of control. I am not feeling myself," she said, bowing her head to me.

I touched her shoulder gently. "No harm done. I would like us to be friends. Please, come to my room in twenty minutes, and bring a jug of wine with you so we can toast to our friendship, and a fruitful future together under the rule of my father," I said, smiling at her.

She nodded before I took my leave. Eren followed close behind me as I made my way to my room.

He grabbed my arm, pulling me into a quiet corner. "What in Azeer's name was that all about?" he demanded.

I shrugged. "I was just trying to ruffle her feathers. You taught me that," I smiled at him with an arched brow.

"Why do you want her to believe I am sleeping with you? What could you possibly gain by making an enemy of her?"

"She is clearly territorial of you. She wants you to want her and desire her, without the stupid contract. I just applied pressure where I knew it would hurt, and she exploded like a bomb."

He shook his head in frustration. "You are too good of a student," he laughed.

"Is the student surpassing the teacher?" I asked playfully.

"I didn't say that, princess. What are you going to talk about in your room?"

"I'm going to make amends with her. I don't want her to take out her frustration with me on you. Maybe I can get her drunk enough that she will pass out, and you can have a night to yourself."

He smiled at me, then his gaze fell. "Thank you for the thought, but it would take a wagon full of wine to get her drunk. Don't think I haven't tried."

I reached out, placing my hand on his arm. "One day, this will all be over, and you will be able to live your life the way you see fit. You will never have to bed another female you don't want. You will be free. The greatest power comes from surviving the darkest of nights ... remember?" I whispered, hoping his own words would bring him comfort.

He nodded as I walked past him to my room.

Otar was waiting for me. I winked at him, confirming the plan was on track. The small vial of blue poison sat on my nightstand. I placed it in the drawer and gathered the evidence he was going to plant in her room.

A knock came at my door. Otar disappeared, making his way to her room. I took a deep breath and opened the door to see Lady Calavi standing between my guards with a jug of wine. I smiled, allowing her to enter. I showed her to the seating area as I gathered two glasses.

"Where are your servants?" she asked.

"I thought you would like to speak freely, so I sent them all away.

My lady will be back at the end of the night to help ready my room," I replied. I poured us both a glass and handed her one first.

She took it, her cold, dark eyes drilling into me. "What is this really about? What do you want?" she asked.

"Only to apologize for my behavior, like I said." I took a sip of wine and smiled at her.

She slammed her glass on the table. "Eren says he has never touched you, so why lie?"

"You assumed I was talking about Eren when I spoke of my passions. I could have been speaking of another. Plus, Eren is a rehearsed liar. He could have been lying to you this whole time."

She laughed. "I've known him since he was a boy. I can tell when he is lying to me. Who do you think trained him? He has never touched you. Don't act like he has."

"Yes, I forgot. You forced him to your bed when he was a child. How noble of you." I placed my wine on the table next to hers. "Oh, don't worry. He didn't break your contract. I pieced everything together myself. You aren't the most discreet rapist."

"Then you know I can have him whenever I want, regardless of who else he chooses to bed. He will always be mine, and you will always have to share him with me."

"What makes you think I want him in that way?"

"Come now girl. I am old, but with age comes a keen insight. Why else go through all of this? You care for him, and the human part of you can't stand the thought of him with another."

"I do care for him, as a friend, but I am fully aware he could never be what I would need. Even if you weren't in the picture."

"Doesn't stop you from hoping," she said, narrowing her eyes on me. "I see the way you laugh and smile with him. I've seen many females of multiple races over the years fall for his charms and wit. You aren't the first, and you won't be the last, yet I remain a constant." She stood, brushing her hands through her dress as she walked around the couch. "Word of advice, princess: guard your heart where he is concerned. He will give you the greatest pleasure and then leave you in pieces as you wonder to yourself why you weren't good enough. I've seen it a dozen times. That's why he and I work. We take and give what we can, and don't expect a single morsel more."

She left my room while I sat fuming at her words. "Otar!" I yelled, taking my glass of wine with me, moving to my nightstand.

He appeared next to my bed.

"Is it done?" I asked.

"Exactly as we planned, wicked one," he confirmed with a smile as I dumped the poison in my wine.

I handed him the vial and nodded. "You know what to do with it."

"In her pocket it goes," he said, disappearing from my sight.

I swirled the glass of wine and then made my way back to the sitting room. I slammed the whole glass back into my mouth and waited.

It took five minutes to take effect. My stomach cramped with pain causing me to double over from the feeling. It felt like someone was ripping my insides out with a hook. My body began to burn with fever as I tried to yell out but couldn't. I fell to the ground, the glass shattering around me. The last thing I remember was my heart pounding so hard I thought it was going to rip through my chest.

Chapter Fourteen

As soon as I opened my eyes, I screamed in pain, grabbing for my stomach. It felt like I had consumed acid and the substance was eating away at my insides, keeping me alive for the ride. Vena was at my side in an instant. She held a bucket to my face as I purged everything that remained in my system. I fell back into the bed while she waved her hands over my body, taking note of my condition. My father appeared behind her.

"The last of the poison is gone. The ulyrium will continue to work its way out of her system, but the worst of it is over. She will be weak for the next few days, but will recover fully," Vena said with a smile.

I reached for her hand and smiled. "Thank you," I whispered.

She nodded.

I looked at my father for answers. "What happened?" I asked, coughing as my throat burned.

"An attempt was made on your life," he confirmed.

I acted surprised. "Who?"

"Rismera Calavi," he said.

I paused, letting it sink in. "But why? I have done nothing to her."

"Members of the court have come forward with accounts of outbursts and different hostile interactions the two of you have had the past few days. You should have come to me immediately. I don't know what I would have done if something happened to you," he said, dropping his gaze to the bed.

I took his hand and tried to squeeze it, but I was too weak. "Next time, I will, I promise. But I am alright. I am alive and I will recover."

He smiled, rubbing his hand through my hair. "Yes, you will. You have to." He cared about me. Not because I was his heir, but because I was his daughter. He truly cared for me.

"What happened to Lady Calavi?"

"She is to be executed in the throne room in the next hour for her treason."

"I would like to be there. To see justice be served."

He smiled and nodded. "If you are feeling strong enough, of course," he said, rising from my bed. "Vena, stay with her until she is ready for the execution. If anything changes, come to me immediately." Vena nodded, turning back to me. He left the two of us alone.

"Do I look as terrible as I feel?" I asked.

She giggled. "A little paler, and you have dark circles under your eyes. Nothing makeup can't hide," Vena assured me.

I tried to push myself up, but needed her assistance. She gave me a glass of water, then busied herself around my room in an agitated state. I could tell by her body language, she wasn't telling me something.

"Vena, come here and tell me what is going on with you. You're making me sick with the back-and-forth pacing."

She laughed, taking a seat next to me in my bed. She huffed as her eyes flickered from side to side.

"Out with it."

"Your friend ... Levos Atros. Can you tell me about him?" she asked.

I looked at her as a small smile stretched across my face. "You're interested in Levos?" I clarified.

"I don't know. Maybe. We had a few brief interactions when he was here last, and I can't get him out of my head. Especially since he is returning this evening. What does he think of the dark alfar? Be honest."

I laughed to myself. I spent the next twenty minutes telling her about him. By the time I was done, she seemed more intrigued by him, which I wasn't sure was a good thing. Levos still loved Madison and was hurting. This would most likely end badly, but I wasn't a matchmaker.

Atalee arrived in my room to help me dress. I was able to stand on my own but had to take each step slowly. She used the makeup to make me appear as if I hadn't almost died. She put my hair up and dressed me in a loose and flowing gown. I made my way to the door and opened it to see Eren waiting across the hall. He smiled, making his way to me. He reached for my arm, but I held out a hand to stop him.

"I'm fine, really," I said, staggering down the hall towards the throne room.

He walked next to me with his head held down. "I'm ... I'm sorry I got you into this," he whispered.

I stopped, turning around as fast as I could. "You have nothing to apologize for, and I never want to hear those words in reference to this situation again. That is an order, do you hear me?" I said.

He nodded as I turned and entered the throne room.

I made my way up to my throne next to my father and the queen.

Otar appeared by my side, smiling with glee. "How are you feeling, wicked one?" he whispered.

"Blissfully optimistic," I said, winking at him.

He laughed, tilting his head from side to side. "We should do this more often."

"If I need an accomplice, you are the first on my list, always," I said.

He dragged one of his long fingers through my hair. I allowed the action as Eren watched from below.

The court was now seated and the guards brought Lady Calavi into the room wearing restraints. She looked awful. I could tell she had been beaten thoroughly last night and possibly this morning. They threw her on the ground in front of us. She looked at Eren with tears in her eyes and mouthed the word, 'please'. He ignored her, looking back towards the wall.

My father rose. "Rismera Calavi, you are charged with treason and attempted murder of the heir to the Kingdom of Doonak. Your assets are now the property of the crown. You have disgraced this court with your unforgivable behavior and are sentenced to death," ordered my father.

She cried on her knees. "Please, my king. I would never attempt to harm you or your family. This is a mistake. I had nothing to do with this. I swear to you," she yelled.

My father held out a hand to me. I took it, pulling myself up from the throne.

"Would you like the honors?" he asked.

He helped me down the stairs and then took his seat back on his throne. A guard pulled a ulyrium sword from his belt and handed me the hilt. I took it, feeling the weight pull at my muscles. I walked over to her, gripping the sword as tightly as I could.

She shook her head at me, crying. "Please, princess, I would never hurt you, I swear," she said franticly.

I knelt down, looking into her disgusting, dark, and unfeeling eyes. She was selfish. She had robbed a child of his innocence. She had made him her sex slave and for that, she deserved this and whatever awaited her in the afterlife.

I tilted my head, letting her see behind my well-crafted mask. "Beings like you," I whispered low enough to insure no one else could hear, "don't deserve to live."

She stopped crying. I watched as she began to put the pieces together.

"You take," I continued, "and take, and take from others without a single thought of their well-being. You're disgusting and should have been disposed of long ago." I pulled away so I could look into her eyes. "As I am sure you've heard, I don't have the tolerance for those who take others against their will. Tell King Lysanthier hello for me when you get to Hell." I stood from the ground, sporting a victorious smile before turning my back on the bitch.

"You!" she yelled.

"Otar," I called causally. Before Calavi could say another word, my accomplice appeared in front of her with all six arms visible as he began to tear her to pieces. His gleeful screams of joy startled the court while they watched my creature enact my revenge. A sword through the heart was too kind. She deserved to suffer.

I made my way back to my father just as Otar had finished playing with her limbs. The court clapped in approval as the guards attempted to gather the larger pieces of Calavi, trying to clean the mess we had made.

Otar, now covered in blood, screamed for joy. In a blink, he appeared at my side, licking the side of my check in thanks before disappearing from the throne room.

I turned to look at Eren. His eyes were on the floor, apparently lost in thought.

Shit. He was putting it together. He was too clever not to notice her last few moments. I bided my father a good night, claiming I was still exhausted from the poison.

As I exited the throne room, Lady Fellwood appeared out of the shadows with a grim smile on her long, hollow face.

"Lady Fellwood," I said formally. "It is nice to see you, but I am still unwell from the poison. I must be—"

She reached out her hand, grasping my arm tightly. "Well played, princess," she whispered into my ear. "More clever than I anticipated. Luckily, Lady Calavi was no friend of mine. She got what was coming to her."

She pulled back, taking in the sight of my face. I fought to remain unfazed, but terror began to stir inside of me. "I am unsure of what you speak, Lady Fellwood. Lady Calavi brought this fate upon herself."

Lady Fellwood chuckled, nodding slowly. "That she did. No worries, Genevieve, your secrets are safe with me. I hope your recovery is swift," she said before returning to the other court members.

I took a moment to gather myself before Otar appeared at my side, seeming to sense my panic. With Calavi's blood drying on his leathery skin, he took my arm and pulled me out of my panicked state. Winnow Fellwood would be another loose end I would have to see to before long.

I had just gotten to my bed when Eren came barging through my doors. Otar went into a defensive stance at the edge of the bed. Eren was calm and collected as always, but I knew the conversation we were about to have might not be so composed.

"Otar, please give us some time. You are free to roam the land," I said.

Otar growled and then disappeared.

Eren walked slowly over to me, examining my state.

I laid my head down on the pillow and exhaled in relief. "What can I help you with, Ambassador Lyklor?"

He took a seat on the edge next to me. "Please tell me you weren't responsible for Lady Calavi's death," he whispered.

"I guess in a way I was, since I was the one she tried to kill and got caught for it. Why? Don't tell me you'll miss her."

"You are more dangerous than I gave you credit for. Clever and deadly."

I smiled at him. "I don't know what you mean."

"You can stop now, I know you. Gen ... what were you thinking? Poisoning yourself. What if they hadn't discovered the origin of the poison in time? You could have died."

"Otar was my fail-safe. He had an antidote ready just in case they took too long. I planned everything perfectly. No room for error. And now, you are free, and the bitch is dead."

"You shouldn't have taken that risk. You put yourself in great danger. Especially if you had gotten caught. I am not worth it. You need to put yourself first. She was mine to deal with, not yours," he said firmly.

I sat up, trying to read him. "Are you angry because she is dead, or because you weren't the one to kill her?"

He rubbed his hand over his face as he stood from the bed. "No, I am not angry about either, I just ... I am the one that is supposed to be protecting you, not the other way around."

"Now we're even. With the whole life-saving game," I smiled at him.

He laughed as a bright smile spread across his face.

He sat next to me again, taking my hand in his. "Thank you ... truly," he whispered.

"You are free. To do whatever you want. No one owns you and you can truly move on and heal. You showed me how to heal from my pain, I just wanted to be able to do the same for you."

He tightened his hand around mine. "You are too soft for this world. I fear it is going to be the death of you."

"Please, don't underestimate me. Many have, and now they're dead."

He laughed, nodding his head. "Yes, I'm aware. Is there anything I can do for you?"

I smiled. "Can you take the discomfort away, please?"

He exhaled and nodded. "I can do that," he replied, reaching his hand slowly to my face. I fell to the pillow and closed my eyes as his smooth skin danced across my cheek. His fingertips made my skin erupt into goosebumps as he trailed them down my jaw. Whiskey and oranges filled my senses as I relaxed into a deep and comforting sleep.

I woke before dinner, feeling a little fatigued, but completely healed. I had to be on my game. Gaelin and Daealla would have already arrived, and I couldn't show them that I was weak. I got dressed and headed to Eren's room to go over the details of our little theatrical display for the evening. I could only imagine how happy he was to no longer be summoned to that bitch's room. I remembered the feeling after Lysanthier had died. It was one I would never forget.

I reached his door and knocked twice. A servant opened it, allowing me to pass. I walked into his seating area, which was also his study, with a smile on my face, feeling happy for him. The double doors opened to reveal Icici as she finished dressing. My smile dropped at the sight of her. She locked eyes with me and grinned with delight. Eren came from behind her, bare-chested, wearing only pants.

"Good afternoon, cousin. I wasn't expecting to see you here this early. Have you come to join us? I mean, it could be fun. One hot body, one cold. I am sure the sensation would be fantastic, don't you think, Eren?" she said.

He passed her, grabbing his shirt and sliding it over his torso.

"Leave, Icici," he demanded.

"Oh, come on now. Two Drezmores are always better than one," she said, walking over to stand in front of me. She drew her cold fingers down my face as I pulled away from her. "You look a little pale, cousin. Still sickly? You should use more makeup. Though, I don't think there is enough in the kingdom to make you look even remotely alfar."

"Icici," Eren barked.

She smiled, taking a step back. "Thanks for freeing him up for me, by the way. Now with that devil gone, I get him whenever I want. I owe you one," she winked before leaving.

I felt so uncomfortable, I would have misted out of the room if I knew how. I just stood there, forgetting why I had even come.

"Did you need something?" he asked.

"I ..." I couldn't even form a sentence. I shook my head, trying to get a hold of myself. "I came to see how you were doing. I take it you enjoyed yourself?" I asked, feeling sick to my stomach at the thought of my cousin in bed with him.

"I am grateful to have my freedom, thanks to you," he said, handing me a cup of tea.

I turned away from him, still attempting to gather myself. "Your first few hours of freedom, and you spent it with her?" I asked.

He exhaled, putting the cup back on the tray. "If it bothers you so much, I will stop sleeping with her at your request," he said plainly.

I closed my eyes, feeling stupid and childish. "No. You are free to sleep with whomever you want. I'm sorry, I just don't like her much, but I guess I can understand the ... physical appeal."

He walked over to me, leaning down to catch my eyes with his. I looked up, taking a deep breath in, remembering who I was. "How are you feeling? Ready for tonight?" he asked.

"Yes, I am. The faster the treaty is signed the faster, they can go home."

"Exactly. I appreciate the check-in, but it wasn't necessary. Did you need anything else?"

I shook my head taking a step towards the door. "I will see you at dinner," I said, pulling the door open before he could say another word.

I went to the balcony of my room and looked out into the setting sun. How could he sleep with her? After the way she treated and taunted me? She was a foul female, and yet he still found her desirable enough to bed.

I pulled out my ragamor whistle and blew it as hard as I could.

I needed to escape, by myself. Tarsyrth appeared at my balcony, latching onto the side of the mountain nearby. I quickly mounted him, taking off into the sky. I spent the next few hours flying. I cleared my head, preparing for tonight's task.

I found myself at the edge of the border, peering into The Frey. I pulled the blue stone from my pocket and stepped through.

I sat on a bench in the center of a town I had never visited and watched the people busy themselves with work and life. A few took a hard look in my direction, but none were brave enough to approach. I watched while children ran through the streets. Couples walked hand in hand through the marketplace. Their lives were simple, yet complete. Time passed as I lost myself in thought, enjoying the simplicity. I made my way back to the border and called for Tarsyrth. I flew back to my balcony and dismounted him, now ready for tonight's theatrical performance.

I took off my jacket just before Atalee appeared in my room. She exhaled with relief at the sight of me.

"Oh, thank Azeer," she gasped. "Guards, tell everyone the princess is safe."

"What is going on?" I asked.

Eren ran through the door, followed by Lily. They just stared at me.

"What?" I asked.

"Princess, you do not leave these walls without someone with you, or at least informing someone of where you are going," instructed Eren sternly. "We thought something had happened. We searched everywhere."

"I'm sorry, I didn't know I needed a babysitter to go for a ride," I replied.

He exhaled again, looking to Atalee. "Prepare her. I will be back when the court is seated," he said, leaving the room.

Lily rushed over flinging her arms around me.

"I'm sorry I worried you. That wasn't my intent," I told her.

"It's okay, I am just glad you're back. Now, wait until you see what I have made you," she said. Atalee ushered me into the chair and began her magic.

I stood in front of the mirror admiring the craftsmanship that went into my look. I didn't recognize myself. My hair was straightened like the alfar's. It was long and went past my bottom. It shined and glistened in the light. My eyes had black liner on the lids, making them appear as if they were bigger than they truly were. Silver dust garnished my cheekbones, and my face was completed with a burgundy lip.

Lily had outdone herself. I wore a dress made completely out of diamonds. They were sewn onto a sheer fabric that revealed every mark on my body. I was practically naked. The diamonds were strategically placed to cover my private parts, but most of my breasts could be seen through the fabric. It was extremely form-fitting and had two long slits on either side up to my hip bones. The sleeves started at the ends of my shoulders and went down to the middle of the back of my hands. Diamonds were scattered on each sleeve. The back was completely visible down to the top of my bottom.

I felt uncomfortable and exposed, but this was what it was going to take to get our treaty signed. Me dangling on a hook in front of Gaelin, again. I didn't know how it was going to feel to see him. To hear his voice or look into his eyes. I had to stay strong and ready for anything.

Atalee brought out a diamond crown and placed it on my head. It had an emerald gem in the center of it. Diamond earrings hung from my ears and my star pendant, the one he had given me, was perfectly displayed.

A knock came at the door. Atalee went to open it and then left the room. I stood in front of the mirror. Small shivers ran up my spin in anticipation of seeing Gaelin in the flesh. I knew this day would come, but it didn't mean I was ready for it. In the mirror, I saw Eren staring at me from the doorway. I turned, walking over to him in silence. He looked me up and down slowly, seeming to take note of every strategically-placed diamond.

"Are you going to say something, or just stand there," I snapped, uncomfortable from his lingering look.

"If that dress doesn't say 'fuck me', I don't know what does," he said, with a heat behind his tone.

Laughter exploded from me, relaxing my nerves. He smiled as he watched my expression. He was wearing a solid black suit with his normal silk trim, but this time it was white. His jacket was shorter, stopping at his bottom. His hair was slicked to the side and his face was radiant.

"I had a last-minute idea to push Daealla over the edge," I said, breaking our awkward silence.

"Go on."

"I thought I'd have Otar follow in behind me. He could take a place in the back and then disappear once the dancing began, but she would see him. The thing that killed her father."

He grinned, reaching his fingers out to my chin. He brought my eyes up to his. "How something so bright can be so dark, I will never understand. I think it's brilliant," he whispered, dropping his hands from my face.

I called for Otar as Eren entered the throne room first. My father and the light court were already seated. Otar was overjoyed to bring more pain to Daealla, so he did what he was told without a fuss for once.

I waited nervously until I heard the announcer clear his voice. "Rise, for the heir of Doonak, Princess Genevieve Drezmore," he said in a deep, booming voice.

The doors opened. I took a deep breath and took my first step. At the head of the table, my father sat with the queen next to him. There was an empty seat for me, then Eren to the left of my chair. Queen Daealla, Gaelin, and Levos sat across from them, now turned in my direction.

Daealla locked her eyes on me and then on Otar as he walked behind with his teeth bared. She sucked in air and held her breath, making a disgusted face. I smiled, proud of myself. I got to the middle of the room and stopped, waiting for the music to begin. Soddram approached first, bowing, and then taking me into his arms. The music began as we slid across the floor.

The dance was seductive and intimate, but I felt nothing when he touched me. Within seconds, Avalon cut in, twirling and bending me low as he smiled into my eyes. Next, Therosi pulled me close against his toned body. His handsome, devilish face scoured my figure as he licked his lips with delight. I smiled, pretending I was flattered.

The middle of the song began to play when Eren tapped Therosi on the shoulder. Eren took me into his arms and glided us across the dance floor, just like he had so many times before. His eyes entrapped mine, preventing me from looking anywhere else.

His hand slowly glided down my bare back, savoring my skin with each touch. He flung me around, then I brought my leg up to his side, as the dance called for. He held me there for a moment, sliding another hand along my leg up to my hip in the most pleasurable and seductive manner. I closed my eyes, arching my back as I enjoyed the feeling of a male for the first time since before Lysanthier. Something I never thought I'd be able to do again.

He pressed his lips softly against my neck before he pulled me up. I looked at him, shocked by the action. That was not a part of the original choreography. He winked at me, pressing his body closer to mine. He twirled me around, pulling my backside into him as he trailed his fingers down my arm, slowly taking his time while he grazed the side of my breast and then continued to the slit in my dress.

I turned back around, face to face again before he spun and dipped me, just in time before the song came to an end. I was panting, out of breath from the excitement of it all. He pulled me up slowly, never taking his eyes from mine. The court applauded as we stood locked to one another, but I didn't care. In that moment, everything but Eren faded into the darkness. He took my face with his hands and kissed the side of my cheek softly. I felt his lips move to my ear.

"How did I do?" he asked.

I dropped my head, not wanting to give him the honest answer. I almost forgot it was all for show. I enjoyed his touch. The feeling of his body against mine. The feeling of his lips against my neck. I pushed the thought of him from my head. I couldn't go there. It would only lead to another broken heart.

He bent down to search for my eyes. "Princess," he whispered, "you're blushing."

I gathered myself and smiled at him. He nodded, offering his arm so he could escort me to my seat.

The court sat as we got to the banquet table. My father leaned over and kissed me on my head proudly. Eren took a seat next to me and undid his napkin. Gaelin was directly in front of me, which gave him a front-row seat to our production. I found the courage to meet his gaze.

His beautiful yellow eyes were filled with so much pain, I could barely stand it. A crown adorned his shimmering head of white hair. His cream suit hugged his well-built body. His lips were frozen into a straight line.

I smiled at him softly, trying to get a reaction, but he simply diverted his eyes to his plate. Eren addressed Levos and laughed at something he said. What it was, I didn't know. I was too busy hating myself for what I was doing to Gaelin.

"Quite the show you two put on, Princess Genevieve," said

Daealla from across the table. "Ambassador Lyklor, I never realized how passionate you were until just now." She narrowed her eyes at him seductively.

He smiled at her, turning his eyes to me. "Passion is easy when you have the right partner," he said.

Her seductive gaze flashed to anger as she looked away from him.

The rest of the night was an uncomfortable mess. Negotiations began and got ugly halfway through. Daealla lost her temper while Gaelin tried to keep everyone together. In the middle of the debate, Eren would casually lean over into my ears, whispering stupid things that I couldn't help but laugh at. He drew his fingers through my hair and noticeably slid his hand under the table to my thigh. Gaelin took note of it all.

Finally, the negotiations ended. We got what we wanted. They had foolishly agreed, and the plan worked. I got up from the table first, excusing myself back to my rooms. I couldn't stand to be in the same room as everyone for another second. I felt guilty for what I had done. Before I could make it back to my rooms, Eren pulled my arm, getting my attention.

"What?" I snapped.

He pulled his touch away uncomfortably. "I ... I just wanted to make sure you were alright after all of that. I know the physical aspect must have been unsettling for you," he said, more caring than I had ever heard him sound.

I took a deep breath, calming myself. "I'm fine. It wasn't as bad as I thought."

He smiled, placing his hands in his pockets. "You know ... for a moment there ... I could have sworn you were enjoying yourself."

"Maybe for a moment," I admitted, laughing at myself, still in disbelief my body had acted the way it had.

"Then what is the problem? If it's not me, then what?"

"Oh, you're always the problem," I chuckled. "It's just ... I didn't like hurting him like that. He doesn't deserve this. He never harmed me. He tried his best to protect me, but some things were out of his control. I feel horrible for what I just did."

Eren exhaled, walking slowly towards me. He placed a hand on each of my arms and looked into my eyes. "You have nothing to feel sorry about. He may have not intentionally harmed you, but he put you in harm's way, and then stood by and did nothing about it while you suffered. He deserves to suffer, if only a little," he said with a smile. His eyes flashed down to the star pendant that sat displayed upon my chest. "He gave you that, didn't he?"

"Yes, but that's not why I wear it. It reminds me of the stars, and my freedom." I said softly.

He smiled at me, allowing his hands to fall from my arms. "Get some sleep. I'll see you in the morning." He turned to walk away.

"Eren," I called out.

He stopped, turning back around.

"I forbid you from sleeping with Queen Daealla," I blurted.

He hung his head and laughed. "Princess, I wouldn't touch her if she was the last female on this planet," he replied.

"I find that hard to believe."

He chuckled, walking away and leaving me in the hallway.

CHAPTER FIFTEEN

Atalee helped me out of the dress and makeup before I bathed, allowing the night to soak away. I dressed in my nightgown, still feeling weak from the poison. She cleaned up the room and made sure the fireplace had enough wood.

"Would you like anything else tonight, your majesty?" she asked.

I smiled to myself. "A bottle of whiskey and a bowl of oranges please," I replied.

She nodded.

Ten minutes later a knock came at the door. I went to answer it, thinking it was Atalee, but there stood Gaelin with both of my guards at his side. I was stunned by the sheer nerve of him to come to my private quarters. I nodded at the guards and allowed him to pass.

I closed the door, wrapping my arms around myself for comfort. He walked through my rooms, taking in the way I now lived. I didn't know why he was here or what he wanted. Atalee came into the room with her eyes wide as she looked at him. She bowed and then put the bottle of whiskey and oranges on my table before leaving.

He took a seat on the couch in front of the fireplace. I walked over hesitantly, sitting down beside him. His familiar scent flooded my senses, bringing back memories both good and bad.

He exhaled and then turned to finally look at me. "It's good to see you safe," he said with a forced smile.

"It's good to see you too. I wasn't sure if you were ever going to speak to me again after the Otar incident."

He smirked. "I would have thanked you if I had the chance. You did what you had to."

"I'm glad you see it that way." A few moments passed in silence.

"Levos tells me you've been able to move past everything. That you are growing and thriving here," he said.

"Surprisingly, yes. My father is supportive and caring, something I never thought I'd have. I'm with Lily again and I am learning about our history and politics, while learning how to protect myself. Overall, I'd call it progress."

"And Lyklor? Are you two ..."

"No. It was just a dance. He is a friend, that is all," I confessed. We had gotten the treaty signed, there was no need to torture him anymore.

"Be careful who you call a friend, Gen."

"Yes, I've been warned by everyone, but what can I say? I am an optimist."

"I've missed you," he blurted. There it was. The phrase I didn't want to hear. "There hasn't been a day that has gone by that I haven't wondered how you were," he admitted, looking into the fireplace.

"I'm sorry you were hurt in all of this. I never wanted to cause you pain. Everything I did was to try and support your vision for Urial."

"I know your intentions were good. I am just sorry you got hurt so much along the way."

"It made me stronger in the long run. That is the way I look at it now."

He turned towards me with a soft smile, studying the details of my face. He reached out and gently brushed his knuckles down my jaw to my lips. "I wish things could have been different. I wish I was someone different so I could have given you everything you deserve." He leaned down and kissed my lips gently. It wasn't a passionate kiss, nor a seductive one. It was a kiss to say that he was sorry. It was full of pain and regret. He pulled away slowly as we both smiled at one another.

We spent the next two hours filling each other in on the months we had been apart. I told him about my education and the rag-amor, how the city really functions and how Lily had fallen in love with Zerrial. He told me how unstable Daealla was. He tried to reason with her, but she threw his position in his face every chance she got. He prayed for an heir just so he could remove her from power.

At the end of the night, he hugged me tightly and kissed me on the forehead before returning to his rooms. I exhaled, glad the awkwardness was over. I walked over to the table and poured myself a glass of whiskey. I peeled the flesh of the orange and twisted it to release the scent. I dropped it into my glass and twirled it under my nose before taking a slow sip.

The proportions weren't exactly the same, but it was close enough. I closed my eyes, enjoying the flavors. *What was I doing?* I couldn't go down this road. It would lead me nowhere. I put the glass back on the table and headed for bed. Gods, I hated human emotions. Why did I have to inherit that part of my mother? Out of all my human traits, that was the one I would get rid of in a heartbeat.

The next morning, I got up and dressed, preparing for the light alfar's sendoff. I left my hair curly and loose allowing it to travel down the length of my back. I wore a gold dress that covered everything but my cleavage. I figured everyone had seen enough of me the previous night. The door opened as Atalee finished making my bed. Eren stepped inside, dressed in his formal long jacket. He peered around the room.

"Did you lose something?" I asked.

"Heard you had a visitor last night," he replied.

I rolled my eyes. "I did, and?"

"Oh, nothing. I just didn't see that coming. I may have a blind spot when it comes to you. I'm going to have to fix that."

I snickered. "Nothing happened. We just talked. He kissed me, but it wasn't that type of kiss," I confessed, hoping to make him a little jealous.

"I was unaware there is more than one type of kiss."

"Never mind, it's none of your business. Bottom line, nothing happened. We had a good talk and then he left."

Eren nodded walking over to the table where the whiskey and oranges sat. He smiled, tilting his head in amusement. "Princess, if you wanted me to tuck you in, all you had to do was ask," he said, taking the glass in his hand.

Embarrassment flooded through me so fast I thought I was going to pass out. "Can we go now," I asked, moving past him towards the door.

He grabbed my arm, pulling me back in front of him. "Not until you tell me why you have a bottle of whiskey and oranges in your bedroom."

I turned my head away from him. "Can you just forget you saw it?"

"Not likely."

I exhaled, feeling my cheeks burn with embarrassment. "Your scent is ... comforting to me. I don't know if it's because I associate it with peace, or if it's because of the way it makes my body relax, but I ... enjoy the smell, okay?" I said, pulling away from his grasp.

He grinned, laughing softly to himself. "Do you think of me ... when you drink this?" he asked, twirling the liquid under his nose.

"No. I think of sleep and that is it. Now can we please go," I spat, storming to the door.

I made my way to my father's side as the light alfar exited the base of the mountain. The horses were saddled and already prepared for the journey ahead. Levos came up to us and bowed respectfully. He stopped in front of me and smiled. I threw my arms around him and gave him the biggest hug I could muster.

"Now that we're on good terms again you should come to see me and bring your ragamor. I demand you take me flying," he said.

I laughed. "Of course. Anytime you want."

"Take care, sweet Genevieve. I miss you already," he said, kissing me on my cheek.

Daealla only nodded in our direction as she passed us to get to her horse. Gaelin bowed in front of my father and then stopped in front of me. His eyes were once again filled with the pain of having to say goodbye.

He reached out, running his hand through my loose hair. He leaned into my ear. "I will always love you. Never forget that," he said, kissing me on the side of my head before turning to join the others.

A piece of my heart broke in that moment for him. He would never have what he desired. I hoped he would find someone else who loved him in return, because that person would never be me.

"You want to tell me again how nothing happened?" said Eren, coming up next to me.

"It didn't," I said firmly.

"*I will always love you. Never forget that,*" he mocked Gaelin.

We watched as they took off towards Urial.

"At least he's capable of love," I said firmly before storming back into the castle.

Forcing the thought of Gaelin and Eren from my mind, I found myself in front of a door with the carving of an eye in the center. Before I could muster the courage to knock, it opened, revealing Winnow Fellwood on the other side.

"Well, hello Princess Genevieve," she said in her formal tone. "I've been expecting you."

I took a deep breath and entered, against my better judgement. She shut the door behind me and made her way to a seating area in front of the fireplace. "Tea?" she offered, gesturing to the chair besides hers.

"No thank you," I answered, taking a seat. "I've come to discuss what you think you know about the late Lady Calavi."

Fellwood stirred her cream into her tea, bringing the liquid slowly to her lip before answering. "I only know what Azeer allows me to see," she answered vaguely.

"And what did you see?" I asked, taking the bait.

Her eyes turned to me, followed by her lips turning up into a grin. "Princess Genevieve, I'd be lying if I were to say I am not offended by your aggressive tone. Have I been nothing but trusting and supportive of you since you've arrived at court? Did I not help reunite you with your family, saving you from a life as a concubine? What have I done to earn this hostility?"

I took a moment, relaxing slightly in the chair. "You're right, Lady Fellwood. I am sorry for my tone. I just ... the entire situation with Lady Calavi is still so fresh and traumatizing. I wish to put the entire happenstance behind me."

"I think that'd be for the best," she said, patting my arm with her hand. "Your future is so bright, sweet Gen. It would be a shame for you to waste it. Regardless of what I know or ... think I know, your secrets are always safe with me."

"She was an evil female," I whispered.

"That, I will not disagree about. My gift showed me long ago how the ambassador rose to his station."

My eyes widened in surprise. "You knew?"

"I know many things about the members of this court, and of others. Something I am sure you can relate to, but it is not always my place to divulge the secret deals and conspiring's of others. Only if it harms the throne do I confess what the gods show me. And I only see the benefit of being rid of a predator such as Rismera Calavi."

"Thank you," I said softly.

"No need for that," she said, standing to her feet. "Now, is there anything else you'd like to accuse me of before you leave?"

"I'm terribly sorry," I confessed, standing to my feet.

Her face softened. "No need for that. Wouldn't be the first time

I was targeted because of my gift. But I do ask, next time, you come and ask me directly first. That way, we can have a pleasant gathering instead of a hostile one."

"Deal," I agreed, taking my leave.

As I left her room, I couldn't shake the feeling Winnow wasn't being completely honest with me. I wanted to believe the kind and gentle female who was the reason I was now reunited with my family, but why bring up my dealings with Calavi, if not to serve some purpose of her own?

Something wasn't adding up. My saving grace was that she had no proof of my direct involvement with the setup. It would be her word against mine, and she knew it. So, what was she after? Was this her attempt to scare me? To let me know I was being watched? Regardless, Winnow Fellwood was an alfar that could not be trusted.

The next few weeks passed quickly as I returned to my normal routine. Combat practice, teachings, and courtly matters. I got to go on more of the hunts with Eren and his group of friends, which never disappointed. I was getting better at killing and tracking.

Some days I prayed something would come through the rift so I would be able to kill it.

The Jestu celebrations came and went, but this time nymphs and incubi attended. I was shocked to see that the nymphs would even grace us with their presence, but Eren explained that though they were aligned with the light court, we still were on good terms with them, and they were welcomed to the celebration. I read between the lines. They were good fucks, so why not let them join?

Their long bodies swayed to the music. The intrinsic colors of hair and skin shimmered in the candle lights as they allowed those around them to explore their long, thin, bodies.

The Incubi, the perfect combination of beast and humanoid, took anyone and anything that crossed their paths. Once engaged in sexual intercourse, their dark, batlike wings expanded, allowing their chosen lover to stroke and caress the thin material. The sensation seemed to entice the Incubi even more as the groans of pleasure and satisfaction echoed through the cavern.

I only stayed an hour, still uncomfortable by the very public displays of affection. Eren would come and check on me before he retired. I wasn't huddled in a corner, so I took that as a win. I had Atalee make sure that there were always oranges and whiskey in my room. Even though I refused Eren when he offered to use his gift to ease me to sleep, I still craved it.

The search for the name Narella continued to lead us nowhere. Otar would have brief moments when he would start to remember small details of his past captor, but it would dissipate before he could tell us anything we could use.

Otar got himself killed two more times over a two-week period. Apparently, since I could bring him back, that gave him a pass to be reckless with his body. He had it out for the fairies, which I couldn't blame him for. They were disgusting little beasts I would have liked nothing more than to obliterate.

I had two visions that helped with hunts we were on. I was recovering faster, but the pain from using my power was still unpleasant. So was the beating Toreon gave me daily.

One evening, after I had just completed combat training, barely making it back to my room for a shower, I grumbled under my breath, knowing I had more training to attend with Eren. I pulled on a loose dress that was lightweight, not caring about my hair, and made my way to his room. I flung open the heavy doors, letting them fall shut behind me as I dragged myself to his couch and plopped down. He was sitting on the floor by the fireplace in his black pants and a loose button-up shirt.

"They work you good?" he asked, writing something on a piece of paper.

"Every day, all day," I said, turning to see what he was working on.

Drawings were scattered across the floor. Portraits and landscapes done in charcoal surrounded him. I slid off the couch to the ground next to him, picking up a portrait of a young woman.

The execution and line work was remarkable. I picked up another, studying the delicate strokes of the hair and the brows.

"Did you draw all of these?" I asked.

He shrugged. "It's my way to escape. Kind of like you do with your books," he said, handing me the book he was drawing in. I flipped through the pages. There were drawings of my father, my uncle. Then there were drawings of naked women, some of which I recognized. My cheeks flushed. I continued flipping until I stopped at Icici's portrait.

The shadows of her face were delicate and well crafted. The detail in her eyes and of her lips were precise and perfect, as if he had studied her for hours. My heart dropped. I forced a smile onto my face handing him back the book, not wanting the next page I turned to be of her naked sprawled out on his bed.

He chuckled, turning a few pages to another drawing.

This one was of me. My face wasn't as long as Icici's, but it was defined and well represented. My nose was small and recognizable as were my lips and chin. My eyes stood out on the page, just like they did in real life. My inadequate ears were present with small tips at the ends, hidden beneath my full bushel of hair.

I turned to the next page to see another picture of myself. This time I was smiling. I turned to the next page. I was laughing widely, with my nose crinkled and my eyes shut. I turned again to another page where I was sleeping peacefully in my bed. Eren reached for the book, closing it before I could continue.

"They're beautiful. You are very talented. Did you take lessons?" I asked.

"Trial and error," he said, collecting the papers and placing them into his portfolio.

I bit my lip, trying to hold back the question I so desperately wanted an answer to. "Did you draw the one of me sleeping from memory or in person?"

He stopped, turning his eyes up to mine with a half-smile. "Are you going to have a panic attack if I said in person?"

"No, I just ask that you tell me next time. I can at least put some makeup on or do my hair or something." I giggled uncomfortably.

"Don't get me wrong, you look striking all done up, but that isn't really you. When your face is bare, and you can see the natural pigment of your cheeks and lip. When your hair is loose like it is now, curling and waving in all different directions. That is the real you. That is the you I like to draw."

I felt a warmth I hadn't felt in a long time begin to well up somewhere deep inside of me. I studied his face as he turned away, appearing slightly uncomfortable by his admission. He was vulnerable and real in this moment. He wasn't hiding behind a mask or having to put on a front. He was himself.

I watched his chest rise and fall with each breath. How his lips pursed together while he continued to collect his drawings. The way his jaw moved and tensed. His black hair was casually brushed to the side. I allowed my eyes to trail down to his strong neck and wide shoulders. I found myself wishing I could touch him and explore him in ways I never thought I would want to do again with another. But with him, it was different. He was my safe place. His touch didn't repulse me. It comforted me. It always had.

I exhaled a long, deep sigh of sexual frustration. When I breathed in, the need to have him intensified. My body started to ache and throb for his touch. Eren took a deep breath in, closing his eyes as he tilted his head back. He slowly brought his face down and opened his eyes to look at me. The silver swirl of his irises lit up.

"That smell. Do you smell it?" he asked.

I didn't know what he was asking and frankly, I didn't care. I reached out in that moment and hesitantly placed my hand on his. His fingers slowly fluttered underneath mine as the palms of our hands traced against one another. I trailed my hand up his forearm to his biceps. I could feel his rippling muscles under his thin shirt.

When I got to the collar of the shirt I pulled it back, revealing the imprint I had wanted to touch for so long. To trace the lines with my hands and then my tongue. He watched intently while I studied the mark. I gently ran my fingers against the bare skin of his neck and then shoulder. His skin felt like velvet. He inhaled at the contact, closing his eyes seeming to enjoy my attention.

I shifted, getting to my knees as I slowly brought my other hand up to his face. I hovered above, straddling him in between my legs tracing the lines of his face. His hands slid up my thighs, firmly planting themselves at my hips as he fought not to lose control. I ran my hands through his thick silky dark hair. He moaned at the feeling. I couldn't help but smile, taking joy in his satisfaction.

The need was building inside of me with each breath I took. It was almost unbearable. I could feel the warmth in between my legs, and I knew it would only take one touch from him to send me over the edge. I brought my lips to his neck, kissing down his skin while my fingers worked at the buttons of his shirt.

Before I could register what was happening, I lost control of myself. I slammed him back to the floor placing myself on top of him. I pulled his shirt apart to reveal that perfect torso I wanted to devour. I leaned down, placing my mouth to his imprint and he pulled at the top of my dress, taking my neck and shoulder into his mouth with passion. His hand buried itself in my hair pulling my neck down harder into his mouth.

Oh, the feeling of him was more than I could have ever imagined. I swirled my tongue around his marking before I moved to his chest, making sure my hands never left his body. I kissed, licked, and bit my way down his abdomen until I got to his pant line. I slid my tongue along it as he arched and moaned with pleasure. I brought my mouth back up to his neck as I fought with the laces of his pants.

I needed to have him inside of me. I needed it more than I needed to breathe. He kissed my chest and roamed his hands over my heavy, full breasts that were still covered by my dress. My nipples hardened at the contact. He dragged his hands down in between my legs, allowing the fabric of my underwear to act as a barrier. His finger grazed the area, feeling the warm moisture that had already saturated the thin cloth. I could feel his entire body ignite with gooseflesh underneath me.

Before I could get his pants down, I felt his hands tighten around my arms, pushing me back. I stopped, looking down at him in confusion. He took a few deep breaths in, looking at my face with wonder. His eyes were ravenous like a wild animal.

"It's you," he said, in a deep and raspy voice, taking another deep breath.

"What?" I asked, annoyed by the interruption.

"Lavender and ... sandalwood. It's your pheromones. You are a manipulator ... like me," he said, pushing me off him to the side.

I leaned against the couch, straightening my dress as he stood from the floor, pulling at his shirt. "I don't understand," I said, moving to the couch. I felt my cheeks flush with embarrassment.

"Your pheromones just now caused that to happen. Yet, somehow, they affected you as much as me," he said, buttoning his shirt.

I frowned, not wanting the beautiful sight to be taken from me. I relaxed, realizing what I had just done. What I had wanted to do. What almost happened.

"Oh gods, Eren, I am so sorry. I didn't know," I said in complete humiliation.

He paced, still trying to regain control of himself. He appeared to be just as embarrassed as I was. "It's okay. The good thing is,

I can help you with this gift. I can teach you how to use it and control it," he said.

He stopped in front of me, still breathing heavily. His eyes locked onto mine again. Time seemed to stop as he slowly reached to move a small strand of loose hair from my face. His fingers grazed across my cheek. I felt that warming sensation begin to rise inside of me again. He breathed in, his eyes widened with recognition, but he didn't remove his hand from my skin.

Instead, he pulled my face into his, our lips meeting in the most passionate and aggressive kiss I had ever experienced. I moved onto him, ripping the shirt open with force once again. Buttons went flying everywhere as my hand trailed down his abdomen trying to get inside of his pants. I grinded myself on top of him, feeling the pressure in between my legs build. He moaned inside my mouth while his hands slid under my dress and up my bare thighs. I pulled away to breathe as he took my neck back into his mouth, biting and sucking, tearing at the neckline of my dress.

He yelled in frustration, tossing me to the side of the couch. He stood up putting distance between us. I took a deep breath, so sexually frustrated that I wanted to cry. It wasn't just the pheromones. I wanted him, now more than ever. He stood off to the side, his shirt parted, revealing his sexy chest and that delicious marking. I fixed the front of my dress, waiting for him to say something— anything. He looked at me, eyes still hungry. I tried to purse my lips, but a smile escaped. I heard him laugh under his breath.

"Okay, we obviously need to figure out a way around ... that, if I am going to help you," he said, tightening his fists. "Mm, your scent is more potent than a succubus, princess," he said, turning his head away from me while he tried to calm himself.

"Is that a bad thing?"

He laughed, turning those entrancing silver eyes on me. "Not at all. Especially for whatever male or female you are trying to seduce."

I smiled. "Why were you able to resist?" I asked with disappointment.

"Maybe because I have a similar gift. I don't know, but believe me, it was hard, extremely hard."

I stood up slowly, still hungry for more of him.

He tracked my every move. "Princess, remember, the pheromones are controlling you. You need to relax and think."

"So, you're saying you wouldn't take me if it wasn't for the pheromones. You don't desire me? You've never once thought of bending me over and taking me on my desk in between lessons?" I said, my voice husky and unfamiliar. I let out a long breath as I filled the air with my scent.

He inhaled, trying to step away from me. "I am not a monk by any means, but I would never take you if you weren't fully in your right mind," he said, his hands flexing like he was fighting the need to touch me.

"Eren, I am in my right mind. For the first time in a long time,

I feel good, but I want you to make me feel better," I admitted, trailing my hand down the center of my cleavage.

He watched my every move: his breath quickened with arousal. "Listen to me, you need to breathe in and out slowly. Think of Lily, your father. Think of all your friends back in The Frey. Think of flying, and how much you love flying," he said desperately.

I took a step back as his words started to break through whatever alter ego this was. None of the things he said made me forget how much I did indeed want him. But I suddenly realized that he may not want me in return. All of his reactions towards me the past few moments could have been solely because of my powers. *He is sleeping with my cousin,* I reminded myself. Why would he want me when he could have her?

I dropped my head, the reality of the situation finally settling in. I took a few steps back, inhaling deep breaths, making sure the scent was gone. I looked up at him as he exhaled in relief. I was so ashamed and embarrassed. The first male I tried to get with after everything had to be the same guy my cousin was screwing. What was wrong with me?

"I'm so sorry," I said, barely able to speak.

"It's fine, really," he said kindly.

Without another word, I bolted for the door. He called after me, but I couldn't bear to look at him.

The memory of his touch replayed over and over again in my mind. How good he felt. How wonderful he tasted. For the first time in my life, I wanted another, and it wasn't because I was relying on them to protect me or because I had to keep them happy. No. It was because I truly desired him. I desired a male who would never be faithful. Who would never love me. Who wouldn't hesitate to use me to elevate himself. I knew what he was, who he was, and yet I still wanted him.

CHAPTER SIXTEEN

I avoided Eren the rest of the day. I busied myself in political matters with my father and uncle. The sacrifice to Azeer was less than two months away, and the thought of innocents being burned alive unsettled me to the core. My uncle oversaw selecting the humans that we would sacrifice. He looked for people who were gravely sick, broken, and compliant. I read over each of the human's files as he compiled a list for my father to choose from.

I didn't know how I was going to be able to stand and watch as their flesh melted from their bones, but I knew I had to. This was going to be my kingdom, my life, and somehow, I had to learn to adapt.

That night after dinner, Lily and I discussed the upcoming ritual. After living among the humans and now alfar, I didn't know where I truly stood with the whole process. As I had learned more about Azeer and Maleki, I understood why the dark court had continued them after the great war, but that didn't mean I would ever be okay with sacrificing even a single innocent life.

When I ascended the throne, maybe there would be something I could do to stop these barbaric rituals. After all these centuries of our devotion and worship to Azeer, maybe it would be enough to sate his jealousy and worry regarding our allegiance.

I told Lily about my new power. I hadn't even told my father or my uncle yet. I wanted to understand exactly what I could do with it before I told anyone else.

I left out the details of me attempting to devour Eren when I told Lily what had happened. I couldn't help but wonder if Icici was in his bed at this very moment. I pushed the thought out of my head as Lily talked about her work.

Vena ended up in my room an hour later. She and Lily were friends, so the three of us were comfortable around each other. Vena fell onto the bed with a smile stretched across her face. We both looked at her with suspicion. She laughed as she told us about her most recent correspondence with Levos. Apparently, she had approached him when he and his court were here weeks ago. They stayed up all night talking before he had to take his leave.

They had been writing to each other since then. She was over the moon that he was showing an interest. I kept my mouth shut and listened. I wondered how genuine his affections were. I knew how much he had loved Madison. I had seen it with my own eyes. True love, between a human and an alfar. Lily was giddy as she wrapped her arms around her in an embrace.

After they left, I couldn't stop my mind from floating to Eren. I poured a glass of whiskey and peeled the orange skin from the pith. I stood out on my balcony, taking in the deep rich scent. I looked

JESSICA ANN DISCIACCA

out into the stars wondering where my life would go from here. After the sacrifice, the next thing on the agenda was my marriage. A marriage I would have to learn how to live with. I took a sip of the amber liquor, clearing my mind of worry and basking in the deep darkness of the night sky.

The next morning, I woke up and sat at my vanity, staring at myself. My face was fuller than usual. My body was still tight from all the muscle I had built while training, but no longer frail and sickly. The dark court had done well for my overall health. I was pulling the brush through my hair when Eren appeared behind me. I followed him with my eyes in the mirror as he made his way to my side.

He looked down at me. "Are we going to talk about yesterday?" he said softly.

"I'd rather just focus on discussing how to control it," I said, without looking at him.

"I put your combat training on hold for the next few days until we can figure that part out. We don't need you in a room surrounded by males when you go off. It'd be a feeding frenzy," he said with a smile.

"Good idea. When do we begin?" I asked, walking over to my armoire. I pulled out a simple dress and changed into it out of his sight.

"Today. I thought it would be best to be somewhere less private while you learn. The grotto will be quiet, yet public enough."

268

"Where is that?"

"In the city, towards the bottom. We didn't get that far on the tour when you first arrived. I think you will enjoy it."

I followed him through the castle down into the city as we descended into the base of the mountain.

"Can we get some hot chocolate after?" I asked, remembering how good the drink was.

He smiled with a nod. "You're the princess, remember. You can have whatever you desire."

I rolled my eyes. *Not everything I desired*, I thought to myself. I kept quiet the rest of the journey. We finally entered a long narrow tunnel that curved back into an open cavern. A beautiful glowing pool of silver liquid sat in the center of the rocky surface. It shimmered and glistened as small beams of light illuminated the water from the bottom. Soft candlelight lit up the dim room.

Vibrant plant life surrounded the edges of the pool and climbed the walls of the cave. Diamond-like crystals hung from the ceiling, the light bouncing throughout their prisms. A table of fresh fruit and wine was in the back. Two other alfar were soaking lazily in the pool.

"Your verdict?" asked Eren.

"This should have been the first place you took me that day—after the hot chocolate, of course," I said, still in awe of the beauty that surrounded me.

"Come on, let's take a seat by the edge over here," he said, pushing me forward. The very touch of his skin to mine set my blood on fire.

I closed my eyes, pulling away from him as I tried to calm myself. "Maybe no touching," I said, as he stopped to look at me.

"You sound like Otar."

"It ... it sets me off. So, like I said, no touching." I followed him to the edge of the gorgeous pool. I dragged my hand through the liquid. It felt like pure silk. Warm and thicker than water, it fell off my skin without leaving any residue behind. Eren sat down with his legs crossed in front of him. I faced him, waiting for the lesson to begin.

"Do you remember what started the release yesterday?" he asked.

I nodded.

"Well, are you going to tell the class, or should I guess?"

"I remember. Now tell me what to do with it," I said firmly. I wasn't going to tell him that I had been undressing him with my eyes and obsessing over tracing my tongue along his imprint. Or the feeling of how good his skin tasted and felt. *Focus, Gen! Dammit!*

"Okay. Moving on. When I release my gift, I have to have physical contact, but I don't think that is the case with yours. I smelled your pheromones before you touched me. I have to focus on the physical contact between the other being and myself. The warmth of their skin to mine. This allows me to activate my power. When

I exhale, I relax and release the pheromones into the air. My touch to the person acts as a target for them to land onto.

"I can only affect those who I am touching. Since yours is airborne, you could possibly be able to control an entire room. What did you experience inside yourself when you noticed the change begin to happen yesterday?"

I closed my eyes. "I had a burning sensation that started deep inside of me. As it grew, it affected every nerve in my body, setting them on fire. I eventually lost complete control as my body begged me to—" I stopped, opening my eyes to see him smiling smugly. "I think you can fill in the blanks from there," I finished.

"So, I think your gift is hormone based. You will be able to control someone through lust," he said bluntly.

"Great, the one thing I love so much," I said.

"It is very powerful, believe me. If you can control yourself, you will be able to make others do whatever you desire. Now, about the controlling part. The best way to do that is for you to experience the feelings of the gift repeatedly until you get used to it and can project the pheromones out instead of allowing them to take hold of you. So, practice it is," he said, scooting closer to me.

"You want me to practice on you?" I asked in disbelief.

He nodded.

"But, what about yesterday? I would never forgive myself if something happened and I took advantage of you because of this stupid power."

He laughed, dropping his gaze to his lap. "Princess, you wouldn't be taking advantage of me, I promise," he said in a deep, sensual tone.

I dropped my eyes, a sense of excitement and warmth spreading through me at his admission.

"Plus," he continued, "I am the only one that stands a chance against your power. That is, until you master it. It will grow as you use it and learn to control it. Eventually, even I won't be able to resist you."

I tried to hide the satisfaction that brought me, but my face betrayed me. I turned my eyes to the pool, trying not to look at him. "So, what is first?" I asked.

"Activating the gift. We will start small. Try to do exactly what you did yesterday to get the warmth inside of you going. Then, once I feel it taking hold, I will tell you to stop. You will calm yourself, refocusing your mind on something else as the pheromones dissipate into the air."

I nodded, sitting up straight in front of him. He watched me closely.

"Can you—" I whispered shyly, "—can you close your eyes, please? I can't do it while you're looking at me." He did as I asked, exhaling deeply. His broad chest rising and falling. My gaze followed his neck up to his strong chiseled jaw and then to his lips. That was all I needed. Just to focus on those lips. I would have done almost anything to feel them against mine again. To feel that full, sensual mouth grazing across my neck, down my chest. Stopping at my breasts as he took my hard nipple into his mouth. Softly flicking it with that delicious tongue of his.

Without warning he flung forward towards me, taking my mouth with his passionately. I wrapped my arms around his neck, pulling myself on top of him. Our lips moved in sync, exploring and learning the way we both worked. He tightened his arms around my waist as his hands cupped my bottom, pulling my pelvis into him.

Stop, Gen, this isn't real, I thought to myself. *You need to stop.* "No!" I heard my body roar. I needed this, I wanted this more than anything. I forced my mouth to pull away from him, pushing myself off as I fell back onto the floor. He took a deep breath, shaking his head to clear it. I wiped my mouth, still able to taste him. I closed my eyes, reveling in the memory. He looked at me, running a hand through his now tousled hair.

"Sorry," I whispered.

"You stopped, that is what counts." He licked his lips and placed his arms over his knees. "Did you ... did you want me to kiss you?" he asked hesitantly.

Shit. I sat back up slowly, not wanting to answer.

"If we are going to figure this out," he said, still gasping for breath, "you have to answer my questions. It's nothing to be embarrassed about. You are dealing with a very potent power."

"Yes," I answered softly. "That was the last thing I was thinking about before you reacted."

"Interesting. No verbal command needed. How did you stop yourself?"

"The thought of me forcing you to do something physical. I couldn't," I said honestly.

He let a few minutes pass before continuing.

"If you're ready," he finally said as he regained control of himself, "let's try again. This time, I want you to use your fear of forcing me to do something I don't want as an anchor of sorts. Something you can hold onto or ground yourself with, so you won't go too far. Something that will allow you to pull yourself back from going completely over the edge. I want you to focus on that while projecting what you want from me. This way, you are still effective yet in control."

I nodded, taking a deep breath. "Keep your eyes open this time," I added. I focused myself, diving into those beautiful mercury eyes of his. I didn't smile, I didn't blink, I just focused. How did I not melt at the sight of him the first time I had seen him at the light court? He was a magnificent being in so many ways. I felt the warming inside of me begin.

I didn't let it take control this time. Instead, I focused on his touch. The way his skin felt against mine. He was gentle and tender, yet I felt his desire. I wanted his fingertips on my skin.

Eren looked into my eyes as he extended his hand out to my face ever so slowly. His fingers slid back against my cheek as he rubbed lightly. I leaned into his hand, closing my eyes to enjoy the moment more purely. Now, all I needed was his scent. A moment later, the air around me filled with whiskey and oranges.

I opened my eyes to see Eren still looking at me. His eyes were full of hunger and desire as his breathing deepened. He swallowed before slowly leaning in towards me. I took his hand from my face, holding it tightly.

"Eren stop," I whispered.

He brushed his lips against mine trying to get a response from me.

I dropped my head, putting out my hand to push him away. I took a deep breath in, trying to clear the air. "Eren," I said, pushing him further back. Finally, he blinked a few times as he came to.

He dragged his hands over his face and laughed. "I am going to need either a room full of females or a very cold shower after this," he said. "Okay, new development. You can control powers with your persuasion. Good to know."

"I think we're done for today," I said, getting to my feet. He pulled himself upright and chased after me.

"Gen, wait," he said.

I turned back to him. "I am fine. Really. It's just too much for today. I need to take this power slow." Without another word he nodded and followed me out of grotto and back into the city towards Hertus's cafe. We ordered our drinks and sat at the table outside of the cafe window.

"Are you up for one more challenge for today?" asked Eren.

"Does it involve you?" I asked.

"Not this time, princess."

"Why not?" I shrugged.

"You see those two behind me?" He said, nodding at an alfar female and male that sat at the table. "Project your pheromones to them, except this time, I want you to make them want each other. I think you've had enough action for one day," he said, winking at me.

I smiled, as my own plans for the two alfar took root. "Sure."

I focused on the couple, placing my cup on the table. I took a deep breath in, remembering the warmth that was inside of me that was now my new power. I exhaled powerfully and heavily as I pushed my power towards the couple, only enough to ignite the desire I could feel already there. Eren inhaled, closing his eyes as the scent wafted past him. The scent hit the couple causing their bodies to relax. Their eyes looked heavy and drugged as they slowly stood from their chairs.

They walked over to Eren, one on either side of him as he sat back in his chair with an eyebrow raised in my direction. They began sliding their hands down his arms and in his hair while he laughed, shaking his head in amusement. I smiled, standing from my seat.

"And where do you think you're going?" he asked.

"You said you needed a distraction after our lessons, so you're welcome. But I don't plan on sticking around to watch," I said, leaving him and the others behind me.

The next few days were trial and error. I was getting a grasp on my new power, but it was a constant battle to prevent it from taking complete control of me. Eren seemed to enjoy being teased to death, which didn't surprise me, but didn't help my position. I wanted him with the pheromones and without them. I took advantage of the brief moments where he lost control and touched or kissed me, but I couldn't enjoy it because I knew it wasn't real.

I finally told my father and uncle about my new development. My father didn't say much but my uncle was overjoyed. He asked questions and begged for a demonstration. He was definitely the more outgoing and enthusiastic brother.

My uncle and I continued our lunches every few days. He told me stories about my cousins growing up. He spoke of his late wife with admiration. My favorite stories were those about him and my father when they were young. They would get into so much trouble around the kingdom. The version of my father that he described didn't even seem plausible. He was so different from the one I had come to know and love.

I decided it was time to start practicing my gift with other alfar. I asked for Therosi's help one afternoon after my combat lesson. He was more than willing to assist. He was attractive and charming, so it would be easy to activate my gift, but he wasn't Eren. I couldn't fully control myself because of how badly I wanted Eren when we practiced, so I thought if I tried on another I didn't want, I might be able to stay in complete control.

We met on one of the ledges of the mountain. The wind was cold, and snow covered the rocky surface. I sat down on a blanket next to a fire the servants had created. Therosi strolled out from behind the wall with a bright smile on his face. I rose to my feet as he approached. He bowed, taking my hand, and kissing it softly.

"Princess Genevieve, I have been looking forward to this all day," he said, taking a seat on the blanket.

"Thank you for agreeing to help. I know it's an odd thing to ask."

"Not at all. I am honored to help my future wife in any way I can." He reached over, taking my hand in his.

I smiled, dropping my eyes to my lap. "Confident, are we?" I asked.

"You are quite the motivation, Genevieve."

I smiled, flattered by the compliment.

"Shall we begin?" he asked.

"Yes. All I need you to do is just sit there."

"I can do that," he said, smirking at me. I focused on his face, calming myself as I allowed the warmth to flood through my body. I exhaled deep and slowly as my pheromones flooded the air. Therosi inhaled, closing his eyes as the scent devoured him. When he reopened his eyes, they were full of hunger and lust.

I exhaled again, realizing I was able to keep myself calm and in complete control. I smiled, happy that my plan had worked. I felt his hand reach for my leg as I brought my eyes back up to his. He watched me intensely breathing in deeply again. I backed away, realizing what he wanted.

"Therosi, stop," I said, pulling away from his touch.

He reached for my face, gliding his fingers over my cheek. I turned away, holding my hand out to stop him from getting closer. My palm pressed into his firm chest, keeping him at bay. "Therosi, take a deep breath in. The pheromones are gone. You can clear your head now," I tried again.

He crawled over to me, only inches from being on top of me. He studied every detail of my face before leaning into my head softly. I pushed him away forcefully, realizing I couldn't snap him out of it. I got to my feet, putting as much space between him and me on the platform as I could.

He rose, moving towards me, reaching his hand out. I readied myself for a fight. Gods, I was stupid. What was I thinking asking him up here all by myself? I was still new to my gifts. I thought as long as the person wasn't Eren I would be able to control them.

He moved quickly towards. I pulled back my arm, ready to strike, when a ragamor slammed into the edge of the mountain ledge, sending us both to the ground. Therosi sat up, shaking his head as my power released its hold on him. He looked over at me as he stood.

Therosi rushed towards me, a hand outstretched to help me to my feet, when he fell to his knees, grabbing his head in pain. He screamed as his veins bulged from his forehead and neck.

Eren came up beside me, holding his hand out towards Therosi. He pulled me up with his free hand without even a look.

"Stop, let him go," I demanded to Eren. "It wasn't his fault, it was mine."

Eren dropped his hand as Therosi fell to all fours.

I rushed towards him, trying to help him to his feet. "I am so sorry. I didn't mean for you to get hurt," I said to him.

Therosi's eyes snapped to Eren, rage flooding over him. He threw out his hand towards him. Eren's skin began to burn red as sweat poured from his forehead. I looked back at Therosi. He was boiling Eren's blood from the inside.

"Therosi, stop it. Stop it now!" I demanded.

He dropped his hand, pushing himself up off the floor. I stood in between both males as they stared at each other.

"Are you okay?" I asked Eren.

He nodded.

"You?" I asked Therosi.

He gave me a small smile.

"Your power, by the way, is—" Therosi stopped, taking in a deep breath of satisfaction.

"What?" I asked.

"It's the most pleasurable thing I have ever experienced. I felt like I would die if I didn't touch you. Azeer, I thought I wanted you badly before, but now, after this—" Therosi took a step closer towards me.

I blushed, dropping my eyes.

He slid his fingers under my chin, bringing my eyes up to his. "I must have you, Genevieve. There is no other I want to possess as badly as I want you." He leaned his head, brushing his lips softly against mine.

Eren's hand slid in between us, pushing Therosi back away from me. "I think you've touched her enough for one day," Eren said with bite.

Therosi laughed. "I cannot wait until the day I marry her. Then, you will be sent back into the wild among the beasts where you belong," said Therosi. "Princess," he said, bowing towards me before leaving.

Eren turned towards me with a look of betrayal. "Planning on taking one of your future husbands for a test run, were you?" he asked.

"No, that was not my plan. I just thought I'd be able to control it if I tried it on someone else."

"And what made you think that?"

I didn't want to admit my feelings for him.

"Just a theory, which I was unsuccessful in proving, obviously."

He laughed, rubbing the back of his neck with his hand. "I came to tell you that I will be leaving and won't return until tomorrow. There are a few creatures that came through the rift this morning. A hunting party is leaving in the next hour to track them down."

"I'll go get ready. I'll meet you at the gates," I said, rushing past him.

He grabbed my arm to stop me. "No. You won't be coming this time. Jestu is tomorrow. Because of your position, you are required to attend, which means you're going to have to sit this one out."

I huffed, disappointed. "I have an idea. Why don't you stay, and I will go? You enjoy the celebration at least. I can't wait to get out of there."

He laughed, pulling me in closer towards him. "Unfortunately, that is not possible, but I like the way you think." He paused, looking down at me in silence for a moment. "Try not to use your power until I get back. Especially at Jestu. And for once, do as I tell you." He let go of my arm, pushing me gently away from him.

"What does my power feel like to you?" I asked nervously. He swallowed, placing his hands in his pockets and looking out into the horizon.

"Your power is maddening. In that moment, I'd rather die than not have you," he said without looking at me. "As the pheromones fade, so does the sensation, and I am able to recognize reality from illusion."

An illusion. Yes. That is all it was between us. A fantasy, not reality.

"Good luck on the hunt," I said, walking back into the castle without another look in his direction.

CHAPTER SEVENTEEN

I sat in the room as the court celebrated Jestu. Even though hundreds of alfar and humans surrounded me, I felt alone and as always, out of place. My hour finally up. I calmly made my way back to my room. I undressed, sliding a black, thin, silk negligee over my body. I let my curls down from the pins in my hair and removed the theatrical makeup, revealing the girl I knew.

"Glad to see you're still in one piece," said Eren, strolling into my room.

I turned around and moved to the bed where my robe was lying out for me. "Knock please, Eren," I said in aggravation.

"I will work on it," he said, as I tied the rope around my waist.

"Did you catch the creatures?"

"Every last one of them. I am effective, I will give myself that."

I let a small chuckle pass through my lips, standing with my arms folded in front of me. "Fishing for a compliment, are we?"

"I just spend the last day with a group of males who do not appreciate my finer qualities. I am entitled to a compliment now and then."

"Well, you won't be getting one from me. If you hurry, I am sure

Jestu is still in full swing. Maybe you can try your luck there."

"Princess, I'm hurt. I thought we were friends."

I smiled, pulling back the blanket to my bed. "As you can see," I said, trying to end the flirtatious banter, "I am alive and well. Your obligations are fulfilled."

He walked slowly towards me, taking a seat next to me on the edge of the bed. He was freshly washed, with a clean shirt and pants adorning his lovely body. "I'm curious ..." he started.

"Here we go," I said.

He elbowed me in the arm. "Why Therosi? Is he your top contender in the battle for your heart?"

"What? No. I hate that I have to marry someone I don't want. I've tried talking my father into letting me choose, but it's not the way of the dark court, as you well know. I just needed a change."

"Did I do something to make you feel uncomfortable? If I did, I apologize, that wasn't my intention. I fought your gift as hard as I could, I promise you."

"No, you did nothing wrong. You've done everything right," I said, fiddling with my hands on my lap.

"Then, why Therosi?"

"I needed someone that wasn't you," I admitted. He looked at me with confusion. I bit my lip and stood to pace in front of him. "I ... I needed someone I didn't ... oh for the love of Mary, I didn't desire," I finally blurted out. I brought a hand to my face nervously.

"Desire? But I just thought it was your power influencing you," he said softly.

"It just magnified what was already there," I said hesitantly. I brought my eyes back to him, watching as he thought in silence. He stood to his feet and made his way over to me. "I guess I am not broken anymore," I said playfully, trying to break the tension.

"You were never broken. A little banged up, but never broken."

"Maybe we should take a break from the whole training thing. I need to clear my head and refocus. Plus, with the sacrifice coming up and my impending marriage, I'd like to just focus on all of that for now."

"You can't run from it, Gen. You can't be afraid of your power either. You need to embrace it and learn how to control it. But maybe we can find you another teacher, so things don't get too out of hand," he said, smiling down at me.

"I'm sorry if I made you uncomfortable."

"Princess, you forget who you're talking to. Nothing about sex makes me uncomfortable, I can promise you that."

I laughed at him, gently removing his hands from my shoulders. I tried walking past him, but he grabbed onto my arm, holding me still. He bent his head down into mine, taking in a deep breath. I froze, not knowing what to make of the action.

His hand slowly moved down my arm to my waist stretching across my abdomen until his grip tightened. My heart pounded in my chest, every nerve on alert. I held in my pheromones, wanting this to be real, not an illusion. He pulled me into his body, combing his other hand through my hair until he made his way to my face. He traced his fingertips along my jaw to my lips, taking his time as I parted them slowly.

He pulled my chin up, so my eyes met his. I melted, loosing myself in the beautiful swirls. He was calm and gently, leaning down slowly into my face. He kissed me tenderly, moving from my forehead down my cheeks. His hand around my waist flexed as the other slid over the curve of my body.

He stopped at my lips, brushing his against mine. I welcomed the softness of his mouth. I stretched out my neck, bringing my lips closer. He kissed me faintly while his hands undid my robe. He pushed the fabric back from my shoulders allowing it to fall to the floor.

His hands slid down my bare arms as I reached up to take his mouth with mine again. I tangled my fingers in his hair, pulling his head down to me. I dragged my hands across his firm muscular chest, needing to feel the skin underneath. I pulled his shirt off, throwing it to the ground.

I turned my focus to his body, taking in every detail of his perfectly formed figure. He watched, brushing my hair from my neck. I kissed down his chest and then traced my fingers around his beautiful imprint. I felt his fingers slide under each of the thin straps of my negligee. He pulled them down to my arms and the silk fabric fell to the floor, leaving me in only my underwear.

He took a deep breath in, holding it as his hands traced the outlines of my breasts and abdomen. His thumb circled my nipple tenderly, and he watched as my body lit up from the action. I stepped into him, needing to feel my body consumed by his.

My bare breasts pressed against his smooth silky skin. He took my mouth again, sliding his hands under my bottom as he lifted me into the air. I wrapped my arms around him, kissing his neck as he carried me to the bed. I never wanted the connection to end.

He placed me down at the edge. I scooted back, slowly removing my underwear while he watched my every action. I tossed them to the side, leaving me completely bare in front of him. I laid back and spread my legs for him as an invitation. He stared at me for a few moments without moving. His breathing was heavy. His eyes scoured my body.

He moved to the bed, sliding his hands up my legs, kissing my knees, working his way up. His soft and tender mouth dragged up my abdomen and in between my breasts before he kissed my lips.

He allowed his body to press fully against mine. I could feel his hardness beneath his pants, begging to be let free. I reached down to undo the tie. He grabbed my hand, preventing me from continuing. His heavy eyes looked up at me. His lips parted revealing that devilish grin I had come to adore. He shook his head, telling me to wait.

He took my nipples into his mouth, swirling his powerful tongue around each just like I imagined him doing. I arched my back, pressing more of my chest into his mouth. I moaned with pleasure from the sensation that each lick, bite, and suck caused me to feel. The heat between my legs grew, causing my sex to become wet and swollen. This need ... this desire was one I had never experienced before ... and now that I had ... I never wanted to be without.

He made his way back down my stomach and then to my inner thighs. He teased the area at first, before finally allowing his mouth to consume the most sensitive part of me. His tongue gently licked from the bottom up, causing my entire body to shutter from the action. Before I could take another breath, he pressed a kiss to my sex, causing me to whimper.

As his lips moved across my wet center, my legs began to shake uncontrollably while my insides throbbed and begged to be filled. I ran my hands through his hair as he pleasured me in the most satisfying way I could have ever imagined. He started fast, slowing as the sensation built before taking me into his mouth fully holding me there until the feeling was too much.

After a few moments, my body couldn't take it anymore. A powerful release came causing my pheromones to spill from my body. He breathed in deeply, moaning with delight. He rose and stood at the edge of the bed. I slid down to the floor, still sated from his talents. I looked up at him as I untied his pants. I pushed them past his perfectly toned legs down to the floor. His hardness was long and thick.

I took it in my hands, stroking him gently while I studied what he liked. His head fell back as his body tensed from my action. I tenderly kissed the tip of him while both of my hands continued to slide down his shaft. My tongue, traced the head of his dick, tasting him with each pass.

The taste of him was maddening. How smooth and soft he was in my mouth caused me to lose control. I quickened my pace, needing to take more of him, needing to please him any way I could. His fingers tangled through my hair.

I moved in rhythm, making sure to trace my tongue along the base and tip. He pulled my head back, picking me up as he bent down to take my mouth with his. He wound his arms around my waist before misting us onto the bed. His body pressed me firmly into the mattress while his hands traced every curve.

I wrapped my legs around his hips, begging him to enter me. With him, I no longer felt scared or repulsed by the act. I wanted to please him. I wanted him to take me and use me however he wished. I wanted this. I wanted Eren.

He moved his length, positioning it at my entrance. I was already warm and wet, completely prepared for him. He moved his lips down to my neck and I heard his breath panting. My hands traveled across his strong broad back as I tilted my hips up to him. He hovered over me with his eyes closed before gently pushing against my entrance. I watched his expressions closely noting the pleasure he found once inside of me.

He was larger than anyone I had known, but I didn't pull away. I wanted him to consume me. I wanted all of him. I felt him slide against my walls as I let out an uncontrollable moan of ecstasy. He opened his eyes, looking down upon my face. I breathed heavily, allowing my body to adjust to him. Finally, he reached the depth of me, fully buried inside. He bent down and kissed me softly.

He moved in and out slowly at first, making sure I was okay. He was being gentle, too gentle. I knew why, and though a part of me adored him for it, that wasn't what I wanted. I wanted to know Erendrial completely. I took his face in my hands, pulling his eyes to mine.

"You don't have to be so gentle," I said softly.

He smiled, kissing my lips. "I want this to be enjoyable for you."

"It is, but I want you to take me the way you desire. I'm not glass. I won't break."

He smiled, taking my mouth with his. His hands tightened around my waist as the motions of his thrust became harder and more passionate. I yelled with pleasure as his body caused mine to release. Lavender and sandalwood filled the air, along with whiskey and oranges. We breathed in, drugged by each other's scent.

He sat up on his knees, taking my legs in his arms and placing them around his shoulders, allowing him to thrust deeper. I felt my insides clench as he moved. Everything inside of me erupted. I needed more of him, somehow, I needed more. I sat up onto his lap. As he continued to slam against me, I bit and scratched and sucked on every inch of skin I could get my hands on. He did the same, taking my neck into his mouth and sucking hard until my skin felt bruised.

I arched back and moaned as he left no inch of my body unexplored. I pushed him down against the bed, slowing for a moment allowing me to appreciate his beautiful figure. His silver eyes flickered as his mouth parted seductively. I caressed his chest down to his abs, tracing the ridges and grooves with my fingers. His hands tightened on my hips as one of his thumbs found its way to the bundle of nerves between my legs.

I began to move on top of him, slowly at first. His finger swirled around the sensitive area. I gradually picked up my pace. Eren closed his eyes as his entire face tensed. I felt my pheromones release again as the warmth inside me burned hot like fire. I yelled in pleasure as he roared, coming to a finish. Our bodies were both damp with sweat from our dalliance.

I collapsed onto his chest, wrapping my arms around him and closing my eyes in complete satisfaction. I felt a smile stretch across my face followed by a small laugh as I listened to the beating of his heart. His breathing finally calmed as we both relaxed.

A few moments passed before I realized he wasn't touching me. His arms and hands were out to his sides, not making contact with me whatsoever. I unraveled my embrace and pushed myself up to look at him. His face was tilted to the side and his eyes refused to meet mine. I felt my heart drop into the pit of my stomach.

Something was wrong.

I pushed off to the side of the mattress, grabbing the covers and pulling them up to my chest. As soon as he was free of me, he got to his feet, collected his clothes and dressed without a single glance in my direction. I pulled my knees into my stomach, trying to figure out where it had gone wrong. He slid his boots on, before reaching for his shirt.

"Did I do something wrong?" I whispered.

He stopped, rubbing his forehead with his hand. "This was a mistake. I shouldn't have—it can't happen again," he said.

My perfect moment evaporated. Everything about our time together was perfect. Every kiss, every touch. How could it be a mistake when it felt so right?

"Okay," I replied disappointedly. I held my face down, tightly gripping the blanket to my chest. It took everything in me to hold back the tears that fought to be released.

"Look. I can't effectively do my job if I am sharing a bed with my future queen. Our relationship, even a purely sexual one, would get in the way of my influence and my objectives. Also ... I can't give you what you want."

"And ... what do I want?" I asked.

He turned towards me, still unable to make eye contact. "At the end of ... of whatever this was, you were waiting for me to hold you. You want emotion and monogamy. Two things I am incapable of giving."

I felt my chin begin to quiver, but I hid it as best as I could. Eren turned without another word and left my chambers. Tears fell from my face, but I did not sob. I felt like a hole had been carved out of my chest. I thought after we were together, he would feel the same, but I was wrong.

The first sexual experience I chose to explore after everything, and I chose to have it with Erendrial Lyklor. I knew how this would turn out, but still, somewhere I couldn't help but hope. I lowered my head, still holding onto the covers. I pulled the pillow his head had just occupied to my face. I inhaled, still able to smell the scent of oranges and whiskey. My body felt amazing, but my heart was once again shattered.

Chapter Eighteen

*B*e strong. *Be brave. Don't let your weakness show. Bury your emotions. Be more alfar than human.* I stood in front of the mirror, telling myself this over and over again in my head. I made my way to combat practice and worked off my aggravation and anger on Toreon and Varches. The twins still couldn't figure out why my black weapon radiated green instead of blue, which hurt their egos.

I made my way to lunch with my uncle, where we discussed light court relations and political matters. It was a good distraction from the failure that was my personal life. I retreated to the library after and found a dark corner to curl up in and escape from reality into a fictional world.

Lily caught up with me before I returned to my room to prepare for dinner. She could tell something was off, but I just blamed it on court matters. In the hall, I passed by Icici and a group of males. She smiled mockingly as if she knew what had occurred the night before. The very sight of her made my stomach turn. I didn't allow myself to think about her and Eren together. I couldn't.

Atalee prepared my hair and makeup in silence. Snow began to fall outside on the balcony. It was peaceful as I went outside and caught the small flakes on my fingers, stretching out my tongue to welcome the frozen delight. That night, I picked a light blue dress to honor the snow. It was a lighter color than anyone in the court ever wore, but I didn't care; I was a royal.

The dress was made entirely of lace, allowing you to see most of my skin underneath. I paired it with my silver crown and crystal earrings. I touched the small star pendant around my neck. I was free. That was all that mattered. I walked over to the door as Atalee made her way out. Eren stood outside, waiting to escort me to the throne room.

I gave him a small smile as the guards closed the doors behind me. He looked me up and down slowly, taking note of the dress. I ignored his glance, remembering his words from the night before. He extended his arm to me, and I took it as if nothing had happened. The very feeling of his touch was hard to bear.

"Are we good?" he asked coldly.

"Of course," I said, trying to sound unfazed. "A fuck is just a fuck."

He turned his head towards me in surprise, but I didn't allow my mask to fall.

I maintained my cool and collected composure for the next few weeks, even though my heart remained empty and heavy. Eren acted normal, as if nothing had happened. He made jokes, which I laughed at, trying to return to our normal banter. At night when

I closed my eyes, I would dream of Eren with Icici. I heard their sounds of pleasure, saw the joy in both of their faces as his hands devoured her body. I would wake, heart heavy and eyes full.

I used the projection sphere to replay the memory of our night together. I searched for signs of regret on his face, but there were none. There was desire, longing, intimacy, and passion. I swore there was feeling in his eyes, but I feared I was just seeing what I wanted to see.

One night after dinner, Eren was escorting me back to my room when Icici stopped us in the hall. She bowed politely as she looked from Eren to me. Her dark eyebrows raised as her cold eyes narrowed on me. *Great, here we go again.*

"Cousin, I've recently learned we have more in common than just our blood," she said.

"You can read too? Oh, wow, I am so happy for you," I said.

She snickered, raising her head higher than mine. She leaned into my ear and spoke loud enough that Eren could hear. "His tongue is my favorite part. The way he devours your sex, starting fast and then slowing right before he holds your orgasm, prolonging the pleasure, causing you to completely loose control. Oh, and let's not forget how wonderful that dark head of hair looks in between our legs," she said.

"Don't you have somewhere to be, Icici?" asked Eren.

My throat closed and my heart managed to crumble a little more as she described the same experience I had with him.

"Is that an invitation, ambassador?" she asked. She looked back at me and smiled. "Though, I was surprised when my eyes and ears informed me that the whole process only took about ten minutes before he ran out of your chambers. He usually takes me at least six times before the sun even rises. Each session lasting, what Eren, an hour at the least? Though, by the look of you," she said, pausing to look me up and down. "I can understand why he left without seconds. I can't blame him. He obviously prefers me over you." She smirked before moving on.

I clenched my fists together to avoid ripping her head off with my bare hands. I didn't even look at Eren. I couldn't. I straightened my posture and made my way back to my room without a word.

That night, I told the guards I would receive no visitors. I got ready for bed and tried to push Icici from my mind. As I brushed my hair my stomach began to turn. I barely made it to the bathroom before I vomited up my entire dinner. I didn't feel unwell. I blamed it on my bitch of a cousin.

The next day I buried myself in politics. My father had chosen three humans that would be sacrificed to Azeer. I read over their profiles carefully. An 83-year-old man with bad lungs. A 38-year-old woman who had lost her whole family to sickness and wished to join them. And a 53-year-old man who was a killer and rapist. What a batch.

Eren entered the meeting room I was currently occupying. I smiled at him, turning my attention back to my papers. He walked over casually, peeking over my shoulder. "Human sacrifices have been chosen?" he asked.

"Yup. A sick old man, a lonely widow, and a rapist. Azeer will be pleased," I said.

He chuckled to himself. "He hasn't complained yet, so I would trust your father's judgment."

I nodded, pushing the papers back into the black folder as I sat back in my chair. Eren perched on the table corner near me. "Listen, about Icici—"

"Eren, please, there's nothing to talk about," I said, pulling a book in front of me.

He was silent for a few moments. "I don't prefer her over you, and our encounter didn't last as long because of how enjoyable it was," he said quickly, as if he had to get it out.

I rubbed my temples, not in the mood for this conversation. "My cousin has a unique personality," I said, not knowing what else to say.

"She's just doing this to rattle you. She thinks if your mind is distracted, you will be an easy target for her to taunt and terrorize."

"But why? What have I ever done to her?"

"Icici sees everyone as competition. It's her defect. She is used to being the most beautiful and charming female in the room." He paused, placing his hands in his pockets and shifting his eyes to the floor. "Ever since you were introduced, that is no longer the case."

I pushed the small flutter of his flattering comment down into the base of my stomach, trying not to read too much into it. "I don't need any more distractions, especially where the two of you are concerned, believe me."

"What do you mean?"

I exhaled in frustration. "Ever since you and I were ... together, I've dreamt of you and Icici in that way. For whatever reason, my mind likes to torture me with too many details I don't wish to speak of."

He exhaled in annoyance as he stood to his feet.

"What?"

"Come on, Gen, think. Why would you have the same dream every night? If it's not a vision, then where is it coming from?" he asked, leaning in towards me.

Shit. Icici's gift was power over nightmares. "She's been toying with my mind for weeks," I said in astonishment.

"Yes, and it isn't the first time. She was the one who constructed all those rape dreams when you were dealing with the aftermath of Lysanthier."

"That bitch! Why are you just now telling me?"

"I informed your father and he put a stop to it. He didn't want you to know, just in case there was a chance of you two mending your relationship."

"I am going to cut off every one of her limbs and feed her to the fairies," I said with a sneer.

"Oh, that reminds me. We are receiving the fairy court tonight at dinner," he said.

"You are just full of information, aren't you," I snapped, standing to my feet. "What will my father do to Icici?"

"I don't know, but I am sure it isn't anything pleasant."

"When you tell him, please leave the details of the dream out. I don't want him knowing we—"

"Of course, neither do I," he said, smiling at me. "Oh, and cover up tonight. As little skin exposed as possible. It makes them hungry. So that means the blue dress and diamond dress are off-limits."

"You're memorizing my wardrobe now?"

"Only the ones worth remembering," he said, winking at me.

"Tell me about them. The fairy king and queen," I said, changing the subject.

"The rulers are a brother and sister. Twins. Who are also married."

"Why does their race still exist?" I said, disgusted even more by them.

"Strong, fast, they fly, they're reckless and unfeeling. Brutal, underground hives. Would you like me to continue?"

"Smartass," I said, feeling my stomach begin to turn. Before I could say another word, I rushed over to the wastebasket and threw up, feeling dizzy and clammy. I pulled my head from the bucket as Eren offered me his handkerchief.

"Everything alright?" he asked concernedly.

"Yeah, I must have eaten something that didn't settle right. I don't feel ill," I said, thinking back to last night's vomit session.

"Anyways, their names are Pyra and Phasis. Ten other fairies will be attending. They will only be staying a night. They are coming to discuss a dispute between the nymphs and their hive."

"Always fun at the dark court," I said, walking towards the door. The sigil in my left wrist began to burn as the arrow spun, leading me towards Otar's dead body. I gasped in pain. "Dammit, Otar. You pick the most inconvenient times to get yourself killed," I yelled, holding my wrist.

Eren laughed. "Come on. We should have time to find the little fucker before dinner."

We found Otar's body on the bank of a lake that was fed by a large waterfall. We brought him back to the castle and Eren waited outside until I resurrected him. Once he came to, Eren re-entered, curious what had killed him this time.

"Very grateful, yes very grateful as always, wicked one," Otar said, shaking the ash off.

"What got you this week?" asked Eren.

Otar sneered at him. "I am not talking to you, ungrateful alfar bastard," he said, turning his back to him.

"What did I do now?" asked Eren.

Otar appeared in front of him, teeth bared. "Do not play stupid. Stupid is the last thing you are. You know exactly what you did you selfish, narcissistic pansy. Someday, I swear to you that I will cut off your precious dick and I will shove it down that smart mouth of yours. Then, I will take your puny testicles and replace your eyeballs with them," spat Otar. He must have sensed my pain after Eren's and my relations.

"Otar, please tell us what killed you," I said, trying to get his attention.

He calmed at the sound of my voice, backing away from Eren to where I was sitting in a chair. He sat on the floor and laid his head on my lap, placing my hand on his head. "As you wish, wicked one. It was a harpy this time. I tried to make sex with it and she attacked me. I defended myself, but I was still turned on and distracted. I leaned in to take a bite, and she shoved her sword through my heart and threw me over the waterfall, where I drowned."

I snickered, covering my mouth with my hand. "You tried to have sex with a harpy?" I asked. "I didn't even know you had sex, Otar."

"I've learned a thing or two at your delicious court, wicked one. Some of your subjects even enjoy me," he said, lifting his head to smile at me. Suddenly, Otar grabbed his head in pain as a loud and unsettling scream erupted from deep inside of him. I looked to

Eren to see if he was hurting him, but he looked as confused as I was. I reached out to comfort Otar, but a third arm came flying out of his side, slashing into my arm.

Eren appeared, pulling me away from him. He turned to attack Otar, but I stopped him.

"No, wait," I said, concerningly. "He's in pain. He didn't mean to. It was just a reaction,"

"You forget what he is, Genevieve," Eren huffed. "You are too trusting with it."

Otar finally relaxed, looking down at my blood that dripped from his talons. He looked at my arm as Eren wrapped it in a clean cloth. Otar made his way over to me hesitantly.

Eren held out his hand to stop him. "That's close enough, you reckless fuck."

"I ... I never want to hurt the wicked one. I never would," he said, looking sad for the first time.

"It's just a scratch, I'll be fine. Are you okay?" I asked.

"I ... I remembered," he said with excitement.

"Remember what?" I asked.

"Narella. She works for a male. An alfar who has great power. He is from this world, but not. His name is Alaric. He takes and takes and then controls," said Otar as he began to pace from side to side. Eren and I both perked up, eager for the information.

"What else, Otar?" I asked.

"He wants more power, more gifts. That is why he has come

here. He is after the—" Otar stopped, scratching at his head. "He's after ... Ah, fuck, it is gone!" he yelled, kicking my bedpost repeatedly.

"Otar, it is okay. You've given us a lot. You will remember in time. You did good," I said.

He smiled, making his way over to me. He glared at Eren who was standing on the other side of my chair. Otar leaned into my face, secretively. He pointed his finger at me as his expression turned serious.

"He does not deserve the gift. Do not tell him of the gift. It is your gift and my gift, you hear me? You hear me, wicked one?" he snapped.

I looked at him, confused. His eyes flickered to Eren and then back to me. I nodded, still unsure of what he was talking about. He smiled and then disappeared from in front of me.

"What secret are you two keeping? Now that I know the thing can have sex, my mind is spiraling with possibilities," said Eren.

"Seriously? What is wrong with you?" I asked in annoyance.

"Your gift, his gift. It must be some gift," he said, winking at me.

Atalee entered the room to prepare me for dinner. "Atalee, sweetheart," Eren said, "cover the princess as much as possible. No skin showing beside her face." He turned back to me. "I will not be here to escort you. Therosi will have that honor. You can thank your uncle for that. I will be preparing for the fairy court, so I will see you at dinner." He bowed, leaving the room.

I moved to the vanity as Atalee pulled thick dresses from the armoire.

"Atalee, change of plans for tonight's look," I said, smiling at myself in the mirror.

CHAPTER NINETEEN

By the time I was finished, I looked like I belonged in a brothel. My hair was slicked back into a tight bun that sat at the base of my neck. Diamonds scattered throughout my dark hair. I wore a formfitting, see-through red dress. There were small pieces of red lace that covered my nipples, bottom, and front, but everything else was on full display. Two long slits rode up both of my thighs to my hips, revealing my hip bones. My arms were bare, and my back exposed. I wore a bright red lip and gold diamond earrings.

I made my way to the door where Therosi was waiting. His mouth fell open as I exited. I smiled, flattered by his reaction.

"Trying to make a statement, are we?" he asked, extending his arm to me.

I took it as we headed towards the throne room.

"Just trying to piss Lyklor off," I said, walking with pride.

"Need any help from me?" he asked with a wink.

"I'll keep you in mind."

We got to the doors as the announcer called my name. I dropped Therosi's arm as the doors opened. I walked with pride and power to my throne. My father rose, kissing my cheek before we took our places. Eren stood off to the side, shaking his head, annoyance on his face. I smiled, satisfied with myself.

The fairies entered five minutes later and made their way to the platform. Pyra was uniquely beautiful in her own way. The fairy's sharp teeth were retracted to reveal a set of human-like teeth. Pyra had long red hair that trailed to the floor. Her blue-tinted skin shimmered. Her chocolate-brown eyes took up most of her face. Her features were long and sharp, like most of her race. Her body was lean with not a trace of fat. She wore a thin gold leather dress that accentuated her breasts.

Her brother had long silver hair that trailed down his back. He had thin lips and a strong jaw, with a wider-built body than his sister but still very lean. He wore a black leather vest trimmed with gold and tight-fitting pants. His chocolate-brown eyes, rimmed with silver lashes, locked onto me, taking me in as if I were his favorite dessert. I smiled and nodded at him, egging him on. He smiled back and bowed.

"King Drezmore, Princess Genevieve, thank you for receiving us at your court," said Phasis.

"We are honored to be in your presence again," added Pyra.

"We welcome you to Doonak," greeted my father. "I am glad our friendship continues to flourish, even during these times of uncertainty. Please, join us." He, gestured to our dining table. They nodded and the servants showed them to their seats. We followed behind our guests as the court began to feast. My uncle sat next to my father and Eren sat next to me. Pyra was across from my father, gazing down the table at Eren, and Phasis was placed across from me.

"What in the fuck are you wearing?" whispered Eren in an aggravated tone.

"A dress," I responded.

"I didn't give you those instructions for my benefit. Phasis already wants to rip your skin off by the looks of it."

"Then we can use that to our advantage."

He pulled back, looking at me as if I had lost my mind. Phasis was indeed staring with a glimmer of desire and greed. I smiled back, making sure he knew I saw him. Eren kicked me under the table to stop. I took my fork and slammed it into his leg. He groaned, leaning forward in pain.

"Please, tell us what has occurred between you and the nymphs," said my father.

"They have accused us of stealing their goods and taking their people as food," started Pyra.

"We have done neither of these things, yet the light court is now involved, demanding justice for the lost nymphs," continued Phasis.

"We have flown over their lands, yes, but we are not stupid," Pyra said with a sneer.

"We do not eat nymphs. They are too woody and watery for our liking. Besides fucking, they aren't good for much else," added

Phasis.

"Now, the light court has begun to send infantries into our lands. They take and beat and threaten our people. They have brought some of our court back to Urial for interrogation," said Pyra.

"They have disarmed our traps, scared off our animal food sources, and have attacked our hives," said Phasis.

"We have tried to send our ambassador to their court, but they will not receive us. We've heard that you've recently made peace with the light court," Pyra said with a gleam in her eye. She looked to me and smiled widely.

"After the brilliant actions your daughter took against their former king and members of their court," Phasis said, winking at me with a seductive smile.

"We were hoping you could speak on our behalf. Act as the middle line of communication between us and the light court," Pyra pleaded.

"We cannot afford to go to war with the light court and the nymphs while protecting our people from the creatures of the rift," Phasis explained.

The twins' connection apparently allowed them to finish each other's sentences seamlessly. It was interesting to watch them interact with one another. I finished my first course and sat back in my chair. I spread my arms across the armrest, arching my back so my chest was protruding out towards Phasis. *Let's see how pissed I can make Eren.*

"What proof does the court have of your crimes?" asked Eren, glancing sideways at me.

"Only nymph witnesses. The light court sent a group of their warriors to the nymphs' village three months ago," Phasis continued.

"We swear on our treaty, we have not taken their people," Pyra spat.

"And we should be able to at least fly over their territory. We wouldn't set foot on their land, but the air is free space. They ask too much," Phasis growled.

The king looked to Eren and nodded. "I will make contact with both the light and nymph ambassador in the morning," Eren said. "I will attempt to arrange a sit down with the four of us so we can clear your name and negotiate the terms of your treaty with the nymphs."

Phasis and Pyra both grinned, looking at each other and then us. It was disturbing to say the least.

"We thank you for your assistance," Phasis said.

"We remain in your debt, as always," added Pyra.

Phasis's eyes never left me, which made eating a bit uncomfortable, but I welcomed the attention. Pyra was talking to my father and uncle as the plates were cleared from the table. Phasis leaned casually forward.

"The black creature, he is yours, is he not?" Phasis asked me.

My eyes widened, remembering Otar's tiff with the fairies. "He is," I answered.

Phasis chuckled in amusement. "He is quite entertaining. I think we've killed him three times now and yet he keeps coming back for more."

"Yes, he doesn't like your kind very much."

Phasis eyes deepened as if he was trying to devour me. "We can be ... misunderstood. As the dark court often is. We are not as bad as other races like to make us out to be."

"Really? Because I've almost been eaten twice, thanks to your kind."

"Tell me their names and I will deliver you their heads by morning." He smiled.

"It doesn't change the fact that your appetite for human flesh is a bit excessive."

"Princess Genevieve, when I look at you, I cannot deny that hunger grows inside of me, but I wouldn't eat you. At least, not in the way you are thinking."

I swallowed hard at his blunt declaration of desire. He smiled, leaning back into his chair as he watched me squirm. Eren looked at me as if to say, 'you deserve this'.

"Are you usually this direct, King Phasis?" I asked.

"Only when I see something I desire." He stood, walking around the table towards me. He held out his hand. "May I have the pleasure of this dance?"

"King Phasis," my father interrupted in a protective tone, "please remember who you will be touching, and her importance and station."

"How could I ever forget?" Phasis replied.

I took a deep breath and gave him my hand. He gently wrapped his long fingers around mine as he led me to the dance floor. He pulled me into his chest, placing his hand on my bare back as he began to lead.

"You're so ... warm," I pointed out. Being this close to him was like bathing in the sun on a late summer afternoon. "I'm sorry, was that rude?"

He chuckled. "No, not at all. I am warmer than humans, yes. It's how our bodies produce more energy to fly. Do you enjoy it?" he asked.

"It is comforting, yes," I replied honestly.

"You are stunning, by the way. I am very pleased with the outcome of an alfar and human. They should make more of you."

I laughed, taken off guard. "Thank you, but unfortunately not everyone shares your opinion."

"Their loss," he said, reaching his hand up, drawing a finger along my collarbone. "I want you."

I swallowed hard again. "I don't know how to respond to that," I said honestly.

"Agree, and I will spend what time I have left here serving you in every way your mind can fathom. I've never seen anything like you before, and I am desperate to have you. To see how your body moves, what sounds you make, what you taste like." We stopped moving as his eyes drilled into mine.

"I ... I," I stuttered, uncomfortable by his boldness.

"Please princess. I've never begged for anything in my life, but I will beg for you if that is what it takes."

"May I cut in?" Eren said, bowing to us both.

"No," snapped Phasis, in the same way Cerci, the fairy I had encountered back at the light court, had reacted to a challenge. The untamed animal underneath the pretty clothes and polite manners made his appearance at last.

Eren smiled, taking my hand slowly as he pulled me from Phasis's clutches. "King Phasis, King Drezmore would like to consult you on negotiation tactics for the upcoming meeting with the light court. Your presence has been requested," said Eren calmly.

Phasis exhaled, turning his head back to me. "Consider my offer. Please, princess," he said, kissing me softly on the cheek with his warm lips. He backed away, not taking his eyes from me.

Eren pulled me into him as we continued to dance. "Satisfied?" he asked.

"More like thoroughly disturbed, and yet slightly turned on," I said, trying to get a rise out of him.

He started laughing as his grip tightened. "You are going to get killed."

"Not intentionally. Phasis promised he wouldn't eat me, so

there's that."

"He may not kill you, but he will take a few bites out of you. I guess that's fine if you're into that."

"How do you know?" I asked curiously.

He exhaled. "I had just been appointed ambassador. I was young and stupid and slept with Pyra during my first visit to their hive. She took bites out of me so deep that the wounds took days to heal."

I started laughing uncontrollably. The court looked at me like I was crazy, but I couldn't help myself.

He smirked, trying to swallow his laughter as he held my shaking body.

"You were an idiot in your youth, weren't you?"

"I was too smart for my own good. Needless to say, I learned my lesson."

"Well, maybe her brother isn't like that. The things he promised seemed enjoyable enough. After all, he did beg."

"Oh, did he?"

I nodded with a smile.

"You should be honored," said Eren, before leaning into my ear to whisper, "but under no circumstance are you to be alone with him. I am serious, Genevieve," he said firmly.

"But he's so warm," I said playfully.

He pulled back, looking as if he was offended. "If I remember correctly, we were both rather warm after our dalliance. Heat was not the problem."

I dropped my eyes, pulling away from him. "I thought we were done talking about what happened between you and I?"

He stepped in closer towards me, taking me back in his arms. "I didn't realize it was a sore spot for you. I am sorry."

"Yeah, being called a mistake less than five minutes after the act will cause that type of behavior," I said.

"You weren't a mistake, but the act was. I already explained and you know how much I hate repeating myself."

"I remember." The turning in my stomach started again. I tried to swallow to make the puking sensation go away. I pulled away from Eren, running out of the room into the hall. I found a potted plant just in time to relieve myself of my dinner. I hugged the vase, feeling like a disgusting mess.

"That can't be good for the plant," commented Eren, holding out a handkerchief for me. I took it and stood to my feet. "I'm going to have Vena come to your room and check you out. Twice in one day isn't a good sign. Also, there will be extra guards stationed at your door. Remember what I told you. Under no circumstance are you to—"

"Yes, yes, I know. I won't sleep with the handsome fairy king," I said.

He tilted his head, as if to ask, 'are you serious?'. "Go back to your room. I will get Vena," he said, signaling to two guards to escort me.

Atalee helped me out of the dress as I wiped the makeup off my face. I got into my nightgown as Vena and Lily came into the room. Atalee left as I got into bed.

"What is going on? Are you okay?" asked Lily, crawling on the bed towards me.

"Eren says you've thrown up twice today?" asked Vena. "Have you eaten anything odd or noticed any other side effects?"

"No. I get a little dizzy before I throw up, but I feel fine otherwise. It started yesterday," I replied.

"Well, lay back and let me take a look," said Vena. She started from the top, running her hands from my head, down my face to my chest. She checked both arms slowly and then moved to my abdomen. She ran her hands down towards my legs but stopped before she went any further. She pressed her hands against my stomach while she concentrated.

"What? What is it? Did you find anything?" asked Lily.

"Shh," demanded Vena as she focused. Her eyes widened before she pulled her hands away from me. She swallowed hard, bringing her eyes to mine, covering her mouth with her hands as a smile sprouted on her face.

"What is wrong with me?" I asked, bringing myself to a seated position.

"You're ... pregnant," she said slowly.

I felt like the wind had been knocked out of me. Lily gasped.

"What?" I whispered in shock.

"You're about four weeks pregnant. I can hear a faint heartbeat, but it is strong for this early in the developmental stage. I can also feel the dark magic it already contains. You're going to have a strong one on your hands," she said, smiling faintly.

I shook my head, reaching for my stomach. "No, no I can't be pregnant. I can't. This isn't happening," I said, starting to freak out. Lily grabbed my hand for support. I turned back to Vena. "What happens if they find out I am pregnant? I'm not even married yet."

"Since you are the heir, nothing. The baby will be safe and next in line to the throne, but the alliance your father plans to make with your marriage may be in jeopardy. Unless the child is one of theirs," said Vena.

"No, it isn't," I admitted.

"Who is the father, Gen?" asked Lily.

I looked at her and shook my head. "It doesn't matter. He wouldn't want it. What do you suggest I do, Vena?" I asked.

She looked uncomfortable. "We can get rid of it if you don't want it. It will be painless and quick. If you want to keep it, I suggest trying to move up a marriage as soon as possible so you can pass the child off as your husband's. Do you want to keep it?" Vena asked.

"I ... I don't know," I admitted. Lily squeezed my hand. I looked back at Vena with assertiveness. "Vena, please, do not tell anyone about this. I am begging you. I know you are loyal to your family, but please. No one can know."

"Gen, you are my family too. This is your business, no one else's. Your secret is safe with me, no matter what you choose. You can trust me," she said, touching the side of my face.

"Thank you," I said as a tear escaped my eye.

"Of course. I will give you two some privacy. I need to get back to dinner anyways. If you need anything, don't hesitate to send for me." I nodded as she left. I turned to Lily and began to sob.

She took me in her arms.

"I don't understand how this could have happened," I whispered. "I was with Gaelin multiple times and never got pregnant. I thought alfar had a hard time getting pregnant. It was supposed to take years, decades even. I was with him one night, one damn night and this happens," I said, pulling away from Lily.

"Gen, who is the father? Maybe he can help," Lily said.

I shook my head. "He called our night together a mistake. He regrets it. Plus, he hates children. He'd most likely tell me to get rid of it or even do it himself."

"Are you going to ... get rid of it?" she asked. I squeezed my hand against my stomach. There was something living inside of me that I had created. An innocent child. It didn't ask to be born, yet here it was growing and thriving within me. Vena said the little one was already powerful. A fighter, just like its parents. I smiled at that fact.

Something inside of my heart bloomed in that moment.

Though I had only known of its existence for ten minutes I already loved it. I wanted to protect it and care for it. I looked at Lily and smiled.

"I'm going to keep it," I whispered.

She smiled, throwing her arms around me with a little laugh. "I'm going to be an auntie," she yelled, clapping. I laughed at her. "A child is a gift, never forget that." Her words triggered the conversation from earlier today with Otar. My eyes widened in shock.

"Otar!" I yelled, getting up from the bed. "Otar! Come here!" He appeared next to Lily.

She screamed, falling off the side of the bed. "I am never going to get used to that," she said, standing to her feet.

He chuckled, turning his attention to me. "You yelled, wicked one."

"The gift you talked about earlier. It was the baby, wasn't it? You were talking about my child," I said in a panic.

"Well of course. It is *our* child," he said.

"What are you talking about?"

He grumbled in annoyance. "The bastard Lyklor may have fathered it, but I will take care of it. Take care of both of you. You and I share blood. The child shares your blood. Therefore, what's yours is mine."

"How did you know?" I asked.

"I heard it fluttering around in there last week. Very active, our offspring is. I can't wait to teach it how to rip a fairy's heart from its chest."

"Thank you, Otar. You may go," I said, moving back to the bed. He smiled, disappearing into thin air.

Lily looked shocked as she sat on my bed, eyes locked onto me. "Erendrial is the father? Gen, when ... how?" she asked in disbelief.

I held my head, getting back into bed. "I have the worst taste in males," I whispered, snuggling into her. I told her everything as she stroked my hair and listened. I held onto my stomach, no longer feeling alone.

CHAPTER TWENTY

L ily stayed with me all night and was still in bed when I woke up. We got dressed just in time to receive Vena. I told her I wanted to keep the baby. I then asked her all there was to know about alfar pregnancies.

She told me that I'd be able to feel the baby flutter in a week or two because of its power.. The incubation period usually lasted ten to twelve months. I'd be able to continue training.

In the middle of her run-down, Eren came into the room, radiant and smug as ever. He looked at the three of us and tilted his head. "Princess? Everything okay?" he asked, looking at Vena.

"She's completely healthy. Just must have had a bad reaction to the fairy king," said Vena.

"Well, no need to worry about him. Just got done sending the horde home. Though, I will say, Phasis was very agitated that you didn't come to tell him goodbye," added Eren.

"I'm so sorry. I completely forgot. We got to talking and I must have lost track of time," I replied.

"No need to worry, I covered for you. Now, I thought we'd finally get you up to speed on misting. Up for a challenge?" he asked. I looked at Vena and she nodded it was alright.

"Sure, but we have that meeting after lunch with my father and the chamber council, remember?"

"Of course, I do. It is my job to remember," he said.

Lily, Vena, and I stood from the table. Vena gave me a quick hug followed by Lily. They left without another word. Eren watched as they exited.

"Did I say something, or have they always been that awkward?" he asked.

"We were just having breakfast together, that's all. Where are we going to practice?" I asked.

"Let's get some fresh air. I know a clearing in the woods we can go to." He walked over to the balcony and called Eeri. I called for Tarsyrth.

We rode out about twenty minutes from the castle. The clearing was by a freshwater spring. The ground was covered in snow, but the sun was shining brightly.

"Okay, give me the breakdown version. I know you like to hear yourself talk, but we don't have all day," I said playfully, trying to act normal.

He laughed as Eeri shot into the air. "Who's the smartass now?" he said, moving past me. "Rules of misting. Rule 1: you need to have seen the place you are misting to in order to get there. Rule 2: you can't mist large distances. A few miles at best, if you are lucky, but it will take time for you to become that skilled. And rule 3:

don't lose focus while misting or you will arrive at your destination in pieces."

"See where you are going, don't go too far, and focus. Got it. Now what?" I asked.

"Now, I want you to focus on that tree over there," he said, coming behind me and pointing into the distance. "When you mist, you need to allow the dark magic to roll over you like a blanket. Let it out of you and allow it to lift you and take you where you desire. Imagine yourself floating on top of the air, weightlessly drifting towards your destination. You will feel yourself lighten. Close your eyes and imagine the place you want to end up. Then, in a flash, you will be there."

"How do I let the magic out?" I asked.

"The warming inside of you that you speak of with your other gift. That is your magic. You need to let it devour you. Let it out with no restraints."

I took a good look at the spot that I was supposed to reappear at. I readied myself, closing my eyes and focusing on the dark magic inside of me. I felt it deep inside, announcing its presence. I focus on it, willing it to grow. The warmth spread through me like it did when I used my offensive power. It crawled up like something clawing around inside of my body. The feeling was unsettling, but I focused on it, allowing it to take complete control. Once I could feel its claws digging in every inch of my body, I opened myself up, focusing on the place I wanted to go.

My body begin to lighten as if I was floating. I focused on that feeling and suddenly my body was being pulled towards my destination like I was falling off a cliff. I held onto the image of the place I was going until I slammed into something hard. My face smashed into the tree trunk, bruises instantly forming underneath my skin. I stumbled back, rubbing my face softly in pain. I opened my eyes to see Eren on the other side of the field. I jumped up and threw my fist into the air.

"Yes!" I yelled. I was so excited. "I can mist, I can mist!" I shouted, laughing with joy.

Eren appeared by me, smiling with a small chuckle. "Alright, alright, stop yelling. You did good, now we just need to work on your consistency and distance. Maybe next time, try not to slam face first into your destination."

We made it back to the castle just in time for the meeting. We took our seats and waited for my father to begin. We discussed the fairy negotiations, the light court, the rift, and the upcoming sacrifice, which was now less than two weeks away. At the end of the meeting, my father opened the floor for any other matters. I swallowed and bravely raised my hand.

"Yes, daughter. What would you like to discuss?" asked my father.

I took a second, trying to be brave. "I would like to discuss my upcoming wedding. With the new regime in the light court, I was thinking it would be beneficial to speed up the timeline on my marriage. What if we held the tournament the same time as the sacrifice ritual? The sacrifice and my union would be an honor to Azeer, and the process of conceiving an heir can begin sooner rather than later," I said, feeling my stomach tighten.

My father and Eren both looked at me with confusion. The council whispered quietly about my proposal. I raised my eyes to Eren. He mouthed, 'what are you doing?' but I didn't respond.

"That sounds like an excellent idea, Princess Genevieve," said my uncle. "It will solidify your position, the union will strengthen your throne, and you and the light royals can begin the race to conceive the next heir."

I moved my hand to my stomach. We already won that competition. I just needed to find my little prince or princess a father who wanted it.

"I will take the request into consideration. If that is all, meeting dismissed," said my father, waving his hand in dismissal. "Daughter, please stay behind for a moment."

The room emptied while I sat back in my chair, eagerly waiting to speak with my father alone. Once the last council member exited, the guards closed the doors so we could speak privately.

My father refused to look at me. He leaned over the table, lacing his fingers together while he slid his thumbs across one another slowly. "What is this about wanting to move up the wedding?" he finally asked.

I leaned in closer to him, trying to appear innocent. "I have thought long and hard since our last conversation on the matter. Living here, among our people, has reinforced my sense of purpose ... of duty. I am ready to play my part and do what is needed. The faster I conceive an heir," I paused, reaching out to touch his arm. "Your grandsire, the stronger our family becomes."

"Has your heart grown for one of the contenders?" he asked, his eyes finally meeting mine. "The Servi male, perhaps?"

I forced a smile to appear at my face. My heart was a treacherous organ I wished to be rid of, yet because of it, I now carried the most important thing in my life deep within my womb.

"I've taken what you told me that morning at breakfast into consideration. My marriage will be a contract that will strengthen our line. My happiness can wait."

My father studied my face for a moment, seeming to uncover every lie I had allowed past my lips. With one fluid motion, he rose to a standing position, allowing the chair to move backwards with force. He stormed towards the door.

"The ceremony will remain as scheduled," he blurted.

I rose to my feet in protest. "But Father, this is what's best for the kingdom."

He froze at the door, one hand on the handle before turning back and pointing his finger towards me. "I am the king of this kingdom and I know what is best. I am also your father and until I say there is to be a wedding, there will be no wedding," he snapped, pulling the door open faster than the guards could move.

I yelled in frustration, allowing a few moments to pass in order to put space between us before I exited the room myself.

Eren appeared out of nowhere grabbing me by the arm. "What in the hell was that? Why would you want to move the wedding up? You don't want to marry any of those idiots. What is going on?" he asked.

"Nothing. I am just focusing on my job and my duties. This will strengthen the kingdom and my position, as my uncle said. I'm going to have to marry one of them, so why not just get it over with?"

"Maybe your father will still change his mind and let you choose. If you gave him time, it could happen. He likes making you happy."

I turned slowly towards him, taking in his face. I wondered what features our child would inherit from him. As long as my eyes won in the gene pool, the child would be safe. No other person had silver eyes like Eren. It would be a dead giveaway.

"And who would I choose, Eren? I am not going to be happy regardless if the matter is forced on me or if I get to choose. There is no one here that can give me what I want. I am just trying to focus on my position. Drop it, okay?" I said, walking away from him.

The next few days leading up to the sacrifice were calm. I got better at misting, now able to go up to a mile away from my position. I started talking to the baby every chance I got. It was nice to not be alone. Eren walked in a few times and thought I was going crazy, talking to an empty room but I played it off. I felt the baby move at the end of week five. It was a little flutter that tickled my belly button. The first time it happened it made me jump, but I was happy that it announced its presence so soon.

Vena checked on me daily, making sure everything was progressing along as it should. My father denied my request to move up the wedding, which meant I would have to tell him about my condition. I decided to wait until after the sacrifice ritual. He didn't need anything else to worry about right now.

I wondered if he would be happy about the baby. I wondered what kind of grandfather he would be. He loved and adored me, so I presumed he would show the same affections to his grandchild. Another Drezmore heir, ready to take the throne.

At night, I no longer had nightmares. Icici was beaten and expelled from court until the ritual. I tried not to focus on her. I focused on my future and what it would hold for me now.

Each night I would pour myself a glass of whiskey with an orange twist, savoring the smell. I wished I could share my happiness about our child with Eren, but I was afraid of what he would do. Would he trick me into getting rid of it? Would he somehow use the child to his advantage? Or would he simply not care? I shared my fears with Lily. She just listened, unsure of what to say.

The day of the sacrifice arrived. I sat in my room, not wanting to leave, but my presence was expected. I bent down, holding my still-flat belly in my hands. I smiled, feeling the little one wake from its slumber.

"Good morning. Hope you're comfortable in there. Thank you for not making me throw up last night. I finally got a good night's rest," I said, giggling to myself. "Today is going to be a hard day, but maybe someday, during my reign, or yours, we can get rid of this disgusting tradition and start a new one, where humans and alfar are equal and live in complete peace. Oh, little one, I can't wait to meet you. You've already made me so happy. I can only imagine what it is going to be like to hold you and kiss you. Just do me a favor, and please have my eyes," I whispered as fear gripped me.

"Talking to ourselves again, are we?" asked Eren, bringing in a plate of food. He put it on the table next to the whiskey and orange slice. He glanced at the items for a moment but said nothing. "You missed breakfast again, so I brought it to you. Don't get used to this treatment. It's a big day and we don't need you passing out."

"Thanks, but I'm not hungry. And you will do whatever I command Lyklor. I am your princess," I said.

"Like you'd ever let me forget."

I giggled, turning back to the vanity mirror. He appeared in the frame and placed his hand on my shoulder gently. My whole body erupted from his touch. Gods how I missed it.

"If at any time you need to leave today," he started, "for any reason, just let me know and I will cover for you. I know this is going to be hard, but you can do this. You must."

I smiled softly at him. "I know and thank you. I appreciate it."

He nodded; his hand lingering until he finally removed it.

The festivities began as the sun started to set. The bodies would burn all through the night—the longest night of the year. We gathered outside at the stone temple that had been constructed in honor of Azeer. It was open to the elements, with large archways covered with red roses and vines. A massive cylinder stood in the center of the structure with three hollowed carvings the size of coffins. In the front lay an altar made from white marble.

My father and I made our way to the first step of the temple. We bowed in honor of Azeer and stood to the side. My uncle and his children bowed and then took their places behind us. Eren appeared out of nowhere at my side. He looked at me and nodded reassuringly. I gave him an uncomfortable smile.

After the whole kingdom was gathered, the priestesses escorted the three human sacrifices to the center cylinder. They stepped into the cocoon-shaped platform as the priestess strapped them against the walls. They didn't yell, they didn't protest. They stood in their tomb of death, silent and unfazed. The priestesses began to chant, dancing around the cylinder oven as music played softly in the background.

My father stepped forward, grabbing a torch and stepping up to the platform. He walked up the tall flight of stairs and dropped the flame into the center of the oven. Flames licked and flickered through small openings in the structure. The three hollowed areas where the humans were strapped lit like kindling as their screams erupted. My father returned to his place by me and nodded at Eren.

Eren stepped forward, holding his hand out towards them. In seconds, their screams ceased. Their hair lit first, evaporating without a trace. Their skin blistered and boiled as the heat devoured them. The smell was unforgettable. I covered my nose, trying to hold in the tears that so desperately wanted to fall. I had had enough. I turned to Eren and nodded. He stepped forward as I retreated into the castle.

I made my way to my rooms and let out a vicious scream. How was I going to endure that every year? How could I allow my child to see that? I wiped my face, going to the table and preparing my whiskey and orange comfort. I went to the balcony and stared out into the night sky.

"Will you be okay?" Eren's voice came from behind me.

I didn't bother turning. "I have to be," I replied.

He came next to me by the ledge. He looked down at the glass in my hand. "I can help with that, if you want me to," he said.

"No, this is enough, but thanks."

"They felt no pain but the initial burn. I made sure of it."

"That was a small kindness, but it still doesn't change that they are dead before their time. I don't know how I am ever going to get used to that: watching helpless humans be burned alive for a god they don't believe in. For a god I am not sure I even believe in. I just ... I need a distraction to get my mind off it. Tell me something funny, or something stupid that you did in your youth. Something that will take my mind off their melting corpses," I said in a panic.

He took my arm, turning me towards him. He pulled the pin in the back of my hair that kept it from my neck, allowing my loose curls to fall down my back. He traced the edges of my face before lifting my chin so he could look into my eyes. His demeanor was calm and comforting.

"I'm here. Let me be your distraction," he said softly.

I sucked in the air around me, not believing what I had just heard. "But I thought—"

"It will only be for tonight," he interrupted, "but at least you won't have to think. At least for a while," he said, running his hands through my hair.

I felt a small tear run down my cheek. He removed it before it could fall. I dropped my head, unsure of what to do. I wanted him. I thought of him every night. I longed for his touch and taste. It would just be one night. A distraction. Something to make me feel good and forget. I brought my eyes back up to his and nodded.

"I promise, after tonight, I will never ask you to touch me again. You have my word," I said with a heavy heart. After tonight, it had to be done. If I was to protect my child and its future, I could never be with its father again. I had to cut him off completely, or the court would figure it out and eventually, so would he.

He didn't nod or say a word in response. He leaned in slowly and took my lips against his. I melted at the first contact. He wrapped his arms around me as we stumbled back into my bedroom. He unfastened my dress, tearing it from my body. I ripped at his jacket and tore through his shirt to get to his flesh. He undid his pants as we fell into bed, completely enthralled in one another.

He kissed my body with passion and vigor as I pushed my fingers through his hair, enjoying every sensation. He sucked on my neck and tore at my underwear until there was nothing left between us. He kissed my mouth again as he pushed his way inside of me. I closed my eyes, trying to just focus on the amazing feeling of his body against mine. I didn't want to open my eyes. I didn't want to look into those eyes that I wanted so much to love me. It would be easier to move on if I didn't watch this happen.

Eren kissed my face as his hands tangled through my hair. I moaned with pleasure, not allowing my pheromones to be released. His breathing quickened as he continued to pleasure both of us. He moaned and laughed lightly as he nuzzled his nose into my neck. I kept my eyes shut, even though I desperately wanted to take in his smile—to see him laugh.

He slowed, hovering over me as he brushed the loose strands of hair from my face. I could feel his eyes on me as he stopped moving.

"Gen, open your eyes," he said softly.

I did as he asked, looking up at his beautiful face.

"You don't have to hold back," he whispered, "I told you: you can use me however you want. I'm yours for the night." He kissed the side of my face lightly.

My heart broke into a thousand pieces in that moment. Use him. He was allowing me to use him, just like Lady Calavi had for all those years. He didn't want this. He was fulfilling his duty to his princess.

"Get off," I whispered, trying to hold myself together.

He stopped, pulling his lips away from my neck as he looked down at me. "What?"

"Please, just get off," I said, turning my face away from him.

He rolled to the other side of the mattress, still looking at me. I sat up and grabbed my robe at the end of the bed, covering my bare body.

"Did I hurt you?" he asked, reaching for me.

I pulled away and stood. "No. Please leave," I said, not daring to look at him. I heard him get out of the bed as he gathered his clothes.

"Gen?"

"I said leave!" I shouted.

He stood for a moment, just looking at me, before finally exiting my room. I went back out onto the balcony and curled myself into the corner as I cried. I held my stomach, remember there was something more important to live for than myself. There was someone more important to protect. To make happy. To love.

CHAPTER
TWENTY-ONE

T he next morning, I got up early and forced myself to eat. I got dressed and told Atalee I was going for a ride. I called Tarsyrth to my balcony and took off into the sky, making my way to the border and crossing into The Frey.

I bought a horse and rode until I reached my old town. My home. I stuck out from the plain townspeople with my black leather pants and long leather jacket that flapped in the wind. My boots came up to my knees, keeping the snow from getting inside.

I sat on a bench outside a small, run-down cottage. I pulled my jacket tightly around my body, trying to keep the winter cold at bay. The cottage wasn't chosen at random. It was the home of the three young children I had given cakes to at the festival just before Lily was taken, which seemed like a lifetime ago.

I watched as they ran out of their front door and jumped directly into the snow. They laughed and screamed in excitement. Their pants had holes and their coats were barely holding together, but they didn't care. They didn't allow their means to define their happiness.

It wasn't too long ago that I was in the same position. I smiled as I sat, laughing along with them. They began to throw snowballs at one another, filling their hair with small white flakes.

Would my child laugh like them? Would they be happy in the dark court?

Eren appeared next to me on the bench out of nowhere. He wore a long black jacket that went to the ground. He folded his hands into his pockets, not making eye contact.

"You know, when I told you that you had to tell someone when you left the castle, I meant, you actually had to tell someone where you were going. Especially if you cross the border into The Frey. There's paperwork and a waiting period," said Eren.

I shook my head, holding back my smile, not taking my eyes off the children.

He allowed a few minutes to pass, perhaps mustering the courage to discuss the previous night.

"Over the years," he started, "I think I've learned a great deal about myself. I know my strengths and I am aware of my weaknesses ... and sex is not one of those weaknesses. I have never been asked to leave a female's quarters, let alone asked to get off mid-act. Needless to say, my ego is a bit bruised, and I would like to understand what happened last night."

I took a deep breath, still looking out into the field. "I didn't free you from one sex contract to bind you to another, Erendrial."

"What?"

"Last night, you told me I was free to *use* you in whatever way I wished. In that moment I knew you weren't with me because you wanted to be, but because you were trying to fulfill an obligation or duty. If I allowed you to continue, I'd be no better than Lady Calavi. I want the person I am with to want to be with me. To want to pleasure me and allow me to bring them pleasure because they desire me. Not because they feel an obligation based on my title."

A few minutes passed as he tried to compose a response. "You are nothing like Calavi. I wasn't there because you forced me. I wanted to be there. I wanted to help you."

"Sex doesn't mean the same thing to you as it does me. It means something to me. I need it to mean something, or I will end up losing the part of myself that I've worked so hard to recover." Another long moment passed between us.

"Why me? After everything you've been through, why was I the one you choose to start again with?" he asked.

I closed my eyes, trying to find the courage to tell him. "I started having visions three years ago. At first, it was the same vision every time I closed my eyes to sleep. The same image. A male, but I couldn't see him completely. He was surrounded in darkness, but I could hear him laugh. I could see his smile. Images of his hands and the jewelry they were adorned with. But the most vivid part of the vision was a black marking, starting from his lower neck, extending over his shoulder and down his arm.

"For years, I thought maybe the gods were sending me this image for comfort. Maybe he was my guardian angel, making sure I knew I wasn't alone. I would take comfort in the vision during nights when I was cold or hungry. Then, when I got to the light court, I continued to rely on those images. Even when I had to lie next to Gaelin, I would still dream of the angel.

"That night I came to you about the battle with Otar, I saw your imprint. I realize that my angel wasn't an angel at all, but a demon sent to torment me. I forced myself to stop seeing you for as long as I could. But when the king began to take me, I relied on those images to get me through the darker parts of the experiences. They were familiar and something else to focus on besides what my body was being put through.

"When I began to get to know you, I thought the images meant something more. That there was a reason why I had been seeing you for so many years, but I was wrong. I tend to overthink things as you well know."

He sat uncomfortably still, then turned his attention to the field in front of us.

"Do you know them?" he asked, gesturing to the children.

"Not really. They were starving, so I stole enough money to buy them each a cake at the summer solstice."

"So now you're stalking them?"

I smirked. "No, I am just watching them play. It makes me happy." I paused, examining his facial expression as he tracked the running children. "Seeing them doesn't make you want one of your own someday?"

"I wasn't made to be a father. A child, even an alfar child, needs nurture and stability. I can't provide either. A child also makes you weak. It can be used against you. Why expose yourself so blatantly? Plus, I'd be tied to its mother for the rest of my life. Not something that is on my to-do list."

I gripped my stomach, feeling the loss for my child. At that moment, I knew it would never know its true father.

"Why do you love the humans so much?" he asked. "Besides the fact that your mother was one, of course."

"They aren't as weak as you all think them to be. They're smart and relentless. They are constantly beaten down, yet they continue to get back up. They're loyal and dedicated and their love knows no bounds.

"If they weren't under the thumb of the alfar, I believe they could create and discover great things. Given the resources, they would build towers that would reach into the clouds. They would write and create art. They would compose symphonies and discover remedies for illnesses. They would explore and conquer. I bet they would even learn how to fly. You underestimate them on so many levels. You oppress them and use them, yet here they still are, loving the life they were born to."

He sat silent for a few moments. "We should be getting back," he said.

Before we left, I walked towards the children. Their mother and father came out of the house as I approached. The children ran behind their parents, staring at me with a bit of fear and curiosity. The mother studied my face.

"I remember you," she said softly.

I smiled, reaching into my jacket, taking a bag of gold coins from my pocket. "This should get you through the next year with ease," I said.

"What do you want in return?" asked the father firmly.

I looked at their beautiful family. A father and mother. Siblings. Something my child might never have. "Only for you and your children to be warm and happy." I smiled at the three little faces before walking back to Eren.

When I was a few feet from him, I felt a zap begin at the base of my back and run up my spine. I collapsed as it reached my brain. Eren rushed forward, catching me before I fell. The pain was excruciating, but I continued to recover faster with each vision. I stood from the ground as he offered me his body as a brace.

"What did you see?" he asked.

"The light alfar. They're coming to court. They've been chasing a horde of creatures that they can't kill. The things won't stay dead. The creatures have crossed into our borders, and I just saw how to take them out permanently."

"Guess we should really be getting back then. Hold on," he said, wrapping his arms around me. He misted us to the border and called Eeri from the sky. I was too weak to fly, so I flew back with him. By the time we reached home, I was fully recovered. Firel, Eren's secretary, rushed to meet us as we arrived. He informed us that the light court was indeed already here.

The doors of the throne room swung open and Eren and I marched to the front. Our black jackets fluttered behind us as the pounding of our boots echoed through the massive room. Gaelin, Levos, and a group of ten guards stood in front of my father. I took my throne as Eren firmly planted himself at my side with his mask of intimidation beautifully on display. Gaelin smiled at me, as did Levos.

"Good of you two to join us," said my father. "King Atros was just telling us of a group of creatures that have broken through the rift. They have killed them, yet they keep resurrecting themselves."

"Yes, I know. I had a vision of them, and I know how to keep them dead," I said with a smile.

My father winked at me, turning proudly back to the light court. "Well, it seems like we are going to have a hunt tomorrow. My daughter will lead the attack. Do you have any objections, King Atros?" my father asked.

"As you wish, King Drezmore," Gaelin replied.

"Excellent. Why don't we meet in my private study in ten minutes, and we can go over our plans," said Father, rising to his feet. Gaelin nodded.

My uncle, Eren, and I went straight to my father's study, wanting to get a head start on the preparations. "What did you see, daughter?"

"The creatures are nocturnal. In order to kill them, you have to dismember them and then burn their bodies to ash. Once they are charred, you bury them in a deep grave, covering the remains with resin," I said.

"Doesn't sound too complicated," commented Eren.

My father smiled at his brother, slapping him on the shoulder.

"Well," said my father, "it seems like you two have everything under control. We will leave King ... Fucker? Isn't that what you call him, Lyklor? Yes, King Fucker to the two of you." My father turned to his brother as they both laughed. The sight brought a smile to my face. They exited the room as we waited for Gaelin.

Once he arrived, we filled him in on the details and then derived a plan. We would take off as the sun set the next day to search the grounds for the creatures. According to Gaelin, they had to be within a twenty-mile radius of the castle. We would dispose of them where they fell, making sure to mark the graves so we could go back and check to make sure they stayed dead this time.

That night, both the light and dark courts ate and laughed together in peace. I retired early, trying to gather my strength for the hunt tomorrow. It was the first one my father entrusted to me. I had to make him proud. Even though I shouldn't have been going anywhere in my current condition.

Atalee was preparing my armor for the next day when Eren appeared in my room.

"Is knocking beyond your comprehension?" I asked.

"I just like rattling you a bit," he said, winking at me. Atalee left as we stood in front of one another. After all the admissions I had made today, I didn't know how to act around him.

He took a step towards me, seeming nervous as he took my face in his hand. He pulled my waist into his and looked deeply into my eyes.

"Let me make last night up to you, princess," he said, rubbing his nose against mine.

I swallowed, gathering the strength I needed. I pulled his hand from my face and then my waist, taking a step back.

"I made you a promise. You would never be forced to touch me again," I said heavily.

He took another step towards me, rubbing his hands along my arms. "Yes, but I didn't accept. Last night wasn't an obligation, nor did it have anything to do with pity. I wanted to be with you. I want to be with you now, tonight."

I studied him for a moment, trying to get past the many masks he was known to wear. "Why now? What changed your mind?"

He shrugged, allowing a soft smile to appear. "I guess you could say you're wearing me down, princess."

I swallowed again, telling myself I had to remain strong. "Eren, you were right. You can't give me what I need ... what I want. I want to be loved. I want to know that I am enough for someone. I don't want to have to worry about what court member is screwing you when I am not looking. I need a person who just wants me, and that person will never be you," I said softly.

He took a deep breath in. "Why? Why do you need a commitment? Isn't being together like this enough?" he said.

"Because I have feelings for you, and it would destroy me to have you one moment and then have to share you with another in the same breath," I said as a tear ran down my cheek.

He ran a hand over his face in frustration as he looked back at me with heavy eyes. "I can make you happy with what I can give," he said, still trying to compromise.

"What you can give me isn't enough, Eren," I whispered as a guard came through the door.

"Princess Genevieve, King Atros," the guard announced as Gaelin walked through the door.

Eren's eyes went deadly as he looked at Gaelin and then back at me. "Can he give you what you want? Is that why he is here?" Eren whispered to me in a harsh tone.

"What? No, of—"

"Don't," he snapped, backing away from me with his hands up in a defensive position. "King Atros," he said, bowing to Gaelin. "I hope you two royals have a fan-fucking-tastic night together. I will see you both for the hunt. Should be a good one," he said. He turned, slamming the door behind him.

I did what I had to do. It couldn't continue, no matter how badly I wanted him. He wasn't capable of loving me or our child.

I had to put the baby first.

The truth was, I had truly fallen in love with Eren. He was my person. The one I had chosen. The one I had given myself to completely. Though, I'd never be enough for him. Knowing that should have minimized my feelings, but how could I ever feel anything but love towards him? He had given me the thing I hadn't known I desperately wanted until it happened. My gift. My joy. My child.

CHAPTER
TWENTY-TWO

*T*here is no fucking way in Azeer's name that Gaelin Atros
is better in bed than me! No way! I thought as I stormed
through the halls. Fucking emotions. Why couldn't she just be
like every other female and not give a damn? Just focus on the
now and what I could offer her physically. Oh, no. Not Genevieve
Drezmore. She needed *feelings* and *monogamy* and yet she chose to
sleep with me. Even though I specifically clarified multiple times
what I was and wasn't capable of.

Azeer! Why did she have to be so difficult? *It's done, Eren, it's
over.* She's probably already under the pretty prick by now, but it
isn't going to faze me. She made her decision and now she must
live with it. Never again will I offer myself to her. Gaelin claims to
love her, so he can have her. He can deal with all her complicated
emotions.

"Ahh!" I yelled, picking a vase up from a nearby table and
throwing it into the wall across from me. I stopped, slicking my
hair away from my face before gathering myself. *Get it together,
Lyklor. Look on the positive side.* Instead of having one warm body

tonight, I could have as many as I wanted. Yes, that is what I'd do.

I headed down to the gentlemen's club in the city where I knew a few of the girls would be elated to see me. I had neglected them for too long. I had some making up to do. I chose a lively blonde, a curly redhead, and two dark brunettes. One had curly hair, the other straight. All humans of course. I led them back to my room and spent the rest of the night devouring their warm and supple bodies.

The next day I didn't leave my room and neither did the girls. I wasn't required to do anything before the hunt, and since our precious princess was having her needs cared for by King Fucker, my schedule was at last free.

I had each girl multiple times throughout the day. Watching as they pleasured each other. Licking up and down their bodies until they were completely sated.

We all fell asleep halfway through our mid-day exploration. When I woke, four beautiful naked women were sprawled across my bare body. I looked down at each one and felt nothing. I slid from the pile, taking the one with curly brown hair with me. I bathed with her, bending her over and taking her one more time before I had to be on my way.

I closed my eyes, imagining she was someone she wasn't. I tangled my hands through her dark curls, remembering the feeling of Gen's hair. Even though this woman was human, she still didn't feel as good as Gen had. She didn't sound the same or smell the small. Azeer, that smell. I would have done anything to smell lavender and sandalwood. Everything about this one was ... wrong.

I wasn't going to lie to myself. I picked this one last night because of the resemblance she bore to Gen. I didn't know if it was because I wanted to punish her in the princess's stead, or because it would be easy to replace her face with another's. I slowed, looking down at the woman. I pulled away, unable to continue. She wasn't what I wanted. She turned back with her dark brown eyes ... not green.

"Is everything okay, ambassador?" she asked.

"Get your clothes and go," I said, standing from the tub. I dried off and dressed as the other women began to wake up. A knock came at my door. I strapped on my weapons and readied myself for the hunt. One of the girls answered the door. When I rounded the bathroom threshold, Gen stood among them with a calm face. She looked each of them up and down and then locked onto the dark-haired one that resembled her.

"Looks like I missed the party," she said, turning her gaze to meet mine.

"Your invitation must have gotten lost. Sorry about that," I said, walking towards the door. I took a deep breath as I passed her. Azeer, her scent made me crazy, yet I was surprised I didn't smell Gaelin on her. She walked ahead of me as we made our way to the front gates. She was clearly pissed, for which I smiled proudly to myself.

"You're ten minutes late. The others have been waiting," she snapped.

"As you just saw, I had my hands full. Had to make sure everyone was satisfied before I left."

"Disgusting," she snarled under her breath.

"What? You're the only one who gets a pre-hunt dalliance? By the way, how was Gaelin? Just like you remembered. Did he give you enough love to fill your impossible quota?" I asked. She turned quickly, backing me up into the nearby wall. Her face was firm and intense.

"Not that it is any of your business, but I did not screw Gaelin last night. He hasn't touched me since the light court. I, unlike you, have what we call restraint. But thank you for proving the point I was trying to make last night. You are incapable of caring for anyone but yourself. You don't care how your actions make others feel, as long as you get what you want," she said, holding her position for a few moments.

I looked into her breathtaking eyes and saw the hurt that she was feeling. That I had put there. She hadn't slept with Gaelin, which made me glad, but also made me feel foolish for what I had just allowed her to see. I had never publicized my intimate relations with anyone, yet with her, I wanted her to see. I wanted to hurt her. And I had succeeded in that.

She turned away and continued down the hall. I followed at a safe distance. *Head clear, Eren. You can't be worrying about her right now.* I had a mission to accomplish; then, maybe after, I'd speak with her and try to explain. But what was there to explain? This was who I was, even though I never allowed her to see it. I had told her and she still expected different results.

We rounded the corner to the doors where Evinee stopped us with a young alfar male at her side. He was tall and well-built, with a slender torso and waist. He had one blue eye and one green. His hair was a dark caramel brown and cut in a shaggy fashion. His imprint could be clearly seen, as the black marking started at his left eye and trailed down the side of his face in a thin line, down his neck, and into his shirt.

"Princess Genevieve, Eren," said Evinee, bowing to Gen. The boy bowed as well. "This is our newest recruit, Tryverse Feynar. His power is illusions. He is an artist when it comes to the mind. He can build mental walls and make you forget things, replacing them with other memories you never actually experienced." Evinee smiled in excitement.

"It is an honor to serve you on this mission, Princess Genevieve," he said, giving her another small bow.

"How old are you, Feynar?" I asked.

"Thirty-eight, Ambassador Lyklor," he said.

"But he is already extremely gifted with his powers and his battle tactics. Believe me, he will come in handy," said Evinee, obviously taken with the young alfar.

"It is always nice to have an extra set of hands. Welcome to the hunt, Tryverse. I look forward to seeing you in action," said Gen.

She nodded and then headed to the platform to call her ragamor.

King Drezmore and his brother Rythlayn Drezmore were standing at the edge to see us off. The king kissed his daughter tenderly, looking down at her with an adoring expression.

"Good luck, my daughter," the king said softly.

"She won't need it," interrupted Rythlayn, pulling Gen into an embrace. "From what Torean tells me, she's a Drezmore on the battlefield through and through."

"I'm learning, but I still gave a long way to go," she said humbly.

"I wouldn't say that," said a female voice from behind me. Lady Winnow Fellwood, the court seer, approached Rythlayn's side gracefully. She looked at Gen with a soft smile.

"Lady Fellwood," Gen said, with a nod. "What do I owe this honor?"

Fellwood looked a Gen for a long moment before speaking. "It is exciting to see your success," she said quietly. "I am so thankful to Azeer he gifted me the vision of you all those months ago. How far you've come in such a short amount of time."

Rythlayn chuckled. "Yes, well, that is to be expected. Drezmore stubbornness and all."

Gen elbowed her uncle playful.

"Well," continued Rythlayn, "we ought not keep you any longer. The faster you go out, the faster you'll return. Happy hunting, niece."

"Thank you, uncle," Gen replied.

Winnow Fellwood approached Gen, moving her lips to her ear and whispering something to her. When she pulled away, Gen's smiled beamed from ear to ear. Winnow nodded, taking her leave from the platform.

The light court was already on the ground, mounted on their slow and useless horses as the sun set on the horizon. We took into the sky and the search for the creatures began. Two hours later, both the light and dark court had found nothing. I flew next to Gen.

"We should take to the ground. It's hard to see anything up here at night," I suggested. She looked aggravated and stressed. I knew what this mission meant to her; she didn't have to tell me. It was the first hunt her father had trusted her with. She didn't want to disappoint him.

She exhaled and nodded. "You're right, but I think—" She stopped as her whole body went stiff, and her eyes widened. Black consumed the whites of her eyes as she lost complete control of her body. She was having a premonition. Before I was able to take a breath, she slid off Tarsyrth's back and was sent plummeting to the ground.

I sent Eeri diving towards her as her limp body flailed in the open air. I leaned against Eeri's back, trying to increase her speed, to get underneath Gen before she hit the ground. Eeri's strong wings flared out, steadying her in the air as I opened my arms to catch Gen.

She fell hard into my body, but she was alright. I slid one of my hands back into Eeri's slit and moved Gen's hair out of her face with the other as she began to wake. She looked around in shock and confusion.

"It's okay, I got you," I whispered, checking her over to make sure she was truly okay.

"Guess we never considered what would happen if I had a vision while flying," she said, embarrassed.

"When we get home, I think we should have straps and a saddle made for you, just in case," I said, smiling at her.

She laughed faintly, as I looked down upon her beautiful face. My fingers still stretched through her hair. Her body, cocooned into mine for safety. She looked up at me, and everything around us faded away for a brief moment.

I shook my head, trying to snap myself out of it. *No, you idiot, you are not doing this. Especially with her. It cannot happen. You are smarter than this. You've worked too hard to let her destroy everything. You have nothing to gain and everything to lose.* I pulled back, letting my hand fall from her hair.

"Hang on. I'll take us to the ground," I said, sliding my other hand back into the slit. She wrapped her arms around my neck, her body laid against mine. Her hair tickled my face as it fluttered in the wind. We made our way down to the others and I helped her off Eeri. She gathered everyone around to tell what she had seen.

The creatures were in a nearby cave just south of our current position by a wide creek. We took off towards the location, looking for the creek and cave she had seen. Twenty minutes on foot and we stumbled across the exact location from her vision. I pulled my black sword, activating its dark magic. The light court guards looked amazed as they stared at our advanced weaponry.

That's right, light pricks. Be jealous, you incompetent, inadequate pieces of crap, I thought with a smile. Our first group scattered near the mouth of the cave. As soon as they entered the darkness, creatures spilled from every surface, crawling from the walls and ceiling like insects. There had to be at least five dozen of them that emerged all at once.

They were the most backward creatures I had ever seen. They walked on all fours, bent backward with their stomachs facing up instead of their backs. They had arms and legs, but they were tall and lengthy, bent unnaturally as they scurried towards us. Their faces were deformed and oddly shaped, with no eyes and a large mouth full of teeth. Their necks spun around, allowing their faces to turn in every direction.

We attacked. The creatures fought with their legs and feet, bending and flipping in unpredictable patterns. Their long horn-shaped nails on the end of their feet slashed and stabbed anything that came close. I heard Gen call for Otar and he appeared instantly. Good. I hated the little asshole, but he wouldn't let anything happen to her.

One creature came charging towards me. I flung my blade at its leg as the thing came snapping forward quicker than a whip. My black blade cut through the leg without resistance. I went for its other leg and then its head, dismembering the creature as Gen had instructed. I charged into the ever-growing pile of creatures as the dark and light fought side by side.

Otar flashed from creature to creature, using his six sharp hands to tear through them like confetti. I guess he was good for some things. I turned towards Gen, making sure she was on top of things. Her face radiated pure, evil delight as she sliced and chopped the creatures to pieces. Azeer, there was nothing sexier than a female who knew her way around a sword.

Gaelin appeared by her side, defending her back as they worked through the crowd. Someday, I would kill him. Though it was low on my list of things to accomplish, every time I laid eyes on him, the task rose a few hundred spaces.

After forty-five minutes of chopping and dicing, the last of the creature's horde was torn apart by none other than the Ambassador of Lies and Manipulation. We were all exhausted, but the job wasn't done. We made camp a quarter mile from the creek as we gathered the remains of the creatures to burn. It was going to be a long night. We made a burn pile and set their bits and pieces on fire as the foulest smell filled the air.

We rotated groups of males and females to dig the deep graves that would house their ashes. Gen, of course, insisted on being one of the first to volunteer, so the others would have some time to rest.

The light court helped, using their powers to move the dirt and roots out of the way. I went into my tent and undressed, removing my blood coated armor. I washed my face and changed into a loose shirt and clean pants.

I heard Otar's voice outside, laughing as he mocked the light alfar about their dead king and stupid queen. I couldn't help but smirk at his brilliant methods of torment.

I sat in the chair, pouring myself a glass of whiskey. I thought of all the ways I could apologize to her for what she had seen back home, but that wouldn't change the fact that she had seen it.

I rubbed my eyes, trying to clear my head. One female. To be with one female for the rest of my life. It seemed so unnatural and wasteful. Why would anyone want to be with one being and refuse the joy others could bring them? Though, since I had been with Gen that first time, I hadn't experienced another that felt the way she did. If I was honest with myself, I had been looking for a reason to bed her again and the sacrifice ritual opened that door for me. I had played on her pain and offered my comfort, making it seem like I was doing her the favor, when really, she was giving me exactly what I wanted.

Ambassador of Lies and Manipulation. Azeer, if that title wasn't accurate. Still, the humiliation of that night haunted me. I wanted so desperately to redeem myself with her, and then she refused me, which only deepened the blow. I shot the amber liquid down my throat and screamed in aggravation. Dammit, this female was making me lose my mind.

Hypothetically, if I were to try the whole one female thing, what's to say she'd even give me a chance after this afternoon? What if I screwed up? Which I was sure to do. And then there was the whole emotional side of things. *I don't know what the hell love is. I don't even know if she truly does.*

Though, since her arrival, I had seen a change in the king. He was so cold and unfeeling before he discovered her. Now he joked, smiled and doted on her, even kissed her in public: something I had never seen him do even with his wife or concubines. Then there was Lily and Zerrial. He had changed for her. He had committed himself to her ... a human.

The king was happy. Zerrial was happy. Was it because of the love they felt for those around them? Gen did make me happy. She made me laugh and smile more than I ever had, even around those I trusted the most. I liked anticipating what smart things would come out of her mouth. I would find myself making stupid jokes just so I could see her nose crinkle as she laughed at my stupidity. And then there was the way she handled Calavi. Azeer, how masterfully she conducted herself.

She was smart and deadly. She was clever and calculative. She was truly my equal. I liked that I couldn't predict everything she did. It kept me interested and guessing. Could I give her what she wanted? Could I love her? Then there was the matter of her marriage. The thought of any of those stupid pricks laying a finger on her made me want to commit treason.

I stopped, straightening in my chair. I did want her. I wanted to be with her, and I *could* deny others as long as I had her in my bed each night. That was where she belonged. Under me, besides me, on top of me.

I smiled at the memory. I took another shot of whiskey and stood up, gathering my courage as I made my way to her tent. I would win her over. I would give her what she wanted, and then whatever came next would be up to her. I didn't know if I could love, but if anyone could make me feel that emotion, it would be her.

I got to her tent and flung back the openings, expecting to see her seated at the table, but the tent was empty. I looked back at the guards.

"She went to bathe at the creek, Ambassador Lyklor," one of them said.

I nodded, stepping inside to wait for her. I looked over at the bed in the middle of the room. I imagined how I would take her tonight. Every position, every angle. No one would be getting sleep in the camp; I could promise them that. I smiled, imaging her bent over the wooden table. Then on top of me as I sat in one of the chairs. Her legs sprawled across my lap.

I made my way over to that same wooden table, dragging my finger across the surface with a smile. Whiskey and a bowl of oranges waited for her in the middle. The scent that reminded her of me. She would accept me. She wanted me and couldn't escape it. Couldn't escape us. The alcohol and fruit were proof of that.

The flaps of the tent fluttered open. I turned with a smile, expecting to see my beautiful princess, but instead, Gaelin's tall, broad figure tramped inside. I glowered at him, changing my mask from seducer to tormentor. I sat in the chair that I would soon take Gen in as he stopped a few paces in front of me.

"Looking for something? Because I can assure you, you are in the wrong tent," I said, peeling back the flesh of an orange.

"What are you doing here?" he grumbled.

"Waiting for *my* princess, of course. You?"

"Where is she?"

"Getting clean for me." I winked at him.

He cleared his throat as his hands tightened into fists. I couldn't help but chuckle. Gen was right, I drove him crazy.

"She is too smart to allow you anywhere near her," he snapped. Oh, he was going to make this too easy for me.

"Would you like to compare notes, or would you just like me to tell you how many times I made her cum the first time?" I said, taking a bite into the orange, the juice spilling to my chin.

"She wouldn't."

"Oh, but she did. Begged for it actually. I had to fight her off for weeks until I eventually gave in. She can be quite the seductive little minx. Though, I wouldn't expect you to understand, since she had to bed you in order to survive."

"She would never choose you over me, Lyklor," he said, walking towards me assertively.

I stood, meeting his dominating stance with my own. After he calmed a bit, I poured a glass of whiskey and took an orange peel, twisting it before dropping the peel into the whiskey. I held it up to his nose, twirling the amber liquid in front of him.

"Smell that?" I asked calmly. "Whiskey and oranges. She has the combination everywhere, if you hadn't noticed. In her study, her seating area, even her room. It's the scent she smells when she is with me. It's my scent. The smell she can't get enough of. I would think it's safe to say she's already chosen. You lose, Atros."

He growled and flipped the table over. The glass from the bowl and whiskey shattered on the floor. The guards appeared instantly in the doorway. I held my hand out to them and smiled, signaling I was okay as I drank the whiskey from my glass, amused by his temper tantrum.

"You don't deserve her," Gaelin roared. "You will destroy her. Everything good inside of her, you will corrupt and take. Because that is all you do is use and take. She deserves better than you. You do not deserve her!"

"Oh, and you do?" I asked, my temper beginning to flare. "Please, enlighten me. How is the alfar who forced her to be his mistress, forced her into a life of servitude, forced her into his bed, deserving of her? Oh, and let's not forget how you just stood by idly and did nothing while that vile, gruesome, disgrace of an alfar king, who you pledged your undying love and loyalty to, raped and destroyed her every night! In what world do you think she could ever love you? That she would ever allow you to touch her, let alone be with her? Tell me, Gaelin, please, because based on the evidence, you have no room to judge my actions."

"I never forced her into my bed. She chose to give her maidenhood to me. And my hands were tied with Lysanthier. You know there was nothing I could have done," he said, lowering his voice.

"She gave herself to you because she was trying to stay alive. Because she wanted you to keep her secrets. Because she wanted to find her sister. You say you love her, but your actions say the opposite." My rage was getting the best of me. "How could anyone allow the person they love to be mutilated and tortured while you lay under the same roof?" I screamed.

"If you were a true alfar male," I continued, "you would have killed the bastard long before he even had the chance to hurt her. Even if it meant losing your position, or even your head. You could have even gotten her out. Sent her back to The Frey. But no, instead of getting her to safety, you were selfish. You wanted to keep her, even if it meant allowing her to be beaten, raped, and destroyed.

"You sat there and said nothing. Did nothing! You choose to ignore what was happening to her, because it made *you* feel uncomfortable. Because it made *you* angry. She was on her own, dealing with all of it by herself and where were you? Pouting in the corner like a bitch." I sneered at him.

He dropped his head, burdened with my words. "You're right. What happened to her is my fault. I live with that every day, and yet I can't let her go. I don't deserve her," he said in defeat.

I finished the whiskey. I had pushed him far enough. "Neither of us do," I said, breathing deeply.

A guard appeared in the doorway. He was out of breath and sweating. He was badly injured and bruised as he panted for breath.

"What is it?" I demanded.

"The princess. She was taken," he said, falling to his knees.

"What? What do you mean taken?" I yelled, walking towards him.

He shook his head as fear flooded his face. "She was bathing at the creek. Another and I were keeping watch. Something attacked us from behind. The other guard's head was ripped clean off without hesitation. They beat me and I thought I was going to die. I passed out just before they took her. I am sorry, Ambassador Lyklor. I am so sorry," the guard cried.

I picked the coward up off the floor and unsheathed my ulyrium dagger, preparing to end his life.

"Stop!" yelled Gaelin from behind me. He approached as I held the fucker up off the ground. I was shaking in rage as I peered into his eyes. "He's the only one that can identify the creatures that took her. We need him for that, then you can kill him."

"For once, you make a good point, Atros," I said, dropping the guard to the floor. I stormed out of the tent into the center of the camp. "Everyone, gather, now!" I demanded. They surrounded me. "Princess Genevieve has been taken by a group of unidentified creatures!" Otar appeared next to me in a fit of rage.

"What? What do you mean she's been taken?" he yelled, stomping his feet on the floor as he grabbed at his head. "Where were you? You are supposed to protect her, you stupid fuck! Ah, the gift, the gift! No, no, no!" he yelled as he went into complete frenzy. His back erupted into spikes along his spine as his other four arms appeared on the sides of his torso.

I grabbed him by the neck, bringing his haunting yellow eyes to mine. "We are going to find her," I said firmly.

"What does she matter to you? You don't care. All you do is take and hurt. I will find her. I will protect her and my gift!" he yelled, disappearing into thin air.

I looked back at the crowd of alfar.

"Leenia," I demanded, "go back to Doonak. Inform the king and gather as many able bodies as possible. The rest of us will begin to spread out and search for any sign of her or the creatures. She was taken by the creek. Any findings, report directly to me. Let's move!" I yelled.

My stomach turned as a panic I had never experienced before spread through me like wildfire. If something had happened to her ... no, she would be alright. She was strong. She had to be alright

CHAPTER
TWENTY-THREE

A whole day had passed, and nothing. We found nothing. The guard that had allowed her to be taken barely saw the creatures, so he was unable to give us anything of use. King Drezmore sent more alfar to help with the search. We spread out, searching every inch of our kingdom. There was no sign of her or the creatures the guard spoke of.

I tried to stay focused, but my worry was beginning to undo me. My mind raced with a million different ways she could be suffering at this very moment. I couldn't stop thinking the worst. Otar was a psychotic mess. Thankfully, Gen's order still held, and he couldn't kill any of us, but that didn't stop him from destroying everything he encountered.

At the end of the second night, Gaelin followed me as I retired to my tent. We scoured the map, trying to find any other piece of land we might have overlooked. We hadn't traveled into The Frey, but that was protected land. The creatures couldn't cross the border that we knew of.

"What if they took her into the rift?" asked Gaelin.

"We have no record of the creatures that cross ever returning into the rift. What do they want with her? That's what we should be asking. Yes, she is an heir, but what do they want in return? Killing her would get them nothing. They must want something. They're holding her as a bargaining chip," I said.

"Ask the creature, Otar. See if he remembers re-entering the rift or what they might want with her," suggested Gaelin. I nodded.

"Otar!" I yelled. Nothing. "Otar!" Still, nothing. "Guard!" I demand. One appeared in the doorway. "Find Otar and bring him to me immediately."

"I have all of Urial looking as well. They are fanning out from the center of the castle to see if they can catch anything we might have missed," said Gaelin.

"I'm sure your wife is just thrilled with this turn of events," I said with hatred.

"I don't care what she is thrilled about. All I care about is finding Gen."

"Another thing we can agree on," I said.

The guard came back into the tent holding Otar's limp body in his arms. "What in Azeer's name happened?" I said, throwing my arms out.

"We aren't sure, Ambassador. We found him like this behind one of the tents. I believe he is ... dead," said the guard.

I walked over, taking note of the creature. He had no wounds that I could see. His breath smelled rancid, but no signs of poison.

His talons were retracted, which meant he didn't die fighting.

"Of course, you go and get yourself killed when I actually need you, you worthless creature," I said, shaking my head. "Put him over there in the corner for now. The princess will want to revive him once we find her." I turned back to Gaelin with exhaustion.

"We should get a few hours of sleep before heading out again," he suggested.

I rubbed my hands through my hair. "I don't think I could sleep, even if I tried."

"Well, at least rest. We will find her," he said, his face stoic.

"We have to," I added.

I scoured the maps again after he left. I looked through the documented creatures for any similarities to the description the guard gave. I had to be missing something. I knew these lands better than anyone and yet, I still couldn't find her. I pushed the papers off the table in frustration. It was late and most of the camp was asleep. I placed my thumbs along the bridge of my nose and closed my eyes.

"Where are you, princess? Where are you, Gen?" I whispered.

"I can help with that," said a female voice.

I snapped my eyes to the opening of my tent. A beautiful humanoid with snow-like skin, long blue hair, and dark eyes stood tall before me. Ivory leather hugged her very desirable figure tightly. I stood slowly, trying to act natural.

"And who are you?" I asked.

"Doesn't matter. Do you want to find your princess or not?" she asked with a smile.

I tensed my jaw. "I'm listening."

"There's an underground cave you and your little rats missed. It's in your territory, not too far from here. Head northeast and you should stumble upon it. The entrance is at the base of a mountain. It is covered in poppies. She is there," she said with a nod.

"And why should I believe you?"

"Oh, I'm sorry. Have you had any luck with your search yet? No, I didn't think so," she said.

"Why are you helping us? What do you want in return?"

"Nothing. I owe the half-breed a life debt. I am just repaying that debt."

"Then why not help her yourself? Why waste time coming to me?"

She raised her eyes slowly to me, as if I had hit a nerve. "I can't interfere with the creatures, but I can send in the cavalry," she said with a smile before disappearing into thin air.

I took a deep breath, rushing out of the tent. "Everyone, we move now!" I demanded. I gave directions and we headed northeast. My heart raced with anticipation. *I'm coming, princess.*

We found the entrance to the underground cave at the base of the mountain covered in poppies, just like the mysterious female had described. The entrance was small and well hidden. Easy to miss. Easy to hide. I made my way in, followed closely by Zerrial, Evinee, and Gaelin. It was dark and damp, but we continued down into the ground, following a single path.

The cave eventually opened into a small room, lit only by the small crack in the ceiling that allowed the moon and stars to squeeze their way through. We lowered our torches, searching for anything, but we were barely able to see. As we walked in, we spread out.

"Whoo," yelled Evinee, stumbling back towards me. "Watch it, everyone, we're on some type of cliff."

"Do you smell that?" asked Zerrial.

"It's oil," said Gaelin, bending down towards something wet that lined the walls of the cave. "It looks like it travels the length of the cave, like a lighting system maybe." I looked at the others; they nodded. I touched my torch to the oil. The flame spread along the path streaming through the cavern.

The light swirled around a ramp that we stood at the top of. The whole cave lit up in seconds. As it reached the bottom of the cave, the flame zigzagged and turned to outline an inverted pentagram. In the center of the pentagram was a body. It was female. My heart stopped. I misted to the center of the symbol as the others followed behind me.

Her hands and feet were bound with ulyrium cuffs. She was naked. Completely exposed. Her face was not beaten. Still as beautiful and flawless as always. From the neck down, her figure was almost unrecognizable. Long strips were gouged out of her skin. She was missing fingers and toes. Bitemarks covered every inch of her. Some were clean and others looked like an animal had torn through her flesh.

I fell to my knees beside her, taking in the nightmare in front of me. This was more brutal than I had ever seen the fairies or any other creature do to another. I felt myself shaking as I swallowed, trying to hold it together. Under her beautiful sun-kissed skin, an orange substance colored her veins. Gaelin moved towards her.

"Don't touch her!" I yelled.

He stopped, backing away, as did the others. I took my black blade, cutting her hands and feet free from the chains. I cradled her perfect face in my arms, covering her body with my jacket. Her skin was cold and didn't respond to my touch. I moved the stiff, blood-streaked hair from her face. "Princess, please wake up. I'm here. Come on, time to go home now." Nothing. "Gen, it's time to wake up. Please say something, please." I waited to hear her insult me or come back with a witty response, but there was just silence.

I sat there, numb as I looked down at her. This couldn't be happening. This wasn't real. It was a dream. A nightmare Icici had constructed. This can't be real. I felt a hand on my shoulder.

"Eren," said Evinee behind me. "She's gone."

I swallowed, realizing she wasn't going to open her eyes. She wasn't going to smile. I would never see her nose wrinkle as she laughed again. I would never get the chance to dance with her one last time. I would never get the chance to talk or tease her. I would never get the chance to make her happy.

I gently slid my arm under her legs and cradled her against my body. Without a word I stood and walked up the ramp and out of the cave with her in my arms. I called Eeri and took off, not waiting for the others to catch up. Her hair tickled my face, just like it had on our first flight together when I brought her to Doonak, but this time she smelled different. There was no lavender, no sandalwood. Only blood.

I landed at the entrance still holding her close to my body. I made my way to the king's private chambers, where Firel informed me he was waiting. The crowds of alfar stared at us in silence, but I didn't stop. I didn't look. The doors of his chambers opened. The king and his brother stood by the fireplace in the middle of a conversation. They turned to me and their faces dropped in despair.

I walked towards them, not daring to let go of her. The king slowly approached, moving her hair from her face. He traced the smooth lines of her jaw as tears silently began to fall from his eyes. He went to remove the jacket, but I stopped him, having to close my eyes to keep the memory of her tortured body out of my own head.

"Don't. You don't want to see, my king," I said slowly, almost unable to speak.

He took her hand in his. He looked at the three fingers she was missing on her right hand. He broke, collapsing to the ground as he sobbed more violently than I thought him capable of. His brother rushed to kneel beside him, placing a hand on his shoulder for comfort. It took all I had to keep it together. I stood still, waiting for my orders.

"Take her to Vena in the medical wing. Tell her to do a full examination," ordered Prince Rythlayn.

I nodded, heading out of the room.

I got to the medical wing, where Vena was laughing with another healer. She turned to look at me and her face fell. Her eyes scanned my arms, taking in the body of her dead cousin. She walked over, trying to figure out if it was really her. She shook her head as tears fell from her eyes. She covered her face to hide her emotion.

"No, no, please tell me this is some type of sick joke," she said, taking a step away from me.

I swallowed, wishing it was. "Your father has requested that you do a full examination of her ... of the body. Will you be able to do this?" I asked coldly.

"No, no I can't. I can't do that to her," she said, as her friend wrapped her arms around her shoulders.

"I will help," said the other healer. "You can do this. We have to. We have to, so we can figure out what did this to her."

Vena took a few deep breaths to calm herself. "Put her on the table," she said.

I walked over to the cold metal table and laid her body down, unable to remove my arms from her. I squeezed my eyes together and willed myself to pull away from her, but I couldn't. My grip tightened on her body as I felt my heart convulsively beating in my chest. Vena's hand ran along my shoulder.

"I'll take good care of her, I promise," she whispered.

I slowly removed my hands from her, taking another look at her beautiful face. I ran my fingers along her jaw and then lips as I finally pulled away. Telling myself not to look back, I marched out of the medical wing and headed for my room. Other alfar called for my attention. I ignored them, not able to think of anything but her.

I entered my room, slamming the door behind me. I felt like I was going to explode. I shook uncontrollably as I looked down at my hands, still covered in her blood. The same blood that made her warm. The same blood that rushed to her cheeks as she blushed. The same blood that pumped through her beautiful heart.

At that moment, I lost complete control. I screamed as I moved through my rooms, smashing and destroying everything. I threw tables against walls, broke every piece of glass and pottery. I ripped at the fabrics and pillows that were scattered throughout my quarters. I started on my books, tearing the bindings and pages out of each of them, until I stumbled across my drawings of her.

I slid down against the wall as I held them in my hands. This was all I had left of the female who completely captivated me. Her smile and happiness. Eventually, my memories of her would fade, but these drawings were forever. I flipped to the one of her sleeping. The night I had put her to bed, after she had entrusted me with her deepest torments. She looked so peaceful that night. I couldn't help but draw her.

I held the pages, trying to commit every detail to memory. I kept breathing, trying to hold back my emotions. Those same emotions I thought I was incapable of feeling. Knocks continued to come at my door, but I ignored them. I couldn't let them see me like this: so weak and affected by her death. I just needed a moment. Just a fucking moment.

CHAPTER TWENTY-FOUR

The king sent every able body to track the monsters that had killed his daughter. We thoroughly examined the cave, but the creatures had left nothing behind.

The king was broken. He did not speak unless necessary. He didn't eat and barely slept. I waited for him to call for my death at any moment for failing to protect his daughter, but the order never came.

The next morning, I readied myself to go back into the woods to assist with the search, when a knock came at my door. My servant opened it and bowed. I turned to see the king gracing my doorway. I bowed automatically. This was it. I would soon be dead.

"My king," I said.

He walked into the room, examining my quarters. "Redecorating, Lyklor?" he asked sarcastically.

"Something like that," I replied.

He turned towards me with his arms behind his back. "How did she do on the hunt? Before—" he stopped, unable to finish the sentence.

"She was exquisite. She was able to trigger a vision that showed their location. Without her, I don't know if we would have found them that night. She fought masterfully. She was the first to volunteer to begin digging a burning, even though she was exhausted. She was a true leader," I said.

"I believe she would have made a good queen. She would have made a difference."

"Yes, she would have."

He held his head I saw the pain stretch over his face.

"Your Highness, I have failed you, and for that, I do not deserve to live, let alone hold a title. I accept whatever your punishment is."

His tall form hunched as if weighted down by his heavy heart. "The creatures are unpredictable. I was told how hard you searched for her after. They say you haven't slept the past few days. I do not put the blame on your shoulders. Plus, you are effective at your job, Erendrial. Too effective, some might say. It would be a pity to lose you."

"Thank you, Your Grace. It will be an honor to continue to serve at your table."

"I just wish I had something of her left. I only knew her for a few months, but in that time, I felt like she had always been with me," he said, rubbing his temples with his fingers.

I moved to my study, grabbing one of my drawings of her. I walked slowly towards him, holding the paper out, hesitant to part with it.

"What is this?" he asked.

"A small piece of her," I said.

He turned the paper over. His eyes widened as he took in her beautiful smile. He traced the lines of her face and then grinned. "Thank you," he said softly. "Come, we will be late."

"Was there a meeting I was not informed about?"

"My niece has finished her examination of her body. I thought you'd want to hear what she has found. It may help in finding the creatures that did this to her."

I bowed, trying to fight the tremor of pain at the thought of seeing Gen's dead body again.

We made our way to the medical wing where Prince Rythlayn awaited us. Vena stood by the table that held Gen's body. Her hair had been cleaned. A sheet covered her body only allowing her face to be seen. Vena stepped forward with a folder in her hand. Her face was long and tired and paler than usual.

"Uncle, Ambassador Lyklor," said Vena, with a nod. "Shall we begin?"

"Yes," said the king, inhaling a deep breath to prepare himself.

Vena opened the folder and began. The details of the horror and pain Gen had gone through in her last moments almost made me double over. Vena stumbled through the ongoing list of ways she was tormented, stopping every so often as tears ran down her face. Finally, she concluded that the final death was due to liquid ulyrium that was pumped into Gen's veins. She closed the folder, waiting for further instruction.

"Prepare her for the burial ceremony. It will take place tomorrow afternoon as the sun sets. Her clothing should cover everything up to her neck. Only her face will remain visible," said the king, before turning to leave.

I stepped forward, taking another look at her. "How much suffering is one being supposed to endure?" I whispered to her. "You deserved so much better."

The search continued, but we came up empty-handed. We knew there were four of them. They had to have sharp teeth and claws to rip flesh, but that was it. We didn't know their habitat, hunting style, mass, preferred diet, nothing. I sat at my desk, twirling the glass of whiskey in my hand as I thought. I had to find these things. For the king, for her, for myself. I just didn't know where to look.

"Giving up so fast, are we?" came a haunting female voice.

I launched to me feet. The blue-haired woman stared back. Rage flared inside me as I grabbed the dagger on my desk. "What in the hell are you doing here? How dare you show your face, after what you led us to," I said with fire snapping through every cell in my body.

"I didn't know she was already dead; I assure you. And I am here because I can be," she replied, standing straight without a single bend in her posture.

I misted to her, but when I reappeared, she was behind my desk where I had just come from. I charged at her, blade ready to attack. She held out her hand and I crashed into an invisible wall. With a flick of a finger, she had me flying through the air, slamming into the opposite side of the room.

I stood up, ready to charge her again. She held her hand out. It felt like her fingers were strapped against my neck as I fought to breathe. I grabbed at the invisible restraint, but there was nothing there. She lifted me off the floor, holding me there until finally releasing my body. I fell to the ground gasping for air.

She looked at her nails, unimpressed. "I have a very short amount of time, and you are wasting it with your fit of immaturity and stupidity. Do you want what I have brought you, or not?"

"She is dead! You failed to uphold your end of the life debt," I said, standing to my feet.

"Yes, little alfar, I am fully aware of how a life debt works. Either I save her life or avenge it, which I am hoping to recruit your help with." She tilted her head as my eyes widened. "Good, you're listening. My present is wrapped and waiting for you at the front gate. Keep them in silver." She turned, about to leave.

"Wait!" I called. She stopped, turning back to me. "Why go through all this trouble for a half-breed?"

She paused, looking to the floor. "She was selfless and kind to me, when she had no reason to be."

"What is your name?" I asked, taking a step towards her.

She smiled. "Narella. Nice to formally meet you, Erendrial Lyklor," she said, before disappearing into the air.

I paused for a second, her name ringing through my ears. She was the powerful being Otar had told us about. I took a deep breath before rushing out of my room to the front gates. The guards flung the doors open to four humanoid beings, bound in silver, kneeling in front of me. I smiled at the thought of how much suffering I was going to cause these bastards.

Their bald, hairless skin was black as if covered in tar. They steamed like they were on fire. Red veins streaked the whites of their eyes, and their irises were black. They had normal-looking teeth, from what I could tell. Their bodies resembled that of a human.

"Guards! Take them down to the torture chamber. Keep them in silver," I demanded. "Inform the king that we have found his daughter's killers."

I allowed the alfar in charge of interrogation, which happened to be my Doria, to do her job, though I desperately wanted to be a part of it. I wanted to hear them scream, pleading for mercy. To suffer. Just like she had. I wanted to rip out their eyes and force them down their throats. I wanted to stick a flaming hot rod up their asses, burning their holes shut. Azeer, the things I wanted to do to them.

The next morning, the court stayed clear of the throne room. No one was to enter until the burial ceremony began that evening. Gen's body lay alone, waiting to be honored. I headed down to the torture chamber to see if there were any developments.

As I entered, Rythlayn Drezmore and Winnow Fellwood exited side-by-side. I stopped, surprised by their presence.

"Prince Rythlayn," I said, "Lady Fellwood."

Rythlayn forced a smile. "Ah, Ambassador Lyklor," he said, patting me on the arm. Lady Fellwood bowed slightly. "Come to see the devils that stole my sweet niece from this world?"

"Actually, yes," I replied stiffly.

"Well," he continued, "Unfortunately, I wasn't able to get much out of them just now. Disgusting, vicious creatures, they are. I took my time carving a few of them up, for the light they robbed us all of." The prince's face fell in sorrow.

I turned my attention to Lady Fellwood. "Did you come to torture the demons as well, Lady Fellwood?" I asked.

"No, Ambassador Lyklor," she said softly. "I was hoping Azeer would gift me with a vision to explain their motives for doing such a thing to our princess, but regretfully, none came."

"There's still time, Lady Fellwood," Rythlayn said, wrapping his arm around her shoulder. "Now, if you'll excuse me, Lyklor, I must see to my brother."

"Of course, Prince Rythlayn," I said, moving to the side to allow them to pass.

As I entered, Doria was in the room with the creatures, sending electrical impulses throughout their bodies. They screamed and laughed as they burned. She let her hands fall and stabbed one of them before walking towards me.

"We have a problem," she said, washing her hands.

"Great, more problems," I replied.

"This is serious, Eren. I think ... I think they're demons. Like Lucifer and Christ demons," she said.

I kept calm outwardly as I yelled in my head. "What makes you believe that?"

"The inverted pentagram you found Princess Genevieve's body in. The state of her body. The appearance of the creatures and the fact that I can't kill them. I've burned them, stabbed them, ripped them apart, even cut off one of their heads. It all just grows back. Also, there is the silver factor. According to our history, that is what can hold them, but only a declaration of Christianity or the Flame can kill them, as you well know.

"They're very blasphemous as well. They know the Christian scriptures and history. I used holy water and that seemed to harm them the most. I sang a disgusting Latin hymn, and they went ballistic. Everything points to demons," she finished.

"I want to talk to them," I said.

"Eren, that isn't a good idea. They are evil and sadistic creatures. You can't trust anything they say to you."

"Open the door, Doria."

She exhaled and nodded. She followed in behind me, locking the door. They were chained side-by-side to silver sheets of metal. Something moved under their skin, likes worms in the ground. Bugs swarmed in and out of their mouths as bile fell from their lips. One swung his head back and forth as if singing. Another laughed for no reason. I approached and all four sets of eyes snapped towards me. They all smiled and began laughing.

"Why her?" I asked bluntly.

"Why not her?" one asked mockingly.

I clenched my jaw, trying to remain calm.

The one at the end made a surprised face as he began shaking in his chains. "He's the pretty one," it said.

They all looked at me with excitement.

"Yes, he is. The pretty one we saw."

"Oh, how splendid it is to meet you, pretty one."

"Yes, splendid indeed."

"What are you talking about?" I asked.

The one that seemed to be the leader flashed a set of sharp teeth that descended out of his gums, covering the set of normal teeth.

"We saw you ... in her mind. Yes, she thought of you while we had our fun."

"She thought you would come for her. Save her even; but she

was sorely mistaken."

My heart felt like it weighed a thousand pounds.

"She thought of you for comfort," said another one.

"Yes, when we tortured her, her mind would go to you."

"We saw all kinds of memories of the two of you together."

"We wonder, did you enjoy her body as much as we did? She was fantastic!" said the one on the end as he laughed and rattled his chains.

I was going to tear them limb from limb for eternity if I had to. "Shut up," I said calmly.

"Oh, did we upset you? We don't mean to. It was fun being you, though," said the leader.

"What are you talking about?" I asked.

The leader smiled. "We played a little game with the half-breed. Since you were what she thought of to comfort herself, we changed our form to appear as you.

"Oh, yes. The horror in her eyes was magnificent. At first, she was excited to see you, but then once we began, the fear and pain was delicious."

"Not as delicious as what was inside of her though."

"Oh, oh, I want to tell him, please. Let me tell him."

"Silence!" snapped the leader, turning his eyes to me. "I will tell him." He stayed silent, holding my gaze as the red engulfed the white of his eyes.

"Are you going to speak, or would you like me to guess?" I said, crossing my arms over my chest, trying to remain calm.

He licked his lips. "During our fun, we discovered the little half-breed was keeping a secret. So, we reached in and tore her little secret out of her womb with our fingers. It took a few passes, but we got the little bundle of joy out."

"Oh, how she cried. I almost felt sorry for her." The demon laughed mockingly.

My mind was scrambling. No, she couldn't have been. We were only together one night. It would have taken more than that. My chest began to rise and fall quickly as my heart pounded. I felt Doria's hand on my shoulder.

"Eren, they're liars. They're trying to get a rise out of you," she whispered.

"Oh, no sparkles. We aren't lying. And yes, the pretty one was its daddy."

"Yes, we saw in her head. She dreamed of the three of you together. That was another one of her safe memories."

"Yes, I forgot about that one. How sweet the little family was. The child was a female with silver eyes. Just like you, pretty one. She liked your eyes," one of them laughed.

It took everything I had to stay upright. My throat began to close in on itself and my vision became blurry. I took my eyes from them, focusing on the floor. It was a lie.

"If you don't believe us, ask the sister," one snapped.

"Yes, she knew. She was thrilled about becoming an aunt."

I picked up the nearest silver blade and began slashed them to pieces. I cut off their heads, arms, legs. I poured holy water all over their skin as they screamed and hollered. I yelled with them in a fit of rage. Blood splattered from their bodies, covering me from head to toe. I threw the sword to the floor, watching as their bodies already beginning to heal.

I rushed out of the room back to the main hall. I couldn't keep my mind from jumping from thought to thought as I fought the urge to kill everything I saw. The court turned to me as I staggered through the halls, taking in my bloodied appearance.

I made my way to Zerrial's room, not waiting to be announced. I barged in to find Lily in a chair, crying softly while Zerrial tried to comfort her. They both looked up at me in shock as the blood dripped from my face and hands.

"Zerrial, out," I demanded.

He stood, shielding Lily with his body as he raised his head to me.

I took a deep breath, trying to calm myself. "I am not going to hurt her, but I need to speak to her in private. Please, wait outside," I asked as nicely as I could muster.

Lily stood up, placing a hand on his chest. "It's okay. I'll talk to him," she said softly. Zerrial turned to her and kissed her on the head endearingly. He walked past me, eyes still spewing threats. After he was gone, I tried to refocus my head. I was still shaking.

I dropped my head and closed my eyes as I fought the tears.

"Please tell me she wasn't pregnant. Please tell me it wasn't mine," I whispered.

She sniffled as she brought her hands to her face. "How did you—" she started to say, before she cried fiercely.

At that moment, I broke. I began to do something I had never done before in the entirety of my life. I cried. Now it all made sense. Why she was pushing me away. The trip to see the human children in The Frey. Her sickness. The way I would catch her talking to herself. She was talking to it. Our child.

I fell to my knees as I tried to cover my face, but the sounds that were coming from me were foreign and unfamiliar. I felt Lily's small hands on my shoulders as she pulled my head into her chest. I had failed to protect them both. They both died and I couldn't stop it from happening. It was the worst pain I had ever felt in my entire life.

"Why did she keep it from me?" I asked softly. I pulled away from her, gathering myself.

"She knew you didn't want children, and she believed you didn't want her. After she found out, she thought if you knew you might slip something in her wine to make her pass the child. She wasn't going to take any risks. She put the child first from the moment she found out it existed."

"That was why she was trying to get the wedding moved up," I said. "She was trying to make it seem like it was her husband's child."

"Yes. But when the king denied her request, she decided she was going to tell him after the sacrifice, but then the light court arrived."

I dropped my eyes, feeling more guilt than I ever had in my life. "Lily, I would have never hurt her. I would have never hurt our child," I said.

She closed her eyes tightly. "I'd never seen her so happy. Especially when it began to move." Lily laughed at the memory. "Vena said it already had great power and it was going to be a handful." Another tear escaped my eye. "She would have been an amazing mother."

I stood to my feet, trying to calm myself.

She took my hand and pulled me into her embrace. "I'm sorry for your loss," she whispered.

I just stood there, unable to move my arms to embrace her.

I headed towards the throne room. I couldn't think. I needed to see her. I grabbed a towel from one of the tables, wiping the blood from my hands and face as I pushed my way through the throne room, closing the doors behind me.

She laid on a shining black stone table. A green dress embroidered with gold stitching covered her body completely up to her neck. Her gold crown sat on top of her head and her curly black hair draped either side of her chest. I walked slowly towards her. I traced her beautiful face with my fingers as I hesitantly laid my hand over her stomach.

"I am so sorry. To the both of you. I am so sorry," I said while tears streamed down my face. I collapsed on the side of the altar, fell to the floor and sobbed. If I had known about the baby, she never would have been on that hunt. She never would have been taken. She'd be in her room, preparing for dinner. Instead, she was dead. She was dead because I pushed her away. Because I couldn't swallow my pride and accept what we both wanted.

I sat on the floor, leaning against the large black stone altar as everything inside of me went numb.

I lost track of time; my mind escaped, not wanting to face reality. I didn't see anything. I didn't hear anything. I didn't feel anything. I was utterly vacant.

"Erendrial?" said the king softly, kneeling towards me. My eyes snapped to his as everything inside of me woke. I felt like I had just been dreaming.

"Your Majesty," I whispered, trying to be formal.

He placed his hand on my shoulder, steadying me. "Go back to your room and get cleaned up. The ceremony will begin in thirty minutes," he said kindly. He gave me a small smile as he helped me to my feet.

CHAPTER
TWENTY-FIVE

I slid into the throne room, not wanting to talk to anyone. After the honoring ceremony, Genevieve Drezmore would join her ancestors in the crypt near Azeer's temple. I would only have my memories and drawings to remember her. I gathered my offering and made my way to the king's side. He turned to me and nodded as if asking, 'are you alright?' I nodded back with a faint smile.

Everyone was in attendance, including the light court. Queen Daealla stood emotionlessly next to Gaelin, who looked devastated. Levos stood at his side, unable to look at Gen's body. Prince Rythlayn and his children flanked the king's other side.

The music began to play as the dark magic in the ceiling sparked with lightning. The king stepped forward, kissing his daughter on the head as he tried to hold himself together. His brother comforted him.

The court moved through the processional, bowing towards her as they paid respects and placed their offerings of herbs and flowers on her altar. I fell into line, waiting my turn. As I approached, I took one last look at her beautiful face. I placed my bundle of lavender with an orange peel wrapped around the stems on top of her womb.

When the crowds had cleared, the priestesses began their ceremonial send-off. After, Lily's sweet voice floated through the air as she held back her tears. The house of Sylour created images of stars around the room to honor her. Her favorite sight. The house of Tiflon created a dazzling display of snow that fell around her. Her first encounter with Tiflon flashed in my memory. It had been the first time I had really seen her smile since she had left the light court. I remembered how beautiful each snowflake had looked against her dark hair. Peaceful, this was the definition of peaceful. She would have loved it.

The ground began to crack around the altar where Gen's body lay. Lavender and small sandalwood trees shot through the rock, growing at the base around her. Her sweet smell filled the air. The court smiled, as did her father. I looked to Gaelin, knowing he was responsible for what had just occurred. His face was wrecked with sorrow and regret. But I didn't feel sorry for him, because I knew he was incapable of loving her. Not like I did ... had.

Lily continued as the priestess prepared Gen's body with oils before she would join her ancestors. I stared aimlessly at the floor, not ready to say goodbye.

My eyes shot up when one of the priestesses began to scream. A roar of black and powerful fire shot from the altar into the dark magic that swirled in the ceiling. Loud crackling noises filled the room as everyone stepped back in horror.

The altar was consumed by a heat that I had never experienced before. Dark flames licked and flickered across the black stone, devouring Gen's body. A loud bang sounded as everyone moved to the edge of the room, attempting to stay clear of the storm. A vortex of wind and energy zapped around the room, making it impossible to stand upright. The floor cracked with force, as the mountain trembled in response to the power.

Finally, the hell storm halted. The courts looked around, trying to compose themselves. I turned my focus back to the altar as I got to my feet. Gen sat upright, completely bare. Her beautiful eyes blinked as she looked around in confusion.

I rubbed my eyes to make sure I wasn't seeing things, but she was real. She was there. Alive and moving. Her black curls sprung back to life as the long locks trailed down her back. Her eyes flickered from black to green. She looked down at her arms and hands in disbelief, then her legs and feet.

Her eyes turned to her surroundings, realizing she was naked in front of the courts. She covered her beautiful body with her arms, pulling her feet to her chest. Her father walked towards her slowly, mouth open, taking his jacket and wrapping it around her. She flinched at his touch and turned to look at him. He took her face slowly in his hand as he smiled with joy.

"Genevieve?" he asked.

She looked around again at the familiar faces. "Why ... why am

I here? What is going on?" she asked in shock.

He laughed with joy as he took her into his arms.

"Clear the throne room, now!" demanded Prince Rythlayn.

I stood frozen, not daring to look away from her. She was alive. She was breathing. She had come back. I had another chance, and I wasn't going to waste it. I laughed as tears fell from my eyes, covering my mouth with my hand. The crowd pushed past me.

"You too, Lyklor," said Rythlayn, pushing me to the door.

I followed orders, looking back at her as I left. I had to get to her. I had to explain and tell her what I wanted. Lily came flying out of the throne room doors and jumped into my arms as tears fell from her face. I smiled, wrapping my arms around her.

"It's a miracle. She's alive. She came back!" she shouted.

"It is a miracle," I replied. "Do you think the baby—" I stopped, moving my eyes to the floor.

She squeezed my arms. "I don't know," she said with a heavy tone. "But now that you have another chance, don't let the opportunity pass you by," she said kindly.

I nodded as she moved to Zerrial's arms.

I was unable to see her that night, and it wasn't for a lack of trying. Her family were the only ones allowed near her. I woke every few hours and went to her door to see if I would be allowed in, but each time I was turned away. I was dying to know if she was okay. I needed to see her, to hear her, to touch her. I needed to know this wasn't a dream.

After breakfast, I decided I was going to camp outside of her rooms until they finally got annoyed by my persistence. I was there for an hour and had thoroughly terrorized the guards. Lily and Vena exited. I stood to my feet with excitement. Vena nodded and went on her way. Lily walked over slowly with a small smile on her face.

"And? How is she?" I asked.

"Completely healed. Every finger, toe, and piece of skin is back. Physically, she is fine, but her mind is far from it. She remembers everything they did to her. She's beyond traumatized, Eren. We got her to eat and sleep, but she's up now."

"How did she come back?" I asked.

"I'm not completely certain, but it appears your fire god found her worthy of another life. Not only is she alive, but she's come back with a new power." Lily paused while my eyes searched her face for answers.

"Out with it, Lilian."

She smiled. "She's been gifted the Dark Flame. Nothing will ever be able to harm her again."

I laughed in disbelief, happy that she had been blessed with a power that could protect her from anyone, anything. I moved past her towards the door, eager to see Gen, but Lily stopped me.

Her face went soft. "She will see you, but Eren ... they took your form while they did those awful things to her. It was you that tortured and mutilated her in her mind. We explained who you were, and she knows you aren't them, but don't expect her to be the same person you remember."

I didn't know what to say. She was afraid of me. That was what Lily was trying to tell me. She associated me with those things and with the pain she had endured.

I nodded, pressing on the door softly. I walked into her seating area, hesitating before I opened the pocket doors to her room. She sat up on the bed, looking out to the balcony. She wore a white gown. A blanket draped over her legs and her hair fell across her left shoulder. I had never seen an angel before, but I expected they looked like her.

She turned to me, taking a deep breath as she sat up straighter against the headboard. I smiled, walking slowly towards her.

I got to the edge of the bed and gestured. "May I sit?" I asked.

She nodded, scooting over. She looked back out to the balcony. Her skin was sun kissed and her cheeks were pink from the blood running through her veins. I watched as her chest rose and fell. The simplest of actions made me smile.

"I'm so happy you're alive," I said. She didn't respond. I

dropped my head, thinking of what to say. "Can I get you anything?"

"I'm fine," she replied shortly. I uncontrollably laughed at the sound of that sweet voice. It was like music to my ears. She turned her head towards me with a blank look on her face. "What's so funny?"

"Nothing. I just ... I'm so happy to hear your voice. I didn't think I'd ever get to again." She dropped her eyes. I slowly reached out to her hand. As I made contact, she pulled away quickly. I pulled back in disappointment.

"I'm sorry, I just—" she began to say.

"It's okay, you don't have to explain. Lily told me."

She shook her head. "I know who you are. I know you're not them, but I can't get out of my own head. I saw you and felt you, but it wasn't you, I know this."

"It's okay. In time you will get better."

She shook her head as tears rolled down her face. "I don't know if I'll recover this time, Eren. Everything feels ... wrong. I'm broken; they broke me," she exclaimed.

I reached out instinctually to hold her face, but she pushed away, and I paused, remember I resembled the thing that had tortured her. "You are stronger than anyone I've ever met. You will get better. You are not broken. You've been given another chance, and you have people that love you and will be here for you. You will have whatever you need to recover, and I want to help in any way that I can," I said. She sniffled as she gathered herself. I sat up straight as the question I so desperately wanted to ask burned inside of me.

"Gen," I whispered, dropping my eyes to my hands. "Is the baby ... did the baby survive?"

She shook her head. "No."

I took a deep breath, trying not to lose it in front of her. I ran my hand down my face.

"How did you find out?" she asked.

"Lily confirmed it."

"I suppose you're relieved. A weakness you were able to avoid in the grand scheme of things," she said as she gathered herself.

I snapped my eyes back to her. "I would have never hurt you or the baby. I deserved to know."

"I kept the child a secret to protect it from you. You made your opinions very clear regarding me and any child you'd ever sire," she retorted defensively.

I took a deep breath, calming myself. She had just been through something atrocious. I didn't want to add to her pain. "Losing you ... was the worst thing that has ever happened to me. Then, when I found out about the baby, I was quickly corrected. I ... I need you to know that I would have done my best."

She looked back out to the balcony. "Where is Otar?" she asked.

"In the lab downstairs. He got himself killed right when you—" I stopped, connecting the dots finally. "He must obey you because he is connected to your life. If you die, so does he."

She didn't respond. Not even a flinch. "Bring him to me."

"Anything you want," I said with a small smile. I sat, just looking at her. In that moment, I wanted to tell her everything. Everything that I felt for her. How much I cared for her. How much I wanted her. This was my second chance, and I wasn't going to squander it. "Gen, I want you to know that I—"

"Enough, Eren. It's over," she said.

I tried reading her. Looking for her usual tells of nervousness, fear, happiness, annoyance. But there was nothing. She was so blank. The light that shined inside of her was nothing but a flicker now. As if it was fighting to stay lit.

"Gen, I want to be with you."

She laughed, bringing her eyes to mine. "Eren, you can't be serious. This is just your guilt from finding out about the child. You don't want me. Plus, let's be honest. You would only use me to elevate yourself. Knowing that wicked mind of yours as I do, you'd find a way to sit yourself upon my throne, while I sat idle blindly thinking you loved me. I'm not stupid. Give me some credit."

"It has nothing to do with power. I would never manipulate you, Genevieve. Not after everything you've been through."

"This coming from the Ambassador of Lies and Manipulation. How poetic." She just stared at me. Finally, after a few moments her gaze softened and she dropped her eyes. "Plus, I don't think I could ever be with you again in that way. They took what I felt for you and used it against me. Whatever was there is gone."

"We can fix this. I'm willing to wait. To help you in any way I can," I said desperately.

"Let it be, Eren. Just forget about whatever you think you feel for me and do your job," she said coldly. I had to find a way to get through to her. To get her past this. She was still in there. She had to be. "We're done. You may go."

I stood up, not wanting to leave her side. I looked at her beautiful face, taking her in. "I will always be here. Whatever you need," I whispered.

I left her room and made my way out into the hall. She was alive. That was all that mattered. I would get her to want me again. For now, she needed time to heal, and I had to respect that. No matter how much I wanted to be the one she leaned on, the one to hold her, I couldn't be. Not now that those things had poisoned her mind and feelings against me.

I went down to where the demons were held. Doria came rushing down the hall before I made it to the room. "We've got something!" she exclaimed. "One of the demons told us that 'he' asked them to take the princess and kill her."

"And who is 'he' supposed to be?" I asked.

"Not sure yet, but they said he controls them. He has something over them, but I couldn't get them to say what or who. At least we know now that they were working under someone's orders."

I chewed over the information, trying to connect the dots.

"Thank you, Doria. Keep me updated on any other developments. I have an idea on how we can get our questions answered." I turned down to the lab and collected Otar's body.

I went back to Gen's room where she still sat looking out onto the balcony. I placed the creature onto the bed in front of her, trying to act like our earlier conversation didn't happen.

"As requested, princess, your creature. Now, please hurry and revive him. I have a lead and I need him to be able to speak."

She sat up straighter, looking at the creature, and then to me. "Tell me," she insisted.

"Doria has been torturing the demons since they arrived in court. No one told you they were here?"

"No. I guess my father wanted me to feel safe."

"They will never touch you again. As I was saying, Doria was able to get some information from them that I need to confirm with Otar here. So, chop, chop."

"What information, Eren? Stop dancing around it and tell me."

I exhaled, acting like she was a bother. "They were working for someone. A 'he'. They said that he is the one that controls them and told them to go after you. He, I presume is Alaric, but I need our little friend here to confirm it." I thought back to Narella. I wanted to tell Gen about the mysterious female's help in finding her body and capturing the demons, but she had enough on her lap for one day.

"Leave. Come back in an hour."

I bowed with a smile. "As you wish, princess," I said, leaving her to her secrets.

An hour passed and I returned as requested. Otar was screaming and yelling as he destroyed her chambers. She sat on the bed in silence, not even watching him tear through the furniture. I walked in slowly, unsure if I was safe around the creature. She could have very well commanded him to kill me. He saw me and charged forward, throwing me into the wall.

"My gift is dead, dead! Because of you! You stupid, stupid shit," Otar yelled.

"Otar, leave him. He isn't at fault," said Gen calmly. I was. They were my responsibility and I failed. I failed them both. Otar's teeth chattered as his breathing continued to quicken. "Otar, please," she said again.

He calmed, returning slowly to her side. He got into her bed and lay on her lap. She hesitated, but put a hand on his head to comfort him. He was talking about my child. My child was *his* gift. A bit of rage and possession rose inside me at the thought of that thing being around the baby we created.

"Otar, we need to know if you remember anything else about Alaric. The demons that killed me say they were following orders. That someone commands them," she said.

His head popped up as his teeth elongated. "Demons did this to us. Demons! I will kill every last one of them, wicked one. I will destroy and maim and then I will kill Lucifer himself for creating them," yelled Otar.

"Otar, focus. We need to know if Alaric could control demons," said Gen.

Otar shook his head quickly back and forward. "He is powerful. He has the ability to control, but it isn't his own. But demons, no, no, not them. They are celestial beings. Only one thing can control them that I know of," said Otar.

"And what is that?" I asked impatiently.

"The blood of Christ," he said.

I laughed, looking from Gen to Otar. "You can't be serious? You expect me to believe there is a being out there running around with a vial of the Christian God's blood?" I asked.

"No, you idiot, his son's!" snapped Otar.

"That means that Alaric could still be controlling them," Gen pointed out.

"No, no, I remember. He hates demons. Hates all things Christian. He would never use them, even if he could control them. Not without a way to kill them. Which, there is no way," said Otar.

"Actually, there is," said Gen. She lifted her palm. Her hand and forearm ignited into a slow ember of power. At first, the wafts of smoke danced across her palm in ribbons of gray tendrils, before lighting to life in a deep, metallic black flame. Red embers popped and sparked around the edges, but the flame itself was black as obsidian, with small streams of a brownish orange color that detailed the curves and movement of each individual section. The calm fire lapped at her skin as it encircled her arm. It was the most beautiful weapon I had ever seen.

Otar jumped back off the bed in surprise. "You ... you came back because of the Dark Flame?" Otar asked.

"Three days dead and now alive with the gift. Just like Maleki," she said, reabsorbing the flame.

"Still. Alaric couldn't have known you would have that. He can't see into the future. Yes, I remember," said Otar.

"So, who else would want her dead? Someone smart enough, with the right resources to find the blood, find the demons, and stage this. It had to have been someone who knew exactly where you would be that night. Someone inside," I said, realizing the enemy was among us.

Her face dropped as a realization dawned on her. "Icici?" she asked.

I shook my head. "No, she isn't smart enough. Plus, as I said, it's a 'he'. I ... I need time to think," I said. I looked at her longingly, just for a moment. I wanted to protect her, but she wasn't going to let me. At least not physically. "Otar, stay with her. Don't let her out of your sight."

"Of course, you idiot. What do you think I am going to do? Leave her in your care? We all saw how that worked out last time," he snarled.

I dropped my eyes. A knock came at the door. I turned to see Gaelin walking into her room. He nodded at me as he focused on her. I looked back to the bed as my heart cringed a little.

For heaven's sake, I had only come to terms with these *feelings* for a few days and they were already a pain in the ass. If I could remove them, I would. Dammit, Lyklor. This what you get for being such a soft idiot. Should have kept your damn dick in your pants.

"I will check back if I discover anything. Rest well, princess," I said, looking for any sign of emotion, but there was none. She turned her gaze to Gaelin as he passed me on his way towards her.

I left before I had to witness her allowing him to touch her. Just the thought made my stomach cringe. She was mine, not his. She was mine to touch, mine to kiss, mine to comfort. Azeer, I hated this. I had to make sure she was safe. I had to focus on this task and then I would move on to our problems. Prioritize. That was what I was good at.

I went to my room and compiled a list of the alfar that would ever consider taking her life. I had to think objectively and clearly. It was a *he*. He would have a vial of blood on his person. He was smart. He wouldn't allow the vial to leave his side and risk losing control of the demons. Someone who was powerful and knowledgeable. Someone who knew Gen. Knew the inner workings of our operation. Someone she trusted and wouldn't see coming.

CHAPTER TWENTY-SIX

A fter only a few hours of sleep, morning stretched out her arms and was upon me. I got up feeling completely exhausted. The past week was wearing on me. I had barely slept or eaten since Gen had disappeared, and even now that she was alive and just down the hall, she still wasn't safe.

I took a shower, attempting to wake myself. I had to be alert to find the male that posed a threat to her. I came back into my room to find Otar standing in the doorway. I pulled on a pair of pants and walked towards the ugly creature.

"What do you want?" I spoke.

He tilted his head and smiled. "Wicked one had a vision," he said in a low, growling voice.

"Tell her I am on my way," I replied, reaching for a shirt.

"No. She doesn't want to see you," he said with a vicious grin.

I stopped, turning my attention back to him.

"She is finally through with you, and I couldn't be happier about it," he said proudly.

I felt a small sting, but I pushed it down. "The vision?"

"She saw a blur of the male we are searching for. She couldn't make out his person. She said he was surrounded in a fog. He was at court though. He is here among us. The demons cowered as he approached them."

"Not much to go on, but at least it confirms we're looking in the right place."

"Indeed," he said.

"Have you fed since you were revived?" I asked.

He narrowed his eyes. "What does it matter to you?" he snapped defensively.

"You can't feed on her. She's been through enough. She was eaten alive while they tortured her. If you were to drink from her, it could trigger a reaction."

"What do you suggest I eat then, hmm? She has commanded me not to harm another humanoid unless she instructs it. I do not have another option." I sat in the chair, grabbed the dagger from my belt, and made a deep slit in my arm. He looked at me as his eyes twitched with hunger. "Why would you offer me your blood? What are you up to? Is it poisoned?"

"As I said, she's been through enough. From now on, you will come to me to feed."

"Why not just let me wither and die?"

"Because she cares for you. She's lost enough," I said as the blood spilled from my arm.

Otar slowly approached, sniffing the air, his eyes narrowing on the blood. He brought his lips to my arm and clamped down. His skin felt wrinkled and stiff, like the hide of a wild animal. I could feel him sucking his bloody nourishment from me. I tried not to focus on what I was allowing the creature to do. The sucking feeling slowed as sharp teeth buried themselves into my skin. I flinched back with a painful groan.

He brought his eyes up to me with a smile, my blood still dripping from his teeth. "Oops, apologies," he said, giggling. The prick bit me on purpose. I wiped away the blood as Otar disappeared.

I headed out into the hall with my list of suspects committed to memory. I rounded the corner to see Gen leaving Lady Fellwood's quarters, our other court seer. Gen was dressed in a soft blue dress that hung on her body freely. It didn't reveal anything besides the top of her chest. The long sleeves went to her hands where her fingers gripped the fabric. Her hair was loose, dark curls tumbling down her back. She didn't wear makeup or her crown. She was simple, yet exquisite.

She nodded and smiled at Lady Fellwood before she turned towards me. I froze, not wanting to make her uncomfortable. It pained me knowing that when she looked at me, she only saw what those demons had done to her. Had taken from her. From us.

She looked at me with heavy and sad eyes and nodded. I approached cautiously.

"Hello, princess," I said softly.

"Good morning, ambassador," she replied.

I looked behind her at Fellwood's door: at the eye that had been carved into it. The memory of the secret Fellwood had offered Gen before the hunt flashed before my eyes.

"I need to ask you a question?" I said.

She looked at me, unimpressed. "Is this a personal question or one regarding the individual who wants me dead?"

I calmed myself, remaining cool and collected. "Before we left for the hunt, Lady Fellwood whispered something into your ear. What was it?"

Her masked slipped only for a second, revealing the sadness she kept bottled up inside. She was getting good at hiding her truth ... too good.

"That is something I would rather be kept between Lady Fellwood and myself," she answered, moving past me with haste.

Instinctually, I reached out, grabbing her arm in an effort to stop her from leaving. She turned on my in an instant, lighting her flame in a defensive manner. I dropped my hand, taking a step back.

"Gen, please," I whispered softly. "All I am trying to do is protect you and to bring the person responsible for our loss—" I stopped myself, taking a breath. "—for your murder to light. Any small detail could help."

She allowed her dark flame to absorb back into herself, taking a moment to calm her rage and fear. "She told me that I would find peace and the happiness I had been looking for soon. That I shouldn't give up on the life I wanted. That everything would be as it should be and I would no longer know pain." She took a moment. "I thought she meant that the war would be over and I would be able to be with—" she stopped herself before admitting what I already knew.

She thought Fellwood's vision meant that we would be together. Raising our child and ruling her kingdom side-by-side. The guilt tore me up inside. It took everything I had not to take her in my arms right then and there, but I knew that wasn't what she needed, even though it was what I desperately desired.

I smiled, bowing before her. "Thank you, princess. I will inform you if I find anything worth report," I said before turning down the hall giving her the space she needed. I couldn't focus on us. Not now. *Priorities dammit,* I thought to myself. First, find the threat, then worry about these *feelings* later.

The list of potential masterminds. First, the king. Even though he was her father and seemed to truly love her, I couldn't eliminate him from the equation. She would eventually take his throne and his power. To most alfar, the thought of an heir brought discomfort and unease. They would take what their predecessor had built and claim it as their own. I had to check him out, just to make sure.

Then, her uncle and cousin Toreon, for obvious reasons. Next was Gaelin and Levos. They may say they cared for her, but they could be working an angle to get revenge for what she did to their court. The rest of the list consisted of members of the council and high lords from our own court that did not wish to recognize her as the heir. They were against the removal of the clause sentencing half-breeds to death.

I met with my team and gave them marching orders. I trusted these people with my life, which I did not do lightly. This was to stay between us. No one else could know. I sent Evinee to Toreon's room. I would take the king. Zerrial would take Prince Rythlayn, and the others were spread out among the rest of the list of candidates. I assigned Firel to Levos. I needed someone with a strong mind to combat Levos's clever wit.

Though Firel wasn't much of a fighter, he was brilliant, almost in an unsettling way. He was the only one, besides Gen, that I had ever considered my equal intellectually. He could read something and commit it to memory. He could look at a picture and remember every detail. He was truly gifted. That was why I recruited him to my team.

With his unique brain came other tendencies others had seen as weakness. He was socially awkward and didn't do well in large crowds. I never saw him with a female. He would shy away from others and preferred to keep to himself. He didn't trust easily, which made our relationship valuable to him. He was a loyal soldier and a secret weapon.

I met with the king to discuss the upcoming meeting between the fairies and nymphs. I avoid the topic of Gen and the demons altogether, and so did he. Her pain was wearing on both of us, but we chose not to acknowledge it out loud. The fairy ambassador was arriving tomorrow to go over the new treaty we would present to the nymphs. I had my work cut out for me.

I checked the king's quarters as casually as I could, looking for any sign of blood or anything that could connect him to the demons. He wore a formfitting jacket and pants. I couldn't make out any jewelry on his being. The vial of blood could have been hiding under his clothing or in a pocket, but I had no way of finding out. The only resource I could rely on was my ability to read people, which meant I would have to bring up the demons. A topic we were both trying to avoid.

"Your Highness. If I may, I would like to discuss the four demons we have tied up in the basement," I said casually. He didn't look at me. He only nodded as he went over the notes for the treaty. "I am familiar with my history, but I am still puzzled as to how the demons returned to our world. Have you any idea who would have the power to get them here?"

He sat back in his chair. His face was heavy as his brow scrunched in distress. "The only thing I have been able to come up with is the rift. This Alaric character. He is a collector of creatures from different worlds, realms, hells, and times. A demon hasn't set foot in our world for 3000 years. It can't be a coincidence they show up now, when the problem with the rift is so prevalent."

The rift was also my best guess, but according to Otar, Alaric wouldn't risk losing control of the demons and he hated them with a passion.

"Do you know of another way to create a rift or tear in between realms?" I asked.

"Knowledge of that type of magic and power has never been my forte. Ask my brother. He was fascinated with other realms and gods when we were in school. He would have the answers you seek," he said, closing the folder in front of him. "That is enough for today. Please, show yourself out," he said with exhaustion. I bowed and took my leave.

Another strike towards Prince Rythlayn. I quickly headed to the library to see if there were any books that referenced realm jumping or portals. If I was going to catch Prince Rythlayn in a lie, I needed prior knowledge of the subject.

After two hours of searching through the book stacks, I finally asked the keeper for assistance. I waited for what seemed like forever. My patience was wearing thin. Finally, he approached, with only a single piece of paper in his hand.

"What is this?" I asked as he handed it to me. There were eighteen book titles on the page.

"These are the books you are looking for, but they are all missing," explained the keeper.

"What do you mean missing? Where could they have gone?" I asked.

"No one seems to know."

"Who was the last person who had access to the books?"

"All records of anyone who has ever checked them out has disappeared as well. I'm sorry, Ambassador Lyklor, but that is all we have."

I grumbled in frustration as I stormed out of the library. Great, another dead end. Whoever had done this had thought of everything. Now, I would have to face Prince Rythlayn blind; something I did not like doing. I was setting myself up to get caught, but he was the best lead I had.

I called for Zerrial to come to my private chambers. He had observed Rythlayn for the better part of a day. I needed an update on his movements. I only had thirty minutes before I was supposed to escort Gen to a council meeting. Zerrial and the others came into my room and we shut and locked the doors.

None of them had anything of use to report. Zerrial reported that Rythlayn went about conducting his business as usual. He was friendly and respectful to the members of the council he met with. Zerrial was unable to make out if he had the blood on him, but there was nothing out of the norm to report. He had visited Gen and brought her a stack of books to keep her distracted while she healed—ever the doting uncle.

I told them my findings and instructed them to be on the lookout. I gave Firel the task of digging up anything he could find on portals and realm jumping. I dismissed them, heading for Gen's room. I may not be able to touch her or speak to her freely, but at least I could look upon her and listen to her heartbeat, signaling she was indeed alive.

I rounded the corner to see Tryverse Feynar exiting her quarters, the male Evinee had introduced to us before the hunt. Gen was showing him out. He turned back to her and bowed with a smile. She thanked him and whispered something into his ear. What could she possibly want with the young alfar? I quickly added him to my list to check out before I approached.

"Tryverse, good to see you again," I said, standing tall with authority. My hands were folded behind my back as I flashed him a suspicious smile.

"Ambassador Lyklor, always a pleasure," he responded casually.

"If you were looking for Evinee, I believe I just saw her heading down into the city. If you hurry, I am sure you can catch up with her," I said, baiting him to find out why he was in Gen's chambers ... alone.

"Thank you, but that won't be necessary. I found who I was looking for," he said, turning back to Gen, smilingly softly. His tone was possessive and too arrogant for my liking. Yes, I would definitely be checking into this prick.

"Princess, the meeting," I said, redirecting the conversation.

"I haven't forgotten," she replied, closing her door as she exited. "Thank you for your help, Tryverse. I will call on you again soon," she said, placing a hand on his arm. I had to hold my breath to calm myself before I lost control and sent him to his knees in excruciating pain.

"I am at your service, Princess Genevieve," he responded. He locked his eyes on me and smiled before moving into the hall. *Don't ask, don't ask, don't ask,* I kept telling myself. Focus on the mission. Not her. Just the mission.

We walked silently to the chamber where the council waited. Usually, her arm would be wrapped around mine. Her fingers would unconsciously rub along the fabric of my jacket as we walked. I would say something snarky to make her laugh. She would occasionally bump her hips against mine as I fought not to pull her closer, but not this time. She kept her distance while I tried to keep my hands to myself and not reach for her.

I pulled the door open and she entered the room. The council, along with her uncle, cousins, and father were already seated. She made her way to the chair at his right. I took my seat across from her as the meeting began. I took note of any jewelry the council members were wearing. Family sigil, gold chains, diamonds. Nothing that could hold a vial of blood.

The meeting progressed as normal. No one mentioned the newly resurrected princess. We spoke of the light court, who was leaving this evening to finally return to their hellhole. We spoke of the findings we had discovered with the new creatures we had recently killed, the rift, and the negotiations between the races. The last topic listed for discussion was the upcoming tournament for the hand of the princess. The winner would get the privilege of marrying her and becoming the next King of Doonak. The king exhaled as he approached the topic. I watched Gen for any sign of what she might feel, but she just sat stoically.

"As custom calls for," said the king, "the tournament for the hand of my daughter is scheduled to take place seven days from now as the new year approaches. The three candidates include Therosi Servi, Avalon Flarion, and Soddram Yositru. They will be tested in three categories: intelligence, skill, and willpower. I have constructed the tournament myself with the help of Ravion Sterling."

Ravion was what we called a Visitor. He could travel into someone's mind, see through their eyes and also memories from their past. With a touch, he could transfer what he saw to another alfar.

"After the tournament, the normal gifting ceremony between the bride and groom will take place along, with the customary night of silence, and then the wedding. All will take place within three days from the conclusion of the tournament," finished the king.

The table was silent. I couldn't imagine what Gen was feeling. After all she had been through, another male was going to be forced upon her. The night of her wedding, I knew a part of me would die. I had to protect her. I couldn't let her endure another moment of pain.

"Your Highness, if I may," I said softly.

He nodded at me.

"After the recent situation the princess has overcome, may I suggest we postpone the tournament until a respectable amount of time has passed, allowing everyone to mend from what has happened? I am sure the court will understand if the princess needs—"

"That is not necessary, Ambassador Lyklor," interrupted Gen, stone-faced as she looked across the table at me. I swallowed hard, taken aback by her objection. She turned and faced her father. "I know what my station requires of me. I am ready to fulfill my duty on schedule." She swallowed, showing the first sign of emotion I had seen from her in days. Pain. "The faster I can conceive an heir, the stronger our kingdom will be. Which requires our schedule to be kept on track."

I dropped my eyes, thinking about our child. The one that would have sat on the throne next. It took all I had to not destroy everything around me. How could something, someone, I had never seen, never held, never known, cause me so much pain? Her father looked to his daughter in surprise.

"The princess makes a good point," added Rythlayn. "The

tournament and a royal wedding will show her strength and commitment to the kingdom. After everything the court has witnessed, this will work in the princess's favor. It will also raise the spirits of our people with the continual attacks we've endured due to the rift."

"Thank you, uncle," said Gen.

The king still said nothing. His eyes met mine for a brief moment before he turned back to his daughter. "As you wish," he said, standing from the table.

We stood out of respect as he left the room. Dammit! She was so unpredictable lately. Something I used to admire was now a thorn in my side. Nothing I did was good enough for her. She just kept spoiling my attempts to help her.

The next two days were much of the same. The court prepared for the tournament and then the wedding. With every day that passed I became more anxious and annoyed. I was getting nowhere. Firel had come up empty-handed with the portals, and my team had discovered nothing useful the other suspects on my list.

On the third night, just four days before the tournament, Otar appeared in my room, erratic as ever. He pulled at his ears and stomp on the floor, yelling and tossing whatever was closest to him. He finally calmed, his breathing unnatural. I just sat on the other side of my desk watching the thing act like a child. He stormed over to me, pointing one of his long black fingers in my face.

"You fix her! You fix what you broke! Make it stop! Make her happy again!" he yelled, sliding the papers and objects on my desk to the floor in rage.

"Are you hungry? Is that what this is about?" I asked calmly, reaching for my dagger.

He stopped me. "No, you idiot. I want you to fix her! There is so much pain and darkness. I can't take it. Not from her. Not when she used to be so shiny and bright. Now she is dull and dead inside. I feel it. I feel it every moment. No matter what I do, I can't bring it back. The shiny part of her. I can't find it."

"I thought you enjoyed pain?" I asked.

"When it is my own, yes. Not when it is hers. It doesn't fit. It feels ... unnatural. And then there is the screaming at night. The nightmares and the torture she sees when she closes her eyes. She just screams, and screams, and screams. I try to fix her, but she is afraid of me. I don't know what to do with her, but I can't stand this. I may kill myself and just wait until this passes. That would be better than every night of this."

I didn't know what to say to him. "She doesn't want my help. I've tried. There is nothing I can do," I said softly. The new knowledge of what she was going through each night ate at me.

"You made her happy once. I felt it. It make me sick, but she was happy. Do it again. Take away the pain. You must do something. Don't just sit here like the worthless piece of shit you are," he said, grabbing me by the shirt and pulling me into his face.

I removed his hand, grabbed the dagger, and slit my arm. "Eat," I demanded.

"I don't want your blood. I want you to fix her!"

I looked at him with anger as my whole body tensed. "I said eat," I yelled.

He slowly brought his mouth to my arm, never letting go of my eyes. After he was done, he disappeared. I got dressed and made my way to Icici's room. If Gen was having nightmares, I had to make sure Icici wasn't responsible. If she was, I would kill her myself.

I knocked, trying to gather my composure. She opened the door in sheer black lingerie. Her elegant hair was loose around her face. Her eyes were deadly as her mouth smirked with excitement. She leaned against the door, pushing her breasts out towards me.

"Well, well, well. It's been a while, Lyklor. Though, I can't say I am not pleased to see you," she said, moving out of the way so I could enter. She closed the door just before I wrapped my hand around her neck, pinning her to the wall. She gasped for air, but I only tightened my grip. She flailed and fought, but I was stronger and more determined.

"Are you fucking with her mind again?" I growled as I brought my face to hers.

She wrapped her hands around mine, trying to pull free as she shook her head no.

"You better be telling the truth. If I find out you're lying, I swear to Azeer I will come back, dismember you slowly, and serve you up to whatever is desperate enough to eat you. Or, maybe I will just give you to the demons. Actually, that sounds more entertaining. Let's see how you like getting fucked and shredded to pieces at the same time." I said coldly, dropping her to the floor.

"You filthy lowborn. How dare you touch or speak to me in that manner. I will have your head for this," she said, grabbing her neck in pain.

"Please, like anyone would believe a lying whore. Your uncle is just looking for a reason to dispose of you. All I have to do is mention that you might be messing with the princess's mind and he would have your head. Who do you think he'll believe, hmm? You or me? I am not usually a betting male, but if I had to, I'd place the wager on me."

She stood to her feet, eyes wild. "What has happened to you, Erendrial? You've allowed her to consume you. All it took was one night in her bed and you've lost yourself. What are you hoping for? That she wakes up and will love you again? That she will talk her father into making you king? That you will live happily ever after? Please. I know you better than you know yourself.

"She would never be enough for you. Right now, she is a chal-

425

lenge, but once she gives in and you've had her completely, you will tire of her and look to another. You would break her little human heart. You are incapable of giving her what she wants. You would devour her light and destroy her, again, in the process. And for what? A few more rounds in between her warm legs?"

I took a breath, not able to look at her. "I would stop talking if I were you," I warned, gritting my teeth together.

"That's fine. I don't have to talk," she said, making her way over to me. She dragged her hand down the front of my chest until her fingers reached for the clasp on my pants. She pushed her soft and supple breasts against me. I grabbed her hand with force, removing it from my pants as I stepped away. She gave a small laugh in disbelief as she shook her head.

"That ... will never happen again," I declared.

She smiled, arching her eyebrow at me. "We will see."

I turned to exit her quarters.

"For the record," she said, "I'm not as evil as you give me credit for. I saw the report of the examination Vena conducted. Genevieve is annoying and inconvenient, but no one deserved that. I wouldn't make her relive those moments. No matter how much I hate her."

For the first time in over 150 years of knowing her, Icici sounded sincere. I left the room, not looking back.

CHAPTER
TWENTY-SEVEN

P rince Rythlayn finally accepted my request for an audience
after dinner the next evening. I was going in blind, but if he
was innocent, he wouldn't hesitate to give me what I asked for. I
had committed the eighteen titles of the missing books to memory.
That was all the ammo I had, and it would have to be enough.

I made my way to Gen's room, stopping to knock for the first
time ever. Atalee came to the door as I heard Gen yelling in the
background. I stepped in quickly, making my way to her bedroom.
She wore a black feathered gown that hugged her desirable little
body perfectly. Her hair swept up and away from her elegant neck.
Otar stood on the other side of the room, on the receiving end of
her wrath. She had a knife in her hand and held out her gashed
wrist towards him. I gestured for Atalee to leave.

"You stubborn creature! You need to eat. I demand you eat," she
yelled, walking towards him.

I could tell Otar was fighting her command with everything he
had, but he was faltering. "No, no, no! I am fine. I eat. I eat," he
said, curling himself into a corner.

"You haven't eaten since I resurrected you. You need to feed. I can't lose you. I need you to eat," she said, kneeling beside him, shoving her arm to his mouth.

"Princess," I said quickly.

She snapped her head to me, standing in discomfort at the sight of me. "You knocked," she stated.

I nodded, moving slowly towards them. "If the creature says he doesn't need to eat, he doesn't need to eat," I replied.

"How do you know what he needs? He hasn't fed in days," she said.

"Does he look ill or weak to you?" I pointed out.

She looked at him, examining his form as he hid his face from her. "No, but that doesn't change the fact that he needs to feed."

I exhaled, not sure how she would react to me being his new food source. "He has eaten. I've been allowing him to feed on me when he needs to," I said, readying myself for her wrath.

Her gaze whipped to Otar in anger. "And you didn't tell me?" she said with aggression.

"No need to tell. All is well," he said defensively.

She took a breath and then a step back. "Leave now, Otar," she snapped.

"But, but—" he said.

"Now!" He disappeared. She turned back to me, walking slowly with the dagger still in her hand. "Why are you feeding him? Are you trying to gain control of him? Because I assure you that is not how the bond works. He can feed off anyone and no one will be able to control him but me."

"That is not my intent. I don't want the creature. I just thought that allowing him to feed on you would trigger uncomfortable memories of other experiences. I just wanted to give you time to heal. That's all, I promise," I said calmly.

The tip of the dagger appeared at my throat as she bared her teeth. "Stop assuming you know what I need and want. I told you what I needed from you, and yet here you are, still interfering. You have one job to do, which you have yet to complete. Find the one who commands the demons. After that, I don't want to see your face unless I absolutely have to. Am I clear, Ambassador Lyklor?"

I nodded as a knock came at the door. Tryverse Feynar appeared.

"Your escorting services will no longer be necessary," she said, lowering the dagger from my throat. "Do not return to my rooms unless you have completed your task, or I call for you." She tossed the knife into the wall and headed past me towards Feynar.

I turned as she took his arm in hers. I was losing her more and more with each passing day. I had to figure out who the traitor was, so I could focus on her. If I waited much longer, he was going to take my place. He was going to take my light.

After dinner, I met with Prince Rythlayn in his private chambers. I memorized everything in his room. He had a massive collection of books that rivaled my own. His chambers were neat and orderly to the point of compulsion. During my time serving the king, I had never known the prince to act in his own interests. He had always been loyal to his brother. He seemed to genuinely love him.

"Prince Rythlayn, thank you so much for accepting my request for an audience. I am sure you are busy with the preparations for the tournament and ceremony," I said.

He took off his jacket and turned towards me with a smile. "Erendrial, please, you can call me Ryth. The day is over, and I am done with formalities. What can I offer you to drink?"

"Whiskey, if you have it."

"Of course," he said, going to his wet bar. He poured a glass and handed it to me, then sat across from me. "Now, what can I do for you?"

"I have spoken with the king about the rift. Since we don't know where it opens or how Alaric controls it, I thought it wise to understand how rifts are created. If I can understand them, I can hopefully find a way to track its movements, or even a way to prevent them from opening altogether," I said, testing the waters.

His eyes remained on his glass as he trailed his finger along the rim. "How can I help?" he said kindly.

"I went to the library to research the topic, but the resources were missing from the keeper's collection. The king suggested that I speak with you. He said you were very knowledgeable on the subject; that it used to be a focus of yours."

He gave a soft smile as he folded his hands in front of his chest. "Erendrial, I have focused on much during my long life. Though I like to think myself an expert in most matters, that was a long time ago, and I am not sure what help I can give," he said, playing humble, acting like he didn't remember. Innocently ignorant.

"Any information you can recall would be useful," I said.

He turned his attention to the ceiling, acting like he was trying to remember. "The only thing I can recall is that in order to open the rift, you need to sacrifice both creatures of light and dark magic. I found that part interesting, but how you get the thing to open or how you control where, I can't remember. It was over eight hundred years ago when I dabbled in that subject. I will check with some resources I have, to see if they possess any of the texts you seek."

I paused, trying to mask the spinning wheels in my head. I stood, finishing my drink. "Thank you, Ryth. Even that small bit will help. Your knowledge, as always, is invaluable."

He laughed, standing to his feet as he patted me on the back.

"No need for flattery. I am too old for that," he said, leading me to the door. "If there is anything else, my door is always open to you. I admit I do enjoy that mind of yours. I always thought it a waste that you were born lower class. If you were the son of a high lord, you would have made an excellent candidate to be king."

"Now you flatter me, Prince Rythlayn. I am humbled by your opinion of me."

"Let's just say I can see why both my daughter and niece took a liking to you," he whispered. He was trying to bait me. To get a rise out of me by bringing up my personal life. I wasn't going to play his game.

"Two very intelligent and talented females. I am honored to serve your family."

He smiled, opening the door for me. "Good night, Erendrial."

"Your Highness," I said, bowing to him. I left certain he was hiding something. Why else try to rattle my feathers by mentioning his daughter and Gen? He knew more about the rifts than he led me to believe. He was clever and crafty, but he wasn't me.

The next day, negotiations began between the ambassadors of the light court, the nymphs, and the fairies. We would be locked in a room until we could come to an arrangement. Yay, me.

"There is no reason to limit the air above your lands. We have done nothing to earn your distrust," said the fairy ambassador Telvi.

"Taking our goods, destroying our lands, and eating our people would suggest otherwise," yelled Haeza, the nymph ambassador.

"Alright, alright. We have heard from both of you enough for one day," I said. "Ambassador Levos, did the guards your kingdom sent to the nymph's lands witness any fairies landing in their territory?"

"They reported seeing them flying overhead just as two nymphs went missing," replied Levos.

"But did they actually see the fairies interacting with the nymphs?" I asked.

"No," Levos said with exhaustion.

"Did your guards see any fairies traveling with nymphs in their arms?" I asked.

"No," Levos said with hesitation.

"So, how do you suggest the fairies stole the nymphs if no one saw them land and your own guards didn't see them carrying bodies? Did they just magically disappear?" I asked. "Ambassador Telvi, does your race now possess the ability to magically teleport things out of an area?" I asked.

Telvi laughed. "No, Ambassador Lyklor. Misting remains your

court's magic trick," she replied.

I turned back to Levos and Haeza. "Then what right had your court to go into the fairies' lands and hives and enact revenge for a crime you have no proof they committed?" I demanded.

Levos calmed himself. "The evidence pointed to the fairies. They were the only ones in the area when the events occurred," replied Levos.

"Is it not possible that someone could have been framing the fairies? Over the past thousand years, our court has built a strong relationship with their race. We know that nymphs are not their first choice as food. Why would they risk breaking their treaty with the nymphs, along with enduring your wrath, for a treat they don't enjoy?" I asked.

Telvi smiled as the other two sat quietly.

"I will consider your silence to mean that you see my point," I continued. "Now, as for the treaty. The only thing that the fairies are asking is that you allow them to fly over the nymph territory. They will not touch down or make contact with their people. The air will only be used for travel. In return, King Phasis and Queen Pyra have offered to pay two hundred pounds in gold a month. That's twenty-four hundred pounds a year for access to the sky. A very generous offer, if I do say so." A moment of silence passed.

"The fairies must promise that no harm will come to our race," demanded Haeza.

"You have our word," said Telvi humbly. "On that note, Ambassador Atros. We would like you to return the six members of our court that you are holding hostage."

Levos sat up straight with a confused expression. "We are not holding anyone from your court captive. We attacked your hive as a warning, but we never took anyone hostage," he explained.

I pulled away from the table at the news.

"Then where did our six fairies go?" asked Telvi. "We've scoured the lands. There is no trace of them."

"I am sorry, but we are not responsible for their disappearance," replied Levos.

"Ambassador Haeza," I said, leaning forward. "How many nymphs are missing?"

"Six as well," she said.

Six nymphs, six fairies. Six members of light magic and six members of dark magic. The ingredients that you would need in order to trigger a rift opening.

"We will continue to look for the members of your races and assist any way we can," I said, trying to divert attention from the missing humanoids. "Now that we have an agreement, I presume you would all like to return to your own courts." The treaty was signed, and my job was done.

Levos stayed behind after the other two had left. He stood in silence, watching as I collected my papers. "Can I help you with something, Levos?"

"I would like to ask permission to stay in Doonak for the tournament and Genevieve's wedding," he stated.

"Is this at the request of your queen?"

"She is my friend, Erendrial. I care about her. I want to be here for her through this," he said, dropping his formal tone.

I turned my focus towards him. "If she agrees to it, then yes, you may stay," I replied.

He nodded. Vena appeared in the doorway, and he turned to her with a warm smile. She scrunched her shoulders as her face lit up.

I snickered. "Is Gen the only reason you wish to stay?"

He turned back to me defensively. "She is the main reason, yes."

"Enjoy your time in the dark court, Levos. Don't get too comfortable," I said, walking past them.

By the time my duties were done, it was late, but I wanted to inform Gen of what I had discovered about the rift. I went to her room where the two guards informed me she was sleeping. She would want me to wake her for this. Maybe Otar knew something about the rifts, or we could use the information to trigger one of her visions.

The king had granted me access to her chambers whenever I needed it. I didn't know how long that privilege was going to last, but I was still allowed into her rooms.

I pushed the door open and walked silently inside. I slid the pocket doors back to find her curled up in the arms of Tryverse Feynar. They lay fully clothed on top of the comforter. Her head resting on his chest as she curled her body against his. His arms were wrapped around her torso and his head rested on top of her curly hair.

I swallowed hard at the sight. He was holding her. Something I had never done. Something I refused to do when I had had the chance. I heard her exhale while she slept peacefully against him. He ran his fingers along her spine in a comforting and intimate manner. Why him? When had this developed? This didn't make sense.

I stepped back, closing the doors in front of me and exiting her rooms. I leaned against the wall in the hall, unable to breathe. *Come on Eren, get a hold of yourself.* I forced myself back up and continued to my room. It killed me to not know how deep their relationship went. I had to know what I was up against.

"Otar!" I yelled as I got to my room. The little prick owed me. "Otar!"

"What, what? I was just about to catch myself a harpy. This better be important," he said, sitting on my bed.

"Tryverse Feynar. What is the nature of his relationship with Genevieve?" I demanded, still trying to catch my breath from the anger raging through me.

Otar smiled and laughed as his head tilted from side to side. "You saw, did you?" he said hatefully.

"Just tell me," I yelled. My vision grew spotty as I felt my body heating.

Otar slid off the bed and made his way in front of me. "He does for her what you could not. He gives her happiness. He takes away the pain."

"How?" Images of their naked bodies tortured me. "Are they … intimate?"

Otar laughed again. "Oh, stupid male. Who cares? She is happy. Stop being so selfish. You should thank the young male. She is sleeping and eating, thanks to him."

"I know we don't care for each other. But please, just tell me," I begged the creature through my teeth.

He huffed. "I have not felt that type of happiness from her. She doesn't allow me in the room when he is there. She does not smell of sex after he leaves. All I know is she is getting better. She is happy, which makes me … calmer."

I rested my hands on the chair in front of me as my temper began to subside. "You may go," I said.

He appeared in front of me, studying my face.

"What?"

"You will not harm the male, will you?" he asked.

Everything inside of me screamed yes. I had already thought of a thousand ways to kill him on the walk to my room. I wanted to cut off his hands just for touching her. I gritted my teeth together, trying to think reasonably.

"If he brings her comfort, no," I barely was able to say.

"Good."

"But the moment he stops making her happy, he is fair game," I snarled.

Otar laughed as he clapped his hands together. "Exactly how I felt about you; but she still says I can't kill you. Don't worry, that day will come," he said, disappearing into the air.

I threw the chair into the wall, breaking it into pieces.

CHAPTER
TWENTY-EIGHT

The next morning, I avoided anywhere she would be. I couldn't erase the image of her in Feynar's arms. I drew them together as I lay in bed alone. I thought if I could get it out of my head and onto paper, it would somehow ease my pain, but I was wrong. Two days until the tournament. Five days until she would be married. Five days until she would have another male's imprint on her body for the rest of her life.

Doria came rushing into the sitting room I occupied without warning. "What is wrong?" I asked, seeing the distress on her face.

"The princess. She insisted on seeing them," she said, out of breath.

"Seeing who?"

"The demons. She's down there with them now."

"And you just left her alone with them? What were you thinking?" I snapped, darting for the door.

I ran through the halls until I reached the chamber where they were still strapped to the silver sheets of metal. Gen was in a green velvet dress that revealed the length of her spine. On her lower back, the scars she had acquired as a young girl were gone. The rebirth must have healed her body of all scars, which meant she no longer had Lysanthier's sigil branded into her skin.

She didn't turn towards us as we entered. She just stood with her eyes locked onto the four of them. I signaled for Doria to leave as I slowly approached, not wanting to startle her. The demons caught sight of me and began shaking in their chains with excitement. I made my way to her side. She continued to stare at them.

"Their natural faces are uglier than I remember," she said calmly.

"I guess they're not as beautiful as their master Lucifer," I said.

She gave a faint laugh of amusement. My breath snagged at the response.

"I once compared your physical appearance to the fallen angel," she admitted.

"Well, I am striking," I replied arrogantly.

She gave a small smile that faded too quickly. I felt another twinge of happiness and pain. Otar was right. Feynar was healing her. He was doing the thing I couldn't.

"He looks nothing like the chosen one," said one of the demons.

"But we'd be happy to introduce you, princess."

"I am sure he'd be interested to hear how you came back to life."

"Yes, just like Yahweh. Three days in the grave, then poof, a miracle resurrection." They all began to laugh in amusement.

She cringed at the sound.

"They don't know, do they?" I asked her.

"I don't think so, but I can't wait to surprise them," she said. The note of revenge was heavy in her voice.

"A secret?" said a demon.

"Oh, oh, I love secrets. Do tell."

"Maybe it will get them to give us more," I suggested.

She tilted her head, considering the option. The leader of the group lifted his eyes to use.

"Have you two begun trying for a replacement child yet?" asked the leader.

I turned to look at Gen. At the mention of our child, her eyes went completely black. Not a trace of white or green in sight. Another side effect of the Dark Flame, I presumed.

"The combination of you two was delicious. You should consider it. We're going to be quite famished once we get out of here."

Both of Gen's arms ignited with the Dark Flame as she lunged towards the demon. I grabbed for her waist, preventing her from ending its pathetic existence as her flames seared my skin. Their eyes widened in shock and fear at the sight of her flame.

"Let me go!" she yelled. "I will rip them to pieces. They deserve this! They all deserve to suffer in pain!"

I held on as she fought me. "I want nothing more than to watch as you enact your revenge, but we still need them. Their time will come. You will have your revenge. I promise you," I said, holding her close to me.

She calmed, still looking at the creatures with hunger. Her eyes faded back to their natural state, her hands absorbing the new power. I slowly released her, stepping back to her side.

"You ... you have it?" asked one of them.

"Impossible. Not since that fucker Maleki," said another.

"She is of his blood."

"That son of a bitch Azeer. We should have killed him when we had the chance."

"I'm glad you didn't," said a voice from behind us. I turned to see Prince Rythlayn approaching us. "He has been a most gracious god. Wouldn't you agree, niece?" He stopped at her side, putting a hand on her shoulder. The demons refocused as they snapped their mouths shut, refusing to look at Rythlayn.

I examined the prince. He smirked at the creatures, not afraid of them, not disgusted by what they had done to his beloved niece. He stood in front of them without worry, confident as if he knew they could never hurt him. My eyes trailed to the hand that held onto Gen's shoulder. A silver cuff wrapped around his wrist. In the center was a small clear orb. A red substance, thick and bright, slid against its confinement. Blood.

I snapped my attention back to the demons. They didn't laugh. Their taunting had stopped. They were silent. Afraid of the control he had over them. It all made sense. He had been the one with the knowledge needed to create the rift. He knew the hostility between the fairies and nymphs. He used their hatred and distrust against one another to capture and use their people for the sacrifice that was required, knowing they would blame each other for their missing subjects.

He knew the inner workings of our operation. He knew where Gen would be and where to kill her. The rift provided the perfect cover. He had the power and authority to remove the books from the library that could lead back to him. When Gen had her vision of him, she couldn't see him because his power blocked hers. His shielding ability prevented her from seeing his face.

But how did he know where to find us that day in the woods? *Click.* It all fell into place.

Winnow Fellwood. She and Rythlayn had been working together. Tracking Gen's every move. Fellwood revered Gen's power as a seer and her ability to control what she saw, making Fellwood's gift seem inferior. It was no secret since Gen's arrival to court, Fellwood had been tossed to the side by the king.

This was their plan all along. Rythlayn wasn't happy for his brother. He didn't care about Gen. He was enraged about the crown being just out of reach. He wanted to put himself and then his heirs on the throne. He had waited for so many centuries and just when it was in reach, she popped up and took it from him. He supported the law that called for the death of all half-breeds. Only when he discovered his brother's daughter was one did he change his vote.

Fellwood would have been happy to assist a future king if it meant regaining her status within the court and removing her competition in the process. The two of them had been rumored to be intimate from time-to-time, adding another layer to this plot. Not only was Fellwood reaching for her station, but also for the throne.

They both had the resources, motive, and the knowledge to pull this off. But they didn't expect the demons to ever be caught. Fellwood must not be able to see Narella. I had made sure not to tell a soul about her. And now, Rythlayn's niece possessed the one thing that could kill them. He came down here in fear that the demons would make a deal with her to save themselves from eternal death. He was doing damage control.

"Yes, uncle," replied Gen. She looked up at him and smiled as he took her into his side. I wanted to pull her away from his grasp, but I couldn't, not yet. I had to trap him in front of everyone, so the court and his brother would see him for what he was.

"Why are you down here, sweetheart? I assumed you wouldn't want to be near these beasts," he said.

"I needed to see them ... to face them," she whispered.

He turned to me. "And you, Erendrial. Have you come to dismember them again?" he asked.

Her eyes turned to me with questions.

"Though I would like nothing more, I am just here as back up," I said with a smile.

"You've turned out to be quite the protector, Lyklor. My brother and I are grateful for your loyalty," he said.

"I don't deserve your admiration. Even though his majesty has looked past my shortcomings, it doesn't change the fact that I failed her majesty," I said, looking at Gen. Her eyes met mine only for a moment, but it was enough. Enough for me to hold onto to a sliver of hope.

"You fought valiantly and in time, I am sure we all can move past this," he said, looking down at Gen with a smile, his hand still wrapped around her shoulder. "Your father has requested your presence, my dear. He wasn't thrilled to hear you were down here. Best go ease his worry."

She nodded before leaving the room.

His eyes turned back to me. "I heard the negotiations with the ambassadors went well yesterday."

"Would you expect anything less?" I said, smiling at him.

He laughed, putting his arm around me as we left. "Your brilliant mind and sharp tongue never cease to amaze me."

"I'm glad I can be of some amusement to you, Your Grace." We ascended into the palace ... together.

I went to my rooms and began to come up with a plan. I couldn't tell a single soul about what I had discovered.

Rythlayn and his children had spies everywhere, and Winnow might have a vision exposing my discovery before I had time to bring them before the king. Even my own team I had to question. I didn't know how far their reach stretched. Tonight, I would expose them. Tonight, this ended.

Thirty minutes before dinner, I made my way to the king's chambers. I needed him on board if this was going to stand a chance of working. If Rythlayn or Winnow were tipped off at any point, this would turn on us for the worse. I knocked, feeling more nervous than I had ever felt. The servant came to the door and announced me to the king.

"Ambassador Lyklor, I wasn't expecting you," he said, continuing to dress for dinner. I looked at the servant and then back at him. He was observant enough to get my meaning. "Thank you, Tessa, that will be all." She bowed and left. "What is the meaning of your visit?" he asked.

There could be no holding back. If this was going to work, I had to take off my mask. Only for a moment. I took a breath, readying myself. "You have always been kind to me, Your Majesty. You gave me a chance when others thought you foolish to do so. Even though I have failed you in the worst way, I hope I have served you in every other way to your liking," I said.

"You have."

447

"Do you trust me, my king?" I asked.

He stopped, looking me dead in the eye a with question. He nodded.

"Please sit."

He did and I began to tell him everything I had discovered. I told him about Narella, the blood, the nymphs, and fairies. I told him my theory of how Rythlayn's mind operated, and what was in it for Winnow. Rythlayn and I weren't much different in that manner, so it was easy for me to understand him. The only difference was, I truly cared for Gen, whereas he only pretended.

When I had finished, the king sat in disbelief as I watched a part of him shatter. His own brother and trusted seer had ordered the torture and death of his only daughter: a daughter he had come to love more than he may have thought possible. He sat up straight, regaining his composure.

"What do you need from me?" he asked.

"They need to be exposed before the entire court. The court needs to witness the control Rythlayn has on the demons. I propose you make a grand gesture, thanking him and his children for all their hard work with the upcoming arrangements. Elevate them and play to their need for affirmation, so he will be caught off guard. During this time, restrain your nieces and nephew, and I will have Doria bring up the demons. Then I will take it from there," I said.

The king paused, still seeming to be in disbelief. "If you are right, he will die tonight, along with his children and a trusted member of our court, if they had any involvement. If you are wrong, your head will be on the chopping block. Are you prepared to risk your life on this, Erendrial? Are you that certain?"

I paused, already having weighed the question myself. "I am, Your Grace," I said with confidence.

He nodded, standing to his feet. "I will see you at dinner, Ambassador Lyklor."

I got up and left, preparing myself for the theatrical show that I would direct.

We all ate dinner together as we did every night. Genevieve looked exquisite. She wore a bright red dress made of satin that left her chest visible. I noted that the Lysanthier sigil was indeed gone, and she no longer wore the star-shaped pendant Atros had given her as a sign of his affections. She sat between her father and uncle as they talked and laughed as if nothing was out of the norm. Her heart would break tonight. She adored her uncle and two of her three cousins. I didn't know if they were involved with the coup, but I was prepared regardless of which way this went.

Winnow Fellwood soon entered the dining hall, taking her seat among the normal houses she chose to associate with. My mind spun with the possibility of other houses being involved in the attempt on Gen's life. If they were, I would discover them; but for tonight, I needed to focus on those who I knew had a hand in the death of the princess ... and our child.

After dinner, the king, queen, and Gen sat upon their thrones as the king called for the room to quiet. The dancing stopped as the music faded into the background. Everyone sat up, eager to hear the king's announcement. It was showtime.

"Thank you, lords and ladies," said the king. "As we approach the tournament, now just a day away, I would like to take this time to thank a few members of our court that have gone above and beyond during these challenging past few months. These members have shown loyalty, commitment, and dedication every step of the way in order to elevate our kingdom. They have helped build Doonak into a strong and feared powerhouse that I am proud to call my home. I am not only honored to call these four my friends, but also my family. Please help me show our respect and gratification to my brother, Prince Rythlayn, and his beautiful children, Lady Icici, Lord Toreon, and Lady Vena."

The crowd erupted with cheers as the four of them made their way to the front of the platform. They looked shocked but honored by the recognition. Their arrogance would be their downfall. Gen clapped, looking down at the people she thought loved her.

Azeer, I pray that she forgives me for this. As the crowd calmed, Rythlayn bowed and then stood with a smile on his face. I sat, waiting for my chance to attack.

"My king and beloved brother. We are honored by the recognition, but it is not needed. We are honored to serve our kingdom and our house. We are strong as a family and look forward to assisting you and the princess in any way that we can," said Rythlayn.

The king's smile fell at the mention of his daughter. "You have welcomed my daughter with open arms into our family. She cares greatly for you and your children. She speaks of you all with the highest regard," said the king.

Gen gave a small smile at the four of them.

"And we speak highly of her. She is truly a blessing sent from Azeer," said Rythlayn.

"There is another member of our court I would like to thank for his loyalty and dedication to this family," said the King. Rythlayn's face scrunched, perhaps wondering who he had to share his glory with. "Ambassador Erendrial Lyklor."

I stood from my chair as the court clapped respectfully. I turned on my mask and readied myself for battle. Gen's face fell, as did Rythlayn's and his three children's.

I smiled, making my way to the platform. I bowed before the royals, raising my head to the king. He nodded. I turned with authority as I looked down at Rythlayn's three children from the step. I raised my hands and my team surrounded Rythlayn and his heirs. They restrained Icici, Toreon, and Vena with ulyrium cuffs. Rythlayn spun around in shock, turning back to his brother.

"What is the meaning of this? Brother, what are you doing?" he asked in a panic. The king ignored him, waiting for me to present the evidence. Rythlayn's eyes snapped to me as I stood before him, smiling. "What have you done?" he snared.

I laughed. "The real question is, what have *you* done, Prince Rythlayn?" I said. I held his eyes as his face tensed. "Doria, darling. Bring them in." Doria and a set of six guards walked into the room with the four demons leashed and on display. The court gasped at the sight of them. Gen went to stand from her chair, but her father stopped her. Rythlayn looked at the four demons and then back to me as he quickly realized he had been caught.

"What are you doing?" asked Gen from behind me. It took everything I had not to turn to her, but I remained in my mask. I walked past Rythlayn and addressed the court.

"My fellow members of Doonak," I said with my normal amount of arrogance. "Three thousand years ago, King Maleki Drezmore eradicated the demon threat that plagued our lands. He made a deal with our revered god to save our lives and our world. Since then, demons have not set foot into this world, until a little over a week ago, when they brutalized our princess, taking her life in the process.

"With the constant opening of the rifts, at first, we assumed the demons had just come through on their own, but after interrogation and further investigations, we found that the demons were not working alone, nor of their own accord. Someone went through a great deal of trouble to allow these things access to our world. Thanks to Prince Rythlayn, I discovered that you need six creatures of both dark and light magic to trigger a rift. Recently, six fairies and six nymphs have gone missing. Their bodies have not been found.

"I believe the person who controls the demons and the person creating the rifts is indeed the same individual. Now, this alone is cause for death, but this alfar didn't stop there. He ordered the demons to attack and kill the sole heir of King Drezmore, to elevate himself and his children to the throne."

The crowd gasped as they looked upon Rythlayn and his children.

Rythlayn turned to his brother, playing ignorance. "Brother please," he said in a desperate voice, "Lyklor has gone too far. How dare he accuse me or my children of such a heinous act? He is out of line and should be dealt with accordingly."

The king looked at his brother with nothing but hatred. "Please continue, Ambassador Lyklor," said the king.

"Thank you, Your Highness. Where was I? Oh, yes, onto his accomplice." I paused, turning my attention to Winnow Fellwood. Her face fell in terror. "Zerrial, would you do the honors?"

Zerrial appeared behind her, restraining her with force. "No," she whimpered. "You are mistaken. I would never act against the princess nor my king." Zerrial forced her to her knees next to Rythlayn.

"Beautifully orchestrated, my dear," I said tauntingly. "You should have considered a career in theater instead of pursuing one at court. It might have just saved your head. Prince Rythlayn had knowledge of Princess Genevieve's whereabouts the day of the hunt, thanks to Lady Fellwood's gifts.

"Since Princess Genevieve's arrival, Lady Fellwood has felt re-placed ... unappreciated, especially since she is the one to thank for reuniting the king with his beloved daughter. As it is known to many of us, Prince Rythlayn and Lady Fellwood have been in-volved in an intimate relationship with one another for centuries.

"By removing the princess, not only does Lady Fellwood regain her position at court, but also a chance to sit on the throne. Prince Rythlayn had the motive to remove her from the line of succession. He knew how a rift operates, which was confirmed by our king. He is also in possession of the only weapon that can control demons," I said, turning to face Rythlayn.

His eyes widened as his face turned to rage.

"The blood of the one and only Jesus Christ. Guards, hold him," I ordered.

I walked over to him, still smiling as I unclasped the bracelet from his wrists. Gen was in a panic as she watched the truth come to light. The court yelled in anger as they cursed and threw things at Winnow, Rythlayn and his children. Rythlayn jerked towards me as the guards restrained him.

"I will kill you for this, Lyklor," he spat.

I smiled and laughed. "You won't have the chance," I replied, walking towards the demons. I held out the bracelet in front of them. Their eyes widened as their bodies trembled. "Who allowed you into this world?" I demanded.

"The prince. He sent for us," one said.

"And who gave you the order to kill Princess Genevieve?" I asked.

"The prince. He told us where and how to kill her," said another.

"Lies," yelled Rythlayn. "They are lying. This is all an act. That cuff doesn't control a thing. It is just a piece of useless jewelry."

"A demonstration perhaps is in order, it would appear," I said, looking to the crowd for confirmation. "Doria, release this one," I said, gesturing to the one I believe to be the leader.

She hesitated but did as I instructed. The court sat back, ready to attack if things went wrong. The demon shook as the chains fell from his arms and legs. It walked forward, looking around the room. I held up the bracelet and smiled.

"Eat your arm," I demanded.

It looked at me with shock. "Excuse me?" It said in a deep and whining voice.

"Eat. Your. Arm," I said again.

Its sharp long teeth descended from its gums as it began to tear into its own flesh. The crowd watched as it obeyed my command.

I turned to Rythlayn with an evil smile. "Need more proof?" He didn't answer. "Okay, more it is." I threw a bottle of holy water to its feet. "Drink it, then recite the Christian Lord's prayer."

Its eyes widened as it shook its head in fear. "Please, no," it begged.

"Now," I said. It picked up the bottle and drank the liquid. Steam and the smell of burning flesh filled the air as it screamed in pain. When the bottle was empty it began to resight the prayer.

"Our father ..." it started. Its body contorted and snapped in unsettling ways. "Who art in ... heaven." It fell to the floor in pain. "Hallowed be thy ... name." It continued the prayer as its body snapped and broke apart. "Thy kingdom come, thy will be done, on earth as it is in heaven. Give us this day our daily bread, and forgive us our debts, as we also have forgiven our debtors. And lead us not into temptation but deliver us from evil." Its body erupted into white flames as its head spun around and around, faster and faster until the flames consumed its body, leaving only a pile of ash. A declaration of the Christian faith. I turned back to Rythlayn.

"Satisfied?" I asked.

The king rose from his throne as rage blazed across his face. "How dare you betray me in this manner! How dare you stand in front of me and profess your love for me and my daughter, when you were the one to cause her suffering and death. You were the one who unleashed those things upon her! You saw what they did to her. You saw the pain you caused me and said nothing. How could you do this to me? After everything we've been through together. I trusted you. I loved you," yelled the king with more hatred than I had ever seen him display.

"You foolish, blind imbecile," spat Rythlayn. "You were so desperate for an heir that you appoint a filthy half-breed to our throne. You gave our throne to that thing, instead of allowing myself and my heirs to take our rightful place once you were gone. The court deserves better than her. She is not one of us and never will be."

The king looked upon his court. "My subjects. If this is what you believe, then speak now, knowing you will not be punished nor harmed in any way. If you'd rather have the line of succession transferred to my brother and his heirs instead of my daughter, now is the time to speak. I am not only your king, but your servant. I not only serve our kingdom. I serve each of you."

A few moments passed before a member of House Seldomer stood to his feet. "I recognize Princess Genevieve to be the rightful heir to the throne of Doonak and the next ruler in the line of succession," he said, bowing to them.

One after another, the houses rose and did the same. Rythlayn looked around him with his mouth open in disbelief. He had lost and we had won. Winnow dropped her head, tears of fear saturating her face.

"You were saying, *brother*?" said the king.

Gen rose to her feet, walking down the steps towards him as she looked into his eyes. "You hate me so much that you turned those things loose on me? Not only to kill but torture me?" she whispered.

I approached her side in case he tried anything.

He smiled and leaned into her ear. "You should have been put down the moment you were born. You should have never been allowed a single breath. Just like your bastard child," he said. He pulled his head away as her face went into complete shock and rage. Her body shook as darkness engulfed her eyes. She screamed louder than a banshee and the room began to shake with the power seeping out from under her skin.

I stepped away just in time to see her hands and arms ignite in dark flames. She threw the fire onto Rythlayn as she continued to scream, unleashing the pain and suffering he had brought upon her. Rythlayn yelled in agony as the members of the court shielded their eyes. The powerful force billowed from her until, finally, she took another breath. Rythlayn was gone. There wasn't a single piece of him left. No ash, no clothing, nothing.

The court sat in awe of the magnificent power that was tethered to their future queen. None of them would ever lift a hand against her again. Not after this. She marched over to the three remaining demons, her eyes still black as night. She slammed her hand against one of their mouths as the fire tore through his insides, melting his organs until the flames reached the surface and devoured him completely. She took a step back, looking at the last two. She raised her arms as two pillars of black swirling flames ate through them in seconds.

She took a deep breath, holding her head high. She marched back over to stand before her three cousins and Winnow, who knelt before the thrones. Vena and Icici were crying and shaking in fear. Toreon refused to bring his head up.

"Look at me," she said with a bite. They shook their heads, still in shock. "I said look at me!" she yelled.

The room shook again. They snapped their heads up to her, looking into her black eyes.

"Genevieve, please, we didn't know of our father's plans," said Vena.

"I promise, I had no knowledge of any of this," said Toreon.

"Lies, sweet princess," cried Winnow. "We are one in the same ... connected by our gift. I would never raise a hand against you."

Icici sat quietly.

Gen tilted her head towards her. "And you, Icici?" Gen asked.

"I would never subject another female to that type of torture. No matter how much I may dislike them," she responded honestly.

"And how can I believe any of you? How can I be sure you aren't lying just to save yourselves?" Gen asked.

"Ah, I've thought of that," I said, going back to the table and collecting the documents I had prepared ahead of time. I handed them to Gen. "Blood contracts. They will guarantee that neither your cousins nor their line of heirs ever lifts a hand against you or your descendants. If they attempt to move against you or your bloodline, they will drop dead. They will pledge their complete loyalty to you. The contracts will also reveal a black pentagram on their foreheads if they indeed did assist their father in the attack against you," I explained.

She looked down at them as her eyes faded back to green. "Would anyone like to change their minds?" she asked.

They all shook their heads. Gen took the quill from my hand and slashed her palm to sign the contracts. Fellwood was first. Gen took her shaking hand, slicing effortless through the skin before latching her grip onto the seer's. For the first few seconds nothing, Fellwood took deep breaths, squeezing her eyes together just before a black pentagram appeared upon her forehead.

Gen pulled her hand from Winnow's. The seer sobbed, falling to floor, crying for mercy just before Gen blasted her with the Flame, leaving nothing of the traitorous bitch behind.

Vena was next. She slashed her hand and signed the contract before sharing her blood with Gen. We waited, but a pentagram never appeared. Toreon's turn had come. He slit his hand and signed his name before sharing his blood with Gen. We sat back and waited.

A black engraving began to weave into the form of a pentagram on his forehead. The design burned as Toreon cringed in pain. If I was being honest, I had not seen this coming. Gen took a step back, looking down at the cousin who had taught her how to defend herself—who she had spent the first five hours of each day with since she arrived. I watched as another part of her heart broke.

"Why?" asked Icici.

He turned to face her with an evil glare. "Don't act so surprised. You were next. After we had killed the half-breed bitch, we were going to dispose of your intolerable ass. Like Father would ever allow you to ascend to the throne. You're a stain and embarrassment on this family's name, just like the half-breed," Toreon spat.

Gen latched her grip around Toreon's neck. She moved him to the middle of the throne room and threw him down in front of the court. Once he was away from his sisters, she set him on fire and watched as his body dissolved into thin air under the Dark Flame. She marched back over to Icici and waited for her to sign the contract.

Icici was shaking as tears fell from her face. With a hesitant hand, she signed her name and then took Gen's hand. Their blood merged as we waited. The pentagram never came. I gathered the contracts as Gen made her way back up to her father without another word. The room went silent.

"Let this be a reminder to anyone who would think to go against us," said the king as he stood, taking Gen's hand into his. They passed by Icici and Vena without a single glance. I followed behind as the court silently stood and returned to their quarters.

CHAPTER
TWENTY-NINE

I made my way to her room, not knowing what I was stepping into. I knocked on the door and Atalee allowed me through. Gen sat at her vanity, combing her hair as if nothing had happened. Her face was somber and her eyes blank. I moved in, glad not to see Tryverse Feynar lounging across her bed.

She set down the brush and turned towards us. "Good night, Atalee," she said as the female left with a bow. I looked at the table where the oranges and whiskey used to be, but the space was empty. "Why didn't you tell me first?"

"The pieces fell into place little by little. I didn't want to bring this to you until I was sure. As soon as I was, I went to your father," I replied.

"And if you were wrong, you would have been killed tonight instead of them."

"The reward was worth the risk."

"And what *is* your reward, Erendrial?" she asked calmly.

"Knowing you had your answers. Knowing you had your revenge. Knowing you were safe."

She laughed, leaning back in the chair. "Still playing this angle, are we?"

"I assure you; I am not playing any sort of game. What I did was for your benefit."

"What should I do with my cousins?"

"The contracts will keep them in check, I made sure of it."

"Yes, you made sure of everything, didn't you. Always the smartest person in the room," she said. "You know what I've come to realize, Erendrial?"

"That you can't live without me," I said playfully.

An amused smile stretched across her face. "Quite the opposite. I've realized that you are not only the smartest but the most dangerous person here at court. Your power makes you an influencer and a weapon. Your wit and intellect allow you to move faster than the majority of the court. And let's not forget the little army that you've created, who only follow your orders. One member in particular who is conveniently bedding my sister. You've set the whole chess board in your favor, haven't you, Lyklor?"

She was paranoid, and understandably so. Everything she said was true. I was all those things and so was my team. Her sister had conveniently fallen for a member of my family, but I didn't have anything to do with that. When their little love story initially began, I discouraged the relationship. Even though my team followed my orders, I never overstepped when it came to their personal lives. They were free to do and be with whomever they wanted.

"You're right. If I were to make a move against you, the odds are stacked in my favor, but as I've told you before and will continue to tell you as many times as you need to hear it, I am not a threat to you. And you do know how much I hate repeating myself, princess," I said.

She exhaled, dismissing my proclamation of innocence.

"What are you going to do with your last day before the tournament? Spend it in bed with Tryverse Feynar?" I knew it was wrong and I shouldn't have, but I couldn't resist. I need to hear her deny it.

"Who I invite into my bed is none of your concern," she said casually.

I huffed, trying to appear casual. "The young buck can't be that entertaining. He's barely out of diapers."

"You forget, I am younger than him. What does that say about you?"

"That I am a wonderful teacher."

She laughed, standing to her feet. "Erendrial, please. Gaelin could run laps around you," she said, pouring herself a glass of wine.

My heart snapped while my pride took the biggest hit. "You're entitled to your own opinion," I said calmly. But really, I wanted to find King Fucker and rip him limb from limb. It disgusted me that he ever had the privilege of knowing her body.

"What? No smartass comeback? Are you getting soft on me,

Lyklor? Or are you just finally ready to admit defeat?"

"Defeat has never and will never be in my vocabulary."

"We shall see," she said, taking a sip of wine. "So now what? The evil prince and his son are dead. I am once again safe, and you are free to move about the court as you please."

"I still have you as my charge, so I am sure my hands will continue to be full."

She tilted her head and cringed. "Actually, as of tonight, I am no longer your concern," she said, taking another sip.

"What are you talking about?"

"Think of it—as your *reward*. I asked my father to relieve you of your babysitting duties. You were only admitted into my room just now because I allowed it. You are free, Erendrial."

No, no, no. She had to remain my charge. I had to remain close to her. How was I ever going to fix this? To fix us? Everything I had worked so hard to accomplish was now going down the drain.

She walked slowly towards me, a haunting smile on her face. "You should be thanking me. This is best. For both of us." she said softly.

"I don't want to be relieved of my duty," I admitted.

"Too late. You are once again just the ambassador to the dark court."

"Gen, please," I whispered.

"I don't trust you, Eren. I never will. You are too conniving and smart for your own good. I may have been foolish enough to allow you close to me once, but that female is gone ... dead. I appreciate what you did for me tonight. I don't know if I would have figured it all out without your help, but I need you to keep your distance. I can't ... I can't be around you. I don't want to have to look at you every day for the rest of my life."

I grabbed her by the arms forcefully. Her eyes widened in terror.

"Look at me! It's me. The arrogant asshole who trusted you at the light court. Who protected you from the fairies. Who came back for you and took you away from their torturous court. I'm the same person who taught you to control your powers. Who taught you how to mist. Who listened to you when you needed to heal. I am the same male who made love to you. I am not them. I will never be them. Please, Genevieve, don't push me away. I want this more than I've ever wanted anything. I want you," I said, more vulnerable than I had ever been.

Her eyes went blank as she stood in front of me not saying a word. I dropped my hands from her arms as I waited. "Here's your first lesson in defeat," she said softly. "You don't always get what you want." She walked away from me, turning to the balcony.

"I'll do anything," I said as a last attempt to reach her.

She tilted her head to the stars. "There's nothing I want from you. Please leave," she said coldly.

Everything I had done for her, and it still wasn't enough. What else could I do? I tucked my tail, for the first time in my life, and left her behind.

That night I went into the city to the gentlemen's club, trying to distract myself. The human women were beautiful and warm as always, but they did little for me. I couldn't bring myself to even touch them. Azeer, what was wrong with me? I had let her ruin me. This is what I get for letting someone in. For believing I could matter to another. I had allowed her to open a part of me that I kept closed for this very reason.

The next day I went on a hunt with Zerrial, Voz, and Oz. No females, just the males. We tracked down a large, dragon-like creature with scaled armor and a mean set of teeth. It had small arms in the front, which gave us the advantage. In order to get it back to the castle, we had to strap the damn thing to all four of our ragamors. The thing weighed a ton.

That night we went into the city and drank until we couldn't drink anymore. Whiskey laced with ambrosia: my choice of medication for any problem. Firel, Doria, Evinee, and Leenia joined us.

This was my family. A family that I had created and built from nothing. We all had our ways about us, but we were loyal to each other. That was the most important thing I had to remember. I needed only the alfar that sat around me.

The females laughed and drank as Oz and Voz put on a show for us. I have never met two smarter idiots then these fools. Genius by day, jesters by night. Oz and Voz were also from a lower-class family. I had met them when I was sixteen in a rough part of the city. They granted sexual favors for food and money. What money they didn't spend on food they used to purchase scrap metal for their inventions.

With what little resources they had, they created mechanical devices. Gravitational spheres that could remove the gravity in any room. Wind machines and so much more. I recognized their unique skill set right away and so my collection began.

I had known Evinee the longest out of the group. She seduced her way into our little club. I fell for her charms and sarcastic sense of humor. She was a wild animal in the sack and a charmer in public. Due to her sexual talents, she worked her way through the high lords and was able to gather information on them as we needed. She was the perfect spy. She was gorgeous, charming, and deadly.

Next was Doria. She had a unique skill set when it came to torture. Her mind was broken by her father, who abused her in a way that rivals even what Gen had gone through. We ended up killing the prick together. She, of course, landed the final blow.

Leenia came along as we entered our thirties. She was from a fallen high house. Her father had stolen money from the king and was killed for it. Her family was disgraced and banned from court. She desired to reclaim her family's honor by moving up the ranks on her own merit. She was the deadliest thing on a battlefield.

Zerrial I collected straight from the dark court's military. I befriended him by chance one night when we met at an alehouse in the city. He was hard to read and a brute of a male. We couldn't stand each other at first. We initially beat the ever-loving shit out of each other, but after a few glasses, we were rolling on the floor, laughing and joking like we had known each other for decades. We ended up getting into a brawl together that same night. Instead of fighting each other, we tag-teamed some high house pricks, which solidified our bond. He taught me and the others everything he knew when it came to combat and battle strategies.

Firel was abandoned by his parents when he was ten years old. He never speaks of them, and we don't push it. He was the closest thing I had to a child of my own until the one I lost with Gen. He was awkward and odd. The other alfar overlooked him due to his unusual personality and stuttering problem. I found him as something broken that I could fix. A challenge. He latched onto me like a babe to the tit. He absorbed everything I taught him and then went above and beyond. His capacity for knowledge was uncanny.

Until Gen, these alfar had been the ones I had loved the most. They understood me ... saw me for who I truly was. Gen was right. I had collected a powerful army of my own ... but in reality, their gifts and talents meant very little to me. We were connected by the sheer fact that we were all survives. Each of us were dealt a fate that should have put us in early graves, yet here we were ... united ... determined to build a better life then the one we were born to.

The next morning, I woke with a headache, still dizzy from the night before, but I didn't care. I made my way over to the whiskey bottle on my desk. I was going to have to stay drunk in order to endure this day. The day that a husband would be chosen for Gen.

It would either be Therosi or Soddram. Avalon was only chosen out of respect for the queen. Therosi was more skilled with a sword and Soddram was the more intelligent of the three. It would come down to their will power. Therosi had the upper hand in that category. Especially because he desired Gen. He had a small taste of her power and allure and wasn't going to allow anyone else a chance at owning it.

I got dressed and headed down to the labs. Our creature was being dissected this morning and I was interested to see what kept the massive hunk of flesh going. I turned the corner to find Evinee and Gen standing at the observation window. I slowed my pace, realizing my attempted avoidance led me straight into her path. But I was going to have to get used to this. I would serve her someday. Not in the way I wanted, but I would serve her all the same.

"Good morning, everyone," I said, sliding my hands into my pockets.

Evinee elbowed me in the stomach as I stood next to her. "Good morning. I'd ask how you slept after last night's bender, but I can see the answer for myself," said Evinee.

"Remind me never to get into a drinking competition with you again," I said.

"You should know better by now. It's not my fault your inflated ego doesn't learn," replied Evinee.

"One of my many charming qualities. What have they discovered so far?" I asked.

"The thing has three hearts. Its lungs were massive, and the size of one tooth is longer than my whole arm."

"Any answer as to what time or realm it came from?"

"It had claw marks all over its hide, but they think it's from a less civilized place. Somewhere where it is at the top of the food chain," explained Evinee. "Oh, and it was pregnant!"

I grimaced. The word pregnant had changed in an unexpected way for me in the past two weeks. I felt a turning in my stomach as it took everything in my power not to look at Gen.

"Did the offspring survive?" I asked.

"Yup. The twins are determined to train it and make it their pet. Unless Gen here decides she wants it. She does have a rather exotic collection of mythical creatures," said Evinee.

Gen smirked. "I don't think Otar would like a new brother or sister, but if I change my mind I know where to find it," she replied.

"Speaking of Otar, where is the little prick? I haven't seen him around?" I asked.

"He is alive and well. Just had to get him back to his normal diet," she said, taking a quick glance at me.

"How's Tryverse working out for you? Was he able to help with whatever problem you had?" Evinee asked with excitement. Azeer, I was not hearing this. I focused on the creature, trying to tune them out.

"He's been very effective. Thank you for letting me borrow him," said Gen.

"You can have him. He's cute and all, but he reminds me too much of a human, no offense," said Evinee.

"Maybe that's why I enjoy his company so much," added Gen.

"Where is Levos?" I asked, trying to change the subject.

"With Vena I presume," answered Gen. "They've been carrying on for months. He's been ... comforting her after her father and brother."

"Have you spoken to either of them?" asked Evinee.

"Vena a little," said Gen. "She just apologizes repeatedly. I don't carry any ill will towards her. She had already proven her loyalty to me before this situation."

"And Icici?" I asked.

Gen turned her eyes to me. "I expect you know more about how she is doing than I would," she said.

Evinee smiled and hit me in the chest. "You're still screwing Icici? Come on, bag it, and tag it. No need to have the same meal for every course. You need a little variety in your kitchen. I'd be happy to shake things up for you to get that bimbo off your mind. It's been what, two years since our last dalliance? Time for a refresher." she snickered.

I closed my eyes, rubbing my temples in between my hands. She did not just say that. Not in front of Gen.

"I'm quite fine on my own, but thank you, Evinee," I replied shortly.

"Fine, your loss. What about you princess? Care to have your mind blown?" she asked.

I snapped my eyes to both of them. "You did not just proposition the princess in public? Remember who she is, for Azeer's sake."

Gen laughed at us, trying to hide that beautiful smile. The sound warmed my insides.

"Thank you for the offer, Evinee, but I prefer males," replied Gen.

"You'll be singing a different tune in one hundred years. Women are way more fun. We know what we like and how to deliver. Isn't that right, Eren?" Evinee said.

"I'm done with this very uncomfortable conversation," I said.

"When has sex ever been an uncomfortable conversation for you?" Evinee asked.

Ever since I decided I had feelings for the princess. Ever since I had imagined her with Gaelin and now Tryverse Feynar. Ever since I had experienced jealousy. That was what I wanted to say.

"I have a meeting," I said. I bowed to the princess before turning away.

"Oh, come on, Lyklor. There is nothing to do today," called Evinee after me, but I didn't turn back.

The throne room was packed. Every member of the high houses had shown up to watch the tournament that would decide who would have the honor of calling the princess their wife. This tournament only came around every so many hundred years, so the alfar came out of the woodwork to attend. I entered the room wishing I could be anywhere else.

I sat down at the table next to the king. Gen wore a beautiful white lace dress, cut into a V in the back and front. Her curls were loosely pinned to her head with a few fallen strands draped around her face and neck. She wore her diamond crown this evening. She was a vision. The greatest prize any alfar could ask for.

"She looks stunning, doesn't she?" asked the king quietly. He must have caught me staring.

"You have a remarkable daughter, Your Highness," I replied, trying not to be too obvious. And to top matters off, I was miserably drunk. I knew it was the only way I would be able to stomach this evening.

"She looks just like her mother. Besides the eyes, of course. She was the most stunning female I have ever laid eyes on. There was a pull to her that I couldn't resist. I fought it, but in the end, I had to have her. I had to possess her," said the king.

I was unsure how to respond to his very personal confession. "She did a wonderful job raising her," I added.

"That she did. I never got to thank you for what you did with my brother and nephew. I owe you a great debt."

"As long as she is safe, I have all I need," I replied, realizing how sincerely the comment came out. I sat up straight and repositioned myself uncomfortably. The king smiled as he watched Gen move around the room.

"Remember, Erendrial. Life is too short to live with regret. You wouldn't want to live the rest of your long life in the shadow of a reality that could have been yours, now, would you?" he said, standing to his feet.

I was taken aback by his comment. I didn't quite understand his meaning, but I was honored that he felt me worthy of such advice. In all honesty, I looked up to the male. He never held my class against me. He encouraged me and gave me the opportunities I needed to prove myself. He entrusted me with the most valuable parts of his kingdom. He was the closest thing I had to a father.

The king made his way to his throne before Gen followed. The crowd found their seats as the excitement grew in the room. I downed another glass of wine and beckoned the servant over for more. Gen tried to smile, but I could tell it was forced. Regardless of what she said, she didn't want this. It went against everything that made her ... her.

"Thank you all for your attendance tonight as we conduct the tournament that will determine the next King of Doonak and my daughter's future husband," said the king. The court cheered with excitement. "The candidates will be tested in three categories. First, intellect. The second, strength and skill. The third, willpower. The winner of the first and second categories will compete in the third for the honor of my daughter's hand. Ravion Sterling has assisted me in designing the three challenges. He will run the tournament and give direction as needed.

"Now, to introduce our candidates. First, we have Soddram from House Yositru. Our second candidate is Therosi from House Servi. Our third candidate is Avalon from House Flarion." Each male walked up and bowed to the royals. They kissed Gen on the hand as she nodded to each with a small smile. The three candidates lined up in front of the royals, ready to begin. The king turned to me and smiled before addressing the crowd.

"I would like to take this time to remind the court that entry into the tournament is still open until the start of the first simulation. Anyone is free to challenge our candidates for the hand of the princess," explained the king.

I leaned forward as I realized what he was doing. He was inviting me to play. He was giving me an opening to marry his daughter, but why? The candidates for the tournaments were always chosen ahead of time. They were chosen based on alliances and house standings. No one ever entered the competition at the last second. It was just a formality to say those words.

But what if ... what if I could win? What if I could have a chance at marrying her? I tried to think quickly, weighing all the pros and cons in my head.

She would hate me for a couple years at best, but I would win her over. I would break her walls down. For Azeer's sake, what was I thinking? This was crazy. The houses would never accept me as their next king.

Just like you had doubts about them accepting a half-breed as their queen?

But that was different; she had proven herself.

Haven't you proven yourself?

I looked over to her, trying to sort things out. Could I live, knowing she was bound to another? Could I live with the thought that I could have been her husband? Could I watch her belly swell with another child that wasn't mine? The king exhaled, prolonging the process.

"There is no one else that wishes to enter the tournament?" he asked again.

No, I couldn't live with any of those things. She was mine and I was going to claim her as such. I stood from my seat and all eyes in the room locked on me. The king turned my direction with a smile.

Gen's eyes widened in disbelief. My instincts were telling me to sit my ass down, but it was too late. My emotions had gotten the best of me.

"I would like to enter into the tournament for the honor of Princess Genevieve's hand, my king," I said boldly.

I made my way to her, took her hand, and kissed it softly. She did not smile or nod. I took my place in the lineup next to the other three candidates as they all glared at me with annoyance. The court chattered quietly, the shock of my bold move rattling their traditions down to the core.

I held my head high, knowing I would do anything to be with her. To protect her. I wanted another chance and if she wasn't going to give it to me willingly, then I was going to take it by whatever means necessary. The king smiled at me as I bowed to him. I would win this. I could do this. I would make her mine.

ACKNOWLEDGMENTS

In my journey as an author, i've discovered writing has become a place where I go to heal. Each of my character possess something inside of me i've overcome that has impacted and forged me into who I am today. Someone I can honestly say ... I am proud to be.

If I am being honest, the book cannot be dedicated to one single person. Though I still have much life to live, i've witnessed so many strong, passionate individuals that have given me the strength to move past my darkest moments. I pray this book acts as an anchor for those who feel they are a drift in the sea. Know, you are never alone. There are those who have paved the way for you to heal ... for you to succeed. Never give up and always look to the star to guide you home.

Thank you to my dear friend and editor Kara for coming through for me once again. Your belief in me is something that has truly fueled me to continue down this path. I respect you in so many ways and I am glad you are on this journey with me.

To my amazing husband and best friend, Joe. How inspired I am by you. Your support, love, and encouragement has comforted me along this journey. I can't believe I get to pursue my dreams. But it wouldn't be possible without you by my side. Never once, have you discourage me. No matter how many crazy business plans or ideas i've thrown your way have you ever discouraged me from pursuing what makes me happy. I plan to build a beautiful life for us and our family and I am so excited to have you by my side.

To my dad .... Thank you for introducing me to the world of fantasy and magic. I truly believe I got my imagination from you (go figure that's genetic). "You can accomplish anything you set your mind to".... Well, guess what, daddy? My mind is a crazy, adventurous place full of impossible stories, but I believe I can make anything happen, thanks to you.

You weren't perfect ... and you made mistakes, but I never doubted your love for me. You wanted your children to be better ... to do better. Something I now pray each and every night for own own children. Your excitement and support in this journey means the world to me. I know, no matter how old I get, or where I am in my life, your arms will always be a safe place where I can go for a warm and loving embrace.

Though life hasn't always been the easiest, I know there is a spark of magic around every corner of our journey. You just have to want it bad enough. Fantasy has always been my escape ... my safe place, and I am honored to share my adventures with you. Remember ... no dream, no matter how big or small, is out of your reach. Chase it. Nurture it. Breath life into it, because you never know who might need your version of the world in their darkest moments.

ABOUT THE AUTHOR

Hailing from Kansas City, Missouri, Jessica, an Italian American and dedicated teacher with a Master's in Educational Leadership, brings a diverse background, having also graduated with a Bachelors in Fine Art, English, Business, Education, and Communications from Park University in 2015.

Beyond her professional life, Jessica is a passionate creator, finding joy in art and family time. A lifelong reader, she began writing at 16, making authorship a dream now realized during the creation of her own publishing house Dark Flame Publishing . Stay tuned for the enchanting worlds she'll unfold in her upcoming literary books!

Made in the USA
Middletown, DE
01 March 2025

71989159R00269